DANA LECHEMINANT

Houston, WE HAVE A Problem

a sweet romantic comedy

Author's Note

The Love in Sun City series can be read in any order, as standalones or together. Writing this series has been such a fun experience for me because the four stories all overlap and share scenes over the course of a month. Not only did I get to discover the stories, but I also got to discover them *at the same time*. It was a cool experiment to see how this type of project would work, and hopefully it gets you excited for the other stories as you read this one. I've added dates to each book to help you keep track of shared events, if you so desire. :)

Enjoy your time with the Briggs siblings as they simultaneously (and quickly) fall madly in love!

– Dana

Chapter One

Darcy

October 13

YOU KNOW THAT THING where you wiggle a pencil just right and it looks like it's made of rubber? I am so good at that thing. It's probably not a thing I should be good at in the middle of a staff meeting, but as the youngest female reporter for the country's premier sports news agency, I tend to have a lot of downtime.

It's probably not a great idea for me to zone out during these meetings, but I learned pretty early on that I haven't earned enough clout to be able to pick which stories I tell when our editor in chief, Connor McMillan, is throwing out ideas for the taking. I tried once, and shot me down so fast that I still feel the sting even two years later.

Don't get me wrong. I'm a *great* journalist. Some of the stories I've reported have trended for weeks on end. And it's not that Connor doesn't trust me, either. Though that first rejection hurt, Connor has never given me a bad story. But my stories have fallen into a certain pattern of assignment, which is absolutely intentional on his part.

I accidentally stumble across *one* bicyclist taking steroids when I try asking him about his juice cleanse and forget the word *cleanse*, and suddenly I'm the woman who exposes crooked athletes.

It can be fun uncovering secrets that can be dangerous or affect other athletes, but it's certainly not the kind of story I like telling most.

"Paxton."

I snap to attention, also snapping my pencil in the process because my brain thinks it actually is made out of rubber and I grab it with both hands. *Oops.* "Yep." How did I snap a pencil with my bare hands? Am I that strong, or is this pencil awful quality? It came from the supply cupboard, but Enhance media isn't known for being frugal. We're one of the best for a reason.

Connor gives me a narrow-eyed look that says he knows I wasn't paying attention, but he lets that go. He may give me stories I'm not especially fond of, but he has a soft spot for me. Has from the beginning. I like to think it's because of my charisma and charm, but I'm pretty sure it's just his fatherly instinct kicking in. I'll take it.

"Markham has the flu," he says.

I sit up straighter. I don't think I've missed the context of this statement, but that doesn't mean I understand why he's telling me this. "That stinks?" I say.

He fights a smile. "He was covering the Series as Jacobsen."

Okay, now he definitely has my attention. "Like, the *World* Series?"

Nodding, Connor points at me. "You're going to take his place."

Since I can't sit up any higher, I stand. I don't care that everyone else in the room is either snickering or scowling, depending on their interest in covering the biggest championship tournament in baseball. This will be the first time I've had a chance to cover something this big on my own.

"Game Six is tomorrow," I say, as if my boss doesn't know that already. It could be the biggest game ever with how evenly matched the Burrs and the Red-tails are. Right now the Red-tails are ahead by one game, but the Burrs have a good chance of tying things up.

Connor smiles. "Then you'd better go figure out which tech you're taking with you. Let's go talk sports!"

As the room clears out after Connor's usual dismissal, I fight the disappointment that washes over me. I don't know why I would think I could do this story without a tech, but I did. It's not like there are any corrupt players on either of the teams that are in the Series, and this would be my first real chance to talk about the actual sport instead of just the dirty secrets behind it.

"Connor?" I chase after him, hot on his heels as he heads back to his office.

He doesn't look back. "No, Darcy."

"But—"

"Everyone at Enhance goes incognito. You know that." He holds his door open for me, knowing I'm not going to drop this argument.

This is the first time I've thought I might be able to win, so of course I'm going to push back. "I know wearing a disguise is a safety protocol," I say as Connor slips into his chair. "But is there really going to be danger at a World Series game? I'm just there to cover the game, right? So I don't see why I need to—"

"Darcy." That one word carries Connor's full authoritative voice, the one that made me terrified of him as an intern until I heard him humming the theme song from that kids show, *Bluey*, one day. He's only intimidating when he wants to be. "The reason everyone wants to work at Enhance is because we take care of our own."

I pout. "Yeah, but no one knows *how* you do that because no one knows that none of Enhance's journalists are real people." I still remember my first day of working here, right before I started grad school, and the monstrously large NDA I had to sign. I didn't know until two years later, when I finally got hired on to the journalism team, that we have an entire department full of makeup artists and wardrobe designers—technicians, as they're officially called—whose sole purpose is to transform us into other people when we're on camera.

Connor patiently nods despite my unprofessionalism right now. "Did you know that when we switched to aliases on screen, the number of threats our team received on a monthly basis was cut in half? And that's not just because no one knows how to find people who don't exist. Going incognito gives you freedom to step beyond your usual boundaries and tell the stories you want to tell without your personal biases getting in the way. It lets you tell the story the right way."

I let out a deep sigh. "I know."

Chuckling, Connor taps his knuckle on the desk. "Do you know why I picked you for this when I could have chosen a more experienced journalist?"

I wish I had an actual answer, but I don't. "Because you know how much I love baseball?"

"Because I have never seen anyone better at leaving their baggage at the door than you," Connor says pointedly. "I know you hate some of the assignments I give you, but I always know I can count on you to get to the heart of the story without letting your own opinions get in the way. Tamlin Park is one of the best things to ever happen to Enhance Media, and I don't say that lightly."

Tamlin Park. She's the only thing separating me from going back to being an assistant, and I know it. Without her, I never would have gotten in front of a camera, and I can't hate her for letting me do a job that I love. I may hate the career-ruining stories, but Connor always gives me a good story in between to cleanse my palate.

In fact, those more lighthearted stories have become more frequent as of late, which has me wondering if I might have a chance to change up the pattern soon. I probably shouldn't be fighting Connor so much on this when it's company policy, but...

"So, there's really no chance of telling the story as Darcy instead of Tamlin?"

Connor rolls his eyes and clicks on his computer. "No, but I'll tell you what. The next time you give an exposé on illegal drug use in the NFL and get two dozen players kicked out of the league, I'll let you do the story as yourself. You know self-defense, right?"

"Okay, fine, you've made your point. I'll go find myself a makeup tech."

I'm at the door before Connor says, "Oh, and Darcy?"

"Yeah?"

He gives me the kind of smile that seems to make his eyes twinkle. It's the smile that tells me I'm going to like what I'm about to hear. "We've set up an interview with Houston Briggs. I've got a hunch there's something there, so show me what you've got."

I can't hide the grin that spreads across my face, even after I make my way down the hall to see who's available to come with me as my makeup tech tomorrow. Houston Briggs? He's the top starting pitcher for the Sun City Red-tails, one of the teams in the Series, and I can't remember the last time he did an interview with Enhance. For some reason, he's fairly interview-shy nowadays despite being one of the best players in the game right now. That could easily mean he has something to hide, like Connor seems to think.

I wonder what Connor is hoping I'll find. Briggs has always been intriguing to me in the same way I have a weird fascination with nature documentaries that depict hunting scenes with all their carnage. I'm not sure if he's the predator or the prey in this scenario, but I have a feeling something's going to die.

Houston Briggs may seem perfect on the outside, but there's no way he's that good both on and off the field. Whatever Briggs is hiding, I'll find it.

GREY
BIRD
TAVERN

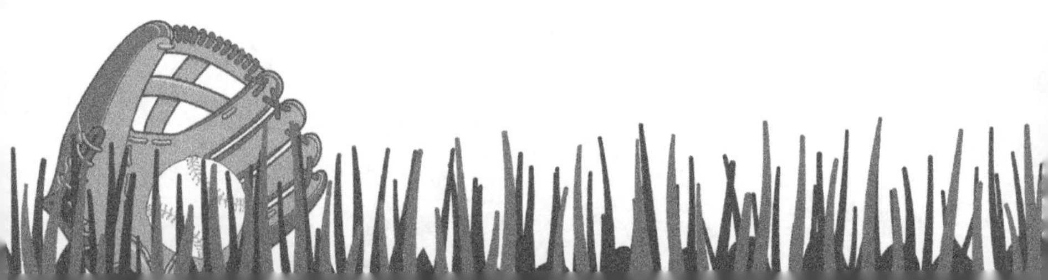

Chapter Two
Houston

October 14

BOTTOM OF THE NINTH. Bases are loaded. Zero outs. Batter has two strikes. We're ahead by one. This pitch could end the game for good or bad. The crowd roars, lights hum, and my heartbeat pulses in my ears. Lars Jensen is at home plate, bat at the ready and a murderous glare in his eyes. He's the Burrs' best batter, and I can see in his eyes that he's determined to knock whatever I throw at him out of the park.

My fingers tense around the ball, shifting the threads exactly where I like them. My shoulder throbs, but I ignore it. Can't show any weakness. It's Game Six of the World Series, and the Sun City Red-tails are ahead of the Oklahoma Burrs. Three games to two.

One throw, and this could all be over. If we lose, we'll have to play another game and potentially lose the Series.

I glance at Hopkins on first base and get a nod. Behind the mound, Badir signals a slider, which historically Jensen can't hit worth crap. It's not my best pitch, but it's probably our best chance at ending this thing.

I take a deep breath, adjusting the ball in my left hand. This is it.

The energy of the stadium changes as I wind up, and the whole place seems to grow still as I release, the ball flying exactly where I want it to. Jensen tenses, shifts, swings. The ball collides with the bat, the sound hitting me in the chest, but it flies high as Jensen takes off running.

Ortiz catches the ball and throws to Hopkins, who misses the guy leaving first base but doesn't hesitate to throw instead. The ball flies to third base just before the runner reaches it and then straight to Badir, who catches the final runner before he can slide home to safety.

My breath slides out of me as the crowd goes wild. The Red-tails storm the field as the victory sets in, my teammates screaming and crying and tackling each other as they surround me.

I'm supposed to share their joy, and I do, but now that the adrenaline is wearing off, the pain seeps in more strongly. My shoulder burns from pitching another full game, as if I need the reminder that I'm not nineteen anymore. I should have been subbed out around inning six, and I'm already regretting my own stubbornness.

Hopkins and Badir grab me, lifting me up on their shoulders and forcing me to plaster on a smile because now the cameras can see me. As long as they can't see the pain, I'm fine. *We won.* I focus on that as much as I can. *We won the World Series.*

The next half an hour passes in a blur as the team's owner accepts the Series trophy. Thankfully the pain dulls as my arm cools and I can start to enjoy the win. It's only the second time the Red-tails have gone this far in the championships, but we've never lost a Series, and that's a big deal. Players will start getting more sponsorships, better paychecks, more playing time. This is everything we could hope for as a team, and the excitement is palpable.

So, why am I glad when my agent pulls me from the crowd?

"Enhance Media wants an interview," he says, hardly looking up from his phone as he leads me to the news tent. Alan Roundy is a beast of an agent, and despite his outward inattentiveness, he's had my back from day one, when I got recruited after my sophomore year of college. He's got some big names on his roster, but I like to think I'm his favorite.

Case in point: he got me a spot with Enhance. The news site is the biggest sports media company in the country, and they can make or break an athlete's career depending on how they spin a story. They can be brutal, but they can also be the best thing to ever happen to one of us.

So far, I've been lucky, and the few Enhance journalists I've spoken to all love me. I mean, I've hardly given anyone a reason *not* to love me. I've never done anything to get on their bad side, and I don't plan on changing that now. I'll take on any of their journalists as long as it's not...

I stop dead the moment I step into the tent and get a sudden sense of unease.

I don't know what it is about Tamlin Park, but I know it's her waiting for me even before I see her, though see her I do. It would be hard *not* to see her. As always, the sight of her in that skintight black dress and heels as she speaks to her cameraman has me frozen, my breath stuck in my lungs. It's like she sucks the oxygen out of a room, suffocating every athlete within a fifty-foot radius, and she does it with a smile. A drop-dead gorgeous smile, sure, but it's the kind of smile that ends careers. I should count myself lucky that I haven't had to personally face her before now, but I guess it's time to meet my doom.

Unless I can pretend I forgot why I came in here?

Unfortunately for me, Roundy is too good at his job, and he notices my hesitation immediately. "Are you going or what?" he asks without looking up from his phone. "We don't have all night."

My attempt at speaking Tamlin's name comes out in a curse I'm not allowed to say on live TV.

Roundy glances up. "Don't make me grab the soap again, Briggs." He doesn't personally care when I swear, but ever since meeting my twin sister a couple of years ago, he's been fueling her drive to clean up my language. It's both annoying and endearing.

He looks around the tent in search of the source of my reluctance. "Why aren't you—oh." His whole face twists in discomfort, which doesn't exactly leave me feeling very confident. "I thought it was Jacobsen covering the Series."

"Clearly not," I growl. Ted Jacobsen would have been a walk in the park, especially because he's a Red-tails fan. He's the kind of guy I'd take out for a beer after a game and talk about golf and the price of ground beef.

But Tamlin Park? She eats athletes like me for breakfast. She's only been reporting for Enhance for a couple of years, but that's been plenty of time for her to make a name for herself as a ruthless shark.

Roundy shifts on his feet as both of us watch her carefully. She's happily chatting with her cameraman, all smiles. To anyone who hasn't seen some of her stories, she looks warm and friendly, and I'll admit a small part of me wonders if she'll keep this interview lighthearted. She can't possibly have any dirt on me, so I've got nothing to be afraid of. Still, my heart pounds in my chest, and my feet are glued to the floor, even as something inside me feels drawn to her like she's got some silent siren call.

"She doesn't look that bad," Roundy mutters, cocking his head to one side.

I mirror him, and I can only imagine how we look right now, both of us with our heads tilted, staring at the gorgeous woman whose laugh rings out over the other conversations in the tent. I doubt we're the only ones captivated. Something about her is mesmerizing.

"This feels like a bad idea, Roundy," I say, but Tamlin chooses that moment to look my way.

It's like a switch flips.

Her unnervingly blue eyes narrow, telling me she's seen me, and her little smirk sparks the part of me that can't back down from a challenge. The friendly, smiling woman is gone, the predator in her place.

"Uhhh..." Clearly floundering, Roundy searches the tent for an escape. But he knows better than anyone that I need to make this appearance. There's no telling what Tamlin might say if I make myself scarce, and she probably already has the nation captivated with her intense beauty as she starts speaking into her microphone. There's something so alluring about her long dark hair paired with those almost unnaturally blue eyes that makes her impossible not to watch. Either her outward charm is all a facade, or the shark is a front, but she is not one to mess around with.

I groan. I'm too tired to deal with this right now. "I'm giving her two minutes. And then you'd better be getting me the hell out of there."

"Language," he reminds me limply, but I'm already marching to my death.

Tamlin gives me her carnivorous smile as I step into the camera's view, not wasting any time as she jumps right into it with her silky voice. "And here is the man of the hour. So, Houston, what's your take on how well the Red-tails played tonight?"

I grit my teeth. She's clearly looking for a sign of weakness, and I won't give it to her. I've seen the way she takes down athletes by knowing way more than she should, and I will not be one of her kills. "We won," I say.

"Barely," she replies. "Some might say you were looking pretty tired in the eighth inning."

My response catches in my throat as soon as I register her words. Anyone would be tired after pitching seven straight innings, but the way she said that... Does she already know my arm's going out? Panic rises in my chest as I fight for a deflection. "Are you forgetting that strikeout I threw?"

"Right before Dalton hit that home run and pulled the Burrs into the lead? That strikeout?" She says this without her smile wavering, and it's unnerving how inhuman she feels. What happened to that woman who was joking around a moment ago? I've seen her do this with other athletes, poking and prodding until something shakes loose, and now I understand how no one is able to throw her off. She's terrifying.

"Luckily for me," I say, shaking off the tension building in my shoulders, "I've got a good team behind me, and we regained the lead pretty—"

"So you admit the rest of the team had to make up for your subpar performance?"

My jaw locks up, nerves settling hot and heavy in my stomach. This feels like a trap. I *know* it's a trap. "That isn't what I—"

"What do you say to all the people who think you're losing your touch in your old age?"

A curse sits on the tip of my tongue, threatening to break free, but Brooklyn would kill me if she heard some of the things I want to say to this woman. My twin probably hasn't watched one of my interviews in years, but she is unerringly sweet and really doesn't like it when I swear. And I hate disappointing her. Heaven knows I've done it way too often lately.

Tamlin is looking at me like she's already won, and I know I shouldn't give in to her taunting. This is her job, and there's a reason she gets paid big money to interview athletes. She digs under our skin and gets the answers she wants, leaving us wounded and full of holes as she moves on to her next strike. I don't know what game she's playing or who she really is beneath this ice cold exterior, but I am so sick of her smug grin. She needs to know she doesn't have any power here.

This is *my* world, and I won't let her take it from me.

Calling on every media training I've ever had, I fix on a smile and look directly at the camera, knowing I am going to regret this in the morning. "Old? I'm just getting started, baby." And then I wink and walk off, ignoring the pained look Roundy gives me as he follows me out of the tent and back to the clubhouse.

But I can feel his words itching to get out.

"Don't say it," I growl, tucking my hat a little lower over my face. I know it's pointless, with my name stitched across my back, but it would still be nice to hide. I don't want anyone else trying to pull me into an interview after that sixty-second nightmare.

Roundy ignores my warning. "Remember that time I told you that it's a good idea to keep your head down until you've made a decision?" He says that as if he's only mentioned it once instead of every day for the last three months.

Pausing in an empty corner of the field, I make sure we're completely alone before I risk saying anything. "I've already made the decision. You know that."

I can feel Roundy's eye roll as much as I see it, and he actually puts his phone away for this, which means he's being completely serious right now. "Are you sure about that? Because you have yet to tell anyone that decision. Me included. Besides, you just told the whole country that you're still in the game when we both know that isn't true."

As if I needed the added argument, my shoulder twinges. Tamlin was mostly right when she'd said I was tired in the eighth inning. What she didn't know was how tired I was before the game even started. I came dangerously close to getting pulled based on the looks the field manager, Hiroshi, was giving me halfway through the game, and that has me more worried than anything. I haven't been subbed out all season, something that's basically unheard of.

That's never going to happen again.

I have a couple of months to rest and recover before next season, but even if I were to look into surgery in the interim, I'm not so sure my arm has another season in it. I don't even know if it has another *game*. Baseball has been my life for the last fifteen years, and without it...

Without it, my life is about to get a whole lot more complicated.

"This probably goes without saying," Roundy mutters, looking back toward the press tent, "but steer clear of Tamlin Park."

I laugh. "Why? We hit it off so well."

"If anyone's going to figure out you're at the end of your game, she is." Roundy has never done well with sarcasm, but he's right. Despite being fairly new on the scene, Tamlin has never done anything by halves.

I rub my shoulder, the burning sensation almost familiar now. "It's going to come out sooner or later," I mutter, though it's not like I need to tell him that.

"I know. But if you let Tamlin Park get her hands on that story, you're going to be out more than a job. She'll find a way to make it some sort of scandal."

He's right. I know he's right. But as my eyes trail back to the tent, I can't help but wonder why she would come after me, of all people. She's so good at exposing dirty players and corrupt management. I've done my best to be as clean as they come, so why me?

No matter her reasons, Tamlin Park is dangerous. And I won't go anywhere near her. *This is my world.*

I just worry it won't be for much longer.

Chapter Three
Darcy

October 16

"HE'S NOT GOING TO crack." I say that to Connor as forcefully as I can, not because I believe it—everyone cracks eventually—but because I really don't want to go head-to-head with Houston Briggs again after that unhelpful interview.

It's bad enough with athletes I *know* are dirty. Ruining their lives always makes me feel dirty by association. Or maybe causation. But Briggs? He's like the golden boy of sports. Never been arrested, never made it in the tabloids for drugs or partying, doesn't even have a speeding ticket. (Yes, I checked.) I don't know why Connor is so determined to find some mysterious story, but I really don't want to be the one to tell it when Briggs hasn't done anything worth this much attention. And yet, something about my incredibly short interview caught Connor's attention, which is why he is determined to get me another chance with Briggs. A chance I don't want.

It's too bad Connor has never reassigned a story just because someone "wasn't feeling it." My alter ego is known for being ruthless, and that's not something Connor will give up lightly, no matter how much I hate it.

Connor rubs his temple, eyes closed as he sits in his chair and contemplates my argument. I hope he believes me and moves on from Briggs, but I'm not feeling very lucky today. I saw not one but two black cats on my way to the bus stop, and one of them watched me with its beady little eyes, like it was warning me that it might cross my path in the near future.

"You're right," Connor says eventually, and my breath catches. I am? But then he keeps talking. "Briggs is never going to give a reporter the insider scoop on his career unless it's a calculated move on his part, and that agent of his is one of the best. He's probably got Briggs locked up tight now when it comes to media appearances. There's no way Tamlin can get what we need out of him."

I never thought I would be so glad to lose such a big story, but I am. I could kiss Connor if he wasn't my boss. And if that wasn't a terrible way to thank someone who is happily married with four kids.

"I'll find a new story," I say, rising to my feet and tempted to fist pump as soon as I'm out of sight.

"Oh, you're not done with Briggs," Connor says, halting my steps. He's got his editor voice turned on, which makes me nervous. He only gets that excited rise in pitch and confidence when he thinks he's on to something. "I know there's something he's hiding, and Enhance will be the one to tell the nation the story. But it won't be Tamlin who gets the scoop. It'll be Darcy."

I blink. Did he forget that whole conversation we had a few days ago? The one where I begged him to let Darcy tell a story? "But I thought—"

"Not on camera, mind you. We still have your safety to worry about." Connor leans forward and grabs his mouse, clicking away, and I can't stop myself from slipping around his desk to see what he's looking for. He pulls up the folder we have on Houston, which is surprisingly small. Usually we have loads of intel, even if it isn't negative stuff. With Houston, we barely have anything beyond his player stats. I catch sight of college transcripts and salary info listed in the folder before Connor opens up a photo of a duplex, but there's not much else.

"Is that where he lives?" I ask, unable to keep the surprise out of my voice.

"Yup." Connor scrolls to a bunch of info we've got on the house, apparently looking for something specific.

The house is way too cute for a pro athlete to be living there. "Not in a penthouse suite or something?"

"There's a reason we don't have much on Briggs," he admits, and I can tell he hates that. Information is the bread and butter of journalism. He finds a phone number and types it into his desk phone without lifting the receiver.

"Sunset Properties," a woman answers over the speaker.

"Yes, I was wondering if the listing on Halladay Avenue is still available?"

"We've had a few offers, but nothing is under contract yet. Are you the buyer or the agent?"

"Agent. However, I was actually hoping I could put in a rental offer. I noticed the short-term lease option at the bottom of the page."

She's quiet for a moment before she says, "Between you and me, the rent he's asking is higher than a mortgage would be even without a down payment."

"That's not an issue. Really, we only need the house for a month or two, but we're willing to pay three months up front, including your commission."

What in the world is happening? Unease settles in my gut as Connor continues discussing fees and payments with the real estate agent, and I grab Connor's mouse to scroll back up to the picture of the duplex. *This* is how he plans to get info about Houston? Setting me up inside the other half of the guy's house? It's ludicrous, and dishonest, and if he is so worried about safety, why in the world would he put me in a house right next to the guy?

"I'll email you the details," Connor says, sounding way too gleeful for a guy who's about to be shot down.

The instant he hangs up, I strike. "No."

Connor chuckles. "What do you mean, no?"

I really wish I was taller, or that I had a pair of my Tamlin heels, but I fold my arms and try to look intimidating. "I mean no, I'm not going to spend a month in Sun City, in a house next to Houston freaking Briggs, just to get a scoop that may not exist!"

Rolling his eyes, he gives me a nudge so he can take control of his computer again and send a message to accounting, probably to pull together the funds to rent the other half of Houston's duplex. "If it takes you a whole month, you're not as good of a journalist as I thought."

"*Connor.*"

He points to the chair on the other side of the desk.

I sit, but only because I remind myself that he's not my friend. He's my boss. This job is the best thing that's ever happened to me, and I'm being reckless by adamantly refusing before I've even been told the details of what he's thinking. "Sorry," I grumble, shrinking a little in my chair.

At least Connor watches me with kindness in his eyes, though he's got that fatherly look that says he still sees me as a kid fresh out of college. I know it's only been two years since I finished grad school, but have I not proven myself to him with all of the Tamlin stories? Maybe he's mad that I didn't get anything out of Briggs when I was at the final game the other day.

"Darcy," he says calmly, "I know it's hard to see the end goal with some of this stuff, but I've been doing this for years. There's a story here; I can sense it. And even if you don't feel ready for a big break like this, you know as well as I do that we don't have anyone else I can send to Sun City for an extended period of time. We don't know how long it might take to get the intel, and you're the only one with both the flexibility and the, uh, availability."

I *know* he doesn't mean my open schedule. I cringe right along with him. "You want me to *date* Houston Briggs? Are you kidding me?"

He grimaces. "No, I'm not saying that. Nor am I saying I like the idea, because I don't, but if you flirt with him, he might give you something. He just ended his fling with What's-Her-Name, the actress, a couple of months ago."

I let out a laugh. "Houston Briggs only dates celebrities and super-models," I remind him, and then I sweep an arm over myself. I wore jeans with holes in the knees and a t-shirt from a boy band concert I went to over a decade ago. Tamlin may wear tight dresses and high heels, but I don't. Between that, my frizzy blonde hair that hates humidity, and my glasses because Tamlin's blue contacts always irritate my eyes for a couple of days, I'm not exactly the pitcher's type.

Connor shifts uncomfortably in his chair, like he wants to have this conversation even less than I do. "Darcy, give yourself some credit. You've got plenty to offer a guy."

"A guy like Houston Briggs? Ha! Connor, this isn't going to work. Don't spend all this money when there's no way—"

"This is happening with or without you," he says, leaving little room for argument. "If I have to outsource, I will, but if you're serious about making it in this field, sometimes you have to do things that push your comfort zone."

I already push my comfort zone. I dress up as someone I'm not and tear people down on live television every other week, and I hate it. But Connor's right. Most of the other journalists have been here for years and have made names for themselves already. Names that carry weight. Until I've better established myself as more than a terror, I have to do whatever it takes to get people to believe the words I say.

And knowing that Connor trusts me with something this big?

Unease starts to build as I realize I'm actually considering this. No, not even considering. I'm doing it. And I can't tell Connor that I'm terrified of spending that much time away from home because a journalist who's afraid of following a story isn't a journalist at all. I'm going to have to pull up my big girl panties and be brave, or I'm going to lose the best job I've ever had. Ever *will* have. Because I know deep down that any other sports news site is not going to have an editor who cares as much for his team as Connor does. He treats us like his family, and he'll do everything he can to make sure I'm safe in Sun City. He's rooting for me in a way no one else will, and I can't let that go.

His final argument is the clincher: "There's no one I would trust more with this assignment, Darcy. If anyone can get this story, you can."

"Okay," I breathe, feeling the word pull all of my fight out of me. It leaves me feeling like a mostly deflated balloon, misshapen and wrinkled. "When do I leave?"

Chapter Four

Houston

October 18

IF THERE'S A SIGHT better than my king size bed, I don't know what it is. Despite what most people think, I'm not a material guy, and there's not much in my house that I couldn't find somewhere else. But this? I paid more for this mattress than I probably should have, but when home is the only place I can (sometimes) get a good night's sleep now, it made sense to pay the premium. Looking at it now—after a week of dodging questions from reporters and the Red-tails owner—I'm almost in tears.

I'm so tired.

As I dump my bag in the corner, my phone starts to ring, and I groan. If that's Roundy, so help me... He promised me at least two days off before he started bugging me again about announcing my departure from the major leagues.

But the caller ID says it's my realtor, so I reluctantly answer the call. Maybe someone has finally bought the other half of my house. "Sheryl. Hi."

"Am I catching you at a good time?"

"Shoot."

"I've found you a renter while we wait for bids."

Kicking off my shoes, I frown at the room in general. "A renter? We still haven't gotten any offers?" I had hoped the high rental price would encourage a purchase over renting.

My shirt comes off next as Sheryl jumps into a long-winded explanation about the market and a townhome complex and something about beetles, and I'm glad she never wants to do video calls. I love my realtor, but she has a habit of saying way more than necessary, and I tend to get a lot done in the meantime.

In this case, it's making my way to the shower. This had better not be a long conversation because I am exhausted and covered in airport grossness, and my glorious bed is calling to me. It might be ten in the morning, but I've been up since two. I desperately need to sleep.

"So I've allowed the three-month lease," she finishes. "Is that acceptable?"

"Fine." I've made it to the bathroom and am down to my boxers, but anything beyond this feels like too much while I'm on the phone. I need to turn the water on to give it a chance to heat up—I haven't gotten around to replacing the outdated water heater—but Sheryl would definitely hear that. "When does the tenant move in?"

Three months isn't ideal, and I was really hoping to get someone in there permanently. But at least the place won't feel so empty anymore.

"They were very eager," Sheryl says, a little warily. "They asked for Sunday. You said it's move-in ready, right?"

I hold back a groan. That only gives me two days to get the place looking habitable after the last tenants left it an absolute mess. I should have just paid someone to clean it up, but I've wanted this place to be mine. Something my fame and money didn't touch. "Right," I say. I don't mean it. "You said *they*. Is it a family?" I hope it is. Give me a family of five with rowdy kids who bang on the walls and scream all night, and I'll stop feeling like the world is empty around me.

"Um, a brother and sister, I think. Their agent was vague on the details, but she passed her background check with flying colors."

"You got a name?"

"Darcy Paxton. I emailed you all the details and the contract."

"Thanks, Sheryl. Anything else?"

"Congratulations on your Series title. I can't wait to see what you do next season."

You and me both, I think with a sigh. Instead, I thank her for the update and hang up, turning on the shower and stepping inside even though the water is frigid. I am so ready for a nap.

A crunching sound wakes me, though I'm not sure if it was real or part of my dream. The details are slipping away already, but I'm pretty sure I was dreaming about waffle fries. I yawn, unsure what time it is but tempted to order in a burger and fries despite the havoc it will wreak on my intestines. I never eat fast food during the season, and my body has lost its tolerance for junk food.

Another crunch makes me stiffen. *Something is in here.* Slowly lifting my head, I prepare myself for some sort of creature ready to pounce—how did it get in here?—when my eyes catch sight of a human silhouette in the armchair. I jolt out of bed as panic hits, but my legs catch in the sheets and I go crashing to the floor.

Familiar laughter fills the room at the same time the curtains open, flooding the space with blinding sunlight.

"Jordan?" I gasp, scrambling to free myself. "What the hell, man?"

"Language," he says brightly.

Sitting up, I groan and rub the elbow that took the brunt of my fall. "Not you too." It's frustrating enough to have to be reminded by both my agent and my sister; I don't need my best friend joining in the game. Why does he even care? He never has before.

He's lounging in my armchair with a bag of Salsa Verde Doritos, grinning at me like he didn't just break into my house. "You gave me a key," he reminds me, as if my confusion is written all over my face. It probably is.

"I don't care how you're here," I grumble, getting to my feet and heading to the closet to grab some clothes. "I care about *why.*"

"I'm here because I haven't seen my best friend in weeks, and he just helped the Red-tails win the World Series. By the way, I am so glad to learn you don't sleep in the nude now. That is not something I need to see."

"You would have deserved it." I glower at him as I come back out in sweatpants and a t-shirt, and then I snatch the chips out of his hands. "No eating in the bedroom. What are you, a caveman?"

"Your sister doesn't have the same aversion to food in the bedroom."

I freeze, a sickening feeling pooling in my gut. "How in the world do you know that?"

"Wow, would you relax? She ate some snacks in her bed after she got that concussion last weekend."

If that was supposed to make me feel better, it didn't. I pretty much forgot the call I got from my twin sister right before Game Three after she fell and hit her head, and now I feel like a jerk for only checking in with her once. I let out a groan, muscles tensing in a way that only aggravates the inflammation in my shoulder. The last couple of weeks have been awful, and I don't anticipate things getting better anytime soon.

"I'm the worst," I mutter.

Jordan smirks. "You're fine. I've been keeping an eye on her."

"Still? It's been a week since…" I cut myself off, staring at Jordan and trying to catch any sign that he didn't heed my warning when I told him to keep his hands to himself last week after I asked him to keep an eye on Brook. Even when we were in high school, he was a ladies' man through and through. I don't know a better man than Jordan Torres, but that doesn't mean I think letting him play with my sister's heart is a great idea. She hasn't dated anyone in forever, and she's always had bad luck with love. I don't want my best friend adding to that bad luck by being his usual, charming self.

If he hasn't been interested in her before now, why would that have changed?

Pointing at me, Jordan shakes his head. "I know what you're thinking, but I've been trying to help her make a move on her teacher crush, so would you stop glaring at me?"

I think he's telling the truth. Jordan is nothing if not genuine to a fault. But I also think he's holding something back because he doesn't seem all that happy about Brooklyn finally making a move on the man she's been pining over for years. I would push for more if I had the energy for it, but I don't. I'm dealing with enough change right now as it is.

"Thanks for looking out for her," I say, leading the way down to the kitchen to see if I have anything in the fridge that isn't rotten. Odds are low. I genuinely don't remember the last time I bought groceries. I don't even think it was the last time I was home, before the Series started. It might be safer to buy a new fridge rather than open the door and find out what's growing inside this one.

"I don't know why I'm so tense," I mutter, rubbing my jaw as I move to the cupboard to see what I can find.

Jordan chuckles. "Sure you do. You've been off since your interview with Tamlin Park."

Does that mean he's been watching all my interviews? "Roundy said the same thing," I admit, though I don't think Tamlin can take all the credit. I went to the team PT after the game because the pain was too much to ignore, and he nearly strangled me when he realized how bad it is. I begged him to keep it between us for now, but that's only going to last for so long.

There's a chance I'll get enough rest before training starts up next year, but there's no guarantee my arm will last through another season. If I get surgery to repair the tears—yep, the team physician thinks there could be multiple microtears now because I've been ignoring the problem for months—I'll be out most of next season anyway. At that point, I'll be twenty-nine and basically starting over, and that doesn't exactly hold a lot of promise for a continuing career in the majors.

As he settles on a stool at the counter, Jordan keeps his eyes locked on me while I start a pot of coffee. "How bad is it?" he asks, reading my mind like he often does.

My half-sister, Micah, is so good at seeing the positive side of things, but I don't think even she could see the good in this situation. Clenching my jaw, I shake my head as I try not to let my churning emotions get the better of me. I don't think I could voice the damage in my shoulder even if I tried.

"I'm sorry, man." And I know he means it. Jordan is the only person on the planet who truly knows what baseball means to me. How much I need it in my life. It's more than just a game and a paycheck I don't need, and even though I know I can't keep playing, my chest aches thinking about what life will look like come spring.

I can't abandon my team, but what good am I to them with a bum arm? This decision shouldn't be a big deal—athletes retire all the time—but I've made sure no one has a clue it might be coming so soon. As soon as I make it all official, the sports world is going to go crazy. There won't be any turning back. I'm not ready for that.

"So, what now?" Jordan speaks out loud the question I've been asking myself for months now. One I don't have an answer for.

Swallowing my fears, I stand up straight and square my shoulders. Dwelling on the future isn't going to do me any good; I need to focus on now. "Got any jobs today?"

"Ha!" He gives me a dirty look. "You know full well I don't. And if I lose any business because you decided to cancel—"

I hold up my hands. "Okay, hey, give me some credit. I *rescheduled*. There's a difference."

"Why?"

"Because I need your help." That's not actually why I did it, but I'll take advantage of his availability.

I'm never going to get the other side of the duplex cleaned up on my own before Sunday, and I know Jordan's not opposed to hard labor. The man started his own landscaping company after all, and he's quickly becoming one of the most coveted companies in Sun City. Granted, I did give his company a shout-out the other day in the hopes of getting him more business, but he's built up a good reputation on his own.

That's why I rescheduled all of his appointments today. He needs a break, and this will be the perfect thing to keep his mind off of work before he gets sucked back into his workaholic tendencies. The man never stops.

Wary, he follows me as I grab a set of keys and head outside, crossing the shared front porch to the other half of the house. I haven't been in here since the last tenants left a couple of months ago, but I still have nightmares from what I saw. How anyone could make that much of a mess is beyond me, and it's going to take more than a few Clorox wipes to get the house in rentable shape.

"I have renters moving in on Sunday," I say as I unlock the door, "and I need to get this place ready."

Jordan swears as soon as the door swings open, apparently forgetting Brook's aversion to cursing as his jaw hangs open. "Dude, I thought this place was on the market."

I snicker at his look of horror. "It is."

"I saw the photos. They're gorgeous."

"The photos are of my place, just flipped," I say with a shrug. "I haven't had the time to get this side fixed up yet, so I had to improvise."

"This looks like a murder scene."

He's not wrong. The last tenants—a husband and wife in their fifties—were painters, something I didn't know until they moved out and left several paintings behind. Some of them weren't bad, but most of them were, uh, *questionable*. They had an affinity for painting gruesome death scenes from moments in history, which meant a lot of splashes of red paint. And I'm talking literal splashes. If I hadn't seen the paintings before chucking most of them in a dumpster, I would have been convinced there was a lot of stabbing and head slashing happening every time I was out of town for a game based on the splattered state of the walls.

If I'm being honest, I'm still a little convinced. I'm tempted to bring in a blacklight to see if there are any traces of actual blood in here, but I'm a little worried what else I might find. They were a strange couple all around.

"Why didn't you just pay someone to come in and—"

"You know why," I mutter, leaving it at that. Jordan knows that after the way I grew up, I hate my bank account almost as much as I hate being given the credit for all of my team's wins. Well, credit from everyone but Tamlin Park. If it were up to her, she would have the world convinced that I'm the reason we've *only* made it to the Series twice in the last eight years. Only she would overlook the fact that we won both times.

Reading my mind again, Jordan chuckles as he picks up an overturned, empty red paint bucket. Yes, *bucket*. The five-gallon kind. He flips it over and sits on the bottom, watching me carefully as he says, "So, how long have you been afraid of Tamlin Park?"

I throw an old paintbrush at him. "I am *not* afraid of her. She's half my weight and always teetering on heels, so I'm pretty sure I could take her."

He laughs. "That's not what I meant, and you know it. You couldn't get out of that interview fast enough."

He's spot on, but for some reason I haven't been able to get the woman out of my head. It's like she burrowed in there and set up camp, just waiting for me to do something wrong. She's not even in Sun City, but I can't shake the feeling that she's nearby.

I do my best to ignore the unease building inside me and deflect Jordan's accusation. "I was tired. Wanted to shower."

"I was tired. Wanted to shower."

"She called you old."

"I *am* old." I huff a little as I grab a discarded garbage bag and start stuffing it with junk. "I'm, like, eighty in pitcher years."

"You don't look a day older than sixty-five," Jordan says. He hops up, bringing his bucket with him to start loading up his own batch of garbage. "What I wanna know is why you don't want anyone to know you're retiring. If you know you can't play, why keep up the charade?"

I wish I had an answer for that.

Even though I remain silent, Jordan keeps talking. He's definitely the kind of guy who regularly has conversations with himself because he's usually the most entertaining guy in the room, and I still haven't figured out why he moved back into his parents' house here in Sun City and started working in a fairly isolated job working landscape maintenance and design. He spent the last decade in California, working for a ridiculously elite PR firm up until a year ago when he randomly dropped his whole life and moved home.

He still hasn't told me why he gave up everything he'd built out there, but I know it has something to do with him working too hard. He and I share that trait, which is not necessarily a good thing.

"But seriously, man," he says, unaware of my concern for him, "you're lucky you walked away from that interview in one piece. She looked like she was ready to eat you alive, and not in a good way. What did you do to get on her bad side?"

"I have no idea," I admit, forcing myself to focus again. Then I groan as I peek into the kitchen. "We're going to have to call in a dumpster for all of this. It's like they turned this place into a demo zone before they left!"

Jordan already has his phone out. "I've got a guy," he explains, reminding me why I have always trusted him with all my darkest secrets. He may not take life too seriously, but he's always there when it matters.

I could really use someone like that right now.

Chapter Five

Darcy

October 20

WHEN WE PULL UP outside of Houston's duplex, my stomach is churning so badly that I'm pretty sure my first act in my new temporary home is going to be throwing up in the well-manicured bushes. Nothing says "welcome home" or "hi, I'm your new tenant" like a bit of puke. Thankfully, I was too nervous to eat breakfast this morning at the hotel, so there's not a lot to lose if I do end up ralphing. Who decided to call it that, anyway? What did Ralph do to be equated with vomiting?

"Looks nice," Jesse grunts, leaning over to peer at the house through my window. He doesn't have much of an expression, which is par for the course with him. "Not what I expected."

It's exactly what I expected because I've spent the last several days memorizing the photos on the listing, just so I feel less anxious about staying in a new place. It may be temporary, but the fact that most of my possessions are packed in the truck behind us makes it feel far more permanent than that.

I turn to the man beside me and give him a wobbly smile. "Have I told you how glad I am that you're here with me?"

His blank face cracks a little, lips lifting in the closest thing to a smile I've ever seen on him. I was more than shocked when Connor told me he was sending Jesse on this assignment as well, both for protection—the man is obnoxiously ripped, like a short-haired version of Jason Momoa, complete with some impressive tattoos—and for his talents with a make-up brush. Connor wants Tamlin to keep pushing things with Houston while I'm here, and I can't become her without Jesse and his magic hands.

I tried once, but I ended up making myself look like a rodeo clown. I had never tried contouring until that day, and I'll never try again.

"Well?" Jesse says, his gaze surprisingly soft as he looks at me. He told me as we packed up the truck back in St. Louis that he would follow my lead on this one, which basically means I'm his boss for the next month, or however long this takes. I'd love to get this over within a week or less, but knowing my luck, that is simply wishful thinking because I still think there's nothing to find. Poor guy is going to be stuck with me instead of back home with his several cats.

Hopefully it's not for long.

"I guess we should get our keys," I say breathlessly. "Houston lives on the left side, and Sheryl said he'll have the keys for us." Apparently, Houston owns both halves of the duplex and has been renting out the other side for a year or so, up until he decided to try to sell the right side instead. I still haven't been able to figure out why a professional athlete who makes twenty-five million dollars a year would choose a little duplex in the suburbs as his home of choice, but I can just add that to my long list of things I'm here to discover about baseball's squeaky-clean pitcher.

"And we're sure this is the right place?" Jesse asks, clearly feeling as uncertain about all of this as I am.

I take a deep breath. "Yep." What I'm less sure about is Houston not recognizing me the moment he lays eyes on me. Granted, my own parents don't know that I'm Tamlin, but they also hardly ever watch sports news. There's no telling what a guy like Houston, who recognized Tamlin instantly from across the news tent, would pick up on. I'm Clark Kenting, AKA I just have to hope my normal Darcy self is so underwhelming that he wouldn't in his wildest imaginings think Tamlin and I were the same person.

At the same time, I have to hope my normal Darcy self isn't *so* underwhelming that he doesn't pay me any attention at all.

Jesse reaches over and grabs my hand, which I didn't realize was trembling until his large fingers wrap around mine. "Hey, little sister," he says, which is what he's been calling me since my first day on the job. He's looked out for me from the beginning, and I love him for it. "You got this. There's no one who can step into the job like you do."

"It's the theater minor. They didn't call me the Improv Queen for nothing." I give him a weak smile. "I'm really glad you're here, Jess."

He gives me a squeeze in return. "I know."

It's just enough courage to get me out of the car and to Houston's front door, but then I freeze with my fist in the air. "They didn't actually call me the Improv Queen," I whisper, back to being terrified.

Jesse chuckles. "I know." Then he knocks on the door.

I stand there with my breath held in my lungs long enough that I start to feel dizzy, but the door doesn't open. I force an exhale and knock again, louder than Jesse did.

Nothing.

"Maybe she told us the wrong side?" I say with a shrug. Jesse matches the gesture, and the two of us slip down the porch to the other door.

To my surprise—and maybe horror—the door is slightly ajar, faint classical music coming from somewhere inside. I peek inside to make sure the front room is empty rather than Houston's living room, and then I give the door a nudge. It creaks open slowly. Ominously. Bare walls echo the music from wherever it's originating, and the whole house seems dark and dim behind all of the closed blinds.

"Creepy," Jesse says, and I don't miss the excitement in his voice. Or the twinkle in his dark eyes.

I grimace. "Only you would think 'Night on Bald Mountain' blasting from an empty basement would be cool," I whisper, giving him a shove forward. Not only does he get excited by the thought of alien invasions and hauntings, but he's way bigger than me. If Connor sent him to New Mexico to protect me, I fully expect him to do his job.

Thankfully, he leads the way down the stairs as the nightmarish music grows louder around us. The room below is bathed in red light, which only seems to make Jesse even more excited. I grip the back of his shirt and take a ninja pose, as if that's enough to save me from getting murdered the minute we hit the cement floor below.

When Jesse steps off to the side, I get my first look at the horror scene. It's so much worse than I imagined, and my whole body goes on high alert. Forget the creepy music from *Fantasia*—the sight in front of me is the most terrifying thing I've ever seen.

A man kneels on the cement, rubber gloves pulled up to his elbows and a scrub brush in his hands. Soapy water coats the floor, but it's the red color that triggers my nausea again. It's all over him too, in his hair, on his shirt, on his *face*. Whoever taught this guy how to clean up blood did a poor job of it, or maybe we've just walked in on him cleaning up his latest kill as the music swells to the climax.

He looks up, narrowed eyes taking us in, and then he flashes a wide, crazed grin. "Looks like my next victims are here."

A scream tears out of me, and I run, stumbling back up the stairs as fast as my legs will carry me. Jesse! But no, he's on his own. He's the one who wanted to go into the serial killer's basement. I make it to the truck, but Jesse locked the doors, and I'm thinking about booking it down the street when a charcoal pickup pulls up in the driveway and a kind-looking man hops out, his dark eyes on me.

"Hey, are you okay?"

I can barely breathe enough to get the words out. "Murderer," I gasp, pointing to the house. "Need to...call...police..." And I'm only just now realizing that this could be one of his accomplices. He doesn't look nearly as frightened as he should, and he did pull into the driveway. What if he's the guy's partner? Did he just drop off the body somewhere?

"Easy," the man says gently, holding up his hands and giving me a smile that makes me want to trust him. Pretty much everything about him is warm, from his dark complexion to his friendly expression. "Take a deep breath, okay? You said there's someone in that house?" He points to the duplex, and I nod. "Did you see them?"

I tuck my arms around myself, finally calming down enough to think a little more rationally. "Of course I saw him. He was—heavens to Betsy, what if he's killing Jesse!"

The man's smile grows. "Is that Jesse?"

My head whips around to find Jesse coming out the front door, stoic as ever. Relief washes over me. "You're alive!"

Jesse furrows his eyebrows. "Darcy?"

"You're Darcy?" The man beside me perks up, and he seems to notice the moving truck behind me for the first time, matching Jesse's confused expression. "You weren't supposed to get here until tonight."

"Why? So that maniac down in the basement would have time to hide the body?" I snap. At this point, I know I've probably overreacted, but my heart's still pounding and I need to put that energy somewhere. "We drove through most of the night," I add. "The place is supposed to be move-in ready."

The man chuckles, shaking his head. "I told him that would bite him in the butt, but did he listen to me? Of course not. Ah, there's your murderer."

I tense as the basement psycho comes through the door and joins Jesse on the porch, covered from head to toe in...purple. Not blood.

"I see you found a way to get the paint out of the cement," the guy beside me says with another laugh.

The one on the porch—who is clearly Houston Briggs now that I'm seeing him in the daylight—scowls at his friend. "It was washable paint," he mutters before his eyes turn to me.

A shiver runs through me. His scowl is still in place, and now that it's directed at me, I'm not sure what to do with it.

"You weren't supposed to get here until tonight," he says, repeating the other guy's intonation and everything.

I can't help but frown. "I thought the place was ready for us to move in on Sunday. Today is Sunday."

He takes the steps down the shared porch, and instinct sends me back a step as he gets a little too close for comfort. At least he pauses, folding his purple-stained arms over his broad chest. Goodness, when he's just in a t-shirt like this, I can see every muscle strain and stretch with his movement. He's not at Jesse levels, but I can see why he's paid for his arms.

He looks me over for a second, his blue eyes hard to read. "Sorry for the scare, but you really should have—"

A stream of water in his face cuts him off, and I jump, turning to find the source. The other guy has the garden hose in his hand and is gleefully washing the pitcher down.

Houston, with eyes shut tight, spits water from his mouth as soon as the hose turns off. "Jordan," he growls.

"Sorry, man, but you looked ridiculous. No one wants to be talking to a landlord who looks like Tinky-Winky."

Houston looks like he's ready to strangle Jordan, but instead he turns his attention back to me. "I apologize for my idiotic friend," he says.

I bite my lip to keep from laughing, which is surprising given I was running for my life a moment ago. Despite his still-present scowl, now that he's soaking wet, I'm less intimidated and more amused by this whole thing. Did I really think I had walked into a murder scene? Now I know not to listen to true crime while driving across several states.

"Actually," I say when I'm sure I've reined in my laughter, "I'm with Jordan on this one. You can hardly call any of this professional."

"Again," Houston growls through gritted teeth, "I wasn't expecting you yet. But you're right. I should have had the house ready for you." He glances behind him to where Jesse is still standing on the porch like a silent, broody sentinel, and all of his muscles tense and tighten as if to try to match Jesse's bulk.

It's a good look for him, let me tell you, even if the display is a little ridiculous.

Jordan gives him another squirt in the face with the hose, killing the pose. "I have an idea," he says, completely ignoring the thunderous look in Houston's expression. "How about the two of you hang out in Houston's living room while he takes a shower and I finish clearing out the basement? And since he seems to have forgotten how politeness works, hi, I'm Jordan Torres. That's Houston Briggs, your landlord, and some people consider him to be sort of famous."

I take the hand Jordan holds out, enjoying his company far more than I'm enjoying Houston's right now. "I'm Darcy Paxton. That's my, uh, brother, Jesse. And what kind of famous are we talking here? TV spot for depression meds? Or local celebrity after streaking through the high school football game?"

Jordan busts up into a laugh so hard that he nearly doubles over and takes me down with him. "Hear that, Texas? Not everyone knows who you are. It's a miracle!"

"I play baseball for the local team," Houston says casually, as if being one of the highest paid athletes in the country is no big deal. "And yes, please come in and make yourselves comfortable. Jordan and I can help you bring your stuff in as soon as I look a little more *professional.*"

"I'd rather get started bringing stuff in," I say, though the thought of gaining access to Houston's house is tempting. I need to play the long game here if I want him to trust me, so I can't look too eager. "We'll stick to the bedrooms and living room for now."

Houston nods once, flinches when Jordan lifts the hose toward him again, and then he stalks into the left side of the duplex without another word.

"He seems nice," I say as soon as the door closes. I can't help myself.

Jordan grins as he begins rolling the hose back onto its stand. "Don't take it too hard. He's had a rough week, and he's not usually wound so tight. He just got back from his season, and he'll warm up in a couple of days."

I meet Jesse's gaze, and we have a silent, micro expression conversation. We've gotten good at that over the years since he doesn't talk much and I'm not allowed to move my face when he's contouring.

Rough week? Jesse says. *I thought they won.*

They did win, I reply. *This must be something else. I'll try to get some more details.*

Think he'll actually say anything?

Guess we'll find out. It's why we're here, after all.

You wanna get a pizza?

Okay, that last part was probably just me projecting, but I'm pretty sure Jesse agrees with me; he's already pulling out his phone as I nod. We've got a pretty good meal stipend while we're out here, which makes me wonder yet again why Connor is so interested in Houston Briggs. The amount of money he's shelled out for this story is honestly ridiculous, and way more than what I'm getting paid to be here. He's looking for something, but I'm not sure yet what it is.

"I'll be downstairs if you need me," Jordan says with a salute, and then he disappears into the house.

"I ordered Chinese," Jesse says, which isn't exactly pizza, but I'll take it.

Then we both look at the truck. Connor hired a moving company to load everything up, but he wanted us to look authentic when we got to Sun City. AKA not like we had the bank accounts of an award-winning news agency funding everything. We have to look like regular Jack and Jill while we're out here, which means moving all of our boxes and furniture ourselves. *Yay.*

"Let's do this," I growl, hoping all of this is going to be worth it.

GREY
BIRD
TAVERN

Chapter Six

Houston

I WILL NEVER SAY out loud that I am relieved when Darcy announces that we've grabbed the last box from the truck, but I am *worn out*. You would think after a full season of keeping myself in peak shape I would be able to move a couple of couches and some dishes, but no. I'm ready to park it on the floor and take a nap right here in Darcy's living room rather than stumble back over to my house and crash on the couch because the stairs will be too much.

It doesn't help that Jordan is still full of energy, and Darcy's giant of a brother barely broke a sweat. Even Darcy seems to have more stamina than me as she laughs with Jordan while they bond over Chinese takeout.

Jordan has been denying up and down for the last few days that he's into my sister, Brooklyn, but there have been some pointed conversations that have me wondering if there's more than new friendship between the two of them. I'm slowly wrapping my head around the idea, but that means I don't like how friendly he's being with Darcy. Okay, so Jordan *is* the friendliest guy in the world. And I can't say that I've seen him flirt in almost a decade, but I hope it doesn't look like *this*. This little banter thing they have going looks more like a sibling thing, so I'm trying not to overthink it so I don't stress out.

Except I *can't* stop thinking about how Brook and Jordan might be secretly dating without telling me. They used to hate each other back when we were teens, and I can't picture them being friendly enough to be anything but reluctant acquaintances. I know I've missed a lot in my siblings' lives since signing with the Red-tails, but I don't like knowing I missed my two best friends forming an attachment. What if it doesn't last and I have to choose between them? I don't have enough people in my life to like the idea of losing my best friend.

So much for not stressing.

"Houston, thanks so much for helping us move our stuff in," Darcy says, still grinning wide from whatever Jordan said that made her laugh. "You want some chow mein?"

My stomach growls just looking at the paper box, but Jordan jumps in. "Oh, Hou doesn't eat anything processed or fried. He's a chicken breast and broccoli kind of guy."

I don't miss the way Darcy's eyes travel over me as I stand by the door. She may not know who I am, but at least she seems to appreciate the hard work I've put in. "I'm guessing you prefer protein shakes over waffles?" she says, laughter in her voice.

Thanks for making me sound like a stick in the mud, Jordan. Though my bed is calling to me, I settle on the floor on the other side of the coffee table from Darcy and accept the container she holds out to me. "It's the offseason," I say, trying not to sound as exhausted as I feel. "And I love waffles. Especially when Jordan makes them." Why did I say that? I've only had his breakfast offerings once.

Darcy glances between us as she chews on some noodles, a lot of questions rolling around behind her brown eyes. "So... Are you two—"

"Friends!" I say quickly before she starts to get the wrong idea. I can see it in her eyes just as easily as I can see how tempted Jordan is to argue against me, just to make things awkward. I will *not* let him try to diffuse this not-tense situation with one of his terrible jokes. "You can ask my sister. Jordan and I are just friends. Definitely friends."

Jordan snickers. Yeah, I probably overdid that one.

Darcy looks like she wants to laugh at me, which is pretty much the expression she's had since she realized I wasn't going to murder her. It's a strange feeling, not immediately charming her the moment she learned my name, and her disinterest has me feeling off kilter. She's clearly not a baseball fan, or at least not a Red-tails fan, and it's been so long since I wasn't an object of desire that I honestly have no idea how to interact with this woman.

It's a pity, because she's definitely cute. With her average height and build, the most I've noted about her body is her strength—she carried several boxes of books up to her room that weren't light—but I keep finding myself drawn to her face. Her blonde hair falls in wavy curls to her shoulders, a bit wild and free. It's not nearly as curly as my sister Micah's hair, but I would imagine it takes her a lot of work to keep it tamed. Her eyes are the warmest brown I've ever seen, like melted chocolate mixed with honey. Her round face leaves her looking soft and sweet, and it's so different from the women I've been dating the last several years that I find it hard to look away. She seems like the kind of person who laughs easily and loves hard. But there's a toughness about her too. She could have sat back and watched the three of us unload the truck, but she was right there in the middle of it all, taking the other end of the dining table and hefting boxes of plates and Christmas decorations. I've never seen anyone like her.

Her brother—Jesse—clears his throat, and when I look at him, he's giving me a steely stare that puts me on edge.

I don't think Jesse likes me very much.

Darcy clears *her* throat, pulling his attention to her, and then the two of them have another silent conversation. They've had a lot of those since their arrival, and it's a clear indication that they are siblings.

"So," Jordan says, breaking the silence. "Where did you guys move from?"

"St. Louis," Darcy says at the same time Jesse says, "Dallas."

I meet Jordan's eye, but we're not at mind-reading friendship levels despite knowing each other since we were fourteen. He's just giving me a weird look.

"We were in Dallas," Darcy amends, "for a little while, but then we went up to St. Louis. Now we're here."

"Why Sun City?" I ask. In terms of metropolises, Sun City isn't anything major. Not like St. Louis or Dallas, anyway. We've got the Red-tails and a USL soccer team, but other than that there's not a lot that goes on here.

Darcy gives Jesse a sharp look before she shrugs. "It just felt like a good place to be for a little while."

"Not very long," I point out. "You only signed a three-month lease."

Another shrug. "Our lives are pretty transient right now. Maybe we'll stay longer than we planned, but it's hard to say what will happen."

"That sounds hard, constantly being on the move."

"Sure does," Jordan agrees loudly. "I don't know why anyone would be opposed to settling down and growing roots." He doesn't look at me, but I'd be an idiot to think he's talking to anyone but me. Either he has been taking notes from Brook, or he sees what I've been ignoring the last couple of years: I've spent too long letting good things slip away from me because I'm afraid to hold on too tightly and risk getting hurt.

It's crazy to think, with the life I've lived, that I would ever reach a point where I want to take that risk, but I do. Terrifying as it is, I do want to settle. Especially now that I know I won't be able to pitch next season.

My shoulder twinges painfully, probably because I've barely had any rest time since the last game.

Like I need the reminder, shoulder... The only reason no one knows about my injury yet is because I have a high pain tolerance, but I am almost never pain-free anymore. It's as constant as my fear of the future.

"I'm guessing your sister lives here in Sun City?" Darcy asks, eyeing me with interest.

I realize I've been subconsciously rubbing my shoulder, and I drop my hand. "Yeah, they both do. And my older brother." Unless he never comes back from Laketown. I swear, if Chad ends up staying in that tiny mountain town for a girl... I always sort of pictured Chad being there as a fixture of my life—the silent support, solid and steady on his own. It's not that I don't want him to be happy, but losing him to a relationship would be like losing the man who pretty much raised me.

I should probably call Chad. I don't remember the last time we had a real conversation that wasn't about sports. The only reason I even know there's a girl in Laketown is because Micah said something about it in our group chat. Beyond her existence, I know literally nothing. Not even if Chad is interested like Micah claims, though it would surprise me if he was. He's only a few months off of his breakup with his stupid cheating girlfriend—good riddance—and probably not in a place to date.

I love my brother, but he's not exactly big on emotions.

Micah thinks he's falling in love, though, and no one is more about love than her. Maybe I should trust her take on the situation, partially because she talks to Chad more than Brook or I do. I've never fully figured out why when they have eleven years separating them and Micah has never really lived with Chad, but sometimes I wonder if I'm jealous of my half-sister for getting more of his attention than I do.

"Well, as much as I love awkwardly stilted conversation," Jordan says, rising to his feet, "I've got a movie night planned with Brooklyn, and no offense, but she's way hotter than any of you."

I groan. This is hardly better than stressing about my brother. "Do you have to call her hot?" This is only adding to my suspicions that they're more than friends, but I don't want Jordan's side to be a casual fling. If he's going to date Brook, he had better be serious about it.

As he heads for the door, Jordan gives me the kind of grin that I know is meant to torture me. "Gorgeous, bodacious, enchanting, bewitching, *delicious.*" He closes the door before I can throw my empty chow mein container at him, but I can still hear him shouting words to describe my sister. "Patient, confident, caring, clever."

He keeps going until his voice fades away, and while I'm glad he sees the awesomeness that is my twin, I still stand by my assertion that he's dead to me if he's only playing with her heart. I should probably ask Brook what's happening on her side of that relationship; she never liked Jordan when we were in high school, and she wasn't afraid to tell me so. What if he's just forcing himself into her life and driving her crazy like he used to? Jordan can be pushy when he wants something.

"Are you guys close?" Darcy asks, her voice a lot gentler than I expected. "You and Brooklyn, I mean."

We used to be. "We're twins."

"And you said you have another sister?"

I frown. "A half-sister."

Why does it look like she's cataloging that information away in her brain? Maybe I'm being paranoid after a week of press releases and interviews. Darcy doesn't even know who I am, and she's probably just trying to figure out her weirdo of a landlord.

Speaking of... I cough, struggling up to my feet like an old man. *Not a fan of that.* "I'll get some replacement light bulbs tomorrow for the basement. I think the last tenants were using it as a photo development room."

At least, I *hope* that's what they were doing. It doesn't explain all the purple paint, but that thankfully came off the cement. Maybe I'll also check out flooring samples tomorrow while I'm at the hardware store and see if that's something I'll be able to install myself. It'll give me something to do other than suffocate beneath the crushing weight of my ever-increasing dread.

"Do you guys need anything else tonight?" I ask.

Darcy shakes her head, still looking at me curiously. Maybe she's just tired like I am. She did just unload her truck after driving all the way from...wherever.

I stand there for a minute, unsure if I should be doing anything else for the two of them. The last tenants moved in in the middle of the night and always stuck their rent checks through the mail slot, so I genuinely have no recollection of what they look like. In the year they lived next door, I saw them only a few times, and always at strange hours.

"I'm next door if you need anything," I say, "but just in case, let me give you my number."

Darcy looks a little too excited about that, so maybe I haven't lost my game as much as I thought, though it's not like I actually want to date my tenant. Even if she does eagerly hand over her phone.

That would be a bad idea.

I add a little caveat before heading back to my place: "Text me if *the house* needs anything."

I have too much to deal with right now to be thinking more about my attractive new next-door neighbor than I already am.

Chapter Seven

Darcy

OH, THE THINGS I could do with Houston's phone number. There are probably only a handful of people who have this number, and to know I'm one of them has me feeling a whole lot of feelings I probably shouldn't be feeling. Especially because I shouldn't be awake right now, staring at my neighbor's contact info. It's the dag nab middle of the night, and I should absolutely be getting as much sleep as I can before I start planning out my approach with Houston.

What does it mean that he trusted me with his phone number so easily? Maybe he was required by law, as my landlord. Maybe he has a phone strictly for work purposes. Maybe the way he stared at me during our living room dinner on the floor was more than just curiosity.

As vain as it sounds, I'm used to people staring at me. As *Tamlin*. As Darcy, I get the occasional notice, but no one usually takes the time to study my face like they're mapping it out. Houston Briggs, on the other hand, spent a good three minutes watching me until Jesse, being the good fake brother that he is, silently called him out on it. I have no idea what to do with Houston's attention. I don't think he was trying to imagine me as Tamlin, or he wouldn't have given me his number. (I should probably praise Jesse for his makeup magic tomorrow.) He was definitely looking for something, though.

But what?

Groaning, I slip off of my mattress, which is currently on the floor because I was too tired to build my frame last night, and creep out of my bedroom. Jesse's snoring softly across the hall, and I'm pretty sure he could sleep through a tornado. He once went with me to cover a hockey game after working a multi-reporter gig the day before and slept through several alarms. I had to convince hotel security that there was a health hazard so they would let me in to shake him awake. So, I don't have to worry about waking him if I go down to the kitchen and find myself a snack.

There's not much down here yet—Jesse offered to grab some groceries tomorrow when he turns in the truck and picks up our rental car—but I grab some leftover sweet and sour from the fridge and head out onto the back patio, planting myself on the steps. It may be October, but New Mexico's dry heat lingers differently from Missouri's humidity. It's still cool, but in a pleasant way. Plus, there are about a million more stars here, and I'm captivated within seconds.

Stargazing, however, leads to a good deal of thinking, and it doesn't take long before I figure out why I can't sleep.

This is the strangest job I've ever done, and I literally have no idea what I'm doing. Yesterday was a fun bit of make-believe, pretending I was back in college, moving into the dorms for the first time. Just like then, just like it's always been, it was me and the guys, the ones who quickly realized I had more in common with them than I did with my fellow girls. Jordan was easy to befriend, and I can imagine he hangs around here a lot with the way he interacted with Houston. I'll be glad to have him as a buffer sometimes because there was only so much pretending I could do with his friend.

Houston Briggs. He honestly surprised me yesterday by helping us move everything even though that's not part of his duties as landlord, and he spent a lot of time laughing and joking with Jordan throughout the afternoon. Like a regular guy. Not like a guy who is hiding some big story for me to find.

What in the world am I supposed to do with him? Whatever Connor is looking for, he thinks Darcy can find it, but I don't know the first thing about espionage. When I'm Tamlin, no one ever questions what I'm after. Sure, I'm pretending to be someone I'm not, but I never lie to people.

Being around Houston as Darcy—as myself—is going to feel so much more dishonest, and I'm worried that my whole life here in Sun City, no matter how short, is going to feel like a lie. That means my budding friendship with Jordan is a lie. If I ever meet Brooklyn, like Jordan wants me to—I'm pretty sure those two are dating and Houston either doesn't know or doesn't like it—that relationship will be a lie too. The only reason I'm here is to get the scoop on Houston, whatever that may be, and then I'll be gone.

Is a job really worth compromising my integrity?

As if the universe is determined to answer my silent question to the stars, my phone buzzes with a text. It's almost four in the morning in Pennsylvania, so why in the world is Carissa awake?

Carissa:

> I interacted with my first patient yesterday! He was the cutest old man who just had a knee replacement, and he is so determined to walk that he just went for it and basically tackled me trying to stay on his feet. It was AWESOME.

I still don't know why she's awake, but I smile anyway. My little sister just started her internship with a physical therapy clinic.

Me:

> You and I have very different versions of awesome.

Carissa:

> Hot dang why are you awake?

Me:

> Why are YOU?

Carissa:

> Because I have the early shift today. First patient comes in at five. Aren't you in Arizona or something?

I hesitate. I could let her misremember and keep my location more of a secret, just in case things go south and someone connects me to Tamlin. Carissa doesn't know that I am ever on TV—she thinks I'm an intern or an assistant and that I'm just working up to actually writing stories and reporting them.

But I don't like lying to my baby sister, so I sigh and type out my response.

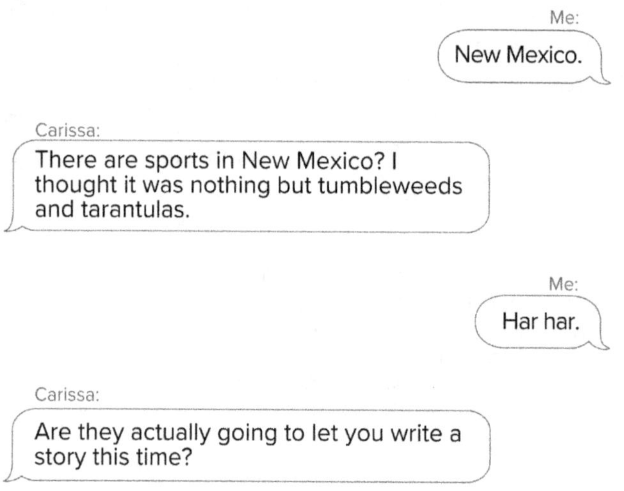

Little does she know that this could be my biggest break yet. She also doesn't know that she's half the reason I work as hard as I do. Yeah, I want to make a name for myself as a serious sports journalist, but I also want to make enough money so that I can keep helping Mom and Dad with her student loans. PT school is expensive, and they had to take out a second mortgage to help cover the monthly costs. Carissa was born to be a therapist, obviously, but she's never been great with money. She has no idea just how much my parents have sacrificed to help her live these dreams of hers, and if I have anything to do with it, she never will.

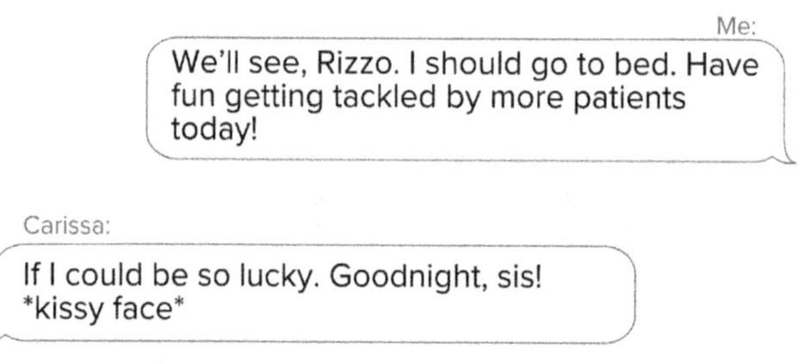

I chuckle and stand to head back to my bed, but a shadowy shape moves just ahead. I shriek, throwing my food in the air and stumbling back. A hand catches my wrist at the same time an arm snakes around my back to hold me steady, and then suddenly I'm pressed against a whole man.

"Sorry!" Houston says, his voice somewhere above my head. Did I know he was this tall? I'm pretty sure when I interviewed him last week,

Jesse put me in Tamlin's tallest heels, so I didn't notice. Neither was I close enough to him yesterday to really compare our heights. But standing here in his hold makes me realize that he probably has more than six inches on me. I'm the perfect height to rest my head against his chest and hang out here for a while.

"I'm going to let go of you, okay? Are you steady?"

"Yep," I say even if I don't feel steady at all. He caught me so easily, and I just got up close and personal with his insanely fit body. I hate how much I wish I had realized that *before* he slowly lets go of me. Now that he's no longer touching me, I'm acutely aware of how warm he is because I'm suddenly chilled without him.

A light flickers on in his hand—the flashlight on his phone—and illuminates the patio beneath our feet. It gives us enough light to see each other, for which I'm grateful because this sheepish smile of his is borderline adorable. That's not something he ever puts on TV.

"I promise I'm not trying to sneak up on you or murder you in the dark," he says lightly. "I didn't think anyone would be up this early."

Hmm, he's calling this early, while in my head this is late. Does that mean he's already slept some tonight?

"Do you always get up at two A.M.?" I ask.

He relaxes a little, probably glad to see that I'm not afraid of him this time. I still am afraid, but I don't think he's going to murder me. I'm more worried that he's going to spell the end of my career as I know it. That could be a good thing or a bad thing, depending on the story he gives me.

"Not all the time," he says, shuffling his feet. He's wearing old man slippers and a pair of gym shorts, which is a really strange combination. He follows my gaze. "I don't recommend walking around outside barefoot at night," he says.

I look up. "Why?"

"There might be scorpions and—"

I yelp, and next thing I know I'm in his arms, my arms around his neck and my feet swinging wildly as he tries to keep his balance. "Oh!" I gasp, not sure if I should laugh or cry. I should get some sleep, is what I should do. "Sorry," I whisper. "I had no idea that I could jump that high."

He doesn't seem to know what to do with me, half a smile on his face. "I mean, you're not super likely to run into any this far into the city, but it's good to be cautious. I've seen a few here and there."

I shake my head, still gripping him tight. And only partially because I'm worried I'm going to die out here. Do people die from scorpion stings? I think kids can, but I'd probably survive as an adult. Man, this guy is strong. He's holding me like I weigh nothing, and he smells so good. Whatever soap he uses, he absolutely needs to keep using it. It's almost enough to make me forget about the scorpions.

"Okay, so here's something you need to know about me," I say, not sure why I'm telling him this. I'm supposed to be getting close to him, not giving him reasons to ignore me. "I am incredibly unlucky."

He raises an eyebrow. "Unlucky?"

"You know, break a mirror, walk under a ladder, open an umbrella inside kind of unlucky. If anyone is going to get stung by a scorpion, it's going to be me because I have all the bad luck in the world."

That gets a little laugh out of him, which I feel deep inside me because I'm still hanging out in his arms. I'm not mad about it. "I'm pretty sure supersti—"

"When I was in the eighth grade, I spilled the salt at breakfast," I tell him, trying to sound as dramatic as possible. This is a true story, but I want to hear him laugh again. I never get to hear athletes laugh when I'm doing interviews because they're always so afraid of saying the wrong thing. "I didn't throw any over my shoulder," I continue, "and later that day, I ripped my pants completely down the seam. I had to wear a pair of sweatpants from the Lost and Found that smelled like old gym socks."

Houston purses his lips. "That's just one—"

I interrupt him. "When I turned twenty-one, my friends took me out for drinks, and a black cat crossed my path on the way into the bar. And you know what happened?"

He thinks for a moment. "You broke a heel?"

"Ha! Like I ever wear heels." I stumble over those words a bit, even if they're sort of true. Tamlin wears heels, not Darcy. But Darcy is Tamlin, and Tamlin is Darcy, and *wow* I need to stop thinking about myself in the third person. I also really need to sleep, but I'm not inclined to move from my current spot. "No," I say, "I ended up puking my guts out most of the night."

Rolling his eyes, Houston is ready with his argument for that one. "I'm pretty sure every twenty-one-year-old does that on their first night out."

"Ah, but I only had water that night because I knew the guys would definitely be getting drunk, and someone needed to be the responsible one."

That gets his attention, pulling his eyebrows low as he holds me a little closer to his chest. How in the world is he still holding me? He's not even breaking a sweat! "The guys?" he asks, and I know he's not jealous but it *feels* like he's jealous. His heart is pounding against me.

I shrug. "All of my friends in college were guys. I relate to them more than I do other girls." And this is usually the part where guys lose romantic interest and turn me into their best bud. Not that I think Houston has any romantic interest, but I may have just ruined that avenue for myself. He does seem pretty close with Jordan, so maybe playing the friend card might get him to open up to me and tell me things he wouldn't tell a girlfriend.

Okay, hold up. At no point did I ever think Houston and I would be an item, even when I was thinking about going the flirting route. I'm pretty sure I wouldn't be able to flirt with him even if I tried, so there's no need to panic just yet.

Houston is quiet for a long time as he studies me again, and I try not to move in case that spooks him. I have to be as open as I can be with him, or he's never going to tell me anything and all of this will have been a waste. I can't imagine Connor loving the idea of me coming back to Missouri with my tail between my legs and no story. I don't think he would fire me, but I'd probably be stuck as demon-spawn Tamlin for the rest of my sad little career.

Yeah, I said it. Tamlin is kind of the worst sometimes.

"You never really said why you came to Sun City," he says eventually, his eyebrows pulling low again. "Or why you picked this house. There's cheaper rent closer to downtown."

I wish I had an answer for him that wasn't *I'm here to try to ruin your career and maybe your life*. "The stars," I say, and we both look up. Sun City is small enough, and we're far enough on the outskirts, that we can see the Milky Way here in the backyard. "I've never seen the Milky Way.

It's kind of amazing, and I don't know if I've ever seen anything more beautiful."

"Yeah," he says, and though I keep my eyes on the sky above us, I can feel his gaze turn back to me. What does *that* mean? It feels like his bright blue eyes are staring right into my soul and searching for the answers to the universe. "I should probably put you down," he says after a minute, but it still takes him several seconds to put me on my feet, which he does so gently that it tugs at something in my chest.

"Sorry for jumping on you. And thanks for keeping me safe from the scorpions," I say, a little breathless.

"The nonexistent scorpions," he replies.

"Like I was saying, if there's going to be a death by scorpions in Sun City, it's going to be me. It's my curse."

He bends to pick up his phone—he must have dropped it when he caught me—and I get a good view of his smile. Hot diggity dog, the man has dimples. How did I not know he has dimples? To my dismay, he taps the flashlight off and plunges us back into darkness.

"Guess I'll have to be around to make sure that doesn't happen," he says, his voice low and rough, and then he disappears into his half of the house without another word.

I, on the other hand, let out a string of words that I *never* say because what in the Sam Hill was that?

Chapter Eight

Houston

October 21

NOTE TO SELF: IT'S a bad idea to have middle-of-the-night conversations with the woman renting your house. Things tend to get...muddy.

I nearly had a heart attack when I stepped out onto the patio and got showered with cold rice along with an ear-splitting scream. I expected Jesse to come running like the guard dog I suspect he is, but Darcy and I remained alone. I'm immensely glad I managed to catch her—the first time—in case she stumbled back into the pool that I haven't had a chance to clean yet. The lights are out, so she probably doesn't know it's there. And I was also glad to catch her the second time, when she jumped into my arms. Both times resulted in a lot of physical contact that made me more than a little confused.

I have dated so many women that that first touch has lost the spark of newness that I always liked about a relationship. The anticipation. Bonnie, my last girlfriend, pretty much jumped me within five minutes of meeting me, so we skipped all the hesitation and awkwardness. It was nice in its own way, knowing exactly where we stood, but our relationship barely lasted two months before we were bored. It didn't matter that she had just starred alongside a slew of A-list actors in her last movie and I pitched a near-perfect game over the summer; our careers did nothing for our relationship.

There was no excitement of a chase. No sense of fulfillment. Even Bonnie thought things were too easy, and we kept the relationship going only long enough for her movie premiere before we called it quits. No one wants to be in a relationship that has no life to it.

I was pretty sure I would never feel that spark until the moment I caught Darcy's wrist, and suddenly I was on fire.

The doorbell saves me from clenching and unclenching my hand like I've been doing all morning, and I jump to my feet, hurrying to the door to grab my delivery. I stuff a few twenties into the kid's hand and take the bags from him, closing the door before he realizes how much I just tipped him. I heard movement on the other side of the wall a few minutes ago, which means someone is awake next door and I don't have a lot of time.

I hope it isn't Darcy making herself breakfast—I'm pretty sure she hadn't been to bed yet when I found her outside and will probably still be asleep. But another part of me hopes it *is* Darcy I heard so she'll be the one who answers the door. Jesse seems great, if a little quiet, but I don't necessarily want to test my theory that he knows exactly who I am and isn't a fan. I may be a bit too cocky for my own good sometimes, but I know I'm likable. It just might take some time to get the silent giant to warm up to me, especially with that awful first impression.

It wasn't my fault that my phone decided to shuffle random music after my playlist ended, and I was elbow deep in paint and soap so I couldn't change the song from that nightmarish but epic banger. Whatever it was, I need to find it again because I have a feeling it would make a killer workout song.

Focus, Hou. Grabbing a couple of plates, I arrange the two meals I bought as haphazardly as I can. The goal is to look as homemade as possible, which is a total lie, but I'm pretty sure a part of me broke when I held Darcy last night and she told me about her superstitions. She is the most open and honest person I've met in a long time, and that makes me desperate to impress her.

There is likely some underlying trauma hiding in that desperation, like if someone like her can see value and worth in a guy like me, it must be true, but I'm more focused on getting these plates of food to my new neighbors than I am on self-reflection.

Priorities.

With a plate in each hand, it takes me a second to figure out how to get the front door open—*put one of the plates down, dummy*—and then I'm on my way, feeling ridiculous and hopeful and entirely unsure how I want this scene to play out. I don't know this girl. She's not even going to be in town for long. Besides, she practically told me we were destined to be friends when she said that bit about only being friends with guys.

But here I am, ready to make a fool of myself because of a few nerve endings triggering.

Nobody tell Micah. My little sister would freak out about me liking a normal, non-famous person and would launch into a full plan to woo my neighbor, complete with balloons and a squirrel. (Don't ask me how the squirrel would factor in. I'm running on a few hours of sleep here.)

When Darcy answers the door—mental fist pump that it's not Jesse—she blinks at me for a second before looking behind me, as if she expected someone else. "Uh, hi," she says, her eyes dropping to the plates of food in my hands. "What's this?"

I shrug, calm and casual. "I figured you guys wouldn't have much by way of groceries yet, so I made you—"

"I have an order for Houston?"

I nearly drop the plates as I turn to look at the completely different delivery guy holding out a plastic bag with my name clearly printed on the tag.

I curse at the same time Darcy says, "I guess now I know why my order was late."

"There may have been an accidental interception," I admit, knowing instinctively that she's fully figured out my scheme so there's no point in me trying to pass it off as a misunderstanding. "I'm a terrible cook."

"I know," Darcy says, taking the bag and giving the delivery guy a wave. "Jordan told me."

I swear again. That traitor. I guess he'll never get over the few meals I tried to make when we were college roommates for a couple of years. After nearly burning down our apartment, I got relegated to dish duty. Jordan handled the cooking.

Thankfully, Darcy seems more amused than anything as she watches me. "He also told me you're trying to watch your language, though that seems to be a work in progress."

"Jordan is dead to me. But he's not wrong. On either count."

"I get the cooking thing," she says, opening up one of the Styrofoam containers from my order and pulling out a fingerful of scrambled egg. I have no idea why I'm so fixated on those eggs as they rise to her mouth, but I am. "If you're a baseball player, you're probably out on the road a lot."

I wish I could go back in time an hour and redo this entire thing; she doesn't sound remotely impressed by me. "Most of the time I feel like I barely live here," I agree. "We've got a chef at the clubhouse, so I'm usually eating my meals there." Not anymore, if I end up retiring like I keep telling Roundy I might do.

"And the swearing thing?"

She asks the question casually, pulling out a bite of hash browns this time, but I still feel like a little kid getting in trouble for using a bad word at school. I don't know how this woman has so easily gotten under my skin, but I'm not sure I'm complaining.

"It's a habit I picked up in the dugout," I tell her, choosing honesty over another lie this morning.

She smiles a little. "Not all people consider it a bad thing. Why change?" I want so badly to know what she thinks about it, even if it shouldn't make a difference in my own goals.

"My sister, mainly. She hates it. But also..." This part is harder, but if I'm ever going to connect with someone enough to actually build a life with her, I have to practice being honest with myself as much as I want to be with others. "Also my mom," I say quietly, feeling the sting of her loss even twenty years later. "She died when I was seven, and she was all things gentle and soft. If she knew what came out of my mouth sometimes, I think she'd die again of shame."

I'm tempted to keep my eyes on my slippers, but Darcy is quiet for long enough that I can't help but look up. As soon as I meet her gaze, her expression softens.

"That's really sweet, Houston. I know that's not an easy change to make, but I think she'd be proud of you for trying."

The language thing isn't even a big deal, but when I first realized my shoulder was going out, something changed in me. I wanted to be more deliberate in my life, in small ways and in big. And lying to my neighbor about making her breakfast because I want to see her smile is probably not the best way to accomplish that.

"I'm sorry for stealing your breakfast and lying to you about making it. I'm trying to live more deliberately, but clearly I can be kind of impulsive. And stupid. Karma caught up to me quickly." I give her my best puppy-dog look.

Though she doesn't smile much, it's still there, playing at the corners of her lips as she continues to nibble at my pathetic offering. "Karma isn't a real thing," she says after a moment.

I raise an eyebrow. "This coming from the woman who thinks throwing salt over her shoulder is going to save her from the scorpions we don't have."

"I thought you agreed to save me. But as long as I see you wearing those ugly slippers, I'm going to be on my guard."

"Hey, I like these slippers."

"They make you look like an eighty-year-old man, Hou."

Oh, I like that. I like that a lot. Not the old man part, but the part where she called me Hou. And okay, maybe she called me that because it sounds like an old man name to match my slippers, but the fact that she's giving me a nickname in the middle of what some might call flirtatious banter is lighting off fireworks inside me.

What would she do if I asked her out? Slam the door in my face, probably. I have a feeling this girl is going to take more than a smile to charm, and I am so okay with that. I hope she makes this difficult for me because if there's one thing I never do, it's back down from a challenge.

GREY
BIRD
TAVERN

Chapter Nine

Darcy

October 22

"Houston Briggs made you breakfast?" Connor looks like he's buffering as he processes that idea. Or maybe he's literally buffering, since the internet in this house is crap. You'd think Houston Briggs would be able to afford fiber internet. At the very least something faster than six megabits download speed.

Maybe he's into gambling or something and has lost all his money. He wouldn't want to be slipping in his career if he was in massive debt from something like that, which would explain his panicked response when Tamlin asked him about getting old. It would also explain why he's trying to sell my half of his duplex.

I pause my dish washing to double check I haven't lost the connection with Connor , and he blinks. "Sorry, I'm just trying to imagine it," he says. "Was it edible?"

I chuckle. "Technically, it came from a restaurant in town, but the thought was nice." Houston told me about his attempt to make Jordan's apparently famous waffles before ordering the food and how he nearly set off the fire alarm. The admission was adorable; I love a man who can own up to his faults.

"Hmm." Connor rubs his jaw, clearly deep in thought. I've been here for two days now, and every time Connor calls, I keep waiting for him to give me a more specific assignment when it comes to Houston. Like, what am I looking for? He said yesterday that I'll know it when I see it, which doesn't inspire a lot of confidence.

You'd think I would have seen it by now.

I've gone over and over that interview, and aside from Houston hesitating slightly when I asked him about being tired, he basically gave me nothing. I doubt that's anything; any pitcher would be tired after pitching a whole game, even one as skilled as Houston Briggs.

"What is that supposed to mean?" I ask when Connor doesn't say anything else.

He shrugs, which is a very non-Connor thing to do. He's the editor-in-chief for a reason, and he usually has all the answers. "I'm curious about why you didn't mention this breakfast thing earlier," he says after a while.

It's my turn to shrug. "It didn't seem all that important, and I've barely seen him since. He sent his friend over yesterday with new light bulbs and to get the internet set up, and I'm not sure if he's even been home much." I did enjoy talking to Jordan again, though. He's a nice guy and one hundred percent in love with Houston's sister, something he confirmed Houston doesn't know. That could get interesting, but it's not interesting enough to be the story Connor is looking for.

"Maybe he's been busy training," Connor says, which disappoints him for some reason. "You may need to fake a house emergency to get him over there so you can have some more interaction. We can't have him forgetting you exist."

Connor doesn't know that Houston gave me his phone number, and I'm not sure I'm going to tell him. That seems like pushing things too quickly too fast, and with how much Houston has been avoiding me since the breakfast incident yesterday, he seems a little skittish. Connor would ask me to start texting him, maybe even assign someone *else* to write the texts for me, and I do not want that to happen. If Houston is going to tell me anything, he needs to know he can trust me.

"So, he brought you breakfast, and then what?"

And then he mowed the lawn without a shirt on, though I'm not going to tell Connor that part. Jesse found me peeking out the front window like a creep, and he's never going to let me live that one down. He hasn't technically said anything about it, but he's got that amused look in his eyes every time we cross paths in this little house.

This little house that is starting to feel a bit suffocating. It's only been two days, but neither of us have gone anywhere or done anything. There's been unpacking to do, but outside of the stuff it takes to make us look like we actually live here, we don't have a lot of personal things. Jesse and I are both unpacked and incredibly bored.

"That was pretty much the last time I saw him," I say, holding back a sigh. "I can try to think of something that would get him over here."

"Or maybe Tamlin needs to make a little push," Connor says.

My heart kicks up a notch. "You want to get Tamlin out? Already? But why would she be in Sun City?"

"She could be snooping around for postseason scandals. Following other members of the team who aren't as squeaky-clean. Trying to get a second interview after Briggs shot her down the last time. Take your pick."

He's clearly thought this through, and I can tell he's not going to give me much of a choice.

The beast is coming out to play.

"You seem nervous." Jesse is working on the final touches on my hair, speaking for the first time since I told him I need to become Tamlin.

I sigh. "I am nervous. I haven't done any of this investigative stuff as Tamlin before, and it'll be a lot harder to blend in when I look like this." At least Jesse has put me in a blouse and slacks instead of a dress; not even a glam girl like Tamlin would wear a cocktail dress outside of sporting events and parties. I'll still be in heels—I need to maintain that height to differentiate Tamlin from Darcy—but at least I'll be wearing pants for once.

I still can't believe how easily Jesse makes me look like a different person with a little bit of makeup. Sure, there's the wig and the contacts, but he always manages to stretch out my face and make my nose look long and thin. My cheekbones look higher and more pronounced. And I always stand more confidently when he's done, though that could also be because of the fake boobs.

These things are lethal. I always envied the women who packed more up front than I ever did until I had to carry these puppies around for a day, and now I feel sorry for everyone with chronic back issues because of what they have to hold up.

"You'll do fine," Jesse says with a chuckle. He tucks the last elegant curl in place and then pins some hair to the side, out of my face. I haven't had long hair like this since high school, but even if I did, there is no way I would be able to do the things Jesse does with it. Mostly because my real hair does not cooperate like Tamlin's. Jesse always seems to breathe a sigh of relief when he tucks my blonde away to make room for Tamlin's gorgeous dark locks because even he thinks my not-quite-curls are a nightmare. "Just be that confident and no-nonsense girl I know is in there, and no one will get in your way."

When my rideshare arrives, Jesse makes sure the coast is clear before I slip out of the house and into the waiting car. We double checked the unattached garage that sits off to the side of the house to make sure Houston's old red pickup—rusty spots and everything—was gone, but there's still a fair bit of risk of someone seeing Tamlin at Darcy's house. Heaven forbid I get stuck in a Mrs. Doubtfire situation without an hour for Jesse to work his magic hands. I may be a decent actor, but I don't think anyone could pull off a cream face without someone figuring out the ruse.

When I reach the Red-tails stadium, my heart is pounding in my throat, but I swallow it down. This is no different from strong-arming my way into an interview at the NBA playoffs when I wasn't technically granted access to the arena. My press credentials get me into a lot of places, but not everywhere, and offseason training is not a place I should be snooping. But here I am.

"Thanks," I tell my driver, giving him a good tip in the app because he only looked back in the rear view mirror a couple of times. Some of my rides have been terrifying because the guys driving are more interested in me than the road. Sometimes Jesse is a little *too* good at his job.

Slipping out of the car, I take a deep breath and force all of my nerves away. Whatever happens, unless I get arrested or something, this isn't *me* snooping around. This is Tamlin. Tamlin doesn't fear anything, and nothing she does affects me in reality. It's all just a game. A meaningless game.

A security guard finds me at the side entrance to the stadium, the one the team uses. "Can I help you, ma'am?"

I flash him a smile. "You sure can. I'm here to meet with Hiroshi Fujimura." I love this smile of mine, not just because it helps Tamlin overwhelm men who think too hard with anything but their brains. Connor paid for an expensive teeth-whitening treatment when I first started reporting, which means this is a Darcy smile too. It makes it so much easier to use when it's a real part of me.

The guard clears his throat, glancing around as if hoping for assistance. "Oh, um, I don't think..."

I titter a laugh as I pull my press ID out of my bag. "Oh, I'm sorry. Hiroshi is expecting me. I was out with him and Deanna last night for dinner at DiMaggio's, and he invited me to have a look around his incredible facility." Thank you, Connor, for the info. Apparently, the Red-tails manager goes to the high-end Italian restaurant every week with his wife. Even if this guard isn't aware of the head coach's routine, using specifics always makes a story more believable. "He said he'd meet me at the clubhouse," I add with another smile.

He looks at my ID, looks at me, back at the ID, and then scratches the back of his neck. He's wearing a wedding ring, which explains his discomfort and tells me I need to choose a different tactic. Subtle flirting isn't going to be enough.

I put my hand on his arm, leaning in close and giving him a sultry look. "Maybe you could show me the way, handsome?"

His eyes grow wide, and he shakes his head wildly, fumbling for his key card. "No, I'm sure Mr. Fujimura will be easy to find."

Good man. I do feel bad about making him so uncomfortable, but it got me into the facility, which is exactly what I need. I head straight for the clubhouse, figuring I'll start at the training room and go from there until I find Houston. I'll have to find the manager at some point, just in case the guard comes asking if we found each other, but I don't plan on hanging around for long. I just need to let Houston know that I'm here and digging, and he'll hopefully be less on his guard when he's at home. If I can strengthen the differences between Tamlin and Darcy, he'll trust Darcy more.

I hope.

A wolf whistle pulls me to a stop, and I turn to find Sean O'Donohue undressing me with his eyes as he heads to the parking lot. The shortstop got traded by the Marlins last year for poor conduct and has been nothing but trouble from the day he got signed three years ago. I think the Red-tails took him on because he's a vacuum cleaner when he's on his game, but they didn't play him a single game this season. I wonder if he'll see the outside of a dugout anytime soon.

I say nothing despite his leers, letting him gawk at me as he walks until he slams straight into a pole and topples to the ground. I snort a laugh and keep walking. Serves him right.

I find the training room easily enough, and though a few players notice me right away, most of them keep working, which is impressive. In my experience, not a lot of athletes would have this kind of focus so soon after a victory. There's a reason the Red-tails have won two Series in the last eight years, and it has everything to do with the dedication inspired by their team captain.

Houston Briggs.

This is one of maybe three MLB teams that has a captain this year. I could probably ask any of these guys why they're so dedicated, and they would credit it to Houston. Yeah, the coaches do their part, and the Red-tails manager is one of the highest paid in that position for a reason. But this team is more unified than most, which makes me wonder yet again why Connor is so determined to find something on Houston.

I wince a little as my mind jumps back to the way he held me on the back patio my first night here. I need to make some kind of separation, or lines are going to blur. Here, when I'm Tamlin, he needs to be Briggs. Not Houston, the guy who thought he could make restaurant food look homemade by putting it on a plate.

Thankfully, Hou—*Briggs* comes out of the team physical therapist's office pretty soon after I enter the gym, and he catches sight of me immediately.

His whole stance changes, tensing like a cat ready to spring as he lets out a curse. "What are you doing here?"

I smirk. Oh, he *really* doesn't like Tamlin, and his glare is in such contrast to the way he looked at me when he brought over breakfast yesterday that it's almost funny. "Just hoping for a little glimpse at the Red-tails' preparations for next season," I say casually before looking around at the guys who are unabashedly watching us. "Gomez, you're looking leaner than last year. Nice work. And Hopkins, you may want to ease up on the bicep curls if you want to keep your range of motion."

Murmurs pick up around the team as I turn back to Briggs, who looks murderous. The best part is he clearly knows I'm right about Hopkins, which seems to drive him crazy as he looks at the first baseman.

"You really need to go," he says eventually, and I can tell he's itching to grab my arm and pull me from the training room. But he won't put a hand on me because he's smarter than that. One unwanted touch, and I could be on my phone in two seconds recording a tearful live video and telling the country that he harassed me. Not that I would actually do that, but he doesn't know that.

It's at this point that I notice he isn't sweaty like the rest of the team. It could be that he finished his workout a while ago, but his hair is too neat and dry to be freshly washed. He's in workout clothes, luscious tan arms on display, but I don't think he's lifted any weights today.

I glance at the door to the PT's office, where he came from, which immediately spooks Briggs.

"How did you even get in here?" he asks, taking a step forward so he's in my space. He's hoping to intimidate me, and even though I know he wears terrible slippers and loves his mama enough to want to stop swearing, Tamlin doesn't know that. She's pretty self-assured, but maybe she would be a little intimidated by this display of machismo. So I take a step back.

Briggs takes that as a sign that he's gaining the upper hand and pushes again with another big step, then another, and before I know it, I'm in the hallway. "Don't sneak in here again, Park, or I'll have you arrested for trespassing."

He does seem the type to follow through with a threat like that, especially when my presence is threatening his team, so I know I've pushed as far as I can today.

Still, I give him a saucy smile and wave my fingers. "I'll see you around, Briggs."

His angry facade cracks, making way for a bit of fear. "I really hope you don't," he growls and then slams the door shut.

And I'm pretty sure I've stumbled onto the right track.

GREY
BIRD
TAVERN

Chapter Ten

Houston

BROOK'S HOUSE ALWAYS FEELS like home. I can't remember back far enough to know what our house looked like growing up or what sort of decorations Mom would put up, but my twin sister got the feel right. Coming here is always peaceful and comforting, which is what I desperately need after *Tamlin Park* showed up at the clubhouse today.

What is she doing in Sun City? Baseball season is over, and we don't have any other big teams here, unless you count the minor league soccer team. She should be off covering college football or infiltrating illegal steroid rings in the NFL or something, but no. She's seducing security guards and making first basemen cry. Hopkins went into a panic about his arms being too big after Tamlin pointed it out.

And no, I'm not bitter that Hopkins listened to Tamlin when he's ignored me over the same subject for years. Not even a little bit. Nope.

"Rough day?" Brook asks as she hands me a water bottle and joins me on the couch.

I groan. "You have no idea. How are the kids this year?"

She recognizes that deflection easily enough and shakes her head. She may be the sweetest person on the planet and shy to anyone who doesn't know her, but Brooklyn grew up with two brothers. Five, if you count our stepbrothers. Brook knows how to hold her own.

"You want to talk about it?" she says, and it's not so much a question as it is a command.

If I tell her the PT forbade me from fully training with the team and now I've got the guys asking questions, she'll figure out something is wrong. I could tell her it's just overuse and I'll be fine in a week, but that would be a lie. I don't think she's all that fond of the lifestyle baseball has given me, but she knows how much I love the game. And I don't want her sympathy.

If I tell her I'm feeling restless, like my life doesn't have meaning anymore, she'll start to worry about me. I'm not depressed or anything, but there's a hole in me that won't seem to heal. And I haven't found anything to fill it. If I tell her that, she will feel it too, and Brook is way too empathetic to share this pain with me. I don't know if it's a twin thing or a Brook thing, but she's the kind of person who shares burdens. I can't put this on her when she seems so happy.

And she really does seem happy. Because baseball season gets crazy, this is the first time in months that I've been around her for longer than a few minutes, and the difference is astronomical. What does that mean? She's been hanging out with Jordan for the last little while, and if he's the source of her happiness... I might have to start getting more used to the idea of the two of them being a couple, though I wish one of them would straight out tell me what's going on with them so I can stop wondering.

I could ask, but I'm not that brave. Just paranoid and tense and overwhelmed.

I have to tell her *something* about what's bothering me, so I tell her the one thing I know she can't fix. "There's a journalist who won't get off my back," I say. Okay, so it was just two times, but she made it clear she isn't going away. Whatever she's doing here, it can't be good for anyone. And I can't shake the feeling that she's here especially for me, like she somehow sniffed out my impending decision. If Tamlin gets that story before I make an official announcement, she's going to twist it into something it isn't.

Brook furrows her brow. "Is it that pretty one you ran away from?"

I gape at her until I figure out why she would have watched that one. "Jordan showed you," I guess. "I didn't run away from her."

"Pretty sure you did. That was the shortest interview I've ever seen. You usually never stop talking because you like the sound of your voice too much."

I grab a pillow and smack her with it. "I do not."

"Keep telling yourself that, Hou. So, is this reporter looking for anything specific? You didn't do anything, did you?"

I scrunch up my face, debating the merits of hitting her again. Whatever I do to her, she has the blanket right to do it right back, and I know she's already planning up her strike for that last one. Brook may look gentle, but she's got a mean swing with a pillow. "Of course I didn't do anything," I say instead of earning myself another pillow smack. "I have no idea why she would be after me when she could help us get rid of O'Donohue once and for all."

Brook makes a face of disgust. "Is he the one that always gives me the heebie-jeebies?"

"That's the one." In fact, O'Donohue came back to the clubhouse after his smoke break sporting a broken nose, which left me wondering what he did during his break. I'm tempted to get maintenance to pull up the security cameras so I can watch. Whoever did that deserves a medal and my profound gratitude because I've wanted to punch that guy from the second he told a lewd joke his first day with the team.

It's probably time to change the subject before I start getting ideas to make that footage go viral. Ideas that include telling Tamlin Park whatever she needs to know to crush his precarious standing to a pulp so I don't have to deal with his nonsense any longer. She would love that. And maybe it would keep her away from me.

I ask the first thing that comes to mind, catching myself off guard with the question. "What's the deal with you and Jordan anyway?" Apparently I *am* brave enough.

Brook turns bright red, and though she tries her best to look innocent, my sister has never been good at hiding her feelings. "There's no deal," she says with an exaggerated shrug. "We've just been hanging out."

"You've always hated Jordan," I point out. It was a source of frustration for me all throughout high school because I could never figure out why she was the one person in the world who didn't like my best friend. I didn't know it was even possible to dislike Jordan, but anytime he was around, Brook was sure to be somewhere else unless Jordan found a way to force her to stay. I'm pretty convinced he kept hiding her stuff in my room so she would come looking for it and get roped into some sort of debate with him. If not having lengthy yet heated discussions with my best friend, she was devising some devious prank to pull on him. She's crafty when she's out for revenge, and I got targeted just as much as he did even though he was always the instigator.

The two of them were exhausting.

Sighing, Brook curls her blanket tighter around herself like it might protect her from this conversation. "I never hated him. And he's mellowed out since high school, so he's a lot less annoying."

"Otherwise known as you want to date him now?"

She chokes and grabs the remote, mumbling something I don't even try to decipher. I honestly can't tell if she's horrified by the idea of dating Jordan or freaked out by those words coming out of my mouth. Her reaction isn't all that helpful, so I suppose I should drop the subject for now. As long as they eventually tell me if something is happening between them, I'll get over the weirdness of it. I just don't want them to leave me in the dark. I have few enough people in my life as it is.

"What movie are we watching?" I ask, and Brook immediately relaxes.

We used to do these movie nights all the time, especially when Brook and I were in middle school. It was a weekly ritual that got us through our dad's downward spiral that started when Mom died and stretched on for the next several years until he ended up in prison for domestic abuse related to drug addiction. Brook and I never really knew him much because he and mom divorced when we were toddlers, but he was our only surviving relative when Mom died so the state wanted to keep him in our lives.

I wish they hadn't. We didn't need our biological father, but we got to watch him sink further and further into addiction and depression while Chad played the roles of Mom and Dad and took care of us. At least until Micah's dad, Lloyd, was able to take us in after our dad went to prison.

I know Brook has gone to visit our dad a couple of times—heaven knows why—but I could go the rest of my life without him.

"Hou, did you hear me?"

I blink, and it's like all the lights turn on around me as I take my first full breath in who knows how long. I turn to Brook, who furrows her brow.

"You were thinking about him, weren't you?"

I nod. I hate that he's tainted these movie nights, but especially lately, I seem to think about our dad a lot more than I used to. I'm pretty sure his sentence is up soon, which makes me itchy. He didn't start off a wreck, but he hit a point where his life fell apart. I'm terrified everything is going to change for me as soon as I no longer have baseball to keep me occupied. What's going to start *my* downward spiral?

"When was the last time you went to see him?"

I glance at Brook but can't stand to maintain eye contact. "When was the last time we were forced to go?"

"Really? Not even once since high school?"

I shake my head as her soft words settle in my gut, feeling an awful lot like guilt. "Why would I? It's not like he was ever our dad."

"Maybe not, but he's gotten better. A lot of therapy and self-reflection."

"Good for him."

Brook watches me for a moment, and then she rubs my arm before grabbing the remote and pulling up *The Sandlot*.

I frown. "You hate this movie."

"But you don't. It sounds like you need tonight more than I do."

Sometimes I really hate that she's a way better sister than I am a brother, but I'm trying. Maybe one of these days I'll find a way to measure up instead of turning out like my deadbeat dad. "Thanks, Blondie. We can watch one of those dumb period dramas next time."

She rolls her eyes right before she smacks me full in the face with her pillow. *Ow.* Seriously, how is she so strong? "They're sophisticated."

"They're boring," I argue.

"Just because you don't have a romantic bone in your body."

I don't really have anything to say to that, so I keep my mouth shut. Sometimes I think I'm romantic, but when things were going stale with Bonnie, I spent enough time with our half-sister Micah, who breathes and bleeds romance, to know a bouquet of roses and a fancy dinner isn't the same as romance. Do I know what *is* romance? Not a clue, which makes this newfound desire to settle down a bit daunting. One of these days I might have to suck it up and ask Brook for help in wooing, but that's assuming I have anyone to woo in the first place.

I settle deeper into the couch and force my focus on Benny and Smalls before my mind starts wandering to a night under the stars and coming up with ways to scare a certain superstitious neighbor into my arms again so I can experience that flood of warmth when I hold her.

We're twenty minutes into the movie, during which I have only thought about Darcy a dozen times or so, when Brook says, "So, what's the deal with this cute neighbor of yours?"

I sit up straighter. I haven't told her about Darcy, which means she's either a mind reader now or her intel is coming from my obnoxious best friend who apparently can't keep his mouth shut. "How do you know she's cute? Did Jordan say she's cute?" I thought he was into Brook, but if he's eyeing other women, particularly the one I'm interested in, I'll kick him in the—

"Wow." Brook laughs, punching me as she sinks deeper into her blankets. "Paranoid much? No, Jordan didn't say she was cute, but he said *you* seemed to think so with the way you were staring at her."

Okay, did *everyone* notice that? Crap, did *Darcy* notice? Maybe that's why she hasn't texted me yet—I creeped her out when I stared at her. And when I didn't put her down after she jumped into my arms. And when I tried to pretend I have any skills in the kitchen after proving yet again that I don't.

Brook giggles. "Didn't she just move in like three days ago? You're relentless."

"What is that supposed to mean?"

"It means you fall for anything with boobs, Hou."

"Don't say boobs," I say with a shudder. "And I do not. Besides, she doesn't even have..." Wow, I am not going to finish that sentence. Darcy is more sturdy than curvy, not that I've paid much attention, but I don't really care about that kind of thing. Not like I used to. "It doesn't matter. I'm not looking for a fling." When Brook raises an eyebrow, I swing the pillow again. "I'm serious! I'm done with casual dating."

"Is that why you broke up with Bonnie Aiken?"

Huh. Brook pretty much never brings up my girlfriends unless she's making fun of me, but she's watching me with a serious gaze. Like she actually cares about this one. Or maybe she cares because it's been two months since Bonnie and I called it quits and I haven't shown any signs of finding someone new. That's strange for me, and Brook knows it.

"Yeah," I say, settling back in my seat so I don't have to look at her. "Bonnie is great, but everything about us was surface level. Pretty much for show, you know? I want something deeper."

"Is Darcy deeper?"

I shouldn't be surprised that Jordan has told her Darcy's name. They've probably had all sorts of conversations about my new neighbor over the last couple of days, and I can only imagine how much Brook is dying to meet this girl. The fact that she hasn't been over yet says a lot about how good Brook is at respecting boundaries. She won't come over and meet my neighbor unless I want her to.

"I don't know," I say, and I mean that. I know almost nothing about Darcy except that she's unlucky—still up for debate—and way too down to earth to want to be with someone like me. That makes her all the more interesting, like she's off-limits or something. I don't even know if she's interested. "But I want to find out."

GREY
BIRD
TAVERN

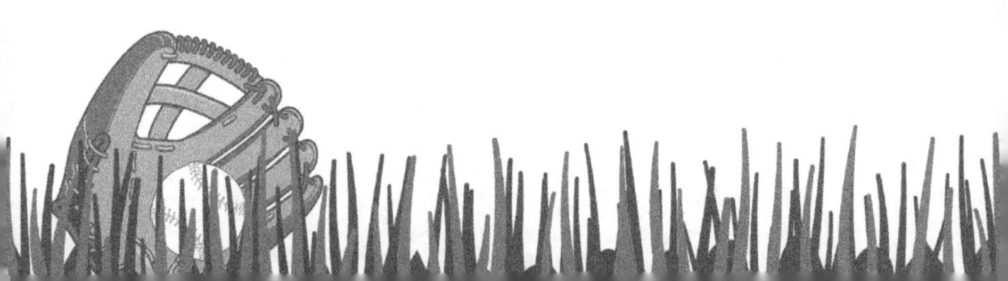

Chapter Eleven

Darcy

October 24

I gotta say, Connor is a genius sometimes. I was complaining to him that I couldn't come up with any good reasons to go over to Houston's house to try to snoop around a bit, and he suggested laundry. I hadn't even thought about how I was going to do laundry, but Connor's idea is perfect for killing two birds with one stone.

Still, I feel a little awkward standing on the porch while it's raining buckets, a basket of my dirty clothes on my hip. Maybe this is pushing the neighbor bounds a little too far, and Houston might not like the invasion of privacy. Maybe it's just me, but the laundry room is a sacred space. It's a place where you can wash away your regrets and mistakes with a Tide pod and a little prayer.

Okay, now that I say that out loud, it's probably just me. Most people probably just throw their clothes in and walk away. But after a girl goes through life spilling ketchup on every white shirt and having tampons leak at the worst possible times, the laundry room becomes something different. I don't make the rules.

I know Houston is in there because I watched him run from the garage to his house twenty minutes ago. Not because I'm a stalker but because I was watching the rain. And maybe waiting for him to show up so I could come over here. A part of me wonders if I should have texted him first, but I still feel weird about having that secret information of his phone number. The minute I make contact through the phone, I can no longer justify not telling Connor that I have his number. Right now, it's easy to pretend that he's still so far out of reach.

I'm stalling, and I know it, but it's weirdly difficult to raise my arm to knock. Yesterday, I walked right into a gym full of half-naked men without batting an eye—though I may have revisited that image a good number of times since then—but knocking on Houston's door is terrifying.

He's had two up-close encounters with Tamlin now, which means he's twice as likely to recognize me. Makeup only goes so far.

"Oh, just get this over with," I growl and then knock loudly, each rap of my knuckles sending a jolt through me. This is seriously ridiculous. I have talked to hundreds of athletes over the last few years, some even as Darcy the lowly assistant getting statements for the writers back when I started. None of them scared me. Not even the linebackers who weigh close to a quarter ton when in full gear. Houston is just a baseball player. Just my landlord. Just a mark who *might* have a secret that I *need* to unearth if I want to keep my job.

The door opens, and my laundry slips from my hands.

Just a guy in nothing but a towel.

I may have seen a whole lot of skin and muscle yesterday, but I'm pretty sure none of the Red-tails hold a candle to their pitcher. This guy's *muscles* have muscles, and it is taking everything in me not to reach out and see if those tan abs feel as solid as they look. If he is this cut and defined while relaxed, I do *not* want to see how he looks in the middle of a workout. (Correction: I absolutely need to see that. Immediately.)

"Uh, sorry," Houston says, clearing his throat. "I thought you were Jordan."

I reluctantly drag my eyes up to his face. "Do you usually greet Jordan in a towel?"

Embarrassment splashes across his cheeks in a splotchy red. "No. I was worried he would come up to my room while I was...never mind."

I have to try so hard not to laugh. "You *sure* he's just a friend?"

"Absolutely. Though, sometimes I wonder why I keep him around."

I've only interacted with Jordan a couple of times, but I quickly figured him out. He's a super friendly guy with no real sense of boundaries, and he pretty much never gets embarrassed. The man carried my drawer full of underwear without flinching and even asked if my lacy black bra—the one I only have in case I someday need something fancy in my normal life—is comfortable or tickles my skin. (For the record, it definitely tickles.) He even told me about his relationship with Houston's sister without batting an eye. I don't think anything fazes the guy, so I can imagine him finding it perfectly normal to start a conversation with Houston while he's in the shower.

Houston seems more embarrassed by his friend than the fact that he's still standing in his open doorway in a towel, which makes sense given the shape he's in. But then he looks down at my scattered laundry and winces.

I drop down to pick it up, but so does Houston, and our heads collide hard enough that I see stars. A curse slips out of both of us—mine is more a collection of random sounds than actual words—and he grabs my arm before any more accidents happen.

Just like the last time he touched me, I feel it everywhere. He really is so warm, and every pinpoint of skin-to-skin between us seems charged with heat.

He frowns at his hand—does he feel it too?—before looking back up at me. "You okay?"

I feel like I've had a collision with a truck, but sure. "I've got a hard head."

He winces. "I noticed. So…" This time when he bends down to pick up some of my clothes, he keeps a hold on me until he's crouched so we don't collide again.

Good gravy, he should not be doing that in a towel that small. Keeping my eyes averted, I gather up the rest of my things and stuff them into the basket, hopping back up so he'll do the same. "We don't have a washer yet," I explain, though my face is heating from more exposure to Houston Briggs than I need. Thankfully, I haven't seen anything that the sun hasn't also seen. Praise the universe for that towel standing sentinel.

Houston looks at my laundry basket as if it might give him more information.

"And Jesse took the car," I add, which is true. He's incredibly bored and went into town to see if he can find a temporary job to pass the time.

Houston looks out at the rain, the wheels turning. "So, you need a ride to the laundromat?" he asks, and he almost seems disappointed by that.

I really hope I'm not reading him wrong and crossing a line when I say, "Actually, I was wondering if I could use yours. Just until we get our own machine. Laundromats and I don't get along." Also true.

To my utter relief, Houston steps aside to let me in. "I have a feeling there's a story there."

"Did you know it's possible to light a dryer on fire if you put something flammable in there? And it turns out when you accidentally dunk yourself in tiki torch fluid, that stuff doesn't easily wash out."

"You won't light my dryer on fire, will you?"

"I haven't swum in any tiki oil recently, but I make no promises."

I pause in the front room, taking it in. It's clean and spacious—he doesn't have a wall separating this room from the kitchen like we do—but it's surprisingly sparse in terms of things to make it feel homey. I know he's lived here for several years, so I have to wonder why it looks like he's as temporary as we are. I guess it makes sense, given how much time he spends on the road, but still. This is his *home.*

"Did you use photos of your half for the listing on ours?" I ask, suddenly recognizing the gray leather couch.

Houston lets out a nervous laugh. "Yeah. I hadn't had any time to clean up your side before my agent wanted the pictures. Sorry again that it wasn't ready for you. Laundry room is this way."

I follow him up the stairs eagerly. The deeper we go, the more intimate the stuff will be. "When did the last tenants move out?"

"Couple months ago."

"Why didn't you pay someone to clean it for you?" It's an innocent question, I hope, but I'm still wondering if he's not as financially secure as he pretends to be. Gambling still seems the most likely, but there are all sorts of things that could get him into trouble.

He leads me into the little laundry room just before the master bedroom—which shares a wall with mine, I notice—and gestures to the laundry supplies. "Use whatever you need," he says without answering my question. "The knob is a little fiddly, so turn it slightly to the right of where you want it to be."

"Got it."

"I'm going to get dressed, and you're welcome to hang out downstairs while you wait to switch your load over."

I give him a smile since he's being incredibly kind about this invasion. "Thanks, Houston."

The red splotches are back on his cheeks, which has *me* blushing too. There is no way he's blushing because I smiled at him, but that's what my heart wants me to think. Why my heart is suddenly in charge, I don't know, but I do know that's a terrible idea.

So I turn and start dumping my clothes into the washer, grateful when he disappears into his room and closes the door.

He hasn't come out yet by the time I make it down the stairs, so I use this limited opportunity to start digging. There's so little in this front room that it doesn't take me long to figure out there's not much to learn about the guy from his stuff. His short bookshelf in the corner is mostly full of baseball books, with a couple of paperback classics that look like they haven't even been cracked open because their spines are pristine. The cactus on top of it next to the modern record player is alive and well, but that doesn't necessarily mean he is good at keeping things alive; it's a cactus. He probably has to water it once a month. He has a pretty decent taste in music; half of his records are classic rock and the other half a mixture of mainstream and indie rock. Other than the TV on the wall opposite the couch, there's not much else going on in this room.

"Who are you, Houston Briggs?" I whisper. I'm dying to know every detail.

"I could probably order a washer and dryer for you guys," Houston says, coming down the stairs before I can peek in the pantry. He's in jeans and a t-shirt now and looking a lot more human. As human as a blond-haired, blue-eyed Adonis can get, anyway. He never looked this good on TV, and I don't think I can blame it all on the camera adding ten pounds. There's something about seeing him away from the pressure of his job. "The last tenants didn't believe in machinery, or so they said, so they did all their washing by hand and hung it out to dry in the back."

"They sound eccentric."

"I guess. I didn't see them much." He scratches his chin as an awkward silence stretches between us. I could easily go back over to my side and have him let me know when the washer is done, but he's the one who said I could hang out here while I wait, and I'm not about to waste that hospitality. "Uh, wanna sit?"

Since he's only got the one couch in this room and it's almost small enough to be a loveseat, when we both sit, we're close enough that I get a whiff of his fantastic soap or body wash, whatever it is. He hasn't shaved today, so he's got some delicious dirty blonde scruff going on.

I like seeing this laid-back version of him. Before my one and only interview with him, I'd only seen the guy on TV and the internet, when he's on guard and careful about what he says or does. He's never had a bad interview, which says a lot about him but also nothing at the same time because it's all just a mask. He's got some good control and isn't quick to give anything away.

I have to wonder if he is always that closed off or if the people closest to him get to see the real Houston. Do his girlfriends get more than the pro pitcher who can do no wrong? A small part of me hopes they don't, which is ridiculous. I'm not allowed to be jealous of women who had every right to date the man, unlike me.

"So," I say, breaking the silence. "You're a baseball player, right?"

That makes him chuckle, probably because he's so used to people knowing exactly who he is. "Yeah. The Red-tails are a pro team here in Sun City."

I widen my eyes appropriately. "Oh, I've heard of them! Didn't you guys just win a tournament or something?" I don't like playing dumb, but I also know how beneficial it can be to stroke someone's ego in the right way. Houston has never been one to take someone else's credit, so appealing to his vanity probably won't get me very far. But giving him the chance to feel like an expert?

He fights his grin as he shifts his body to face me a little more. "The World Series."

"Whoa, you're the best in the world?"

Hello, dimples! "No, just the country, but they call it the World Series. Though, there's a team in Canada, so I guess that counts?"

I'm impressed he didn't make me feel stupid for that one, and my estimation of the guy goes up. Maybe I could play that up, see where his limits are. "Are you on your downseason, then?"

"Yep." Wow, he didn't even try to correct me by casually saying offseason. "It's nice to have a little break before spring training."

"What do you do when you're not playing games and stuff?"

He shrugs, and this answer doesn't come as easily, like he's trying to decide what he actually wants to say. His hesitation makes me wonder if he's telling the truth when he says, "I co-own a few businesses, so I check on them every once in a while."

That is not even close to what I expected, and I lose the act, genuinely interested now. "What kind of businesses?" And better yet, how has he had time to run multiple businesses while being a starting pitcher for a champion team? Jordan told me the other day that Houston does other stuff for work on top of baseball, but he didn't elaborate. I wouldn't have guessed it would be something like this.

Houston must not have expected me to latch on to this topic because he turns a brighter red than I've ever seen him. Maybe no one has ever taken an interest in this side of him before, or maybe I just have crazy eyes. But his lips slowly twist into an amused smile as he probably realizes that I'm not kidding about wanting to know.

"Jordan has a landscaping business," he says.

"Yeah, he told me. You own that with him?"

"Yeah. He was doing maintenance at the stadium when he moved back to Sun City last year, and when he decided to start up his own business, I wanted to help out because he's been my best friend since we were in high school."

Okay, their close friendship makes more sense now, given their history. And Jordan would be extra grateful for Houston's investment and want to repay the favor, even if that favor is hosing Houston down when he looks like he murdered a Teletubby.

"What else?" I ask, inching closer.

"An old neighbor wanted to get into real estate, so together we bought some duplexes and condos to rent out. I technically own the house Brook lives in, though she doesn't know that."

That explains *this* house, but not why he lives in it when he could live anywhere. Why would anyone want a wall-sharing neighbor if they didn't have to have one?

"Why doesn't she know?" I ask.

He blushes slightly. "I wanted her to have a place she could afford on her own—she's stubborn, like me—but she's a teacher, so she doesn't make much. I like to help my family however I can."

Sensing there's more, I grab his hand. Because *that* makes sense. *Not.* Still, now that I've got him, I don't want to let go, and he's looking at our hands with such an intense look that I refuse to break his concentration. It's not like we're *holding hands*—his is sitting palm-down on his leg—but I've got my fingers wrapped around his hand in a way that says this isn't just a casual touch.

I give him another verbal nudge. "And?"

"My stepsister started a bookstore," he says, his voice lower than before. "But she's making so much money that I'm thinking I should tell her to buy me out so she doesn't have to keep sharing her profits."

I'm grinning like an idiot, but I can't help it. This is so different from the man I expected Houston Briggs to be but in the best possible way. I'm not sure this is the story Connor is looking for, but I am more than okay going down this rabbit hole. Houston has lit up in the last few minutes, and he looks like he's lost a lot of the weight that was sitting heavy on his shoulders. He was carrying it so well that I didn't notice it until it was gone.

"I think it's really cool that you have helped so many people out like that," I tell him with full sincerity. "I can't imagine how grateful they are, and it says a lot about who you are when you're willing to put so much faith in people."

That's when his thumb wraps over my fingers, turning this into an active hand-holding situation. His wrist twists, slowly but surely, until our palms are together and he slips his fingers between mine. Every little movement of the process kicks my heart rate up another notch until it's pounding in my chest.

What did I say about laundry? It's a religious experience.

Houston spends a few seconds looking at our hands before lifting his eyes to meet mine, a furrow between his eyebrows as if he's just as confused by this as I am. "I..." His voice comes out breathless, and he clears his throat before trying again. "I don't really tell anyone about the businesses," he says, leaning closer.

I lean too because I'm pretty sure this is all a weird dream and I don't have control over my actions. Especially not when his eyes slip down to my mouth for half a second. If Houston Briggs wants to kiss me, I'm not going to stop him. "Why not?"

"It's... I don't do it for the recognition or the money. I got lucky. My job pays well—too well—and there are a lot of people out there who could be doing great things if they only had the opportunity."

Be still my freaking heart. No, seriously, it feels like it's about to break right out of my ribcage because that is not the look of a man who is planning to stay on his side of the couch. And clearly my body doesn't *want* him to stay on his side of the couch because I'm moving right in and closing my eyes. Holy guacamole, I'm going to kiss Houston Briggs.

An obnoxious buzz echoes through the house right before we make contact, jolting through me like a bolt of lightning. Houston chuckles and pulls back, untangling his hand and getting to his feet. "That's the washer," he explains before offering his hand again to help me up. The contact doesn't last long, and I feel the loss as I follow him back up the stairs.

Was Houston really about to kiss me? That seems so out of left field, but my body is still humming with electricity from his touch. I've seen his last girlfriend—hard not to when her new movie is plastered all over billboards right now—and there is no way I measure up to that. Maybe I'm just an easy score, but it doesn't feel like it. Getting tangled up with his tenant is dangerous in a lot of ways, and he's too smart to get himself mixed up in a situation like that. Especially with Tamlin hanging around Sun City.

That had to have been real desire propelling him forward.

I don't know what to do with that. Why would he be interested in *Darcy*?

Houston clears his throat again as I finish moving my wet clothes to the dryer. "Do you want to come out with me tonight?"

My stomach clenches. "What?"

Though he cringes at my not-so-eager reaction, he presses forward anyway. "I know you're new in town and probably don't know anybody and... My stepsister, the one with the bookstore, she's in town for a couple of days, and my siblings and I are going out to a bar."

"I don't really drink."

"Me neither, but they have some killer nachos."

As surprised as I am by that confession, I definitely can't be around Houston right now, even if nachos sound delicious. I need to talk to Connor and get his take on how I should act going forward. Houston is clearly into me, but putting all of his focus on Darcy might compromise anything Tamlin might be able to accomplish. Tamlin spooked him earlier this week, which means she's probably on to something—*I'm* on to something—and I don't want to risk this whole assignment.

Mostly, I just need Connor to help me keep a clear head. This suddenly doesn't feel like just a job anymore, and that makes this dangerous.

"Thanks," I say, "but I've got some work I need to do tonight. In fact, I should probably get cracking while these are drying."

He looks like a lost puppy, though he hides his disappointment quickly. "No worries."

I grab his arm. "Maybe another time?"

That pulls a little smile out of him, and I try not to pay too much attention to his lips. For obvious reasons. "Sure. Just, you know, text me anytime you're free and I can show you around Sun City."

I force a smile. This is exactly what I should want, but that vulnerability he's giving me in his open expression worries me. I want him to trust me, but I don't want him to fall for me. I *really* don't want to fall for him and muddy these already blurring lines. I'm walking a razor thin line right now. "That sounds great," I say. "I'll, uh, come back for these in an hour or so. Unless you'll already be out?"

"We're meeting up for dinner first," he admits, but he looks like he's thinking hard as he glances around the laundry room. "How about I give you a key?"

Oh, Houston Briggs, you don't know what you're doing. Feeling slightly sick, I nod and follow him back down to the kitchen where he digs through a drawer and pulls out what could be his doom, depending on if he has any skeletons in his closet.

I gulp. There had better not be actual skeletons in his closet. One of the podcasts I listened to on the drive to New Mexico involved a lady who saved the bones of all her victims and put them on wire, like creepy giant stop motion dolls. I stopped listening before I found out if she ever did make stop motion movies with them and instead switched to Disney music for the rest of the drive.

"Come over anytime you need to do laundry," he tells me and places the key in my palm, his fingers lingering there and sending chills through me. "Jesse too."

I curl my fingers around the key, telling myself that I can only use this for laundry. Not for snooping. I don't know why Houston is trusting me so easily, but I don't want to use it against him. "Yeah, no, Jesse is exceptionally particular about his clothes and has to have them professionally cleaned. It's a whole production."

Houston chuckles, taking a step forward into my space. This feels all too familiar, but his intent is the complete opposite from what he did in the training room. He doesn't want me gone like he did Tamlin; he wants to cut the space between us to nothing. "Jesse seems like an interesting guy."

The step I take back is more painful than I want to admit, and I feel it in every microsecond of Houston's disappointment. He's so good at schooling his features to hide what he's really feeling, but it's my job to see past the front. What did I do to make him start falling for me like this? We've barely interacted, and all I did was come over to do laundry.

"I should go," I say, wishing I didn't have to.

He nods once and leads me to the door, opening it for me. "If you change your mind about tonight, we'll be at Grey Bird Tavern at eight. They really do have the best nachos."

My smile is real, but it drops the second I close my front door once I'm inside my side of the duplex. I've got my phone in hand, dialing Connor even though I probably shouldn't be calling him in panic mode like this.

Thankfully, he answers, and he only gets halfway through his greeting before I say, "Houston almost kissed me."

Silence fills the distance between us for nearly ten seconds—seconds that I spend thinking about the way Houston held my hand so timidly—before Connor's voice pulls me back. "Darcy you or Tamlin you?"

The question is so ludicrous that it instantly calms my racing heart. "Are you serious? He hates Tamlin."

"Just checking. What was the circumstance? I thought you weren't going to flirt with him."

"I wasn't! I didn't. I just went over to do laundry, and we got to talking. And then bam! He's going in for a kiss." Granted, I did take his hand, but it's not like that's some big gesture of romance. Old ladies hold people's hands all the time. Fathers with their daughters. Random strangers when they meet.

Okay, a handshake is not the same thing, but still.

Connor makes a thoughtful sound, his chair squeaking in the background as he spins from side to side. I'm not sure why he's still at the office, but I'm glad he picked up. "Well, Briggs does have a reputation."

"He has a reputation for being in monogamous relationships," I argue. "Not for casual flings with his tenants." It's why I decided after I moved in that I should stick with the friendship route, something I told Connor earlier this week. It seemed more likely to get me something.

"There's a lot we don't know about him. That's why you're there, Darcy. I can't shake this feeling that there's some sort of story with this guy, good or bad, and I know you can find it. It's just the matter of *how*."

I groan, pacing the living room as I work through this. "I really don't think he was hoping for an easy score, Connor. It's not his MO, for one, but it also seems like he's actually..." Like he's interested. In *me*. Which is ridiculous.

Connor hums again. "You must have sent him signals, so what's your level of involvement here? Again, you said you weren't going to flirt with him as Darcy, but it seems like maybe you did."

Did I? I would say I don't know how to flirt, but I've done plenty of flirting as Tamlin. The makeup and the outfits help, but it's still me saying the words and making the moves. It's not like I've done it a lot—mostly just to hone in on an athlete's baser nature if that's where the story's going—but I guess it's possible that I was accidentally flirting with Houston.

Or subconsciously. The man is gorgeous, athletic, and quite possibly the most interesting person I've ever met. The more I learn, the more I want to know.

"Maybe I flirted," I admit. "Tell me what to do, Connor. I shouldn't push this, right?"

He squeaks in his chair a few times, adding in some pen clicking this time. I don't know how that doesn't drive him crazy, but it helps him think. "You probably need to pump the brakes for a bit. You've got Houston on a line, but you don't want to reel him in too quickly. We need to make sure he's good and caught before we grab the net."

I purse my lips. "You've never been fishing before, have you?"

"Not once. Just go with it. Do some friendzoning and see what he does with it. I'd rather you stay safe, and there's a lot you can learn just by observing. He's hiding something; we just have to figure out what it is."

I can friendzone; it's my comfort zone and exactly the place I've spent most of my life. But I'm starting to feel weird about digging this deep into a *feeling*. What is Connor looking for? "And in the meantime?"

"In the meantime, try to work out another encounter with Tamlin. Figure out somewhere public that he'll be and let him see you. If he starts getting paranoid, we'll know he's got something worth looking for, and then we can use Darcy to figure it out."

"Has anyone ever told you that you're a little scary sometimes?"

Connor laughs, and the sound is oddly comforting. I know he's got my back, which really helps this whole thing feel less sketchy. He clearly recognizes that I'm uncomfortable with how things are playing out, even if he doesn't know the reason, and he's doing his best to make things work for both of us. He has a job to do, just like I do.

"Now we just have to figure out a place for the two of you to bump into each other," he says.

"I have that info, actually. He kind of asked me out with his family tonight."

"Why didn't you say that in the first place? What did you say?"

Now I'm extra glad I turned Houston down. "I said I have some work to do. I was planning on writing down some thoughts I've been having about why Houston might be so dodgy, but..."

"But it sounds like Tamlin is coming out to play."

"You're going to owe me some good stories for this, Connor."

He chuckles. "You never know. This could be a good story."

"You know what I mean." Doing all this digging into Houston's life is making me realize more and more that I am desperate to get away from Tamlin's terrifying reputation. I want to build people up, not tear them down. "I hate this."

Connor's voice turns gentler. "I know you do. I promise I'm doing everything I can to get you where you want to go. When I said this could be a good story, I mean it could be a *good* story. Briggs has something to tell us, whether he's willing to admit it or not. I could see it in his eyes when you talked to him at the Series."

I grip my phone a little tighter. "What is he hiding?"

"That's what you have to figure out. Let me know how tonight goes."

I hang up and send a text to Jesse, letting him know that he's got a human canvas to play with tonight. Once I've retrieved my laundry—without any snooping at all, I'll have you know—I tuck the key to Houston's house in the very back of my underwear drawer, determined to keep it there at all costs.

GREY
BIRD
TAVERN

Chapter Twelve

Houston

"Who's the genius who decided we should go to a bar when none of us are drinking?" Kit asks that question right after a confused server walks off with our drink order of sodas and lemonades. My stepbrother-in-law looks completely perplexed, as if he's waiting for the punchline to a poorly told joke.

"Nachos," Brook, Micah, and I say in unison. I wasn't kidding when I told Darcy that this place has some killer food, and even though we've just come from eating a massive dinner at one of Brook's favorite restaurants, we've ordered three plates of nachos for the seven of us.

"Trust me," I add, nudging Kit with my elbow.

This bar also does trivia nights on Thursdays, though we made sure not to tell Kit and Skyler that, just in case it might have stopped them from making the two-hour drive to visit us. I haven't seen Kit Morgan in months, since his wedding, and he's like the second brother I never knew I needed. The day he married my stepsister was one of the better days of my life.

Maybe it's weird to like my stepbrother-in-law as much as I do, but when he came to our family reunion last year, he was the only person who saw how much I was starting to resent my casual way of life. He didn't say anything about it until a few weeks later, after he and some friends came to one of my games. He must have seen something in my face after that game—the first time I wondered if my shoulder might be loose—because he started texting me soon after. Now he sends me almost weekly check-in texts to see how my self-rehab is going. I haven't told him I'm likely going to retire instead of playing out the last year of my contract, but I swear he's got this sixth sense. Sometimes I wonder if he already knows.

The guy is basically a therapist but way cooler, even if he is freakishly good at paintball.

I can't decide if he's going to be good at trivia too, but I should probably figure it out before we get to that point so I know which team he should be on. As for the others...

I think Fischer, Micah's...friend? Boyfriend? I honestly don't know what they are. But he has probably already figured out the real reason we're here, with the way he's frowning at the trivia night advertisement on the back of the dessert menu. But I have a feeling that if Micah likes it, he will never say no. He's been giving her longing looks and little touches all night. And Micah *loves* trivia. We used to come here as often as we could, though it's been a while and feels strange without Chad here.

According to Micah, my brother is too busy being drunk on love to come home. As long as he's not actually *drunk*... The last time he got drunk, he said a lot of things I know he didn't mean to say, and Chad doesn't like losing control. Generally, he's as sober as he is antisocial.

I force my attention back to the moment, making another mental note to text Chad soon and check up on him, even though I've ignored any previous notes to make contact with my brother. I love him, but I wouldn't call us close.

Jordan's up for anything, so he'll be fine with trivia. Plus, he's been fixated on Brook all night, so I think he'll do anything she wants him to do. It's a weird thought, considering he used to drive her crazy by pushing all her buttons. I still haven't been brave enough to flat out ask him if he and Brook are hiding some sort of deeper relationship, but I might be having a chat with my best friend later based on the way he's looking at her.

After trivia. I can only handle so much at one time, and right now I am desperate for a distraction from all the love surrounding me.

I'm pretty sure Kit would be up for a bet against me if we split into opposite teams. It's Skyler we'll have to convince. She may have loosened up since being with Kit, but she's never shy about being vocal when she doesn't like something. I'm not sure if trivia night is up her alley.

If she doesn't want to play, we can grab a couple of strangers who are up for some fun. (I'll put them on Micah's team, obviously.) Brook will be with me, which means we'll have Jordan too, and then it'll just depend on if Skyler is a spectator or not. If she doesn't want to play, I'll gladly take Kit on my side.

"What are you scheming?" Kit asks, looking at me warily. He has a right to be cautious; I did swindle him in our first bet—involving a carnival baseball-throwing game—and got to shoot his bare chest with a paintball as his punishment.

I smirk at him. Might as well let him stew a bit until I know the plan. "Nothing you need to worry about."

"Pretty sure we should all be worried," Fischer says gruffly, still studying the dessert menu as our server passes out our drinks.

I haven't quite figured him out, though I'll admit I've been distracted tonight. If I wasn't watching Jordan and Brook poorly act aloof around each other, I was thinking about Darcy and how much I wish she had come with me tonight. Everyone else is paired off, leaving me as a seventh wheel.

I grab my glass of Coke and take a long sip, trying not to let that get to me. Brook would smack me with a pillow if she knew, but I'm not sure I believe Darcy when she said she had work to do. What did I do wrong? I'm not as friendly as Jordan, but I like to think I'm pretty likable. And yet, despite my inexplicably growing interest in Darcy, she keeps pulling back and keeping her distance. Why?

I've been asking that question a lot. *Why?* Why can't I find a relationship that sticks? Why did my arm have to give out on me? Why is Tamlin Park sitting at the bar?

I choke as my eyes lock on none other than the diva journalist herself sitting at the bar and nursing a cocktail. Soda sprays everywhere, most of it from my nose, but I can't even focus on the pain of that because that is undeniably Tamlin sitting there chatting up a guy who's basically drooling on her. I'd recognize her anywhere.

"You okay, Texas?" Jordan asks as Brook and Skyler scramble to soak up my mess with napkins. Fischer is dripping with soda and worse, which isn't going to help him like me.

But I'm already on my feet, barely aware of the mess as I march across the bar and slide onto the seat on Tamlin's other side. She has her back to me right now, which gives me a second to wipe my watering eyes dry on my sleeve, but as soon as I find an opening in her conversation, I jump right in.

"You wanna tell me why you're following me, Park?"

Her body tenses, enough of her skin on display from her navy blue dress for me to realize she's stronger than I would have thought. Her outfits usually draw the eyes...elsewhere...but with her back to me, I can see definition in her shoulders that I wouldn't have expected.

Her manicured nails play with the straw of her drink, which she's barely touched, before she apologizes to her salivating friend and turns to meet my gaze. "Houston Briggs."

The guy behind her widens his eyes. "Wait, you're—"

I hold up a hand, which shuts him up. I'm not over here for a chat with fans; I'm here to get this woman out of my life. "Answer the question, Tamlin."

Everything about her is catlike, from the way she moves to the predatory look in her eyes to the winged eyeliner she wears. She probably came out tonight on the hunt, though I'm pretty sure she can do better than the guy who can't seem to decide if he's more interested in her or me.

Her red lips twist in a smirk. "Oh, Briggs, you must think you're so special if you really think I would waste my time following you around when you have nothing good to give me. I like my stories to be exciting. Interesting. And you..."

I don't know why her assessment bugs me so much. It's not like I want her to find some exposé to ruin me—or even have something for her to find—but it doesn't sit well that she so easily tosses me aside.

"Because I'm old, I'm sure," I say, tempted to ask for a drink stronger than Coke. That's a terrible idea. The last time I had alcohol, I was still in high school, and I nearly cost myself a scholarship when I got benched after showing up to a game hungover. My stepdad would have paid my way if the UCSB scout hadn't come to the next game to give me a second chance, but I like knowing I got where I am on my own merits.

Tamlin laughs, the sound low and sultry. Why does everything she do feel deliberate? From the way she moves and speaks to the expressions she makes. Even that laugh was perfectly controlled, and it's unnerving. "I never said you were old," she says.

"Pretty sure you did," I growl back. I *know* she did because it's been bugging me for the last week and a half.

But she shakes her head. "I was only asking what you thought about other people's comments. You were pretty confident in your answer, unless you want to change it now."

It's only now that I notice her phone sitting on the bar between us, and I tense. "You're not recording this, are you?"

"Why? Is there something you want the world to know?"

"I want you to leave me alone."

She doesn't leave her stool, but she does lift her glass and set the straw on her tongue before closing her lips around it. She takes the tiniest sip, but I still watch every moment of it until she swallows. She may be completely superficial, but she knows how to hold a man's attention, I'll give her that. Tamlin Park is undeniably beautiful, and she knows it.

"I'm going to point out that you're the one who came to me this time," she says, returning her glass to the napkin in front of her. "I might have never known you were here if you hadn't come to say hi."

"I definitely haven't said hi."

She pouts. "I know. It's very rude."

A growl rumbles out of me, as if her felinity is summoning the dog in me. I want to chase her out of this bar—out of this city—but she keeps herself just out of reach. My place in the public eye is a chain holding me back while she walks the fence above my head, taunting me.

"You know what you are?" I say, stuffing my hands into my pockets so I don't clench them into fists.

She flashes a white-toothed Cheshire grin. "What am I, Houston Briggs?"

"You're a real pain in my—" I cut myself off when she cocks her head, like she somehow knows how hard it is not to finish that sentence. Those big blue eyes of hers watch me, waiting, and I'm realizing she will never do what I want her to. No matter how many times I ask her to stay out of my business, she's going to be right there pretending she's here for anyone but me.

She wouldn't have that growing smile if she wasn't trying to get under my skin.

I hate that there's nothing I can do to stop her from burrowing. I hate more that seeing her is starting to feel familiar, like I've seen her more often than these couple of interactions we've had. I can picture her lurking everywhere I go, waiting for me to slip up somehow. How did she get in my head so easily? Our interview only lasted a minute.

"Enjoy your night," I say, not meaning a word, and then I turn to return to my waiting family. Only, Jordan is right behind me, wrapping an arm around me and giving me a look that says he's up to no good.

"Are you going to introduce me to your friend, Houston?" he says. He knows exactly who Tamlin is, and he sounds far too amused right now.

Tempted to slip out of his hold and walk away, I'm all too aware of the way my family is watching this exchange. Kit, especially, seems to have taken an interest, and I don't like the way he's glancing between Tamlin and me like he sees something there.

There's nothing there. Absolutely not.

"Jordan," I grunt and nod toward Tamlin behind me. "Tamlin Park. Tamlin, my friend Jordan."

"I didn't realize you have friends," Tamlin says with a laugh.

"Don't even start," I snap. "You know nothing about me."

"Whose fault is that? I'm not the one who walked away from our interview."

I hate that she's right. And I especially hate that her whole demeanor has changed now that Jordan is here. When I look back at her, she's relaxed and smiling, all traces of the predator gone. In its wake is a woman who looks like she's out for a good time with friends. The one I saw in the press tent before she set her sights on me.

I hate everything about tonight.

Jordan looks from me to Tamlin, his grin growing by the second. "Well, Tamlin, we're in need of a teammate."

My stomach drops. "No."

Jordan ignores me. "Turns out it's trivia night, and Briggs here is one of our reigning champs."

Tamlin's excitement is palpable; I can't decide if it's because she can see my horror clear as day or because she is interested in the trivia game. "Is that so?" she says, slipping from her stool to stand next to us. I have no idea how she moves in those heels, but I don't think I've ever seen her without at least four inches added to her height. Maybe, if she went with a more natural look, athletes would be more inclined to talk to her.

She would also have to stop tearing us down for that to happen, but that is wishful thinking.

"You really don't want to play," I tell her.

I know her answer before she opens her mouth. "No, I think I really do."

I try one last tactic, though I know I've already lost. "The questions get pretty out there sometimes. There's no junior league."

Fire flashes in her eyes, which are somehow still unnaturally blue even in the dim lighting on this end of the bar. "I have a double degree in psychology and communications," she says sharply. "Throw in my Master of Investigative Journalism, and I'm pretty sure I can hold my own. Let's go."

That's...impressive, though I'll never admit that out loud. I can't hold back the question that jumps out of my throat as Jordan leads us back to our table where Brook is waiting for us. "Why would you settle for sports?"

Her eyes glitter as she slides into her chair next to Jordan like we've done this a hundred times. "Because I like them, Briggs."

Kit leans over the edge of the booth wall that separates my team from his. "We've already made the wager, Briggs. Losers have to wear a Halloween costume of the winners' choosing."

"I look forward to seeing you in action," I reply. Then I turn to Tamlin. "You'd better not make us lose, Ginger Snap."

Her face shifts to the most natural expression I've seen her make around me, a mixture of amusement and confusion. "Ginger Snap?"

It sounds stupid now, but sure. I lean across the table, getting as much in her face as I can with the table between us. "You may look sweet," I say, "but you've got an impressive bite."

She clearly thinks my metaphor is stupid, but she leaves it alone, turning instead to Brook and holding out her hand. "I'm Tamlin."

"Brooklyn. Houston's twin sister. Thanks for helping us complete our team."

"Now I know who got all the politeness in the twinship."

Brook snorts a laugh and glances over at me, and it's clear she is already on Tamlin's side. I have no idea how Tamlin did that so easily when she's so awful to me for no reason. "Don't mind Hou," Brook says. "He's been grumpy lately, so it's not you."

When Tamlin meets my gaze, I do my best to convey the message that it is *absolutely her*. If I'm in a bad mood, it's because she put me there.

"Let's just get this over with," I grumble, knowing before we've even started that I'm going to be wearing Kit's costume next week. And I'm not looking forward to finding out what it is.

Chapter Thirteen

Darcy

WELL, I LOVE TRIVIA night, and not just because Brooklyn and Jordan are the *cutest* couple. Not that they're actually acting like a couple. Apparently it's still a secret, and they're trying to act normal, but every time they look at each other, Brooklyn turns red and Jordan has to try to hide his smile before it gives his feelings away.

I don't blame him for being into her. She's so sweet and gentle, though she's not afraid to get loud when she knows a trivia answer, and she is clearly very comfortable in her own skin. It's probably hard not to be when she looks like Blake Lively, but she's also quick to admit when she is wrong, especially when Jordan is right.

And Jordan, unlike before, is quiet tonight except for those rare moments that he throws out a trivia answer. Other than that, his focus is entirely on Brooklyn as she tries her best to ignore him, and it's a miracle Houston hasn't noticed and figured out that they're a thing now.

Not going to lie, Houston is the most entertaining part of the night so far, partly because he's really into trivia but mostly because it's driving him crazy every time I get an answer right.

That's not to say he *lets* me answer right half the time. He's still sulking over me joining the team, and even when I am absolutely certain that I know the right answer, he questions it, like he can't even get it into his head that I might be smarter than him. He's smart too—more than I would have guessed. But if the guy isn't willing to accept that his nemesis got where she is for a reason, he's got bigger problems than losing at trivia night because he won't accept my answers as the right ones.

The longer the night goes on, the more frustrated I get with him, and I am so glad I didn't let him kiss me this afternoon if this is how he's going to treat Tamlin.

I hadn't planned to interact with him tonight. Like Connor said, the goal was simply to let Houston see me, then gauge his reaction before heading back home. I got to the bar early and set myself up in a conspicuous spot, but then I got distracted by the drunk who decided I should go home with him the moment he saw me. I didn't even know Houston was here until he said my name. And when Jordan invited me to join the game? It was too perfect an opportunity to pass up. I've learned a lot about this man over the last hour.

When the game host announces a ten-minute break before the lightning round, I decide to test something and excuse myself to use the bathroom. While Houston hops over to talk to the table next to ours, which holds a couple of his sisters and their beaus, I find a decent hiding place and text the number I was pretending I don't have.

I know, I know, but this is important, okay?

Me:

> This work is impossibly boring, and now I'm wishing I had just come out with you tonight.

Houston grabs his phone almost immediately, and the smile that blossoms on his face, dimples and all, makes my insides catch fire. Or smolder a little, at least. He types back quickly, making my heart jump up into my throat. Maybe this was a bad idea.

Houston:

> Who is this? You're right irregardless. I am way more fun than work.

His little smirk tells me this was *definitely* a bad idea, especially after what Connor told me to do, but I continue forward regardless. (Which is the right word, by the way. Not what Houston used.)

Me:

> Definitely not your needy neighbor who dropped her entire basket of clothes in your living room when she saw a spider. I'm sorry if you find any stray socks.

He takes a little longer to respond to this one, even though he's scrolling through something on his phone, but his response makes me snort out loud and draw a couple of unwanted glances my way. Yeah, okay, it's a little weird to be laughing behind a fake plant, but this is way more fun when I can see his face and all the expressions that come with it.

Unless he's doing his best to hate me, of course. He hasn't even noticed that Tamlin hasn't come back, which could either be because he's actively avoiding me or because this text conversation has him completely riveted. Maybe it's both. He is certainly oblivious to Jordan and Brooklyn behind him, who aren't being even the least bit subtle now about how they feel about each other.

I really shouldn't be encouraging Houston by texting him, but none of this feels like flirting. Connor didn't say anything about not being friends with Houston—the opposite, in fact—and that was my original plan anyway. If I can keep him at a distance physically but build up the friendship this way, maybe everything will work out.

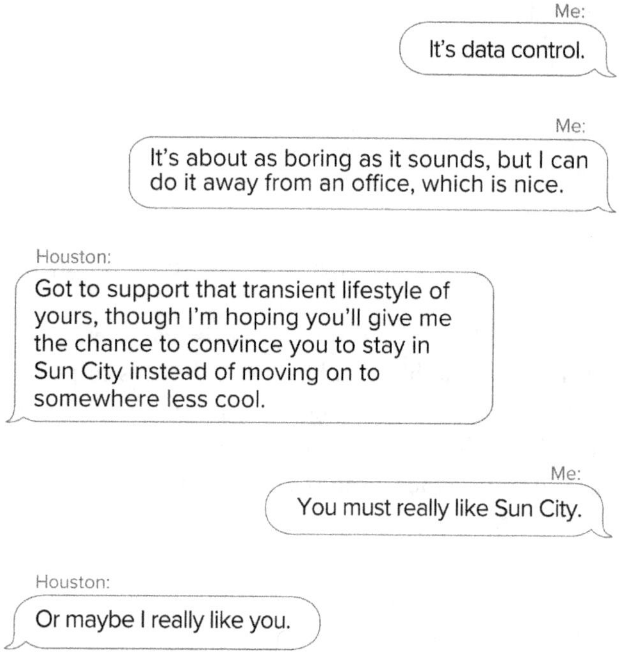

Oh. Okay. Um. Apparently, what I took as friendly conversation, he took as flirting, and I honestly have no idea how to respond to that when he's looking at his phone with so much anxiety in his face. He took a leap of faith with that one, and I'm not sure I have the heart to shut him down like I'm supposed to. The Houston Briggs I'm looking at right now is so much different from the one who's been challenging me for the last hour, and that makes this complicated.

Who is the real Houston? He's always been a ladies' man, but I don't think a serial dater like the world views him would try this hard with a girl like Darcy when he has a history of dating literal movie stars. There's more to him than what the public sees.

And he has good reason to distrust Tamlin when he's watched me ruin the lives of other athletes like him. I don't like that he's this spooked, but I still haven't seen anything that could point to a story. Maybe it's just that I interrupted his game night with his family and put him on edge. That would explain his brusqueness during the game. There's the whole bet between our teams, so I know Houston wants to win.

His brother-in-law, Kit, who has been trash-talking our team all night (for good reason since they're ahead of us by eight), nudges his elbow and says something to him, looking a little worried. It probably means I'm not the only one who has caught on to Houston's disappointment, and I hate the idea of his family knowing how jerky I'm being by not responding to his bold text.

The break is almost over, so I need to get back, but I type out one last text and hope it straddles the line between rejection and encouragement.

Me:

> I'm all for giving chances, and I'm open to learning more about Sun City. I generally believe there's always more than meets the eye, and I like what I've seen so far.

Houston looks at the text right as I slide back into my seat across from him, and his eyebrows pull low as he reads. Maybe if I had put a wink at the end of it he would read into the subtext and know I wasn't just talking about Sun City.

I clear my throat. "Are you in this, Briggs? I can't keep carrying the team forever."

Jordan snorts, fighting laughter, and even Brooklyn stifles a giggle as Houston's eyes snap up to meet mine.

"Oh, I'm in this," he says just as the trivia host announces the theme of the lightning round: sports.

Houston's half-sister, Micah, groans at the other table, and Brooklyn lets out a disappointed sigh. But I lock eyes with Houston, and the tension between us shifts. This isn't just about our team winning anymore. We're in a sudden showdown, he and I, and Houston is hell-bent on making sure all of the answers come from him.

This town ain't big enough for the two of us, his eyes say.

Too bad for him, I've already got my hand hovering above my holster, ready to draw.

"Who has won more grand slam titles? Venus or—"

"Serena!" I shout before the question has even finished.

The host splutters for a second before awarding us the point. "Next question. Who was the first US president to throw the ceremonial pitch in—"

"Taft," Houston growls without looking away from me.

"What year were women allowed to compete in the Olympics?"

"1900," I say.

"Which team won the first NBA game in 1946?"

"Knicks," Kit shouts, beating me by half a second.

"Which female pitcher struck out Babe Ruth and Lou Gehrig?"

"Jackie Mitchell," Houston and I say at the same time.

I blink, shocked that he knows that one. Sure, it's his sport, but I didn't expect him to pay attention to a female pitcher in the first place.

The next question goes to a few tables away from us, probably because Houston seems confused by my confusion, but then the following question—about another female athlete—pulls us away. I answer a second ahead of Houston, my voice wavering a little because he gets that one right too.

The next few questions follow the same pattern, one of us just ahead of the other, until we've hit the last question of the night. We're tied with Kit's team, which means whoever answers this first wins the trophy. The game host is drawing things out to make it more dramatic, giving me the opportunity to study Houston while he studies me. He can't seem to make heads or tails of me anymore, and his frustration still simmers just beneath the surface.

"Who was the first NBA player to shatter the backboard?" the host asks, and I know the answer immediately.

But it sticks in my throat. Houston's expression has fallen, his eyebrows low as he stares at the table, and I can't know exactly what's in his head but I'm pretty sure he hates that I've given him a reason to be impressed. I could easily answer the question and win the game, but I have a feeling he's not going to take it as a victory.

"Chuck Connors," Kit says, and Micah squeals when they're announced the winners for the night, kissing her stoic boyfriend on the cheek as she bounces in her seat.

"Didn't know that one?" Houston asks, lifting his gaze to meet mine. His reluctance to be civil is written all over his face, but there's so much more going on behind those baby blues of his than there was before.

Tonight's outing has sufficiently confused the poor man, and I should probably put him out of his misery. "Hate to disappoint, but I don't know everything. I should go; duty calls." I wave my phone as I get to my feet, hoping to slip out before his family decides to try to keep me around.

I make it just outside the tavern before Houston's voice catches me off guard. He's right behind me, close enough that I feel his breath on the back of my neck. "You're working tonight?" There's an accusation in there, though I can't imagine what he thinks I would gain from a trivia game.

I turn my head just enough to meet his eyes. "I got a bit distracted when I should have been going back to my hotel to write." That's sort of true. I'm going to get crazy bored if Houston is my only story, so I've been thinking I should start looking for something else Connor might like in the meantime. "Thanks for letting me play. That was fun."

Houston frowns, clearly wary of my reply. "Write about what?"

I give him the first answer I can think of. "Little League." Except there are no leagues playing at the end of October, so that was a pretty stupid response.

To my complete surprise, Houston smiles a little, like he couldn't think of anything better than that. "*That's* why you're here? Our Little League teams?"

I'm not about to question this decision if Houston is going for it. "Did you really think I would be here for you?"

"I'd say breaking into the Red-tails training room might have given me that idea."

Right. I did do that. Laughing, I tuck some hair behind my ear and shake my head, trying to come across as calm and carefree. "You don't think I would be able to resist that kind of access while I'm here, do you? But don't worry. Your little team is safe for now."

"Except O'Donohue."

I perk up, mostly because he just said that voluntarily. "What happened to O'Donohue?" Aside from walking straight into a pole, that is.

Chuckling, Houston shrugs. "No one knows for sure, but he ended up with a broken nose during practice the other day. We all have a lot of theories that keep getting worse the longer we go."

When I grin at him, my smile is entirely real instead of the practiced one I usually give as Tamlin. I've always disliked O'Donohue and the way he thinks women are his playthings, and it seems his teammates might not be fond of him either. I could definitely do something with that. Especially if the moment was caught on camera.

"Maybe you should check the security footage," I tell him, choosing to let him see the moment blind instead of describing what happened. "And if you happen to see anything interesting, I'm just an email away. Enjoy the rest of your night, Briggs."

"Wait."

I pause again, curious about the hesitancy in his voice. His stance is just as tense, but there's less of a divide between the Briggs I met at the bar and the guy who nearly kissed Darcy this afternoon. Lines are blurring.

"I'm sorry," he says, the words coming out of him thin and quiet. I know how hard that probably is for him to say, so I keep my mouth shut and let him get it all out without interruption. "I shouldn't have treated you like you didn't know anything. I'm... You're pretty smart for a diva."

He's just full of surprises tonight, and I can't help but grin at him yet again. If he keeps this up, I'm going to forget who I'm supposed to be around him. "Funny," I say. "I was about to say the same thing about you."

Chapter Fourteen

Houston

"So, are we going to talk about that?"

I've just finished finalizing the plan with Micah for an event she asked me to come to in a couple of days—I'm making an appearance to endorse a newly reopened lodge—when Kit asks that question in that calm way of his. The one that sounds completely casual but is closer to digging out a festering splinter with a knife. The worst part is Kit is so likable that you don't usually know he's in there until the splinter is out and you're bleeding. You're better off in the long run, but it tends to sting for a bit.

As Micah and Fischer head back to their car, I glance behind me to where Kit leans against the side of the building with his arms folded. It stopped raining while we were at dinner, but the air is still cool and damp, everything fresh. I can breathe out here, unlike inside that bar that will forever make me think of Tamlin. I really hope she didn't ruin trivia night for me. "Talk about what?" I ask. "Where's Skyler?"

Kit smirks. "She's trying to convince the bartender to trade our trophy for a free plate of cheese fries. And you know exactly what I'm talking about. I don't think I've ever seen you act the way you did tonight. What's wrong?"

I could probably stall until Skyler has her fries and they head to their hotel, but Kit doesn't usually leave things alone. He'll delay if I want him to, but he's not going to drop it. In the year and a half I've known him, he's become a source of insight and reason, and I'm so glad Micah convinced him to come to Sun City this week. I could use his wisdom now more than ever.

I sigh, kicking a cigarette butt that's been left on the sidewalk. "*She's* wrong," I grumble. "She's like an itch I can't scratch and won't go away."

"Isn't she that reporter that works for Enhance Media? The one who did the story on the NBA betting rings?"

"Yep."

"What's she doing here?"

"Writing a story on Little League, apparently."

Kit lifts his eyebrows. "In October?"

"We play year-round here," I mutter, though I'm suddenly starting to wonder if Tamlin really meant it when she said she wasn't here for me. What if she found out that I help coach an underprivileged team? I can't see how she could twist that story negatively, but there's a first for everything. I'll have to be extra cautious at our game on Saturday and make sure she doesn't somehow show up at the field and start taking creepy pictures or something.

"Uh, you okay?" Kit asks.

I don't know what paranoia looks like, but I've probably got it on my face. "I've just been on edge," I admit.

"Because Tamlin is in Sun City?"

If Tamlin was my only problem, I'd be fine, but I've got baseball to deal with, as well as Jordan and Brooklyn's whole thing. They're still inside, and it's taking everything in me not to go see what they're doing. Micah is clearly dating Fischer despite meeting him a couple of weeks ago, and the guy looks at her like she's his sun. I'm not sure I trust him, and with Chad not around to look out for her, I feel like I have to step in. Then there's my inconceivably attractive neighbor who has my head spinning because I can't figure her out.

It's all too much.

I groan. "Because of a lot of things."

"Because of your sister dating your best friend? Or is it because of whoever you were texting earlier?"

I shoot him a glare. "Kit Morgan, you are terrifying. Are you secretly psychic? How does Skyler put up with you?" Then something clicks in my head. "Wait, how do you know they're dating?"

Laughing, he shakes his head as if I'm the most ridiculous person he's ever met. I'm a little bit serious, though, because I swear this man can read minds. That, or he's some sort of micro-expression and body language expert like that one TV show I used to watch years ago. What was it called? *Lie to Me*. Whatever he is, he's got a crazy read on people that I've never understood.

"Anyone who looks at Brooklyn would know she's in love with Jordan, and you don't seem too bothered by that."

I am bothered, but not because I don't want them to be together. If they would just tell me what's going on instead of keeping it a secret... The fact that Jordan is hiding it makes me wonder how serious he really is, and he doesn't have the best track record when it comes to relationships. Neither does Brook, to be honest. I don't want either of them to get hurt.

Kit folds his arms. "And I'm pretty sure anyone who looked at your stupid grin would have figured out that you were texting a girl," he says, rolling his eyes. "What kind of model is she?"

"A model citizen." I give him a shove. "You're not going to leave that alone, are you? I already told you that I'm done with casual."

"That doesn't mean you're ready for serious," he counters. "So?"

This is going to sound horrible, but there's no way to paint it better without flat-out lying. "She's my new tenant next door."

Kit's smile drops, which is pretty much what I expected to happen.

"Don't start," I say. "I know that makes things muddy. And it's not like I planned on kissing—"

"You kissed her?"

"No! Well, almost." If that stupid washing machine hadn't gotten in the way, I might have been able to play trivia with Darcy tonight instead of Tamlin. Kit's still watching me, but I feel weird talking about this. Outside of jokes and taunts with the team, I've never really talked about relationships or dating. It's always been too casual to bother with it, and I don't know how to navigate real feelings.

But if anyone can talk me through something like this, I'm pretty sure Kit can.

"I don't know how to do this," I admit, and the words hurt.

Kit cocks his head. "Do what?"

"Relationships. Real ones. I don't even know this girl, but I can't stop thinking about her."

"It could be rebound emotions you're feeling," he suggests.

I shake my head, though I do consider that for half a second. It's been more than two months since Bonnie, which is a whole lot longer than I've ever gone without finding someone new. "If I wanted a rebound, I wouldn't go for my tenant. There are probably half a dozen women in that bar who would gladly go out with me."

"Cocky, much?"

I roll my eyes. "Just realistic. All I'd have to do is tell them I threw the winning pitch at the World Series and they'd be all over me. But not Darcy. She barely even knows anything about baseball and didn't have a clue who I was when we met."

Nodding, Kit thinks that through. I'm not sure what insights he could have with just that. "So, she's a challenge."

"I guess." Except, it wasn't a challenge to hold her on the patio and talk about scorpions and superstitions. It wasn't a challenge to tell her about my various business endeavors, something I haven't even told Kit about beyond his wife's bookstore. In fact, being wholly myself around Darcy is easier than anything's been in a long time, and that has to mean something.

"I know you think otherwise," Kit says with a chuckle, "but I can't actually read your mind, and I feel like there's a lot happening in there."

Instead of explaining the swirling thoughts floating around in my head, I pull up my conversation with Darcy—at least, I really hope it's Darcy, though she didn't actually say—and shove the phone into Kit's hand.

He reads quickly, and I know the exact moment he gets to my absurd "I like you" text because his eyebrows shoot up, followed quickly by him trying not to laugh. "Sorry," he says as I snatch the phone back. "I think it's cool that you just went for it."

"Yeah, but she clearly doesn't want our relationship to go that way. She even told me the other night that most of her friends have been guys, and I'm pretty sure that means she only sees me as a friend."

"You don't know that. It's hard to infer meaning in a text. Have you asked her out?"

"I did tonight." Though, she might have seen it as more of a hangout than a date because that's exactly what it would have been. "She said she had to work. Whatever data control is, I hate it."

Kit chuckles again, and I don't even care at this point that my life is so amusing to him. I just want him to fix it. He's only a couple of years older than me, but he got to the marriage thing after a bit of a rocky start between him and Skyler. Their whole relationship had been fake until the point Skyler got scared of her real feelings and pushed him away. Pretty sure that lasted like half a day before Kit had her completely in love with him again because that's how good he is. If anyone can navigate complicated, he can.

As if reading my thoughts—no matter what he says, I'm still convinced he can do that—Kit studies me for a moment and then says, "Do you know why Skyler and I worked?"

"Because your entire relationship was based on a lie?" I quip.

Kit doesn't even flinch. "Because we were friends before anything. I trusted her with my darkest secrets, just like she did with me, and we didn't have any of the pressure of a romance getting in our way."

"I'm sorry, but are we forgetting that time I found you two making out on the couch?" Even when they had been fake engaged, they'd been nauseating.

"Sky brings out the best in me because she knows me better than anyone. If a woman you're interested in doesn't do that for you, it's probably because she doesn't know you."

Skyler bursts through the door just then, loaded with not only a steaming plate of cheese fries but a couple slices of cheesecake and what looks like a tankard full of soup. "It's time to go, Morgan."

Kit's eyes go wide as he takes the soup from her. "What—"

"Don't question it, just get in the car before the owner changes his mind about giving this all to me for free. Good to see you, Houston!" Then she's gone, disappearing around the corner toward the restaurant where we parked.

I meet Kit's eyes. "You know your wife is terrifying, right?" I feel like I can say that because we're only related through marriage, and *distantly*.

"Oh, I know," Kit says, and then he gives me a salute and follows Skyler. He throws one last piece of advice at me before he steps out of view. "Let Darcy know you without any strings attached, or you're never going to know if what you're feeling is infatuation or love."

Love? I make my way back into the tavern as that word bounces around inside me. I have known this woman for less than a week, and if this heartburn-like feeling in my chest is an indication of the inklings of something as frightening as love, I'm in big trouble.

By the time I get home, I'm ready to shut myself off from the world and never come back out until things are back to normal. It was so much easier when I had nothing holding me back in baseball, and my dating life was straightforward and easy, and my best friend and my sister were people I could count on to be predictable.

I just saw Jordan kissing Brook, and not in an "it was nice to see you, buddy" kind of way. Nope. It was an "I can't get enough of you and this isn't the first time I've kissed you" kind of way. It was a "drop my to-go container of nachos when I see it" sort of kiss that has been replaying over and over since I went back inside Grey Bird to order some food for Darcy. I was too much of a coward to confront them about it and instead gathered up my nachos and high-tailed it home.

How long have they been together? A week? Or has it been months of making out behind my back and pretending nothing is happening?

Honestly, all I can think about is how Kit was right about them so he's probably right about everything else. I should really be more bothered by this Jordan thing than I am, but I probably don't have the capacity to worry about anything else when my life is already a steaming pile of garbage.

Apparently I'm getting dramatic in my old age, something Brook told me as we were leaving the restaurant after dinner. But whatever.

It's late enough when I finally unlock my front door that I know I should just go to bed and deal with all of these emotions I'm feeling in the morning. But I get stupid when I'm tired, so I don't make it past my living room before I send a text to Darcy. I need the distraction as much as I'm desperate to see her.

I curse, grit my teeth for letting the swear slip, and then type out another text before I get the cops called on me for being a creep toward my tenant.

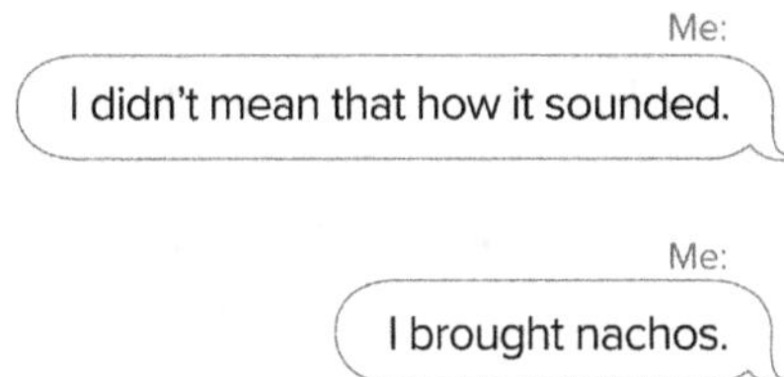

Who wants nachos at ten thirty at night? This was a terrible idea, and I'm going to have to eat them all myself so they don't go to waste. My stomach is not going to appreciate that in the morning, but my tongue is certainly up for the challenge. If I'm going to risk the pain for something, at least it's Grey Bird nachos.

They might be the only good thing to come out of tonight.

Jordan and Brook. *Kissing*. And Tamlin Park is kind of a genius, which is way more attractive than it should be. And Darcy... Darcy seems to have a hold on my heart. I have no idea how she got her hand around it because I barely know her, and I'm not the kind of guy who just lets people in.

None of these things feel like they're going to mix well with everything else going on in my life. Even if I do go to bed now, I'm pretty sure I won't be able to sleep.

My phone pings, and I nearly knock the box of nachos onto the floor (again) in my haste to open the text.

I don't trust myself to be alone in my house with her right now, and I don't trust Jesse to not be looming like some bodyguard if we go into her place. The porch is Switzerland, and hopefully a place I can try to be her friend, like Kit suggested. Even if I've never had a female friend outside of my sisters before and have no idea what that's supposed to look like... I'm just going to wing it.

Darcy steps onto the porch at the same time I do, and her eyes go immediately to the open Styrofoam container in my hands. I should be insulted that she doesn't give me the same look that she gives the food, but I can't blame her for nearly tearing up at the sight of jalapenos, olives, bacon, and enough cheese to block her arteries.

Without a word of greeting, she scoops out a handful of chips and shovels them into her mouth with a moan. "You weren't kidding," she says. Or, I think that's what she says. She has to say it around an enormous mouthful of nacho.

Is it weird that her complete disregard for chewing with her mouth closed is actually making me like her more? Especially because Tamlin didn't even touch the nachos at our table during the trivia game.

Darcy looks freshly showered, her damp hair pulled back in a braid and big, wire-rimmed glasses accentuating her chocolate eyes. I'm immensely jealous of her sweatshirt and pajama bottoms. I should have changed before coming out here so I could relax a little more. I may have dressed up a bit tonight, just in case she changed her mind and came to the bar, so this feels disproportionate.

I'd rather be comfy like her, which is a strange sensation for me. She doesn't make me feel like I'm on display.

"We should probably sit down before I knock these out of your hands," she says after she swallows.

We settle on the steps, and I keep a firm hold of the takeout container so she can use both hands to eat without the risk of losing any cheesy goodness. "I'm glad you like them," I tell her, as if her approval of my favorite junk food is all I've ever wanted in a woman. In a *friend*. I have to remember that distinction unless she gives me any sign that she wants otherwise.

A string of cheese dangles down her chin after her next bite, but she doesn't seem to notice. "How was your night with your family?"

How do I even put it into words? "Eventful," I say. That's putting it way too simply, but whatever. I'm trying not to reach over and wipe the cheese from her chin, and that's taking most of my concentration. "My family was great, as always, and I don't get to see my stepsister and her husband very often, so that was nice." Then there's Brook and Jordan, but I'm ignoring them for now. Poorly, but still. "I had to deal with my arch enemy."

Darcy chokes, breaking into a coughing fit that gets me lamely patting her on the back until she can breathe again.

"You okay?" I ask.

Though her eyes are watering behind her glasses, she nods. "I should probably pace myself," she says with a laugh, and she wipes her chin clean with her sleeve. "I don't want to be one of the lucky four thousand people who choke to death every year. You have an enemy? Who?"

I don't know why I don't want to tell her about Tamlin. It's not like she has any reason to be jealous—the idea of me liking Tamlin is beyond laughable, even if she surprised me tonight. I guess I don't want Darcy to think I'm capable of disliking someone when I have no good reason.

Darcy bumps her shoulder into mine. "You seriously can't say something like that and not give me all the dirty details. Come on, Briggs." She tenses, clearly trying to decide if she likes the feeling of camaraderie that comes from calling me by my last name. I hope she hates it and goes back to calling me Hou.

I let out a sigh, feeling some of my own tension spill out into the damp night air with my breath. *Let her know you.* "She's a sports journalist who may or may not have it out for me."

"So, she definitely has it out for you," Darcy infers.

"No. I mean, I don't know. She says she doesn't, but she doesn't really have any reason to be in Sun City right now when there aren't any sports going on."

"Your team is still practicing, right?"

"We never stop." Outside of a few days around the holidays, we pretty much have practice all year.

"Maybe she's doing a story on what happens during the downseason?"

There's that word again, the one that is almost right but not quite. I love that she's trying, even if she has no idea what she's talking about. It certainly seems like she *wants* to know me, which has to be a good sign. She did come outside despite the late hour.

"Maybe," I say. "She said something about Little League, though I don't know why someone as prominent as her would want to write a story on a bunch of ten-year-olds who spend more time picking dande-lions than they do trying to catch the ball."

Darcy has made it halfway through the nachos and shows no sign of slowing, which is admirable. I don't think Brook or Micah have ever gotten through a plate of these on their own, though Chad and I can both pack them in. I like that she's not afraid to show an interest in food, when most of my past girlfriends have treated eating like a necessary evil.

I should probably stop cataloging everything I like about Darcy, but I can't help it.

"I've never seen a Little League game," she says after she swallows an especially big bite. "Do they really get distracted so easily?"

"You could come to my game on Saturday and see for yourself."

She pauses with her hand inside the container, and I worry I've over-stepped again until she looks at me with excitement shining in her eyes. "Really? Do you play Little League too?"

The laughter that bursts out of me seems to release something in my chest that I didn't even know was trapped, breaking a dam that I've probably been building my entire life to protect myself from anyone getting too close to who I am at my core. I laugh so hard that I cry, and I can suddenly breathe in a way I've never breathed before. And I don't even care that this rupture leaves me exposed because it feels so good to let it out like this.

Besides, there is no way someone as genuine as Darcy Paxton will hurt me.

We sit on the porch for a couple of hours and talk in a way I've never talked with anyone before. We don't say anything significant or meaningful, but it's all so *easy*. And when Darcy can't stop yawning, I bid her goodnight and make my way to my bed with a smile on my face. Despite everything happening in my life right now, there's something about this woman that makes me feel hopeful for the first time in a long time. And I am not going to let that go.

Chapter Fifteen

Darcy

October 25

I avoid Houston at all costs on Friday, which is thankfully pretty easy to do. Jordan shows up next door pretty early but doesn't stay long, and then Houston leaves for practice around nine and doesn't come back until that afternoon, heading straight for the shower. (Which, you guessed it, shares a wall with mine. Not at all awkward and definitely doesn't remind me of how he looked in a towel.) Then he heads back out, maybe to spend some more time with his family who's in town.

The hard part is ignoring the texts he sends me throughout the day, like we're suddenly best friends and text each other all the time. I last about twenty minutes after the first text comes in before I can no longer hold myself back from responding.

Houston:

> I nearly got eaten by one of those fabled spare socks this morning. Do you know where I can buy some sock repellent?

Me:

> I think it's called Sandals.

Houston:

> My stepdad has proven that method is ineffective.

> Me:
> Are you sure? The internet is pretty convinced.

> Houston:
> I have photo evidence that Sandals do not keep away socks.

He texts me again around lunch time, when I'm in the middle of setting up an interview with a golf player in Albuquerque who thinks he's designed the perfect putter. It's close enough to Sun City that I can spend the day watching him prove that his design can make anyone a pro. I don't believe it can, but odds are high that the guy is actually an incredibly skilled golfer and just doesn't know it. I would love to be the one to get him in the spotlight if that's what he wants. No matter the outcome, it should be an entertaining story.

Just not as entertaining as Houston Briggs.

> Houston:
> One of my outfielders isn't convinced that Grey Bird has the best nachos. Please confirm.

Well, how could I let him down?

> Me:
> Can confirm. Ate my not insignificant weight in nachos last night and still wanted more.

> Houston:
> Well now you just sound like a nacho lightweight. Pretty sure you ate more than that.

My cheeks heat. I hadn't really been fishing for a compliment, and I don't see myself as overweight or anything. But I am not petite or slender, and it takes a good deal of effort for Jesse to wrangle me into all of the bits and pieces that make up thin and curvy Tamlin Park. But Houston just heavily implied that he finds me small.

I mean, next to a wall of muscle like him, I am tiny. But I've never *felt* small. I've always been the athletic girl whose muscle makes finding a dress that fits both my shoulders and my small chest next to impossible.

Same with jeans that actually fit my thighs without drowning my waist. I'm not nearly as strong as I used to be, but I still like to head out to the batting cages now and then or play a game of Horse on the basketball court with some of the guys at Enhance.

Before I can come up with some sort of response to his subtle compliment, he texts again.

Houston:

Bardem thinks his wife makes better nachos, but I've seen some of the lunches he brings from home, and I'm not willing to risk a taste test.

Houston:

How's that data control treating you?

My cheeks are going to hurt from smiling this much, and I'm glad Jesse went into town so I don't have to see him looming over me with those judgy eyes of his. I swear, he was two minutes away from flickering the porch light last night when I finally came inside (way later than I should have), and he refused to listen when I told him I'm working on the story. I haven't breathed a word of what happened—almost happened—yesterday while I was doing laundry, but I have a feeling he knows.

Me:

As boring as ever. I get sleepy when I try to describe it to people, but it pays the bills and has flexible hours, so I can't complain too much.

Houston:

I may need you to tell me about it so I *don't* fall asleep. Our manager is droning on and on about how we need to work together as a team to win games.

Houston:

I don't think he realizes that's about as basic as you can get with team sports, but his whole speech feels very coachy, so I guess he's doing something right.

> **Me:**
> Are you telling me you put your Little League team to sleep when you talk to them?

> **Houston:**
> No, I'm one of the cool coaches. I always roll up to games bearing gifts of Fruit Roll-ups and orange slices.

> **Me:**
> Good. I didn't need my weekend to be as boring as my day job.

> **Houston:**
> You're really coming tomorrow?

Even if it's a terrible time to take a step back from this conversation and think about what I'm doing, I set my phone down anyway and take a deep breath. Connor told me in no uncertain terms that I have to be at that game, whether as myself or Tamlin. No one knew Houston coaches Little League, so this is kind of a big deal. It's not *the* big deal—Connor is still talking through strategies for future Tamlin interactions—but this side of Houston isn't going to stay secret for long.

Even if I didn't tell the story, Connor would put someone else on to it.

I wish I hadn't told him.

It will be better if I can control how it goes out and minimize the effect this has on Houston's ability to keep coaching. As soon as the world knows about it, they're going to start flocking to every Little League game in Sun City, which could be beneficial for the teams who don't have a lot of funding. But at the same time, Houston's fame might disrupt games and turn this into a spectacle instead of an outlet for the kids.

Why did Houston have to tell me about this?

Sighing, I pick up my phone and send off a text I don't mean.

> **Me:**
> I wouldn't miss it for the world.

October 26

By the time Saturday afternoon rolls around, I'm pretty sure Jesse is at the end of his rope because I've been freaking out about this all morning. He slips out of the car as quickly as he can when I drop him off at his new temp job—at a tattoo parlor, which, frankly, makes a lot of sense. I've never understood his passion for makeup, but this makes me think he's in it more for the artistic aspect than the beauty. Jesse is definitely an artist, and apparently the human skin is his favorite canvas. He doesn't really care about the medium.

Before closing the door, Jesse peeks in at me. "This is your job," he reminds me. "And going to a game you were invited to isn't doing anything wrong."

Maybe not, but lying to the guy who has been nothing but nice to me feels pretty wrong.

"Just have some fun, Darce. You work too hard." He gives me a little smile and then heads inside to make some people incredibly happy about their choice of tattoo parlor; they're getting the best.

As I drive over to the park where Houston's team is playing, I grumble about what Jesse said. I do not work too hard. I put in the same effort that everyone else does at Enhance, and half the time it doesn't even feel like work. I get to claim courtside seats at basketball games and join bowling leagues. I spent a week covering geriatric Olympics in Los Angeles back when I was just an intern. Even here, despite the growing conflict I feel about what I'm doing to Houston, I spend most of my down time with my eyes glued to college football games, searching for any standouts who might be on their way to the NFL next draft season. How could anyone call that work?

The universe decides to answer that question like it did on the back patio, in the form of a phone call from my mother right as I pull into the half-full parking lot.

I hit every red light on the way here—should have expected that—so I'm borderline late, but it's been long enough since I talked to my mom that I can't just ignore her. She'd be fine if I told her I need to call her back, but I do miss my mama.

"Hey, Mama," I answer as I nearly drop my phone.

"Hi sweetie! How is Missouri?"

Apparently Carissa hasn't shared my whereabouts, which makes this interesting. Do I lie to my mother so she doesn't start asking questions I don't know how to answer? I shudder at the thought. No, I can't lie. I'm doing enough of that with Houston.

"Work is great," I say. "I'm helping with a big story that I'm hoping does really well for me."

"I'm so glad to hear that! When are you going to come visit next?"

While I know she's asking because she misses me, there's an underlying layer of stress in her voice that makes it sound thin. Gripping the steering wheel, I try not to let my worry leak out into my own voice.

"How's Dad?"

Mom sighs. "Oh, you know, it varies from day to day."

My poor dad has been dealing with severe arthritis for the last several years, and nothing seems to help. He's too old to still be working, but I know he's nowhere close to being able to retire in terms of finances. And my mom, who is twenty years younger than him, is probably struggling with how to help him. She's already working part-time for a local CPA who has a home office down the street from them, but she's only ever been a stay-at-home mom. I'm not sure she has the fortitude to work any more than she already does, though she'll do it if she has to. But I know she would rather be spending time with my dad while she can.

"Do you think he'll need to quit the store?" I ask. "Can he still work?"

Dad runs a hardware store but doesn't own it, so he can't sell and live off the profits. He's tried convincing the owner—some guy who lives in New York—to sell it to him, but I don't know if my parents could even get the loan for that. Not while they're still paying off Carissa's student debt. I hate that they are stuck in this endless financial loop, like scooping water out of a leaking boat with a teaspoon, but I hate more that I can only do so much to help. Someday I hope to move up the ranks at Enhance and make some more money so I can help support my parents.

Hard to imagine that happening when I can't even find whatever story I'm here to tell.

"It's getting harder for him," Mom says. "It's okay. He still has good days where he can work full hours."

But what happens if those good days get less frequent?

My job pays too well to quit and move back home to help them directly, but I feel so helpless when I'm states away. My mom puts on a brave face, and I am so glad they have Carissa there to keep an eye on them, but I wish I could do more. I need something better, like a big break story to convince the board at Enhance that I am valuable.

Is that why Connor sent me out here? Am I missing something obvious when it comes to Houston Briggs? I could feel the story just out of reach when I snuck into the Red-tails training room, but I still don't know what it is. What is Houston hiding?

I'm never going to find out by sitting in a parking lot.

"I plan to be home for Thanksgiving," I say. "I should probably go. I've got work to do."

"On a Saturday?"

I know full well that the only reason my mom is calling me is because my dad is at work today too, leaving her alone in the house with her worries. "Yeah. It's not too bad. I get to watch a Little League game today."

"In October?"

I chuckle. "It's a little strange, but that's why I'm here. I'll call you later?"

"Sounds good. Don't work too hard!"

"Love you, Mama."

The game is already underway when I round the bleachers, and I hurry up to an empty seat near the top.

It takes me a second to find Houston amid the many coaches and parents hovering behind home plate, but the instant I see him, my whole body relaxes. I'm not sure I like how quickly he eases my tension.

I see his hair first, blonde locks poking out the front of his backwards baseball hat as he shouts something to the boy who's up at bat. I take in the rest of him slowly, deliberately, because this is the most relaxed I've ever seen him. He wears sweats and a red t-shirt with the team's logo—the Scorpions, ironically—printed on the back, but it's more than his clothes that give him that relaxed look. He is literally relaxed, his limbs loose and limber and his broad shoulders low. And his smile...

He looks just as content as he did when I joked about him playing Little League the other night.

My heart throbs in memory of Thursday's nachos. Not because of the nachos—which were a religious experience unto themselves—but because I practically watched his stress melt away as he laughed. I've spent so much time learning to read people, and I've always been fairly intuitive when it comes to body language. But even someone who hasn't had years of training would have picked up on the way Houston seemed to lose every shred of fear when it comes to Darcy.

If I thought he was falling before, I'm pretty sure our conversation on the steps reeled him in completely.

The opposite of what I needed to do. Houston isn't supposed to fall in love with me. At this point, I barely want him to *befriend* me, but a large part of me treasures the way he looked at me on the porch. I've never had anyone look at me like that, like I bring happiness into his life just by existing.

I wouldn't mind spending a million evenings on that porch, talking to Houston Briggs.

After his batter bunts the ball and hustles to first base, Houston sweeps the bleachers, a bit of tension entering his shoulders. I can't decide if he's disappointed he hasn't seen me or if he's worried he might find Tamlin, but it doesn't matter. The instant his eyes lock on to mine, a full, dimpled smile breaks loose and his energy practically doubles. He gives me a wave—several spectators look at me in curiosity—and I wave back, hating the warmth that spreads through me from that smile meant just for me.

The next kid comes up to bat, and Houston puts an arm around his shoulders, muttering something to him before tapping the top of his helmet and sending him up to home plate.

The kid has a good stance and looks ready to knock the ball out of the park. When he swings at the pitch, he doesn't quite manage a home run, but the outfielders scramble to scoop up the ball, and the Scorpions get one run as the batter makes it all the way to third base.

I desperately want to know what Houston said to that kid. For a ten-year-old, that hit was amazing.

Houston, of course, is beaming, clapping his hands with vigor along with the crowd as if he couldn't be prouder, and my heart melts a little. There's no one here to fanboy over him, so this is all genuine Houston.

"Hi there."

I reluctantly pull my eyes away from Houston to look at the woman sitting directly in front of me. "Hi."

She gives me a warm smile. "I haven't seen you at one of these games before."

I know she's probably curious about my relationship with Houston, but her smile is so genuine and friendly that I can't help but smile back at her. "I just moved to town," I tell her. "Houston thought I would enjoy coming to the game since I don't know anyone in the area yet. I'm Darcy, by the way."

The woman puts her hand on the man beside her, who gives me a smile that's just as friendly as hers. "I'm Molly. This is my husband, Jack."

"Do you have a kid on the team?"

"We have two, actually." She points out her boys and jumps right into telling me about how she and Jack adopted them this year. "Cooper's a little young for the team, but he idolizes his older brother."

"He just *has* to be on the same team," Jack says with a chuckle.

They spend the rest of the game telling me the names of the boys and explaining the rules of the game—I must have looked overwhelmed or something—and I fall a little bit in love with both of them. They both work, but they've done everything they can to get their schedules to line up with these games so they can support their boys.

When Cooper goes up to bat, Molly and Jack leap to their feet and cheer like maniacs. Houston does the same routine that he does for every kid, bending low to talk to the much-smaller kid before sending him off to the plate. Cooper looks nervous but determined, taking his stance with gritted teeth.

He swings and misses on the first pitch, some of his confidence waning.

Jack whistles loudly while Molly practically screams encouragement.

Cooper's second strike has him almost shaking with disappointment, and I can see the fear in his eyes. If he strikes out, the game is over and the Scorpions lose. The crowd's energy shifts, growing quieter as everyone waits for the pitcher's wind up. The ball flies, Cooper swings, and the muffled sound of the ball hitting the catcher's mitt is deafening.

"Oh no," Molly says, tears filling her eyes as the Tarantulas storm the field in victory.

Jack sighs. "He almost had that last one. One second too late."

"Look at him."

Cooper hasn't left home plate, but the bat hangs limply in his hand, the end of it in the dirt as his head hangs low. His shoulders shake, and I know he's trying his best not to cry but can't help it. The rest of his team trudges onto the field to shake hands with the victors, but he doesn't move.

Next thing I know, Houston is crouched at his side and holding his arm in a comforting grip. I can't tell what he's saying, but the emotion in his face gives me a pretty good idea. I can't help but tear up, sympathetic crier that I am, even if Houston isn't crying. I know he feels it, which is pretty much the same thing.

Cooper throws his arms around Houston's shoulders right as his parents get down to the field, and I feel that hug from all the way up here. It's like Cooper's arms have wrapped around my heart and given it a good squeeze, only I'm pretty sure Cooper isn't the one who has me feeling this way.

This is bad. How am I supposed to tell Connor that I'm falling hard and fast for my story? I'm not. Because if Connor thinks I am emotionally involved, he's going to pull me from the story and get me as far from New Mexico as he can. It would probably be good for me, getting some distance from this insanely attractive man, but I hate the idea that someone else will take over and start pushing on the pressure points I have regrettably informed Connor about.

No, I have to stay and see this through, which means I have to slam on the brakes of this attraction to Houston Briggs. I have to friendzone him hard, no gray areas or fuzzy lines, and I have to tamp down these feelings that are more of a nuisance than anything anyway.

I mean, seriously. How is a girl supposed to focus when her heart has taken up tap dancing as a regular hobby?

Now that the game has ended, parents and kids are disappearing quickly to their cars, but I stay where I am. It feels safer up here somehow, and I can still watch Houston in his element. In his *real* element. I've watched plenty of Red-tails games and seen him in action, and while he's an incredibly talented pitcher, he's never shown that level of contentment that he has now as he talks to kids and adults alike. Okay, yes, games are intense, so of course he would be focused while on the mound, but even after games, he's always had an underlying seriousness that used to make me think he was all about the game and winning.

He might still be all about the game, but I'm starting to think he cares more about the other players than he does about himself.

When the field is pretty much empty, one man approaches Houston with his hand on his son's shoulder—the kid who nearly hit a home run. He looks nervous, which makes Houston tense up immediately. A part of me itches to race down there and make sure he's okay, but the conversation doesn't even last long enough for me to stand before Houston reaches into his pocket and holds out his car keys.

The man freezes, then waves his hand as he shakes his head. But Houston practically forces the keys into his hand before saying something to the kid and ruffling his hair.

As the man wanders off with his face twisted in emotion, I make a mental note to see if Connor will pay for a lip-reading course. It could come in handy during certain sports if I have a good view of the coaches and players on the bench. And, you know, when Houston Briggs apparently gives away his old pickup truck.

Finally it's just me and him, and Houston leaps up the bleachers with a lot more energy than I have right now. He flops down next to me, shoulder to shoulder, and fixes his gaze so intently on my face that I heat up like a hot air balloon, his smile the *whoosh* of burning gas pulling me higher into the clouds.

"Hi," he says, that one word feeling like it carries a hundred others with it.

Whoosh.

"Hi yourself."

"What did you think of the game?"

"It was pretty fun, I guess."

"You guess? That's all you can say after you just spent the last hour checking me out?"

Whoosh.

This hot air balloon of mine is going to hit the stratosphere if I'm not careful. I nudge my shoulder into his, hoping that distracts from my blush. "I did not! I spent most of it talking to some new friends."

"I noticed. Jack and Molly looked ready to adopt you." Was he watching me as much as I watched him?

Whoosh.

Silence builds between us, heated and tangible as we gaze at each other, like we're both waiting for the other one to pop the bubble of this moment. As much as I wish we could stay here in a place that feels more like home than anything has in Sun City so far, I can't. I can't tell Houston that I have loved baseball since I was a kid. For some reason, I made him believe I didn't know anything about sports because I wanted to separate Darcy from Tamlin as much as I could, and now I can't be completely honest with him without ruining everything.

I don't want to hurt him, but at this point I think it might be inevitable no matter what I do.

Houston breaks the silence first, though it's clear he doesn't want to. I think he'd be totally down to sit on the bleachers in the sunshine and gaze at me in a way that makes me think my hair might catch on fire.

"So... I could use a ride."

If he's going to bring it up, I don't feel bad asking. "Yeah, uh, did you just give away your truck?"

He laughs, throat bobbing as he throws his head back. I want to bottle up the sound so I can pull it out when I'm feeling down. "Wow, you must have a really high opinion of me if that's your first conclusion."

"So, you didn't—"

"John needed to borrow it. His pickup broke down, and he was going to lose his job if he didn't have something to use while it's getting fixed."

What kind of relationship does Houston have with these people if they feel comfortable asking for such a big favor?

As if he can see the question in my eyes, Houston shakes his head. "He told me Jay was probably going to have to miss next week's game because he wasn't going to have a way to get him here. But I know John's foreman is incredibly strict and wouldn't let him take an unplanned week off."

"That's..." I don't even know what to say, so I just say, "Wow."

Though he does seem a bit uncomfortable about this conversation, his smile still melts me in my seat. It's not like today is incredibly warm, so that's all him. "Anyway," he says, "the team's going to Big Henry's for lunch, and I promised the kids I would go. I can grab an Uber if you're not up for—"

I grab his hand, realizing too late that I already know my hand likes his a little too much. I meant it as a friendly gesture of excitement, but Houston stops breathing. So do I. *Rein it in, Paxton.* "I think that sounds fun," I say, miraculously without sounding breathless. "Will Molly and Jack be there?"

Houston swallows. His eyes are fixed on his hand, which is so completely still that I know he's doing everything he can not to repeat his move from the living room. I'm not sure why he's silently agreeing to my friends-only rule I made for myself, but I am not going to question it when it's better for both of us.

"Probably," he croaks before pulling his hand away and jumping to his feet with a cough. "I want to try to get there before everyone orders, so if you want to take pity on me..."

It's such a bad idea, but I still say yes because I'm not ready to let go of this side of Houston Briggs. Not by a longshot.

GREY
BIRD
TAVERN

Chapter Sixteen

Houston

BIG HENRY'S IS BUSY on a regular day, but on game days? The place becomes a madhouse. The burger joint is a Sun City institution, even though the menu only holds six items and hasn't changed in forty years. The Scorpions fill every booth and table in the place, not just with sweaty kids and their parents but with all the noise and nonsense that comes with them. I know Henry doesn't mind—Little Henry, since his dad, Big Henry, died a couple of years ago—but he still puts up a stink whenever we show up.

The fact that he asked for a game calendar a few months ago and always asks about the final score has me pretty convinced that he secretly likes it when we show up.

When Darcy and I step into the wave of shouts and screams, she leans into me, her eyes a little wide as she takes in the chaotic scene. I'm not complaining, and I even put my hand on her back in case she needs support to deal with all of this. I'm glad she came with me, even if she's throwing out all sorts of mixed signals. I deal with that all the time with Badir when he can't decide what sort of pitch I should throw, so I'll do my best to take things in stride.

Maybe she's just as wary as I am of trying to turn this into more than a next-door neighbor kind of relationship. I have no idea what her dating history is like—technically I don't even know for sure if she's single—but despite my past lineup of relationships, this feels like it's all new to me. I'm perfectly fine if we take things slow and build a friendship first, just like Kit said.

In fact, it might be smarter if I make sure that's what we do. Seeing her in the bleachers, laughing with Jack and Molly and cheering for my Scorpions, had my insides doing a jumbled sort of dance, like my body couldn't decide if I was nervous or elated. I started picturing her being there for every game, cheering on my kids with the same enthusiasm she seems to give everything in her life. I started imagining her showing up with Capri Suns for the boys and a kiss for luck for me, and I think my heart may have latched on to that idea a little too strongly for my liking. It's not about the kiss—of course I want to kiss her. I could barely think about anything else for the first two minutes after I saw her.

But when I imagine that kind of support system, one that goes beyond my siblings, I start to hope again.

And hope is a dangerous thing.

"Is it always this loud?" Darcy asks when a couple of the boys start some sort of screaming contest right in front of us.

I chuckle. "I'm guessing you don't have any brothers."

"Just my little sister."

I tuck that detail away in the mental folder I'm titling "The Real." Things that make Darcy more than just a fantasy or an ideal. The more I can learn about her, the more these intense feelings might make sense. "How much older are you?"

When a boy comes barreling past us toward the bathroom, Darcy jumps back, colliding with my chest and knocking me back a step. My arm wraps around her instinctively, and neither of us move for five whole seconds until I find the will to let her go. It's not easy. At all.

"Sorry," she says.

"Don't worry about it." *Feel free to do it again.* I should not like holding her as much as I do, but there's something solid about her. With most of my past girlfriends, I always felt like I had to be delicate and careful with every touch and movement. Darcy isn't much bigger than Bonnie was, but she seems like the kind of girl I can hold without breaking her.

"She's three years younger," Darcy says, reminding me that I asked her a question about her sister and probably shouldn't be trying to think of excuses to hold her again. Another boy will probably run past us. Or I could pretend to slip on that spot of ketchup on the floor and grab her on my way down. "She just finished physical therapy school and is doing an internship back in Pennsylvania, and she is way too excited about scaring people into healing faster because they don't want to disappoint her."

I like her already. "Pennsylvania. Is that where you grew up?"

"In Ardmore, just outside Philly."

I still wonder how she ended up clear across the country in New Mexico, but I'm grateful for whatever entity dropped her in my lap. "Did you go to college?"

She laughs, raising an eyebrow at me. "What's with the sudden inquisition?"

"I'm killing time while we're stuck in line." It's the excuse that makes me sound less pathetic, but we've almost reached the counter. I don't want to stop asking her questions, so I hope she doesn't mind the inquisition.

"I did go to college," she says. "Back east."

And that seems to be a touchy subject because that's all she says. Whatever data control entails, I can't imagine it's very difficult. I want to know what she majored in—maybe she's feeling unfulfilled—but instead I start talking about myself.

"I went to UC Santa Barbara. But only for two years, and then I got drafted by the Red-tails."

If she thinks it's pathetic that I never got a degree, she doesn't show it. Instead, her eyes have drifted to the menu even though it only takes about ten seconds to decide when your choices are 'hamburger,' 'hamburger with cheese,' 'hamburger with cheese and a pickle,' or a hot dog.

When she says nothing, I scramble to come up with another topic. "Did you have any pets?" I relax at the sight of her smile as she turns back to me.

"If you're going to ask so many questions," she says, "I feel like I should get to ask some too."

"You have questions? Ask away." I'll be an open book for her.

"Is it worth the extra twenty-five cents for the pickle?"

I blink. She wants to ask me about pickles? "I don't like pickles," I say stupidly.

"Well, I love pickles," she replies with a wink. A *wink*! "I think the world is equally divided between people who like pickles and people who don't so everything can stay in balance. Seems like you and I were meant to be friends."

Look, I'm not saying I believe in something ridiculous like soulmates, but...

Darcy pulls her phone out of her pocket, frowning at the lit-up screen before she says, "I should take this. It's my boss. I'll be right back."

While I hope everything is okay, she leaves at the perfect time for me to order our food without her finding out about everything else I'm buying today.

"Did anyone fight you on it?" I ask Little Henry, handing him my credit card.

He rolls his eyes as he processes the enormous bill. Everyone thinks Little Henry gives them all their food for free, and I'd like to keep it that way, even if he doesn't like it. Everyone gives him all the credit because I force him to keep his mouth shut about me paying for it. "They all did. As usual. They might stop coming if you keep insisting on buying everyone's meals, Briggs." To anyone who doesn't know the gruff and burly fry cook, they might think he's worried about losing customers. But I know better. Chad used to take us here when we were kids, when Little Henry was still under Big Henry's wing. He's always been a big softy, just like his dad. He's worried about his customers being mad at him.

"They'll keep coming," I say. I know how much it hurts to accept help from someone better off, but I also know how hard it is to live paycheck to paycheck, like most of my team's parents do. They can pretend they would rather pay for their own food, but when some of these families have multiple kids, Henry's is a splurge, however small, they can't always afford.

"You sure you want the pickle?" Little Henry asks as he hands my card back. "I thought you hated pickles."

I grin. "I do. Yes, I want the pickle."

Grunting, he looks past me to the door. Darcy is just on the other side of the glass, pacing a little as she talks on the phone. "I'm surprised you actually brought one."

I have never brought a girlfriend to Big Henry's, or even to a game. Neither have I talked to Little Henry about my dating life, but he's not so old that he doesn't know how the internet works.

There's no holding back my grin when I turn back to Little Henry. "She's different."

He smiles. "For your sake, I hope so."

I could ask what he means by that, but I probably know the answer. Historically, I haven't made the best dating choices, and none of those women were people I could have settled down with. For a while, that was the point, but now...

By the time Darcy comes back in, most of the boys have gotten their food so the noise levels have dimmed to a dull roar. I managed to coax some boys into sitting with their friends so I could take their table, and it has taken everything in me not to nervously eat all the fries before she can decide if she'd rather have those or onion rings. I don't know why I would be nervous about a phone call, but everything with Darcy feels so temporary. What if her job pulls her away from Sun City before I'm ready to let her go?

What if I'm never ready?

"Everything okay?" I ask as she slides into the booth opposite me. I don't know why I thought she would sit on the same side as me, but I'm disappointed irregardless. Er, regardless.

She sighs. "Fine. There's a big project my boss wants me to work on the day before Halloween."

My heart sinks. I was toying with the idea of asking her to be my date to a gala I'm going to that night, but I guess that's out. Probably for the best, considering I likely wouldn't recover from seeing her in formal wear. I can't picture Darcy in a dress, so I wonder if she would have even said yes if I'd asked.

"Hopefully it's nothing too boring," I say.

Her smile returns as she looks at me, bringing with it a bit of sunshine into my soul. I'll have other chances to ask her out. It's fine. "This one might actually get a little interesting. But we'll have to see."

"I think I'd rather do data control than go to the party I'm obligated to attend that night."

"A party? That doesn't sound so bad."

"It does when you realize it's a charity function and I'm only there to draw a bigger crowd." I hold up my hand, following the words of an invisible marquee as I announce, "Come see the famous pitcher who almost lost Game Six of the World Series when he pitched a home run in the eighth inning."

She snorts. "First of all, that would be terrible advertising. Second of all, are you really that famous? You don't act famous. And I thought home runs were a good thing."

Does she have any idea how refreshing it is to have someone not only not care that I'm moderately well-known in the world of sports but also not even have a clue what that means? If she likes me—jury's still out on that—it's because of *me*. That's something I have to hold on to as long as I can.

"Home runs are good unless it's the other team getting them," I say with a grin. "Fries or onion rings?"

She looks at my offerings and then picks up one of each, taking a bite with the seriousness of someone judging an expensive wine. I could watch her silently debate with herself all day. "Onion rings," she decides, pulling the bag closer to her side of the table. "Unless you wanted them?"

"Nope. I don't like onion rings any more than I like pickles."

"Then why did you offer me the fries?"

Because I care more about your happiness than I do mine. But that would be creepy, so I don't actually say that. Instead, I peek inside my burger and make a face of disgust. "Speaking of pickles... Looks like I ended up with one. Do you want it?"

Her eyes literally sparkle. Well, not literally, but close enough. As she reaches over and pulls the massive pickle off my burger with a wide grin, I can't help but match her smile with one of my own. I'm generally a happy guy, but I feel like I smile more with Darcy than I ever have before.

"See what I mean?" she says brightly. "We're a match made in heaven."

This pickle was *definitely* worth the extra twenty-five cents.

"So," I say after we've both had a chance to dig into our burgers. "I know you like pickles for some reason and grew up near Philly with a little sister. You went to college and may or may not have had pets growing up."

"I did not. Both my parents are allergic to fur."

"Or did they just tell you that so they didn't have to keep telling you no every time you asked for a puppy?"

Her jaw drops. "Oh my goodness, what if that's true?"

Snickering, I shrug one shoulder as I relax deeper into my seat. Though I've done a pretty good job of pretending I have no idea what's going on around us, I'm all too aware of most of the Scorpions' parents surreptitiously watching us. This is probably the most interesting I've ever been. Some of them know who I am—the die-hard baseball fans—but most of them just know me as Coach Houston.

It's a little strange being more than the guy who shows up every now and then, but I can't hate the reason for their interest.

"What about you?" Darcy asks. "Any pets? Did you get along with your siblings growing up? You mentioned a stepdad and his sandals. What about your real dad?"

I choke on a fry when she says that last question. The fact that just a mention of my poor excuse for a father gets to me makes my stomach churn, but it's only been a few days since my movie night with Brook. Maybe the bad juju is still lingering.

I take her questions one at a time after I manage to swallow. "I had a dog when I was really little, but I don't remember him much. He wasn't part of the package when Mom remarried when I was three. After that, we weren't really in a place for pets. I get along with Brook the best, though we have our differences. I'd do anything for her, and I hope she'd do the same for me."

"She's your twin, right?"

I nod, unable to hold back my grimace as I think about my sister. Darcy picks up on my discomfort because her eyebrows pull together, and I make the impulsive decision to confide in her. "I just found out Brook and Jordan are dating," I say quickly.

She blinks, concern still in her expression, but after a few seconds she bites her lip to hold back a grin. "I could have told you that days ago, Houston. Jordan hasn't exactly been subtle. How do you feel about them being together?"

I rub the back of my neck, not sure how to put it into words. "I confronted Jordan about it yesterday and probably didn't have the best reaction." AKA I shouted at him and accused him of being a player, like he used to be. Part of that is because I'd only gotten a couple hours of sleep before he showed up, but really I just had no idea how to put my feelings into words. I rarely do.

"But then I saw the way Jordan was so serious about his feelings for her," I continue, "and I think I'm coming to terms with it. Honestly, I've been trying not to think about it."

Darcy's smile softens into something gentler. "I haven't met your sister, but Jordan really seems to like her. Maybe even love her."

"That's what he said." I believe him, but it's still hard to wrap my head around it.

"What about your other siblings? What are they like?"

I am so grateful for the change in subject. "Chad is eight years older. We tolerate each other most of the time, but there's love there. We've been through a lot as a family, and he was always a rock in my life. The older we get, the easier it is to work through our differences. He's the serious to my fun, but it's not his fault. He never got to be a kid."

"And your half-sister?"

"Micah. She's like a cartoon kitten in human form. She's cute, cuddly, and will take your eye out if you make her mad. Good thing it's pretty much impossible to dampen her mood."

"They sound great, Houston."

"They are."

"And your dad?"

Inside all this chaos isn't exactly the best place to unload this sort of thing, but I'm so desperate to let her know every part of me—which is terrifying, by the way—that I almost don't care. Still, I lean closer and drop my voice so she's the only one who hears.

"He was never much of a dad. My mom was smart enough to divorce him when Brook and I were two or three, but we still had to go back and forth up until the day Mom died. We had to go live with him after that, but Chad was the one who took care of us. At least until my jerk of a dad finally landed himself in prison and we went to live with my stepdad."

Okay. That wasn't so bad. Darcy's expression hasn't changed much outside of a softening around her eyes, which is a lot better than the pity I've come to expect. Not that I ever tell anyone about my dad. Bonnie didn't know anything about my parents at all. I'm not sure she ever asked.

"I'm really sorry, Houston," Darcy says, and then she puts her hand on top of mine.

If she would stop touching me, maybe I would be able to stop comparing her to my girlfriends instead of thinking of her as a friend, but I'm such a sucker for her touch that I twist my wrist and lace my fingers with hers. That can be a friendly gesture, right?

Her blush says no.

"Thanks," I say, not sure how to proceed. I'm probably the one sending mixed signals now, but it's so hard to pretend my body isn't becoming increasingly attuned to her. I notice every movement she makes, down to each breath. "It's actually really nice to tell someone all of that."

She cocks her head. "Have you not told anyone else that? What about Jordan?"

"Jordan met me when I lived with my stepdad," I say with a shrug. "Otherwise known as a super rich man with a literal mansion. I never really talked about life before high school with him, though I'm sure he's picked up on a lot of things. It's not like I ever want to talk about my failure of a father."

"My parents are amazing." Darcy turns a bright red, pulling her hand back. I miss the contact immediately. "I didn't mean that how it sounded. I just... I'm sorry you didn't get to have what I have. You seem pretty well-adjusted, all things considered."

"That's because you have me on my best behavior."

She grins, not at all deterred by my joke. "Is that so? Is there a darker side to Houston Briggs I haven't seen yet?"

I don't know if I would call it *darker*, but there have been moments in my life that I regret. Things I've said or done that will haunt me. "Remember that thing I said about trying to live deliberately? I wasn't always that way. When my pro career started, I didn't take much of my life seriously. I dated around, used words my mom would have hated, got into trouble with my teammates. Nothing...bad...but enough that I didn't like who I was. The only thing I cared about was baseball." I can't help it. Her hand is sitting right there, still within reach, and my fingers cover hers as an electric shock passes through me from the contact. "But not anymore. Trying to live deliberately means making choices that mean something."

Darcy's smile fades into an expression I can't read at all. I wish I had Kit here to interpret, because all I can gather from the intense look in her eyes is that she has a whole lot of thoughts running through her head right now, like she can't decide about something.

Probably about me.

"So, this is deliberate?" she says, sliding her fingers up between mine.

I shiver. "Yes."

"And you coaching a team full of low-income families is deliberate."

That one isn't a question, and though I have no idea how she figured that part out, I nod. "With a pro team in the city, most of the leagues are club teams. AKA expensive."

Leaning closer, Darcy pins me with a look that completely captivates me. A good chunk of that captivation is because of the smirk that twists her pink lips. "Anything else you'd like to deliberately do?"

I might have leapt across the table and claimed that mouth with my own if three Scorpions didn't suddenly appear beside us in a flurry of shouts and whines that equate to begging me to play catch with them before they have to leave.

I hold back a groan, but I barely get to see these boys during the season. I'd be an idiot to pass up this chance to spend a little more time with them while I can.

Chuckling, Darcy frees herself and gestures to the boys. "Go ahead," she tells me. "I'll hang out with Jack and Molly so I can take you home when you're done."

I can't even put into words how much I love that. Especially when Jack and Molly welcome Darcy at their table with open arms and several other parents move over to talk to her. As I head outside, Little Henry catches my eye and gives me a nod of approval, and my heart feels like it's trying to beat out of my chest.

By the time we leave Big Henry's, Darcy has managed to make all of the Scorpions fall in love with her. She got invited to Cooper's birthday party, even though it's not for another month. Six different parents told me how much they like her and warned me about doing anything to mess things up. Half the team begged her to play catch with them, and she's not half bad. (Though, she did get me hit in the stomach with several balls because I kept looking over at her instead of paying attention to the boys throwing to me.)

I would have kept things going and taken her to dinner or something if I didn't have to get ready for Micah's event tonight, which is at a lodge a couple of hours away.

The energy in the car is different as we head back toward home, and I'm feeling more certain than ever that she and I could have something good.

Until she says, "I just need to pick up Jesse really quick, and then we'll be on our way."

Jesse. I'd pretty much forgotten about the behemoth, mostly because I haven't seen him since they moved in. I don't think I'm remembering wrong when I think about how Darcy told my realtor that Jesse is her brother. She told *me* that. And yet, she told me today that she only has her sister.

I'm not sure what that means, but there's no mistaking the fact that he's not her real brother. Not a big deal, but...

Wouldn't she have brought him up at Henry's if there was any kind of relation there? She didn't, and I don't know what that means. But I know what I think, and I think there's more to her relationship with Jesse than she wants me to know. She could have called him a friend, and I wouldn't have flinched, but suddenly I'm wondering if he's more like a boyfriend, which would change everything I know about this woman and the way she interacts with me.

It would make me question everything she's said to me.

So, when we get back to the house with a scowling Jesse in tow, I tell Darcy I've got some work to do and head inside after thanking her for the ride. I don't want to think she's lying to me about anything, but I can feel the dam in my heart get a couple new bricks added to the wall, building back up as a safety mechanism. I'm almost glad I have Micah's thing to distract me for a few hours, except the drive up isn't going to be all that fun.

"You're overreacting," I tell myself as I start up the shower.

But I'm not sure that I am.

GREY
BIRD
TAVERN

Chapter Seventeen

Houston

Does it make me a terrible brother for not really knowing what Micah does for her job before now? Probably. I knew it had something to do with party planning, but I didn't realize she was *in charge* of the thing. She asked me to make an appearance at tonight's event earlier this month, and she gave me the details at trivia night, so I thought I knew what to expect.

I didn't expect her to be so confident and coordinated. I've been watching her all night, and I'm genuinely impressed with my little sister. I probably owe her an apology, but tonight makes me wonder what else I've been wrong about. Maybe Chad doesn't want to be alone. Maybe Brooklyn and Jordan are good for each other and won't split up. Maybe I don't want to be just friends with Darcy even if she lied to me about Jesse.

"Can I get a smile, Mr. Briggs?"

An elbow to my ribs jars me back to the moment, and I plaster on a grin as I look at the camera. "When did you get so strong?" I ask through my smile.

Bonnie titters a laugh that sounds as practiced as any of her movie lines. It's her public laugh, unlike the giggle she lets out in private. "I've always been strong, Hou."

The event guest in front of us thanks us for the picture and rejoins his friends, giving us a moment alone for the first time since the party started.

I drop my smile, knowing I'll have to bring it back in a moment. For now, I turn so my back is to the room. "Have I thanked you yet for doing this?"

Unlike her laugh, Bonnie's smile is as real as ever, though that could be because she tucks herself under Derek Riley's arm. When I called my ex a few days ago to see if she would be willing to show up to the grand reopening of this lodge—thinking it would help give Micah an extra boost—I didn't expect her to bring her new boyfriend. She clearly moved on quickly, with how familiar the two of them are. We only broke up a few months ago.

"I was happy to help," Bonnie says. "Besides, we have some time to kill before we start filming our movie." She's thriving without me, and the fact that she's dating her co-star is doing wonders for her image.

I meet Derek's gaze, feeling strangely inadequate next to him. I'm famous enough that my self-image is pretty good, but standing beside a man who not only has the looks but the acting chops to become a Hollywood legend makes me feel insignificant. Plus, he's got that tall, dark, and rugged look going for him, and more people have wanted a picture with him than with me.

I'm not jealous. I'm just curious who Darcy would be more interested in if she were here.

"You guys are amazing!" Micah scurries up to us, her face glowing with happiness as she hands us glasses of water. "I seriously can't thank you enough for coming all the way out here for something so small." She says that more to Derek and Bonnie than to me, which makes sense. Driving two hours is not the same as flying out from Los Angeles.

Bonnie gives Micah's hand a squeeze. "This lodge is beautiful, and your party is so well-coordinated."

Micah turns a bright red and scurries away as quickly as she came. I don't blame her for being starstruck when Bonnie is not only beautiful and talented but also genuinely kind.

She and Darcy have that in common.

As if reading my thoughts, Derek clears his throat and asks, "Who are you dating nowadays, Briggs?"

We all smile for a photo with a guest.

I shrug. "At the moment? No one."

"Out of character for you, don't you think?"

I've interacted with Derek a few times, when I joined Bonnie at premieres or parties with her friends in between games, but I wouldn't say we've gotten anywhere close to friendship. We hardly know each other, and at this point I know Darcy better than I know the action movie star. I have no desire to talk to him about my dating life.

Bonnie, on the other hand... "Your sister said you might be dating someone."

Another guest wanders up, pausing the conversation long enough for me to figure out how I want to respond to that comment.

"Micah sees love everywhere, and she thinks I'm interested in a sports reporter who has been lurking around Sun City. I'm not, for the record."

"There's really no one?"

I look at Bonnie, trying to figure out why she would care so much. We only dated for a few months, and it's hard to believe she would sound so sad about me being on my own. Then again, Bonnie has this uncanny ability to make everyone around her feel important.

I sigh right as another person comes up and forces me into a smile. "There...might be someone," I mutter. "But it's complicated." In fact, if she hasn't been teasing me about my supposed attraction to Tamlin, Micah has been trying to get a straight answer out of me all night about whether or not I'm dating "the mysterious Darcy." But I haven't had one to give her.

Derek poses with three different women at once, leaving Bonnie to step off to the side with me. To my surprise, she rests her arm around my back, basically forcing me to do the same to her. "I know we didn't date each other for long, Houston, but I know you. I know you don't like being alone. And I know you're scared to be vulnerable. If it's complicated, it's because you made it complicated."

I groan. "Do you think you're a therapist now that you've played one in a movie?"

She smacks my chest. "Don't be rude."

"Sorry."

"I'm just saying you and I worked so well because we both knew it wasn't going to go anywhere. As soon as things become real, it's easy to start looking for reasons why it will fail."

Frowning, I watch the way Derek poses with the women so naturally, no traces of discomfort in his body language. He clearly loves the spotlight, but I know Bonnie doesn't. She's in it more for the acting than the fame.

"So, what's the deal with you and Riley?" I ask. "Is it complicated or easy?"

Bonnie's smile shifts, still firmly in place but far less real. "Things with Derek are complicated. But not for the reasons you think."

"What is that supposed to mean?" Better yet, do I need to have a talk with the movie star and make sure he really is treating her right?

"Easy, Hou. I don't need you fighting any battles for me." Snickering, Bonnie pats my chest again and then rejoins Derek in front of the camera, giving him a thorough kiss as the partygoers around us cheer. She seems happy, at least, though my heart still feels heavy in my chest.

Am I complicating things with Darcy when I don't need to? I could just ask her about Jesse. But I'm not sure I'm brave enough for that, and I fear what the truth might do. What if she's lied to me about other things? I barely know her, and the thought that some of the things I think I know might not be real brings an uneasiness to my stomach.

"Let's get Briggs in this one," the photographer says.

I return to Bonnie's side and paste on my smile, but as soon as the picture is done, I slip away, sneaking onto the back porch to have a moment to breathe. Hopefully Micah doesn't mind, but my ability to remain cheerful is dwindling the longer the night goes on.

Right as I get out into the cool night air, my phone buzzes with a text.

Darcy:

> My arm is so sore after throwing that ball today. Is that normal?

I settle against the railing on the deck, gripping my phone. A couple of people sit around the gas fire pit, but I've got a corner relatively to myself. Which is good when I'm this frustrated. I don't even know why I'm frustrated! Honestly, Darcy's text makes me that much more attracted to her because she's just so real. Unapologetic.

There must be a reason she called Jesse her brother when she first moved in. Darcy doesn't seem the sort to lie.

Tapping my phone against my palm, I consider the best response to her text. I've got a lot of things I would love to say: *Who is Jesse and should I be worried that you're living with him? I'm mad I didn't kiss you today. If I knock on your door with ice cream tonight, will you answer?*

I for sure can't say that last one because it's after nine o'clock, which means even if I left now I wouldn't get back to Sun City until after eleven. As much as I've come to love my late-night conversations with Darcy, they're dangerous.

The text I do send feels sterile and impersonal.

She answers quickly, and I can almost hear her sarcasm.

Right. I learned that just today, which means I was probably a bit too distracted by thoughts of kissing her to bother paying attention.

My thumb hovers over my phone, though I don't like this urge to tell her that my arm is sore too. She likely won't think anything of it, but putting my pain out into the world feels dangerous. What if she tells someone? I don't know who she would tell, but I can picture someone like Tamlin Park getting wind of my arm going out and using the rumor to take me down before I'm ready.

I groan as flashbacks from Thursday fill my head. Flashbacks of Tamlin going from an annoyance to someone genuinely impressive. She's too smart for her own good, and that, plus her beauty, make her feel so untouchable. Like she's not real. And yet she's still in my head, a constant pressure in the back of my mind that's too hard to ignore even though I've got my sights set elsewhere. While Tamlin is every man's dream, Darcy is down to earth and approachable.

But Darcy keeps secrets, and Tamlin isn't afraid to tell the truth.

"Are you seriously comparing the two of them right now?" I mutter to myself. I have spoken to Tamlin exactly three times in my life.

And that's different from Darcy how?

Though I haven't responded to Darcy's last text, I pull up Jordan's number and hit the dial button. I need a distraction, and he's always good for that.

He answers at the last second, sounding out of breath. "Hey, what's up?"

I frown. "Uh, you okay?"

"Of course." Now he sounds like he's on the verge of laughing. "You good? I thought you had some fancy party with Micah tonight."

"I do. Uh, Bonnie's here." And telling him that is supposed to help me?

There's a pause and some shuffling, and then Jordan says, "Are you okay with that?"

"Of course. It's a little weird, obviously, but I'm the one who invited her. It's not like I'm still hung up on her or anything, and she's here with Derek Riley anyway."

"You met Derek Riley?"

I pull my phone away to stare at the screen as if that might help me make sense of what I just heard. "Brook?"

"Uh. Hi. Sorry. Jordan put you on speaker."

Jordan finally admitted yesterday that they're dating, but it's still too weird to think about. I still can't get the image of them kissing at trivia night out of my head, and that's not something I need to dwell on right now when I'm pretty sure I just interrupted a make-out session. It was strange enough hearing some of the things he said about my sister yesterday—all of them good—and inevitably wondering if we're going to end up brothers rather than friends.

I think... I think I'm okay with that.

"You okay, Hou?" Brook asks.

I let out a deep sigh. I need to get back inside and see if Micah's dad has shown up yet. I called Lloyd hoping he would come to support Micah, knowing she wouldn't have told him about this because this is where he married our mom. There are a lot of painful memories associated with this place since Mom's death. But I also wanted Lloyd to come so I could pick his brain about what to do when I can no longer play. He's gotten into all sorts of different businesses, so I'm hoping he has some good ideas. It might make the thought of retiring easier to bear if I have a game plan.

"I'm fine," I tell Brook, even if it doesn't feel very true. "Congrats on the new job, by the way."

There's a thump, and then Jordan says, "Ow!"

"I wanted to be the one to tell him!" Brook complains.

"You really are terrifying with that pillow, Queens."

Shaking my head, I start making my way back across the deck to the open doors. "I'm glad you're getting back into what you love, Blondie." Even if I still don't know why she got out of research in the first place, Jordan says she couldn't be happier about this lab job she's starting up on the weekends.

I feel like everyone's lives are passing me by, while I'm stuck in this big unknown. I don't like it. "You'll have to tell me all about it," I add, hating that I have to say it. Brook and I used to tell each other everything.

"I will," she promises. "Have fun tonight, and tell Micah that she's amazing!"

"Tell Derek Riley that he's the bomb dot com," Jordan adds.

"Yeah, I'm not saying that." I hang up right as I step back into the lights and music.

A small cheer rings out from a group over by the photo backdrop, a nice boost to the ego as they scurry over to get a photo with me as soon as I arrive.

"Welcome back," Derek grunts.

"Everything okay?" Bonnie asks.

My phone buzzes with another text that I read in between photos. It's exactly the kind of text I want to get, but I can't bring myself to feel hopeful when I'm still so confused by the stupid Jesse thing.

Darcy:
I loved seeing you with all those kids today, by the way. You seem like a great coach.

Why do relationships have to be so difficult?

GREY
BIRD
TAVERN

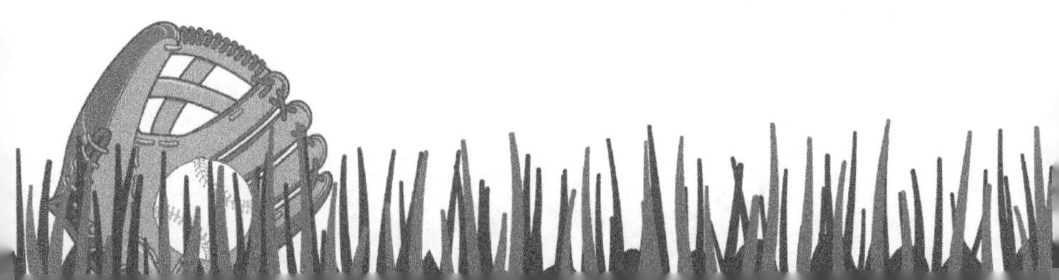

Chapter Eighteen

Darcy

October 30

I MAY NOT WANT to be here, but I can see why Connor wanted Tamlin to come to this gala. It's an annual sort of thing hosted by the World Series winners as a way to give back to their communities and show their gratitude for their fans. Because the dinner is at minimum five hundred bucks a plate, most of the people here are incredibly high profile, from star athletes to team owners to celebrities wanting to build their image.

Thankfully, that means there's a lot more for me to do here than to keep lying to Houston, and so far I've managed to avoid him entirely.

That's not to say I don't know exactly where he is at every moment. It's like I've got a tether attached to him now, and it doesn't matter if I'm on the other side of the ballroom—if he laughs, I hear it. When he moves, my eyes pull in his direction. It's altogether distracting and frustrating, and I only get through five quick interviews before I'm desperate for a break.

Tempted to peruse the silent auction—signed baseballs and mitts, collector's baseball cards, coveted box seats for next season's home games—I instead take a seat at the bar and order myself a soda with a twist of lime to keep me occupied while I subtly watch Houston charm his way across the room.

Seriously, it seems like everyone, no matter how important, wants a chance to rub shoulders with the star pitcher. He takes it all in stride, all smiles despite never having a moment to himself. Tamlin's whole existence is to give me the confidence and the social status to interact with people and dive deep into conversations, but I'm always glad to wash her away at the end of the night and take a break from her.

Does Houston ever get tired of being *on* all the time? I have yet to see him just pause and relax, and he has to be exhausted.

Maybe that's where the story is. He's been playing in the majors for eight years, and while he may be young compared to the average populace, twenty-eight as an athlete of his caliber can't be easy. He hasn't shown any signs of slowing down, no matter what I said in our interview. How long can he actually keep his lifestyle going?

After I've been sitting for ten minutes, working myself up to make the rounds again and talk to more people, my phone buzzes in my clutch at the same time Houston has his phone in hand.

Houston:

> I was hoping we could talk tonight.

What in the world does that mean? He's been avoiding me for the last few days—I mean, I've been avoiding him too, mostly at Connor's request—and this feels so out of the blue. I could easily ignore him and keep my focus on the gala, where it should be, but with the determined glint forming in his eyes, I have a feeling he is more likely to leave the party early and come bang on my door if I don't reply.

We certainly can't have that. Not when I'm here.

Me:

> What about? How's the party, by the way?

He sighs as if he would rather talk about anything except this gala. Is it really that bad? I think it's quite nice, and the amount of money they've raised already is astounding.

Houston:

> It's fine. Probably more boring than your thing. How's your project?

I answer honestly.

Me:

> A little frustrating, but I'll figure it out.

Houston:

> Anything I can do to help?

"Just tell me what you want," I grumble. That isn't fair. If I knew what I wanted, or even if I knew how to tell myself that I can't have what I want, I wouldn't be making such a mess of all of this. Flirting with him at Big Henry's was a terrible idea, hence Connor's instruction to take a step back before I get too emotionally involved. But every minute I spend with Houston convinces me more and more that there can't be any kind of story here worth all this effort. Connor is just grasping at straws at this point and wasting everyone's time.

Houston goes to practice every day without fail. He doesn't drink, doesn't swear—most of the time—and isn't even dating anyone. He's like the Captain America of baseball, the golden boy who has done nothing but good since the moment I arrived in Sun City.

If there's a story here, it's that he's as good as he makes everyone believe. *Better.* I would love to tell that story, but I can't see how that would help Enhance in any way.

It might be time to tell Connor that he needs to pull me back to Missouri before I lose more than my boss's confidence in me. My heart is in grave danger of getting left here in New Mexico.

Me:

No, I have to do this myself. You didn't say what you want to talk about.

Houston:

I don't really know how to put it in a text. Are you going to be up in an hour or so?

Connor told me I have to be at this party until the lights shut off, so no. I won't be home. But how do I tell him that?

Me:

You probably shouldn't come over. I think I caught a bug or something, and I don't want to get you sick.

Houston goes rigid, which is kind of adorable but also makes me think I made a bad decision with that one. Especially when his texts come in rapid fire.

Houston:

You're sick?

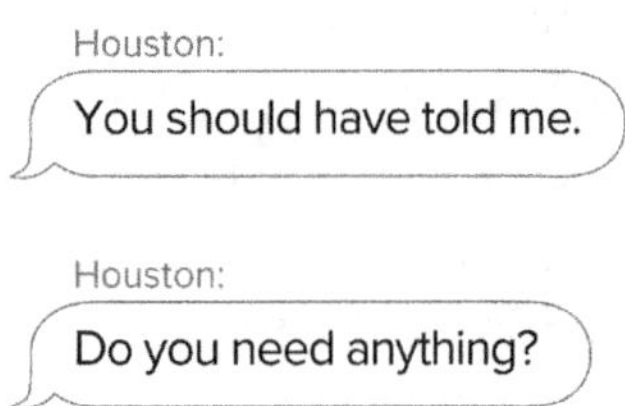

I should have just told him I wasn't home.

"What's a pretty thing like you doing here alone?"

I cringe at the voice that is way too close for comfort, turning my head just enough to see the face of the fifty-something man standing over me. Malcolm Callahan looks even creepier than he does on TV, though I'm glad to see I wasn't exaggerating the football announcer's roving eyes when I decided I didn't like him a year ago. Connor tried to get me to do a TV spot with him once, and I put my foot down. No woman should have to be in the same room as a guy like this, one who is currently undressing me with his gaze. He's not even trying to hide it.

"I'm not doing this with you, Callahan," I say sharply, turning back to my phone.

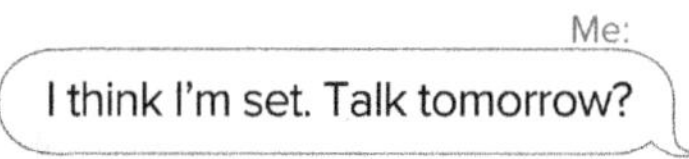

"What are you drinking, beautiful?" Callahan reaches over my shoulder and picks up my glass, bringing it to his nose with a sniff. He's so close that his hot armpit cups my shoulder, sending a shudder through me. "Playing it safe tonight, Park?"

I slip off my stool, my balance wavering as I take a step. The room feels too hot, the music muted as a buzzing fills my ears. Why am I reacting this way? I've dealt with dozens of men like Callahan. They all think they are God's gift to women and that because I wear makeup and pretty dresses, I am asking for their attention. I can take care of myself, and I'm not afraid to throw a punch if the situation calls for it.

But when Callahan slides his hand down my arm and takes hold of my wrist, my body malfunctions, freezing me in place instead of letting me run. I can't breathe. I want to scream but I just stand there and shut my eyes tight as he moves back in, pressing his nose into my neck from behind and breathing in deep while his other hand finds my waist and starts roving. *Stop. Please. STOP!*

"I think it's time to leave the lady alone," a voice says, and cool relief washes over me.

"Houston," I gasp. Something clicks back into place, and I scurry out of Callahan's reach. I don't mean to dart directly into Houston's arms—or maybe I do—but I love the way he barely touches me as he wraps an arm around my back, like he's telling me he's there only if I need him.

"How about you wait your turn?" Callahan snaps.

Houston looks ready to snap too, but in a completely different way. Where he's always been pretty relaxed, now he stands tense and poised to strike. Even when dealing with Tamlin in the past, he's never been this rigid. A fire burns in his eyes that says in no uncertain terms he is more than willing to throw hands if it comes to it. "You're drunk, Callahan. Night's over for you."

"It's over when I say it's over."

The safety I feel standing with Houston is heady and almost overwhelming, but the last thing either of us needs is a fight happening in the middle of a black-tie gala. That's not a story I want Connor to have.

Twisting to face Houston, I grip his lapels and pull myself just close enough to draw his attention. "Dance with me, Briggs."

He blinks, glancing at me. "What?"

"Dance. We don't need to make a scene."

I can see the thoughts running through his head as if they're playing out as subtitles above him. He's doing nothing to hide his expressions, still mostly focused on Callahan. *I absolutely need to make a scene. Wait, did you say dance? Why can't I make a scene? I don't want to dance.* Please *let me make a scene.*

"You are being ridiculous," I hiss. "Come on."

Grabbing his arm, I drag him to the dance floor with no small effort. Every step helps me relax, but it does nothing for Houston, who is so stiff that he doesn't seem to notice when I wrap my arms around his neck.

I never took Houston for the violent type, but he holds his hands in fists at his sides.

"Hands on my waist, Briggs."

Miraculously, he does as he's told.

"Why would you do that?"

He scoffs. "Malcolm Callahan is a slimy perv who shouldn't be allowed to breathe the same air as—"

"I know. But you hate me."

"I don't...hate you." His response, faltering and thin, seems to surprise him as much as it surprises me. It's at this point that he realizes we've been swaying for the last several seconds, and all of his tension shifts from anger to shock. His blue eyes go wide, and when his hands tighten reflexively around my waist, my breath hitches. I've been within seconds of kissing this man, but I've never been *this* close to him.

I try to ease the tension by giving him a Tamlin smirk. "It's okay if you hate me, Briggs. We don't have to be friends. But thank you."

"Why didn't you punch him in the nose? Or run away? Don't tell me you were interested in—"

"I couldn't." I hate that my voice comes out so small, but it pretty much reflects how I feel. Callahan and I are basically equals, even if he's more regularly on TV. To know he saw me as nothing more than a set of curves makes me nauseous, and my knees nearly give out. I'm used to being stared at, but no one has ever touched me like he did, with no regard for my personal boundaries. No one has ever actually crossed the line.

Houston's hold tightens around me, offering support whether or not he knows how much I need it. "Are you okay?"

Those three words hit me hard. He really does have every reason to hate me, especially because of the things about me he doesn't know, but he still came to my rescue when no one else did. He's here now, offering a quiet strength as I struggle to crawl out of the darkness Callahan's advances threw me into.

"I need to sit," I realize out loud when my vision dims at the edges.

I'm not sure how I get to a chair, but as soon as I sit down, I can breathe a little easier. Houston pulls up a second chair and sits knee-to-knee with me, and he waves at someone while I try to just breathe. What is wrong with me?

"Hey, try drinking some water."

I look up right as a server hands him a glass, which he holds out to me with unwavering hands. He looks so steady, and I feel like I might fall apart at the seams. When I don't move, he lifts the glass to my lips and carefully pours some over my tongue. The tenderness of the gesture pulls me up enough to take the glass for myself.

"Thank you," I whisper, all too aware of the trembling in my fingers. "I feel ridiculous."

"Traumatic events have that effect." His bitter words come with some bite to them as well. "Are you good if I leave you here?"

I don't want him to leave. Panic bubbles up again, and he must see it in my eyes because he smiles gently.

"I just want to see if I can get Callahan thrown out. It won't take long." He waits until I nod, and then he's off, far calmer than he was before but with a determination in his steps that sends my heart racing.

By the time he comes back, I've emptied the glass of water and feel mostly myself again, though I do worry that I won't be able to play Tamlin as easily as I usually do. This whole thing drained me in a way I've never experienced before, and I can't help thinking about Houston's use of the word trauma. Was he speaking from experience? Or was he just saying it to say it?

"Are you okay, Park?" he asks as he takes his seat again, his eyes fixed on mine like he's searching for any sign that I might not be.

"I think so," I tell him. "Thank you. Really. I don't know what came over me."

"Callahan came over you."

Rolling my eyes, I manage a little smile. "I *know* that, Briggs. I just mean when it comes to fight or flight, my response is usually fight. Not freeze."

"Of course it is," he replies dryly. "Callahan's lucky he didn't lose an eye."

"I can't argue with you there."

"You're usually so confident." He frowns, as if he isn't sure why he said that. He keeps talking, his words coming faster the longer he goes. "I mean, I saw what happened to O'Donohue. You didn't even give him a second glance. I'm a little disappointed that it wasn't you who gave him the broken nose directly. And at trivia night you didn't once second-guess yourself when you knew the answer, even when I tried so hard to argue. It was..."

I raise my eyebrows when he doesn't finish. "What was it?"

"Impressive," he admits, and then more quietly he adds, "and attractive." He coughs. "Don't let guys like Callahan make you feel like you're any less than you are."

Holy mama, he is not making this easy. If he'd said this to Darcy, I would have had a better grasp of the meaning behind his words, but I have no idea what he's intending Tamlin to get out of this. I'm not so sure he does either, with the way his eyebrows remain bunched up above his baby blues.

"You're surprising, Houston Briggs," I say, wishing I was feeling more confident, the way he sees Tamlin. This night could have looked so different if my life wasn't split down the middle like it is. There wouldn't have been this divide inside me, both sides wanting so badly to be a part of this man's life but knowing it is impossible while the other person exists. Houston likes Darcy, I know he does, but there is so much about myself that I've had to hide to protect Tamlin and the career I've built. And he'll never fall for the woman who could ruin *his* career in a heartbeat if he gave me the right button to push.

The universe—and an ironclad NDA, which Connor unnecessarily reminded me about on Saturday—has decided we can never be together, and I hate that. For both of us.

"Now that you don't look like you might pass out," Houston says, flashing a dimpled smile that digs a knife into my chest, "how about we finish that dance? You can tell me about how you got into sports, and maybe your freakishly large knowledge base can get your mind off of the man I hope I never see again."

It's such a bad idea, but I'm too tired to say no. "I'd like that," I say, taking his hand. Tonight, I don't want to worry about how to move my hand or where to shift my weight when I stand. I don't want to think about which part of me knows which facts. I just want to exist. To dance with Houston Briggs and have a night where I can just be me.

Chapter Nineteen

Houston

You know when there's been something off balance in your life but you didn't know about it until it all shifts and levels out? Well, that feeling is nauseating at first, but then it feels like I'm no longer just out of step of where I want to be.

Tamlin Park is human. Not only that, but she's actually pretty funny when she gets going. I think it's helping her to make jokes that contain thinly veiled insults toward me—insults I know she doesn't mean because she bites her lip every time she says something, like she is cracking herself up.

Everything about her has relaxed while we've danced. I don't know how long we've been out here on the dance floor, or at what point it started to feel like we fit together really well, but so much about this is easy. There's no awkwardness or expectations, just a beautiful woman in my arms as we talk about some of my favorite subjects.

She tells me about getting her undergrad from Harvard—*Harvard*—and then getting her master's from the University of Missouri *while* working at Enhance. It's no wonder she got to where she is while being so young when she's insanely intelligent in a way I'll never be. (I have to ask her how old she is, which she finds hilarious. She's twenty-six, for anyone wondering.)

She doesn't ask a thing about me, which could be because she already knows everything she wants to know, but I don't think so. I think she is trying to put me at ease, telling me without telling me that she's not dancing with me for a story. She's dancing with me because she wants to, or to say thank you for saving her from Callahan. Whatever her reasons, I'm perfectly okay to keep holding her.

Roundy told me on our way to the gala that I had to keep up appearances as if I had no intention of leaving the majors, regardless of what my decision ends up being. I had to schmooze the team's owner and take selfies with sponsors, and I was hitting a point where it all had me feeling numb. My agent knows this decision is one of the hardest I'll make in my life, but he also knows that if I don't pretend everything is good, the decision might be made before I'm ready.

I wouldn't have been able to socialize much longer anyway, but seeing Callahan groping Tamlin gave me a great excuse to take myself out of the game tonight. Even if I was seconds away from punching the guy's lights out. Tamlin was right when she pulled me away. I have no idea how she had the mental fortitude to still be thinking logically when all I could see was red.

She's stronger than I would have thought, and dancing with her tonight, I don't feel like I have to prove anything to her. Somehow, she's shutting out the world for me and removing any expectations.

As the music transitions into a slow song, I slowly pull Tamlin closer even though I haven't actually let go of her since we came over here. "Tell me about the best story you've ever told," I say quietly, desperate to keep this night going as long as I can.

In the back of my head, a little voice is telling me that Darcy is sick at home, wondering why I was so determined to talk to her. It's a voice I want to ignore because I still don't want to face the idea that she lied to me about Jesse and maybe other things too. I don't *want* to confront her, but she's also the only person I've ever wanted to trust with my everything. If I can't trust her, I'd rather know now, before I'm in too deep to protect my heart from being broken.

Tamlin rests her head on my shoulder, tall enough in her ridiculous shoes to do that. I don't even know how she can spend all night in heels that tall, but now that I'm holding her so close, I'm realizing she's shorter than I expected.

I wonder how Darcy compares.

Stop that. You can't be thinking about one woman while you're dancing with another.

Thankfully, Tamlin starts talking, her voice not as husky as it usually is. She sounds tired, and I wonder how long she's supposed to be here. She said her boss forced her to come tonight, just like mine did.

"One of my first stories was about a man who runs ultramarathons," she says with a heavy sigh. "You know the kind where they run for literal days without stopping? I had preconceived notions in my head about why people run like that and what they're hoping to gain, but when I got the chance to talk to him, he completely opened my mind. It wasn't about the notoriety, or the fame, or even about being active and fit."

What else could it be about? "Tell me," I murmur, shifting my hold and curling my fingers around her waist.

She hums a little and nuzzles her face closer to my neck. "For him, it was the idea that he could live mind over body. He wanted to push limits and control how he responded to tough things. It reminded me of my days of playing baseball and proving to everyone—and myself—that I was more than they thought I could be. My town was too small to have a softball team, and I was the only girl on the team. That didn't stop me from being one of the best batters we had."

Pretty sure I just swallowed my tongue. This beautiful, tough, intelligent woman played on a *baseball team*? So much for my life leveling out—Tamlin Park has just knocked me so off balance that I'm not sure I'll recover from tonight.

"I've broken you, haven't I?" she says with a laugh.

I swallow. "Maybe a little."

"What about you? Why baseball?"

If I hadn't spent the last hour or so holding her against me and matching my breaths up to hers, I probably wouldn't answer that question. But for some reason, this space feels safe, and I choose to believe she just wants to see deeper into my heart and understand why I've dedicated my life to something that is in no way easy. If anyone can understand, she can.

I take a slow breath, willing myself to trust this woman after she showed so much vulnerability. Besides, with what I just learned about her, I think she'll understand what the game can be for someone who needs it.

"I never felt important as a kid," I tell her, though the words frighten me. "My mom was dying of cancer. My brother constantly got frustrated by me. I had a dad who didn't want me and a sister who didn't need me, and it seemed like no matter what I did, it was never enough. Then one day in school P.E., we played a game of softball, and I was so determined to hit the ball and prove that I could do something."

"You struck out, didn't you?"

I chuckle, instinctively knowing she's not asking that question seriously. "I hit it out of the park," I reply. "Suddenly, I was the cool kid in the class, like that one fluke swing meant I could do great things. I became obsessed. I stole a ball and bat from the school closet and spent every afternoon at the park hitting that ball as far as I could get it."

"I'm guessing you had to run after it every time," Tamlin says with a gentle snicker.

"The runs were nice. I could get out of my head when I was running and get away from all the doubts that were always a step behind me. My stepdad eventually found out what I was doing and signed me up for a team, and the rest is history."

Snuggling in closer, Tamlin sounds even sleepier when she asks, "What made you become a pitcher?"

"I realized I could stop other players from hitting the ball as well as I did if I threw the ball the right way."

"Ah, so it was self-preservation."

"At first. Then it became a challenge. A way to test my own limits and strength and see how fast I could throw it. How accurate I could be. I wanted to be the best."

She shifts against me, no longer leaning into me but holding herself up again. When she pulls away to look at me, I can see the reluctance in her eyes, but it's like she can't help herself. "Wanted," she says. "Past tense."

I could turn my response into a joke. Tell her that I'm already the best so it's no longer a wish but a truth. But I want to be honest with her, even if it might damn me in the end. "Wanted," I repeat.

Her chin lifts, eyes locked on mine. "What about now?"

Now I have a knot in my stomach and a throbbing in my chest that's telling me she wants me to kiss her. And I want to do it. But four days ago I thought I was head over heels for Darcy Paxton, and this is not the kind of man I want to be. One night of dancing isn't the same as a date. An hour or two of talking isn't the same as really knowing a person. No matter the attraction I feel for either of these women, it isn't fair to them for me to gravitate toward whichever one I currently hold in my arms. It's what my dad did, and I won't be that kind of man.

"Now," I say, dragging my attention from her full, red lips, "I should let you get to bed."

The gala is dying down. We're one of the last couples on the dance floor, and anyone who might want to talk to me is either too drunk to be lucid or already gone. I probably have a message waiting for me from Roundy, telling me I'm free to go. And yet it's so hard to step away from Tamlin, which is as surprising as the disappointment in her eyes. She feels so familiar, like I've known her forever.

A week ago, I expected us to be mortal enemies for the rest of my career, maybe even beyond. Now...

Now, I really need a moment to myself so I can think.

"Can I make sure you're safely on your way home?" I ask her as I stuff my hands into my pockets to keep them to myself.

She glances around the room, blinking as if still trying to break free of the bubble we've been in. I don't blame her. She fits so well against me that my empty arms feel heavy and cold, and if it weren't for Darcy, I would have an even harder time walking away tonight. The old Houston wouldn't hesitate, but living deliberately means I need to think through my actions and recognize that jumping into something like this with both feet comes with consequences.

Especially with someone like Tamlin Park. While tonight she seemed to be natural and authentic, I've seen her make that switch before. I know there's a dangerous side of her. She may not have it out for me—not something I can know for sure—but she still holds a lot of power she could wield against me. If not her, she works for a company that has never been shy about using athletes as pawns to build their following.

"You okay?" Tamlin asks, cocking her head as she watches me. She can probably see all sorts of thoughts running through my head because I'm half-convinced she's a mind reader like Kit. There has to be a way she always knows which questions to ask to trap someone into revealing everything.

I give her a smile that feels more fake than real, but maybe she'll buy it. "There's...a lot going on right now," I say, which is true. "I'm tired." Also true.

Tamlin approaches cautiously, like I'm some sort of wild animal, and then she brushes her fingertips across my cheekbone in a featherlight touch that makes my hair on my neck stand on end. "I'm probably the worst person to give this advice, but hear me out. You can't do it all. If you give yourself one hundred percent all of the time, there's going to be nothing left." Then she leans up, brushes a warm kiss against my cheek, and leaves me standing there as she heads for the door.

Though she's still waiting for a ride when I get outside, I force myself to keep some space between us. She's deep in conversation on the phone anyway, and her ride pulls up at the same time mine does. I'm almost glad I don't have my truck; I would have been way too exhausted to drive myself home after tonight.

The sight of my house brings both relief and increased tension. I'm so ready to crash into my glorious bed, but I don't know how well I'll be able to sleep when I know Darcy is just on the other side of the wall. I only make it as far as my living room before my feet won't go any farther, and I hate that I can't just let things go. I shouldn't have pushed this off for so long, especially because now she's sick and probably—hopefully—dead asleep.

My debate lasts nearly five minutes, and in the end my mental exhaustion wins over the physical. I'll just ask for clarification about who Jesse is. It doesn't have to be a big deal. I'm sure she'll have a logical explanation, and then I can sleep easier until tomorrow.

As I step out onto the porch, movement on the driveway catches my eye and brings me to a dead stop. "Tamlin?"

Her head snaps up, eyes going wide as if she's been caught doing something she shouldn't. Well, obviously she shouldn't be here. Was all of tonight an act? A way to get close to me and get me off my guard?

"Are you following me?"

She relaxes, looking around the street before she says anything. "So, this is where you live? Not what I expected. Not by a longshot."

"You shouldn't be here, Park."

"Would you relax? I'm not here for you."

Why else would she possibly be here?

Probably reading my question in my glare, she waves her phone at me. "I got a tip tonight. Someone who works at a tattoo parlor here in Sun City got in touch with me after he overheard something about a gambling ring that's getting people into trouble because the game feeds are delayed. Pretty standard con, from the sound of it."

She says it so confidently that I have to believe her, and Jesse works at a parlor. I guess it could be him? But... "Now? It's almost midnight."

"I'm not going to let someone else take my story if it's something good."

Also logical, but after I spent the night keeping her safe from the aftereffects of Malcolm Callahan, I can't be comfortable with the idea of her wandering around a strange city in the middle of the night. Sun City has a low crime rate for its size, but unless Tamlin is a black belt in jiu jitsu, she's putting herself in danger.

And Jesse still terrifies me a little.

"I'm coming with you," I say firmly.

Her mouth forms an O as she glances next door. "That isn't necessary, Briggs. I can handle myself."

"Tonight told me otherwise. I'm coming."

"I'm pretty sure I'm not going to get murdered in a duplex basement. Besides, isn't this guy your neighbor? You don't seem the type to live next door to an ax murderer."

Why is she fighting this so much? Growling, I step between her and Darcy's door, not sure who I'm protecting more. "You know nothing about me. Either I'm coming inside with you, or I am personally seeing to it that you make it back to your hotel."

I'm overstepping, and I know it, but it's been a long day and I've lost my ability to keep to my own business. I care about Tamlin too much to back down, and she has to see that. Besides, I'm desperate to check on Darcy, though maybe not quite as thoroughly as I was before. Having both these women in the same place has my heart pounding wildly in my chest, leaving me slightly dizzy.

Tamlin must see that this is a battle she can't win because she sighs heavily and loops her arm through mine. "Fine. But let me do all the talking. This guy seemed pretty skittish."

She knocks, and we only have to wait a few seconds before the door swings open to reveal the hulking Jesse. He scowls at me first—still doesn't like me, apparently—and when his dark eyes take in Tamlin, they double in size.

"Hi," she says loudly, holding out her hand. "I'm Tamlin Park. You had something to tell me?"

GREY
BIRD
TAVERN

Chapter Twenty
Darcy

THIS IS MY LITERAL nightmare. Okay, so I've never actually dreamed of Houston insisting on keeping an eye on Tamlin while I pretend to be a stranger questioning a man who has seen way too much of me to ever act like he doesn't know me. Maybe if Jesse wasn't practiced in sticking adhesive boobs to my non-existent ones we might be able to pull this off, but he and my chest are well acquainted.

"Do you have somewhere we can talk privately?" I ask Jesse after he lets us into the house.

I can see the wheels turning, and he's so lost right now. Poor guy was probably deep into an episode of *The Great British Baking Show*, maybe even half asleep as he waited for me to make it home.

"Sure," he grunts and gestures to the kitchen.

Houston makes a sound of protest in his throat that makes me ache to slide back into his safe hold and never leave. "Tam, you shouldn't—"

"I'll be fine," I tell him. "I'll scream twice if I need you."

"That isn't funny," he grumbles but plops down onto the couch anyway.

As long as he stays there, maybe I can make this work.

When we get to the kitchen, Jesse gives me a sharp look.

"I know," I whisper, pinching the bridge of my nose. "I thought he'd already gone up to bed, and then I couldn't shake him. I told him you have a story for me."

Though he says nothing, I can read Jesse's expression pretty well. *How do we get rid of him?*

I could spend a few minutes in here with Jesse and then call a ride and have the driver circle the block a few times before bringing me back. Easy.

What if he doesn't leave? Jesse's eyes ask.

That's a valid problem, but my brain feels mushy after the night I've had. I'm not on my game, and I'm lucky I thought of the gambling story as quickly as I did. "I don't know what to do," I admit, hoping Jesse has a solution.

His eyes snap behind me, alerting me to Houston's presence right before Houston says, "Sorry to interrupt, but I was thinking maybe I could check on Darcy while I wait? She said she was sick."

Oh, this is bad. Of course he would want to check on Darcy! But what's he going to do when he finds out she's not here? He's going to realize she lied to him, maybe even realize Darcy isn't here because Darcy is me. Not only am I going to be out a big story—assuming it exists, like Connor insists—but I'm going to lose this precious, wonderful man before I'm ready to give him up.

Since I can't answer Houston's question, Jesse mumbles something that even I can't understand until he gets to the last two words: "Lady time."

Houston pinks. "Oh."

Jesse, you're a genius. "Okay," I say, pulling both their attention to me. "I have a feeling you're not going to leave until you know this girl is okay," I tell Houston, "but I can't in good conscience let you invade her space. I'll go talk to her, woman to woman." I point at Jesse. "Take me to wherever she is, and I'll see if she's up for some company for a minute."

Jesse grunts and leads the way, but Houston is so close on my heels that I spin at the bottom of the stairs and put my hand on his chest. "Don't you be following me, Briggs. No woman wants a handsome man to see her when she's indisposed."

"I really need to talk to her," Houston says. "Will you tell her that?"

He sounds so desperate that I find myself nodding, even though I have no intention of bringing "Darcy" downstairs. "I'll tell her."

My phone buzzes before Jesse and I make it to my bedroom.

Houston:

I'm downstairs. Can we talk? It doesn't have to be for long.

Houston:

Please.

Closing the door behind me, I groan and show Jesse the text. Though he gives me a look that is pretty easy to interpret—*This is your fault and you know it.*—I still silently beg him to help me fix this.

"I don't think he's going to leave me alone until he sees Darcy," I mutter. "And even you can't turn me into this without half an hour of uninterrupted time." I wave my hand around my face. "This is impossible!"

Jesse looks around my room for a second and then slips out into the hall, hopefully with an idea. But when he returns with a jar of his favorite face mask, the kind that you lather on thick and end up looking like a swamp monster, I shake my head.

"No," I say with as much force as I can put into the word while still whispering. "You are not Mrs. Doubtfiring me."

Ten minutes later, he's shoving me down the stairs in a bathrobe because there's no way I'm going to be able to change in and out of my fake chest, so I'll just have to hide it.

"Houston?" I speak his name quietly, trying to sound miserably sick as I sit on the stairs and peer at him through the banister rails. He jumps up from his seat on the couch and looks ready to rush to me before I hold up a hand and stop him. "I really don't want to get you sick. I'm worried enough about Tamlin, but she wouldn't take no for an answer."

His eyes stray to the top of the stairs. "She's okay, right? She and Jesse are just talking?"

"What else would they be doing?"

"I don't know." He settles back on the couch, stuffing his hands into his hair. He's untied his bowtie and left his tux jacket loose, and I have to admit this ruffled look is pretty mouthwatering. "It's been a weird night. How are you feeling?"

I cough into my sleeve. Dramatic effect and all that. "I've been better."

"You look really flushed."

That's because Jesse and I just spent the last five minutes scrubbing every inch of makeup off my face. I'm glad it's dim because I didn't want to have to put my blue contacts back in after the blissful relief of taking them out, so I still have Tamlin's eyes.

"I think I'm over the worst of it," I tell him. "Really. A good night's sleep and I'll be back to normal. What did you want to talk about?"

His eyes jump to the top of the stairs again, full of confusion and frustration. I really shouldn't have come on to him so strong at the gala, but I couldn't help it. I'm falling for him, and it doesn't matter if I'm Darcy or Tamlin. Every part of me wants him. I want to know everything about him and see what makes him tick. I want to hear about all his fears and triumphs, doubts and favorites.

I want to know why the universe decided to put me on *this* story with *this* man at *this* time in my career, when I'm well on my way to getting everything I've ever wanted but at the same time can't risk losing my paycheck. I don't see a way for us both to win here.

"What are you doing for Halloween?" Houston asks instead of answering my question.

I frown. "I don't really have plans."

"Come out with me." He speaks with command in his voice but is impossibly gentle at the same time. Rising, he crosses half the room but thankfully keeps his distance. "Come to my siblings' Halloween party."

Yes. I absolutely want that. "Do you always bring a friend to your family events?"

He shakes his head. "I always bring a date."

Oh. I guess I *was* wanting him to be more direct about what he saw in me, but I'm both giddy and terrified hearing the word *date* coming out of his mouth in relation to me.

I swallow. "Are you asking me on a date, Houston Briggs?"

"Are you saying yes?"

"I think so."

"You think so?"

I snort a little laugh. I hadn't meant to say that, and the anxiety in his face is adorable. "I mean I'll go out with you if I'm not still sick. What should I wear? Should I be matching you?"

His eyes drop to my bathrobe for half a second. "As much as I would love to see you matching my costume, you're probably going to want to find one of your own. I'm stuck paying up on a bet I made last week."

"Sounds frightening."

"For everyone else, yes. My only consolation is that Brook and Jordan have to wear the same thing because it was the four of us who lost, not just me."

I am a glutton for punishment at this point, but I have to ask. "Who was the fourth person and why don't they have to wear this horrific costume?"

Crimson floods his face, and he takes a step back as if the distance might help him keep his cool. "Uh, Tamlin, actually."

"Wait, do you know her?"

"Yeah." That's all he says. *Yeah.* I don't know what I expected, but I would have liked for him to have some kind of explanation, even if it's the truth. *She's a sports journalist and did an interview with me a couple of weeks ago. We needed another team member and Tamlin was at the bar. I might have kissed her tonight because she was giving off some serious vibes after I saved her from the creep of creeps, but I'm too good of a guy to take advantage of her.*

I shiver, thinking of the way he was so ready to protect me. And the way he looked at me right before we left the gala. A girl could get used to a look like that.

"You should get some rest," Houston says, misinterpreting my shiver.

I nod. "Are you waiting for Tamlin?"

Another glance upstairs. "I just want to make sure she gets home okay. Or at least on her way. She had a rough night." He probably doesn't realize that I would be inferring all sorts of things from that comment if I didn't know all about what Tamlin went through. What *I* went through.

"I'll go talk to her." I sigh, angry with myself for being annoyed at him when I'm the one causing all of his confusion in the first place. "She's really nice."

"Darcy?" He takes one more step, close enough now that we could reach our hands out through the banister rails and almost touch.

The only thing keeping me from slipping down the stairs and into his arms is the fact that my eyes are not my own. "Yeah?"

"Sleep well."

I nearly scurry up the stairs, though I still have the strength of mind to keep my steps slow and labored. As soon as I'm out of sight, I book it back to my room and fall against the closed door when I get inside.

Jesse raises an eyebrow, ready with the face cream. It's probably my only shot, and his face mask is kind of the best, but this is going to require a lot of lies that are only going to add to my guilt.

"You could tell him the truth," Jesse says when he's almost done lathering my face.

"You know I can't. It would ruin everything, and Connor will never trust me with another big story. Not to mention that whole contract thing you and I both signed."

"But maybe you could be happy here."

"My job makes me happy."

He doesn't argue after that, for which I'm glad. I'm torn enough as it is, and I need to stay focused to make this next part believable. I don't want to think he might be right about what I might find here in Sun City if I stayed. It's only been a week and a half, and already I feel rooted.

Once Jesse is satisfied that I look enough like Tamlin, which takes longer than I'd like because I know Houston is struggling down there, I head for the stairs and pray I can pull this off.

Houston is back on the couch, elbows on his knees and hands in his thick blond hair.

I wait until I've hit the living room before I speak. "Hey, I'm going to stay."

His head snaps up, and he spends several seconds taking me in. Obviously the face mask is throwing him off, but I think the fact that I've put on a pair of pajamas is messing with his head as well, leaving him completely baffled.

I tug at my wig to pull his attention to the dark color. "Darcy seems like she could use some girl time—she practically begged me to change out of my dress and have a spa night. She said I should tell you that I'm fine and I'll spend the night here so I don't have to get a car this late. We'll take care of each other."

"She should be sleeping."

This beautiful man... "She is. She passed out a couple of minutes ago, but not before telling me how sweet it was that you were worried about her. You're a good man, Briggs."

"Will you go to lunch with me tomorrow? After practice."

Did he really just...? I swallow my frustration and hurt when I realize what he might be doing. This man is torn, for good reason, and he hasn't taken either of us on an actual date. It probably says something that he wants Darcy at his family event while Tamlin only gets lunch, so I'm going to have to plan accordingly.

This isn't how it's supposed to go. I'm not supposed to *plan* when I fall in love with someone. I'm not supposed to keep half of me hidden and expect him to be whole and real with me.

Hold up. Did I just think the word *love*? Well that's just straight insanity.

Forcing an easy smile despite my internal panic, I tell Houston, "I would like that. Tell me when and where, and I'll be there."

He relaxes a little. "You sure you won't be too busy taking down a corrupt gambling ring?"

"I have a feeling that's not going to end up being a story for me. But hey, at least it let me meet Darcy, right? Maybe she and I can become friends."

"That sounds great," he says, voice cracking with his own panic.

Yeah, okay, that one was a little mean.

Reaching out, I give his arm a squeeze and pretend I am cool as a cucumber. No freaking out happening over here, no siree. "Go to bed, Briggs. You look exhausted."

"Yeah," he agrees, and then he surprises me by pulling me into a hug that seems to pull me together and hold me there, like he can fix what feels more and more broken the more divided I become. It's the extra squeeze at the end that does me in.

Maybe he isn't as decided as I thought.

GREY
BIRD
TAVERN

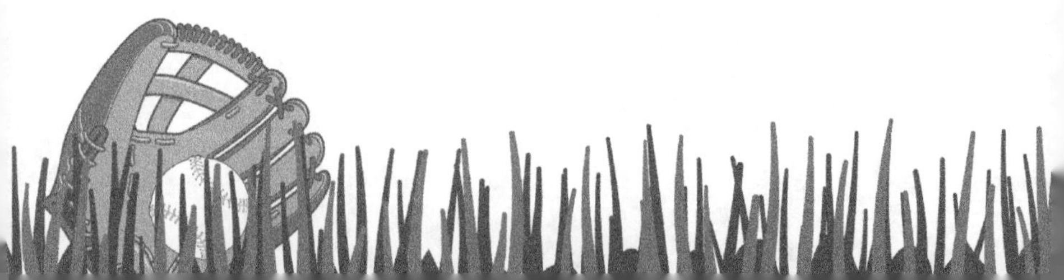

Chapter Twenty-One

Darcy

October 31

"Darcy, I hear you, I really do, but you have no idea what that kind of story could do for us. You know I'm going to run it regardless of if it's you or someone else, but I would appreciate not having to buy a plane ticket to send another journalist out there."

Connor *sounds* reasonable, but he's got that undercurrent of command that makes him a good editor in chief. He'll listen to the requests of his journalists for the most part, but at the end of the day, he has a business to run. I'm being ridiculous, trying to get out of the Little League story, but as soon as Connor found out Tamlin has a date with Houston—from Jesse, the little traitor—he told me I have to start the interview today. No matter what that might do to my budding relationship with Houston.

"You will do the right thing," he said before I launched into my argument a few minutes ago. I'm pretty sure he meant I'll tell the story the right way. And there's definitely a wrong way with this one.

"I'm not going to change your mind," I say as I pace outside the restaurant where I agreed to meet Houston. It isn't a question because I already know the answer.

Connor sighs, his chair squeaking in the background. "I get the feeling you're still emotionally involved with this one."

I want so badly to say no, but I can't. "Isn't that why you sent me out here? To date Houston Briggs and learn all his secrets through exploitation?" I know I sound bitter, but I can't help it.

"I sent you out there to give you a chance to shine. Not to get yourself hurt. That's why I pulled you back before the gala, but it clearly didn't help." Connor is quiet for a second. "Look, Darcy, I'm not supposed to tell you this, but the board wants to start a new division centered around inspirational stories. You know, the kind you love. And they need someone to head it up. Your name came up multiple times."

I nearly drop my phone. A new division? And they want *me* to run it? That's like taking a high school part-timer at McDonalds and asking them to take over the store they've worked at for a month. Okay, yeah, I've been with Enhance for the last four years and have been telling some pretty big stories for the last two, but that's chump change compared to some of the veterans I work with.

"Are you serious?" I whisper, not sure if it's even loud enough for Connor to hear.

"It's not a done deal," he says. "They're waiting to see how you handle this Briggs story, and I'm not talking about the Little League. That's just icing on the cake."

I grip the phone tighter. No wonder Connor was making such a big deal out of this. "What Briggs story, Connor? What am I looking for?"

"I can't tell you that because I don't know. But there are signs that something is lurking under the surface, and if anyone can figure it out, you can. This could be your big break, Darcy. Whatever it is, give it the signature Tamlin flair and make it *your* story. You've got this, Champ."

How am I supposed to respond to that?

He must know how much this is making me internally combust, but he throws one last log onto the flame. "You've always been meant for more than covering football games and dirty players, Darce. And I know you want to tell your own stories and put your name on something you can be proud of. Unless I'm wrong about this story, Briggs could be your ticket to everything you've ever wanted. Think about it: your own office, your own team, enough of a pay increase to get your sister out of debt and give your dad the kind of care he needs. I can't give you that with what you're doing now, no matter how much I want to."

And this, ladies and gentlemen, is why I work for Enhance. Why I work for *Connor*. Yes, first and foremost he's my boss, but he *knows* me. He knows what drives me and where I want to go, and he's always been on my team. He's the coach I always wanted but never had, cheering me on and pushing me to be better with tough love because he sees the potential rather than the flaws.

As much as I want this perfect job he's describing, even more so I don't want to disappoint him. If he thinks I can find a story here worth telling, I have to stick around and find it. I don't know what that will mean for Houston, but I'm going to have to make the most of whatever happens. I don't have much of a choice.

"Hey, Tamlin," a voice says, and Houston appears around the corner, an easy smile on his face. Part of me wants to scream and run away because I so don't have the capacity for this right now, but the sight of him holds me in place. What if this story ends up hurting him? Can I risk his happiness to help my family? Can I choose him over them?

I just have to pray there won't be any casualties when this is all over.

"I gotta go, Connor," I say into my phone.

"Seriously, think about it," Connor replies. "I'll fly you home if you're not ready for this, but I really think you have it in you to take your life by the reins and win this race."

"You really need to work on your metaphors." The laugh that ekes out of me helps to calm my racing thoughts a bit, though there's no hope for my heart with the way Houston leans against the side of the restaurant, patiently waiting for me to finish my phone call. No one should look that good in jeans and a t-shirt. I suppose the worn leather jacket he's wearing is doing a lot for the aesthetic; he looks like he belongs in the fifties in the best way.

Connor chuckles. "There's a reason you're the writer, not me. Good luck."

When I tuck my phone into my purse, Houston pushes from the wall and greets me with a kiss on the cheek that I swear leaves a mark. "Connor McMillan?" he guesses, nodding toward my purse. "Can't get away from your boss even all the way out here?"

"Unfortunately."

"Is he the reason you're still in Sun City?" He asks that question casually, but I can hear the undercurrent of nerves. Houston might be starting to trust Tamlin, but that doesn't mean he trusts Enhance Media. And he has good reason to be wary, whether he knows it or not.

"Let's grab a table," I suggest, nodding to the door. "I think we have some things to talk about."

"Some of the most terrifying words in the world," he jokes as we head inside.

He does seem better today than he did yesterday. Hopefully he got some good sleep—I certainly didn't—and used this morning to think about things and make some decisions. Whatever he chooses after this date, I'll do my best to go along with it.

That doesn't mean I've made my own decisions yet. Can I use him for my own benefit? But it's not just for me. It's for Carissa, who is living out her dream and improving lives. For my mom, who has been taking care of my dad for so long and is tired but will never say so. And for the peace of mind knowing my dad has all the care he needs before he's gone. And even beyond what affects me directly, it's for a chance to tell the stories that often get pushed to the wayside for the big scandals. For the people who deserve a little time to shine in their quiet lives.

But all of that could come at the cost of Houston's happiness.

I don't know what to do.

"Everything okay?" Houston asks as the hostess seats us at a cozy little table in the back. He pulls out my chair for me, hands brushing my waist as he helps me scoot in.

I've never been on a date as Tamlin before, so this could get interesting.

"Just a lot on my mind lately," I say with a little shake of my head. "I'm sure you feel that a lot, being team captain and in such an important position."

"You have no idea."

After a waitress arrives to take our orders, we settle into small talk, which I have no complaints about. I'm going to have to bring up Little League at some point, but I want to enjoy at least a part of this date.

Our waitress returns pretty quickly, looking repentant and wary as she tells me, "I'm so sorry, but it looks like we're out of the salmon."

"Oh, that's too bad," Houston says.

I roll my eyes, though I can't help but smile. I should have expected that. "Typical. How about you give me whatever you know you *do* have? I'm not picky, just unlucky."

The waitress breathes a sigh of relief before returning to the kitchen, which means I must have been giving off "Karen" vibes if she was so afraid of giving me bad news. I'll have to work on that; I want Tamlin to be intimidating to athletes, not to minimum wage service workers.

Why is Houston looking at me like that?

"Are you often unlucky?" he asks quietly.

I nearly swear out loud but manage to keep it in my head. Unluckiness is a Darcy trait, not a Tamlin one. Why does this man have to put me so at ease? I scramble for a way to spin this. "Only when I'm trying to impress a hot guy and prove I don't have the appetite of a linebacker," I say.

Houston pinks a little, fighting the smile that plays at his mouth like he's trying to ignore the ego boost.

I roll my eyes again. "Yes, you're hot, Briggs. I can't be the first person to ever say that to you when you have this whole Captain America look going for you." I lean closer. "Between you and me, I like you better than Chris Evans, and that's saying something."

He opens his mouth, but I'm pretty sure I've rendered him speechless with my boldness. Darcy never would have been able to say something like that, but being Tamlin has its perks. She's never afraid to say what needs to be said, and if that means stroking this man's ego to get him to trust me a little more, then so be it.

Houston clears his throat, turning redder by the second, and I have no idea where his mind has gone when he looks so completely embarrassed by what he's about to say. I didn't think he *could* get embarrassed. "There's no way to not sound like a jerk when I ask this," he says, which is intriguing by itself, "but why do you wear so much makeup?"

Oh, sweet boy. At least he's aware that his question is generally frowned upon by the female society. "Because it makes me look pretty," I say.

"Have you ever thought you might be pretty even without it?"

"I never said I wasn't." And then I wink.

He laughs, and the sound boosts my own mood. He hasn't laughed enough since being around me. There was that moment on the porch with Darcy, when he laughed so hard he cried, but that was pretty much the only time he hasn't seemed weighed down by something. I have firm memories from watching past interviews and videos of Houston Briggs, especially the last time they won the Series. This man used to be nothing but smiles, always a secret joke behind his eyes despite his serious approach to the sport. Either something has changed in his life that has nothing to do with me being in Sun City, or I've dimmed the undimmable Houston Briggs.

New goal: Make Houston laugh as often as possible so he might survive this thing.

Still chuckling, he reaches into his pocket and pulls out his phone. Then he frowns, all of his tension returning. "Sorry, it's my agent. I should probably take this."

He shuffles off to the corner of the mostly empty restaurant, ducking his head as if that might help him be quieter. It's not like I'm trying to listen, but as the conversation goes on, Houston's voice gets louder until I can hear most of his side of the conversation.

"I know," he says with clear frustration. "I'm not trying to make this more difficult than it needs to be." Pause. "No, not yet, but Solano said—" He cuts himself off and runs his hand through his hair. "No, the supraspinatus. It's not great. Yeah. I know. A few more days, Roundy. That's all I'm asking for."

I have no idea what that word was in the middle, but it sounded important and body related, plus he mentioned the team's physical therapist. For not the first time, I wish I had taken an anatomy class or something when I was in college because I'm always a bit lost when it comes to that sort of thing. I'm great with sport rules and terminologies, but biology is not my thing.

As Houston ends his call with his agent, I add to my mental list of classes I want to convince Connor to pay for, along with lip reading. Definitely an anatomy course, and maybe a cooking class in there somewhere for those days I'm on the road a lot or in an undercover situation like I am now.

"Sorry about that," Houston says, slipping into his chair. I can practically see the weight on his shoulders from that conversation. "No rest for the wicked."

I grin, hoping my smile filters over to him. "Are you the wicked one in that context, or is Roundy? I've heard a lot of things about your agent, and I'm curious to know what's actually true."

"I would tell you if I knew. Roundy has always been a bit of a mystery to me, even after working with him all these years."

Our food arrives a moment later, and we slip into talking about the most recent football games. Houston is a sports fan in general, not just of baseball, so the conversation flows easily. Or maybe it's just because Houston is easy to talk to. As he settles more and more throughout our lunch, he becomes closer to the version I've seen of him in interviews in the past. Lots of smiles, plenty of teasing jokes, and a generally light outlook on life. If I wasn't already crushing hard, I could see this man being a great friend. I envy his siblings for their chance to have this side of him in their lives all the time.

I highly doubt I'll get to keep him.

When the afternoon inches closer to evening, cutting down my time to turn back into Darcy, I reluctantly glance at my phone and let out a small sigh. "Duty calls. Thanks for lunch, Houston. I've had a really good time."

I would have preferred a little more protestation from him, but he simply nods. "I'm glad."

"If I'm still in town for a while, we should do this again."

As I expected, he tenses a little, giving me the universal panicked expression of not knowing how to turn someone down. "You're a really great woman, Tamlin," he says, his intonation indicating there is more to that than what he's said.

I roll my eyes, making sure my smile is as believable as I can make it so he knows Tamlin is not going to leave the restaurant brokenhearted. "But?" I push.

He seems surprised by my casual response, which is likely why he says what he does next. "But you're like some fever dream. You're smart, beautiful, athletic. It's like you were made for someone like me."

I smirk. "Some would say that's a good thing."

"But you don't feel real. Maybe it's just because you don't want me to see who you really are, but it's like all I've gotten is the surface you. I can't see what's beneath. What makes you tick. Does that make sense?"

Of course it does. Everything that makes me real and human gets tucked away when I play this part. The real stuff is the side of me he's clearly choosing. But even Darcy is only half a person, and I fear sooner than later he will realize that I've never been honest with him. It's a miracle he hasn't made the connection between Tamlin and Darcy yet, though he's started giving me curious looks, like he's trying to figure out why I look familiar. My time is running out, and I know it.

Reaching across the table, I place my hand over his in the briefest of touches even though I want more. "I understand what you're saying, Briggs. This job means I keep a wall around my heart to protect myself, and it's not something I can just take down. As long as I am on my current path, that is never going to change. I'm sorry I can't be real with you."

But if Connor is serious about this inspirational division, there won't be the same danger in reporting that there is now. I'll be telling happy stories, maybe even be behind the scenes a lot of the time, which means I won't have to hide behind Tamlin. I'll be able to be fully me for the first time in years.

"What about friends?" I say, shivering when Houston's gaze softens in relief. He must not have been completely ready to give Tamlin up, which is mildly concerning but also flattering.

He settles back in his chair, more relaxed than ever as his smile grows and shows off those dimples. "You sure you want to be friends with a guy like me? I'm usually the type you take down."

"Do you have a reason for me to take you down?"

The question was supposed to be a line of banter, but it has the opposite effect that I wanted. He tenses right back up, hard lines forming around his eyes as he fights to hold his grin. "No," he says.

I don't believe him.

I swallow. "I should tell you something. I know about the Scorpions, and I have to run a story about you coaching them." Goodness, he looks ready to run, so I grab his arm, hating that he flinches at my touch. "I don't have a choice," I tell him. "But I don't want to do anything to hurt those kids. If the country finds out you are their coach, they're going to want to show up for the chance to meet you or see you in action, and that could jeopardize the boys' safety or make them too nervous to play. That's the last thing I want. I don't know what to do, Houston. You have to tell me how to protect those boys because either I tell the story, or Connor will send someone else in to tell it for me."

He clenches his jaw so hard that the muscles look ready to snap, and I'm pretty sure this just ruined any chance of friendship between him and Tamlin. He has every reason to hate me, especially because I saved this for the end of our date rather than coming clean right from the start. I would hate me too.

But then he pulls his eyebrows together, looking more thoughtful than angry. "How did you find out?" is his first question.

No way am I going to put his relationship with Darcy in danger too. "I have my ways. I told you I was here for Little League."

"Have you filmed anything with the team?"

"Not yet. But I might have to."

He nods slowly, his gaze distant while he thinks. "Everyone on that team is low income. It's the only way they're allowed to be a Scorpion. We've had to trade players to other teams because their parents got better jobs and started making more. A lot of those parents are proud people—in a good way—and they won't like their poverty being on display."

"Did you buy all their uniforms and equipment?" I ask. Nothing about their jerseys had looked any different from the other team's in terms of quality, and every boy had a decent mitt.

Houston grimaces. "I don't want that to be part of the story."

My breath catches when I realize what he's saying. "You're going to let me run the story?"

"Do I have a choice? But you have to let me control the narrative. *Please*. Do an interview with me at our game on Saturday. You can get your footage of the boys in the background, but the focus has to be on me."

His words may sound self-centered, but they're not. He's desperate to protect the privacy of those boys and willing to use himself as a shield.

I smile, easily agreeing to his terms. "You can decide how much information goes out. We won't mention the team name or which league you're a part of, but maybe it can boost support across the board from those people who might go around to games trying to find you."

"Exactly."

"This is only going to make you more of a golden boy," I warn.

He chuckles. "I don't know why everyone thinks I'm perfect. I'm not. There are plenty of guys who play an honest game and live their lives privately." Then he sits forward, piercing me with a stare that seems to dig inside me in search of the truth he must be able to sense lurking. "So why me? You can tell me all you want that you came to Sun City for the kids, but I know you're here for me. Why?"

It's dangerous, but I answer honestly. "I wish I knew."

GREY
BIRD
TAVERN

Chapter Twenty-Two

Houston

I AM GOING TO murder Kit Morgan.

This is what I get for not being around to help make the bet at trivia night, and I wish I had Tamlin's number so I could blame all of this on her. She's the one who distracted me at the bar. She's the one who knew the answer to the last question but didn't say anything. If anything, *she* should be the one wearing this costume, but that wouldn't even be justice because she would look amazing in this.

"I sort of understand the appeal of tights now," Jordan says, coming up beside me and joining me in the full-length mirror in my closet. "These are comfier than I would have expected. And dang, do I look good."

There is no way on this blessed earth that I will ever agree with him out loud, but the man can rock a tutu.

Yep. Kit's version of a normal bet payout is having to wear a leotard and tutu for the duration of my family Halloween party. He will require multiple pictures throughout the night so we don't change. I'm pretty sure he put Fischer and Micah in charge of the documenting, and I doubt Fischer is going to waste this opportunity to trash me. (I may not have interacted with him much at trivia, but when I talked to him at the lodge opening, I got the feeling Micah's new boyfriend doesn't really like me. Or maybe he does? He's so hard to read.) Generally Kit is pretty tame when it comes to bets, and he should, in theory, be satisfied with the pictures. But once he has them...

If I see any evidence of this night on his stupid woodworking video channel, he's officially dead to me. (It's not stupid. It's really cool. He teaches kids woodworking in a way that makes it appealing to adults too. I have to admit there have been a few times that I've wanted to try building a table or something just because he makes it look so easy.) But he's smart enough to know that sharing a photo of me in a tutu would do nothing but hurt me...I hope.

Jordan puts his arm on my shoulders, and I really wish he would stop making so much eye contact in the mirror when I feel like I am entirely on display. I was once part of a "sexy baseball player" calendar photo shoot and wore only boxer briefs for my May feature, and yet right now I feel way more exposed than I ever have been. Which makes no sense, considering Jordan and I shared a locker room for all of high school and two years of college. There's just something about being in skintight Spandex that makes me shudder.

"Pink is not my color," I say weakly. "Would it make me a jerk to uninvite Darcy to the party over text so there's no possible way she sees me like this?"

Jordan laughs. "Yeah, it would. Besides, you're looking at this the wrong way. This might be just what you need to get her fully on your side. No woman in her right mind can resist a set of abs like those."

He pokes me in the gut. I shove him into my vast array of blazers.

His tumble into my formal wear doesn't faze him, and he hops right back up to start striking ballet poses in the mirror.

"How are you like this?" I ask without meaning to. You'd think, for how long we've known each other, I would have asked something like this before, but I've always kept a decent distance between me and, well, anyone. All of this time I've been spending with Tamlin and Darcy has apparently made me go soft.

I'm trying to see that as a good thing.

Jordan does an impressive jumping twirl before landing in the Heisman pose with an invisible football. The combination of that with his fluffy tutu looks ridiculous, and he clearly doesn't care. "Like what?"

"How do you make it look so easy to not care what people think of you?"

He stands up straight again, eyebrows low. "I care what people think of me."

Gesturing to his leotard, I raise an eyebrow.

"One," he says, "I have never looked better. And two, I absolutely wouldn't wear something like this if you and Brooklyn weren't wearing it too. And three, I only care about the people that matter. If you were to tell me I was acting stupid, you would probably mean it, so I'd listen.

Just like when Brooklyn says I need to stop working and relax, I know she's not saying it to make me feel bad, so I should do what she says."

I narrow my eyes at him. We haven't talked much about his relationship with Brook outside of that short conversation when he admitted to being in love with her the day after trivia. That means I haven't sufficiently warned him not to break her heart. Now probably isn't the time, but I still say, "You'd better listen to her."

He smirks. "I do."

"Good."

He studies me for a moment, fully serious now that he's probably picked up on my own sobriety. "This is bigger than a tutu, isn't it?"

"That's a sentence I never thought you'd say to me," I mutter and then head down to the living room to flop onto the couch. I've still got a few minutes to kill before Darcy's expecting me, and it might be nice to talk out some of the stuff that has been bubbling up since my date with Tamlin today.

Once Jordan has settled on the other end of the couch—our tutus bunch between us awkwardly—he bites his tongue and waits for me to initiate this conversation. I'm glad he can be serious when he needs to be, and I can sense Brook's influence. He usually can't shut up, and I *know* he has things he wants to say.

I appreciate his uncommon willingness to let me take this at my own pace.

It's still weird to think that he and my sister are in love, but from the sound of things, they've been good for each other. That's what a relationship should look like, but I'm not sure I have that with either Darcy or Tamlin. Has either been good for me? Have I been good for *them*? The instant I suspected Darcy of lying to me, I basically ignored her for days. I don't think that would make anyone feel good.

"Do you think I have trust issues?" I ask without context.

He lets out a little laugh, as if he has no idea what to do with that question. "I'm guessing you've given this some thought?" he says slowly.

Not really, but it has probably been festering inside me for a while. Definitely since I made the connection—or lack of—between Darcy's family and Jesse, but I think this is a deeper problem. There has to be a reason I've never been very open in my relationships over the years. One that goes deeper than the fact that I've always been busy with baseball. That never stopped me from constantly having someone to call mine.

Have I been overcomplicating things, like Bonnie said? She told me I don't like to be alone, but that doesn't mean I've ever let someone else in. I'm pretty sure I've been alone my entire life.

"It's a more recent thing that's come up," I say, shrugging. "And I know you trust pretty much everyone, so it's okay if you don't underst—"

"I love how you have all these ideas about me that aren't true." Jordan shakes his head and grins like he's never met anyone more ridiculous. "I know you and I don't see each other as much as we used to, but you clearly need to work on your friendship skills. Who says I trust easily? I have the *hardest* time trusting people."

"Says the guy who fell in love with someone after a week." Whatever happened between them over the last couple of weeks, they both seem really happy to have found each other, so it must be real.

He rolls his eyes. "First of all, I'm pretty sure it's impossible to distrust Brooklyn Briggs. Second, I've technically known Brooklyn as long as I've known you. I may not have been crushing on her back in the day—too busy driving her crazy for that—but I knew her. I knew exactly who she was and what she could do to me if I let her in. Love means vulnerability, which means the risk of getting hurt or *causing* hurt, which means my instinct is to run far away because I can't give up control. But we're not talking about me." He nudges my arm. "Why are you wondering if you have trust issues?"

"I don't know. There's the whole thing with Tamlin Park—I thought for sure she was out to get me, but I've come to respect her and how she does her job after getting to know her. And then there's Darcy's brother..."

"That guy terrifies me," Jordan says with a nervous chuckle. "He was heading out to his car when I got here and wouldn't stop glaring at me."

Sounds about right. "Thing is," I continue, "I talked to Darcy about her family quite a bit last week, and she said she only has a sister. So she's probably lying about Jesse being related."

Jordan doesn't reply, like he's waiting for me to finish my explanation.

"That's it," I say.

"Okay, so you don't trust Darcy because she's not related to the guy who's twice her size and a completely different ethnicity from her?"

"She introduced him as her brother when they first moved in."

He snorts a laugh. "Uh, I've told about a million people that you're my brother, and..." He gestures between us as if I haven't noticed the differences in our complexions: he's dark where I'm light.

Does he really think of me as a brother? A warmth seeps into my chest at the thought. I really *should* work on my friendship skills. Especially now that I'm probably going to have a lot of free time in my future. Jordan has been with me for half my life, sticking by me even when I got drafted and gained an ego I didn't need. He deserves better than what I've given him.

"Family isn't what you're born into, man," Jordan continues. "It's what you make it. You should know that better than anyone, with your dad and everything."

Okay, well, he makes a good point, even if I don't want to admit it. This means he knows more about my dad than I thought, and suddenly I want to talk to Brook about Dad. I don't know if she's talked to Jordan about him, but as far as I can tell, she has clearly figured out how to get past the hurt of being abandoned.

I'm still working on that part.

Okay, I'm starting to see where my trust issues might be stemming from...

"I want to trust Darcy," I say, resisting the urge to run my hands through my hair because I don't want to ruin the style I carefully crafted. I may be reluctantly in a tutu, but I refuse to show up as anything but my best. "But if one little thing tripped me up, what happens when I come across something big?"

"You're talking as if you're expecting something big to come up," Jordan counters. "I don't think that's healthy."

Weirdly, this conversation is helping. Maybe just saying it out loud has been good for me. The first step in getting over my issues. "Thanks for putting that delicately."

"Delicate is my middle name."

I groan. "*Jordan* is your middle name, you dork. So... You're saying I shouldn't expect things to go south? That everything will be fine?"

"You can never know that for sure. But if you're always waiting with one foot out the door, what reason is Darcy going to have to expect you to stick around? Trust goes both ways."

"I think you're right."

"I'm always right."

I punch his arm lightly. "No, I mean, I went to lunch with Tamlin today, and she told me she's running a story on me coaching Little League."

Jordan splutters. "On you doing *what*?"

Oh, right. I haven't told anyone that I coach. Clearly my trust issues are deeper than I thought, and I have a lot to start sharing with my family. "I'll tell you later. The point is she told me about the story so I can make sure the boys aren't compromised, and it was easy to think she'll follow through because she warned me about the story in the first place. She trusted me, and I in turn trusted her. So, you're right."

"Beyond the Little League thing, I'm still hung up on the fact that you're only telling me *now* that you went on a date with freaking Tamlin Park. How did that even happen? And why didn't you tell me?"

Groaning, I pinch the bridge of my nose and pray I don't end up with a headache after the madness that is this day. "I'm sorry, *how* long did it take you to tell me you're in love with my sister?"

He winces. "Fair point."

I'm not trying to turn this back on him, and I know why he was so reluctant to tell me about his feelings for Brook. They are the two closest people I have in my life, and they didn't want to risk that. I don't like that they kept it from me, but I understand it.

Suddenly I remember a conversation I had with Fischer back at the lodge. He said something about Darcy having a reason to keep things from me. I haven't thought much about what he said because I didn't believe him, but now... Maybe he was right all along. I should probably spend more time with my siblings and their significant others. I might have a lot to learn from them.

"Can I tell you about this later?" I ask, feeling restless from all of this uncertainty. "We should probably go get Darcy."

"As long as you promise to answer all of my burning questions eventually, sure. Don't think I'm going to drop any of these things."

"Never crossed my mind. I know you too well." Or maybe I don't. But that's fixable, something I am going to be grateful for, I think. I could use as many good friends as I can get.

I step out the door cautiously, making sure none of my neighbors are out and about to see me looking this ridiculous. I'm so glad Jordan said that Jesse has gone somewhere so I don't have to imagine his expression, but that does nothing to help my nerves as I cross the porch and knock on Darcy's door. I could have warned her to save myself the full brunt of her shock, but I think I was hoping I could avoid this embarrassment altogether.

As the door opens, I brace myself for the inevitable humiliation. But all of that fear vanishes the instant I register what she's wearing.

She's in uniform. *A baseball uniform.* And I would recognize the Red-tails red and gold anywhere without seeing the logo printed on her chest. Her knee-breeches should not be as attractive as they are, nor should the hat holding back her ponytailed curls or the cleats on her feet. It's the mitt that does me in, tucked under her arm so naturally that it's like she just came from a game and forgot she has it.

Is she trying to kill me? Because I'm pretty sure she's sending me right into a heart attack.

"What do you think?" She does a spin, giving me a clear view of the name *Briggs* on the back, as well as my jersey number, twelve.

I force myself to respond. It isn't easy. "Where did you get this? Don't answer that. I don't care."

I can't help myself. I move in until we're practically sharing the same breaths, though she doesn't seem to be breathing at all. My fingers shakily trace the eye black on her cheeks beneath the frames of her glasses, and I'm so tempted to pull her hat from her head to give me room to kiss her that my fingers are on the brim before I remember we have company. I adjust the hat instead, pretending to angle it just right. I need to take things slow. If I want to allow myself the chance to really trust this woman, I can't jump in before I'm ready.

I need to say something, anything, but the only thing I manage is, "You look..."

Her cheeks burn red. I love the way I can so easily see her blush because the only makeup she wears is some mascara and a pink lip gloss that looks a little too tempting. If anyone is real, Darcy is. She really has nothing to hide.

I can't believe how quickly I distrusted her.

"Houston?" she whispers. Her eyes haven't left mine even once since I moved in.

The space between us is practically nonexistent now. "Yeah?"

"Are you wearing tights?"

If there's a better way to kill a mood, I haven't seen it. I glance down, once again self-conscious about how much of me she can see. Only my arms are bare, but that doesn't mean this smooth fabric isn't hugging every bit of me.

Let me just say: thank goodness for tutus.

I clear my throat. "They're more comfortable than they look."

"That was my line," Jordan says with a laugh. He's sitting on the porch railing and watching us like he's having the time of his life. The only thing he's missing is the popcorn. He points at me and then touches his mouth. "You got a little drool there, bud."

I'm going to kill him.

By some miracle, Darcy laughs at his joke and then says, "Looking good, Jordan."

She didn't say *I* look good. Why does that bug me so much?

There's enough laughter in Jordan's eyes that I'm tempted to punch him. He must see my growing tension because he claps his hands together and hops to his feet. "So, are we going to a party or what? I'm driving."

"*I'm* driving," I growl, if only because having the wheel in my hands will help me keep them to myself. Between Darcy in my uniform and Jordan laughing at my expense, my hands are itching to do a lot of things right now.

As Jordan hands over his keys, he leans in close. "If only you could see your face, man. You're totally gone. Have fun tonight."

The sight of Darcy wearing my jersey isn't exactly solving any of my problems, especially after that phone call with Roundy while I was at lunch today. He's putting on the pressure to make a decision—I don't blame him—and I thought I'd pretty much decided that it would be best if I called it quits now and saved myself the humiliation of barely being able to play next season. But seeing Darcy with my name on her back has me picturing her in the stands of every home game, cheering me on until the game ends and I can run up and kiss her for the world to see.

I think something might be wrong with me if that's what I'm picturing after less than two weeks of knowing this woman. But when I pull open the passenger door of Jordan's truck and watch Darcy hop inside and give me a warm smile, I'm pretty sure I don't care that this might be crazy.

If ever there was someone made for me, I think Darcy might be it.

GREY
BIRD
TAVERN

Chapter Twenty-Three
Darcy

"You know," I say, speaking into the silence that has only been broken up occasionally by Jordan humming snippets of songs in the back seat. "At this rate, it's going to be November by the time we make it to your brother's house."

Houston's fingers tighten around the steering wheel. "I'm not going that slow."

I have to lean closer to see the speedometer, and he tenses at my nearness. I know it was mean to wear the baseball uniform, but when I was trying to come up with a costume, I couldn't stop imagining the look on his face. And let me tell you, Houston exceeded my expectations. I thought he was going to fall over or maybe just kiss me with reckless abandon, and oh how I wanted to dive right into that. I'm not sure what held him back, but it was probably a good thing he has better self-control than I do.

"You're going ten under the speed limit," I point out.

Jordan groans. "This is why I should have driven! You're going to have to face your fate sooner than later, and you are rocking that tutu. Besides, what's the point of you being up there if you're not even going to hold her hand, huh?"

Thank you, Jordan!

Houston growls a little, but then he meets my eye for a second, silently asking permission. Considering I'm usually the one making the first contact, the respect he's showing by giving me a chance to refuse has me melting in my seat.

I reach out my hand, and Houston's dimple makes an appearance the moment we touch over the console. It's not like I haven't held his hand before, but this feels different. This isn't a heated, private moment—not with Jordan back there singing what I'm pretty sure is "Kiss the Girl" under his breath. And since we're heading to hang out with all of his siblings, he's basically telling me with this gesture that this thing between us is more than an unspoken attraction.

I wish I could be as confident as I am when I'm Tamlin and tell him how much I like knowing he isn't afraid to show me off tonight.

I spend the drive exploring Houston's hand. His fingers are long, knuckles pronounced, and because he's left-handed he doesn't have too many calluses on this hand. His skin is smooth and warm, and I relish the way my fingers fit between his so nicely. For the most part, he keeps his hand relaxed so I can do what I want, but every once in a while his fingers curl around mine or brush along my palm and send a shiver through me. Every time he does this, a little smile stretches across his lips and brings back that dimple.

I've never had anything feel this natural before. I've been on plenty of dates and even had a couple of boyfriends—nothing lasting longer than a few months—but I don't think I ever would have been this forward with a man's hand before meeting Houston.

Or maybe Tamlin is rubbing off on me.

When Houston pulls up outside a suburban house that looks incredibly warm and welcoming, Jordan is the first one out, shutting the door behind him and leaving us in a heavy silence that feels full of possibility.

Houston and I speak at the same time.

"I should probably warn you about—"

"What exactly are we—"

We share matching smiles before Houston gestures for me to go first.

I don't feel quite as brave as I did a second ago, but I force myself to ask the question anyway. "What are we? I mean, who are you going to introduce me as?"

He shifts so he's facing me a little more. Jordan's truck is pretty giant, so there's plenty of room for him to turn in his seat. "I don't know yet," he says, which honestly is a perfectly valid answer, all things considered. "What do you think?"

What would Tamlin say? It feels a little ridiculous to ask myself that question when I *am* Tamlin, but especially lately I've separated the two halves so well. Too well.

I speak more to his hand than to his face, as if that might make it easier to be honest. "I think I really like you. But I don't know how long I'll be in town, which makes this...complicated."

"Your lease isn't up until the end of the year. We have time to figure out what this is before we make any decisions."

We have only as long as it takes for me to find this elusive story, and then I'll have to cut him out of my life and vanish. I wish I could tell him the truth about who I am because he deserves to know, but Enhance has made that impossible. Even if I *could* tell him, it would only make everything worse because I've been lying to him since the day I met him. Houston is going to end up hurt no matter what I do, and I hate that.

"Maybe we just take one day at a time," I suggest quietly.

I can tell Houston wants more than that, but I want to protect his heart and soul as much as I can when the hammer falls.

"What were you going to say?" I ask when he doesn't say anything about my suggestion.

He glances at the house, his expression hard to read. "I should warn you about my siblings. They're chaotic on a good day, and Halloween tends to bring out the worst of us. They'll...they will probably ask you a lot of questions. Sorry in advance."

I can handle questions. I have to be quick on my feet whenever Tamlin goes to battle, so this will be nothing. But to stay true to the Darcy that Houston knows, I give his hand a squeeze. "Just don't leave me alone for too long," I tell him. "Who knows what kind of unluckiness I could run into here."

We slip out of the truck, and Houston takes my hand back as soon as he can, walking with me up to the brightly lit house. "I have yet to see this unluckiness in action," he says.

"Maybe that's because you counter it with your luck."

He chuckles and then pushes the door open.

A big ball of fur greets me immediately, two paws slamming into my chest as a tongue swipes my face in a slobbery kiss. The impact knocks me into Houston, giving me a great chance to experience up close and personal all of that muscle that is on display beneath the thin fabric of his leotard as he grabs me and holds me close.

"Duke, no!" Houston shouts, but the kisses keep coming.

A whistle pierces the air, sharp and clear, and Duke drops to all fours, his tongue lolling out the side of his mouth as he grins at us. Now that I can actually see him, he's the most gorgeous golden retriever I've ever seen, his fur long and silky and his tail swishing back and forth in a quick rhythm.

A man comes around the corner and commands, "Outside." The dog obeys without hesitation, trotting off until I can hear a dog door flap closed.

Still in Houston's strong hold, I take my first look at Chad Briggs. He has the same coloring as the twins, blond hair and bright blue eyes, but everything about him is more muted than his younger siblings. His hair is more of a dirty blonde and a lot shorter than Houston's, and his eyes are a darker blue, closer to the gray side of the spectrum than Houston's more turquoise color. He looks like the kind of guy who can shave in the morning and have to shave again that night, so he sports a decent amount of scruff, giving him a rugged look that matches the lumberjack getup he's wearing.

Something tells me this is one of his more regular shirts, and this is about as dressed up as he gets.

"Sorry about that," Chad says, pulling out a handkerchief—a hand-kerchief!—from his back pocket and handing it to me. "Duke only does that with people he's excited to meet. He'll be better behaved now that he's, uh, tasted you."

Houston pulls me closer, like he's worried about someone else want-ing to get a taste as well.

Grateful for the chance to de-slobber my face, I smile at Chad. "Don't worry about it. He seems great." I return his handkerchief and then leave my hand there for him to shake. He has a firm grip, and I'm pretty sure he's testing the strength of my response as his eyes travel over me. I can recognize a fellow observer, which could make tonight interesting if I let anything slip that I shouldn't.

"Darcy Paxton," I tell him.

"Chad Briggs. You hungry?"

"Always."

Satisfaction brightens his expression, and he gives Houston an ap-proving look that says I'm off to a good start. Knowing the kinds of women Houston has dated in the past, I can imagine I'll be accepted a little more warmly than the otherworldly models and actresses this family has encountered in the past.

As we follow Chad around the corner to a kitchen and dining room, a wave of smells and sounds hits me, and immediately my mouth starts to water. Jesse and I have been eating well, but there's something to be said for a good homemade meal, something I haven't had since my dad's birthday last June. More than that, I take in the sight of Houston's family all looking so happy and free as Halloween songs play over a speaker on top of one of the cabinets.

Jordan and Brooklyn are dancing in the kitchen, both of them laughing as they attempt some ballet moves that neither one is good at. Brooklyn is more graceful than Jordan, but he's got the muscle to back up his pliés. They both keep looking at each other almost in awe, as if neither can understand how the other fell for them, and it's the sweetest thing I've ever seen.

Micah is directing Fischer on where to put all the food on the table, arranging everything so it looks like a professional spread. She keeps changing her mind, but Fischer doesn't seem to mind. I watched them a bit at trivia night, but I was so focused on trying to beat Houston that there's a lot more I can learn about those two. I don't think they've been together long, which means every time Micah chooses a different spot for a platter of pigs-in-a-blanket, Fischer gives her a little smile that is equal parts "you're ridiculous" and "I love you." He seems fairly subdued and chill, a solid and steady match to Micah's bubbly personality. They've dressed up as Zac Efron and Zendaya's characters from *The Greatest Showman*, and they are both pulling off their respective circus costumes incredibly well.

Only Chad is on his own instead of in a pair, but he doesn't seem to mind as he skirts around Brooklyn to pull a pizza out of the oven. How much older did Houston say he was? Something like eight years, and he's giving off some serious dad vibes as he smiles at the way Jordan picks Brooklyn up and starts twirling her around. Maybe Duke is the only significant other he needs when he's got his family around.

Suddenly, Micah bursts into a fit of giggles and points our way, the first person to notice us. "Oh my gosh, it's perfect!"

I step aside to give her a better view of Houston's tutu, but when Micah comes around the table, it's me she's focused on. She grabs my hand, holding my arm out so she can see the full effect of my baseball outfit.

"Houston, did you die when you saw her?"

Houston grunts something and slips away to help Chad in the kitchen.

I hold back a laugh at his discomfort, but only barely. "You should see the back," I tell Micah and turn to show her.

Micah squeals. "You know what you're doing, girl! What was his reaction?"

I don't know how to put it into words, but I'm pretty sure my blush says it all.

Brooklyn comes to join us, pulling me in for a hug that surprises me. "Sorry," she says. "I know we haven't met yet, but Jordan has said enough about you that I feel like we have. I'm Brooklyn. This is Micah."

Right. They haven't met Darcy.

Clearing my throat, I smile wide. "I'm Darcy, Houston's, uh...next door neighbor?" We never actually came up with a label for what we are.

Brooklyn and Micah both inch closer and glance into the kitchen in unison, where Houston is watching us with concern even though Chad is saying something to him. "I've never seen him like this," Brooklyn whispers. "Are you sure you're not more than his neighbor?"

"He's giving off some serious possessive vibes," Micah agrees.

"That's a bad thing, Mic," Fischer mutters from his seat at the table nearby. What, does he have superhuman hearing or something?

Micah waves him away. "It's not a bad thing," she says. "It just means that he's worried we're going to scare you away!"

"Which means he likes you," Brooklyn adds.

"A lot. Do you like him?"

"It's okay if you don't. He can be a pain."

"But it's about time he settled down and stopped dating people who weren't going to stick around anyway!"

"He's really great and has a lot of love to give, he just has to find the right person who can be patient with him."

"Are you the right person?"

"Okay," Houston says, breaking up the inquisition before I say something I can't take back. "Can we stop scaring my date?"

"Told you," Micah whispers with a wink, and then she settles herself on Fischer's lap instead of her own chair. Rolling his eyes, he wraps an arm around her waist and pulls her against his chest, and she rewards him with a kiss that he happily returns. I don't remember any kissing happening at trivia night, so I have to wonder if their relationship is as new as Jordan and Brooklyn's. What does Houston think about all of this?

As Jordan tugs Brooklyn toward the table, Houston regains my attention by slipping his hand into mine and leaning close enough that I have to lift my head to see up into his face. "I tried to warn you," he says breathily. "They can be a lot."

"I like them," I counter with a grin. I think back to what he told me at the gala about how he got into baseball and how he felt redundant and unimportant. Maybe I can help him out a bit. "I can see how much they care about you."

His fingers curl even tighter around mine, like he's afraid to let go. "And what about you?" he whispers. If he notices his family staring at us, he doesn't mind. "Do you care about me?"

I snort a little laugh, trying to ease the tension before I get lost in his bright blue eyes. *Too late.* "I already told you I like you, Houston."

"Just checking," he says with a chuckle, and then he presses a kiss to the top of my hat. Stupid hat has gotten in my way twice now, and I'll have to ditch it before the night is over.

"Hey, are we eating or smooching?" Jordan asks loudly. "I'm happy to do either, but I want to know which—"

Houston steals my mitt and throws it, nailing Jordan in the chest.

Laughing, I lean up on my toes and channel my Tamlin confidence as I say, "There will be enough time for everything."

Houston's face goes slack, his cheeks filling with color.

I have to pull him with me to the table, and even after we start digging into the incredible spread, he seems a bit in a daze. He's nearly kissed me more than once, but this is the first time I've given him any kind of permission. That makes this feel all the more real, and the anticipation might very well kill me.

Thank goodness for the Briggs siblings, who don't take long to start throwing more questions at me.

"How is it living next to Houston?" Micah asks, starting things off.

"I rarely see him," I answer honestly, and then I take a huge bite of pizza because I refuse to miss out on any of this delicious-looking food because I'm too busy talking. I can be strategic about this.

"You should have seen the way Houston greeted her when she showed up to move in," Jordan says, already laughing before he describes the horror scene I walked into.

"The paint was everywhere," Houston complains. "I was just trying to get it all cleaned up before they showed up."

"They?" Chad asks with poorly concealed interest.

I swallow a bite of the best spinach artichoke dip I've ever tasted. "Yeah, me and Jesse. He's like a brother to me."

"*Like* a brother," Jordan repeats, but he's looking at Houston with his eyebrows high. What is that about?

"What brought you to Sun City?" Fischer asks.

I still don't have a good answer for that one. "A lot of things."

"And do you like it so far?" Brooklyn asks.

This one is easier. "I really do."

"I'm glad Sun City hasn't scared you away with its tendency to be cautious with newcomers," Jordan says.

Uh, I'm not sure what he means by that or how to respond. At least, I don't until he winks at Houston and Houston groans, dropping his face into his palm. Ah, okay, so we're not talking about Sun City. Two can play at this game.

"I wasn't sure about Sun City at first," I say casually. "It's a little too glorified for my taste, but the longer I've been around town, the more I've come to know the city that's under the shiny surface." Houston looks up, but I keep going, pretending I have no idea what Jordan was hinting at. "There are a lot of hidden secrets, but I'm excited to get to know everything I can because I have a feeling Sun City and I could really be something good."

I've left the table stunned, everyone staring at me like they never could have expected someone like me. Houston is frozen solid beside me, and I'm too afraid to look at him in case I was just too bold for his comfort.

Chad speaks first, his eyes crinkling at the corners as he smiles at me. "I think Hou has met his match in you, Darcy."

"I'll say!" Micah chimes in. "All the other women have been too afraid to look at him too hard."

The irony of that comment makes me laugh, and I finally turn to meet Houston's gaze. It hits me right in the gut because he's looking at me with so much warmth and awe that my insides twist themselves into knots. This expression isn't so different from the one Jordan gets every time he looks at Brooklyn. Or the way Fischer smiles at Micah's antics.

Dare I even wonder if Houston is falling in love with me? This is going to end so badly, and yet as I watch him right back while the family changes topics to something less heated, my heart beats with a solid rhythm that seems to say, "I love you too."

That can't be good.

GREY
BIRD
TAVERN

Chapter Twenty-Four

Houston

I'VE NEVER FELT THIS way. I lost track years ago of the number of times I've told a woman I loved her, but I know for a fact I never meant it because nothing ever came close to the way I feel right now. I wish I could say for sure what this tightness in my chest really is. If this is love, it's so different from what I expected. I expected it to be light and easy, like a fire igniting inside me every time I look at the woman who has captured my heart. I imagined trumpets and fireworks and excitement.

This is different. This is contentment and calm. This is a need to protect. This is a fear that I'll never measure up to the man I want to be for her.

As I watch Darcy bob for apples, with her hat backwards on her head and her glasses in her hand, I want to make her happy. I want to see that light in her eyes never dim. I want her to believe that no matter what, I will have her back because she makes me feel strong enough to be that for her. Even when my own life is still at a terrifying crossroads, I feel like no matter what decision I make, she'll make it worth it.

She said it herself that she's leaving Sun City at some point, but there has to be a way I can convince her to stay. If her job is remote, surely it doesn't matter where she is. And if not... If not, that might make my decision easier. If Darcy is going to leave, would she be up for me going with her? It's not like I can play anyway, so what's the point of me staying with the Red-tails and finishing my contract?

Chad joins me on the stairs, where I've been watching Darcy interact with my family for the last ten minutes. "Jordan told me about your arm."

My heart drops into my stomach. "He did what?"

He puts a hand on my shoulder and holds me down before I can get up and strangle my former best friend. "Indirectly," he clarifies with a little smile. "He was talking about his landscaping and how he's glad you're still half owner despite offering to sell your share. I inferred the rest."

I groan. Chad has been a private investigator for the last eighteen years, which is too long in my opinion. "Have I ever told you you're terrifying?"

"Many times. Why didn't you tell me you're injured?"

"Because no one knows." My shoulder twinges in response, even though I only just started working it out this week. It's already sore, and the PT isn't thrilled by the minimal recovery I showed from a week of rest. Hence Roundy getting jumpy about my lack of a decision. I can't skimp on practice for much longer before the team really starts to notice, and my ligaments have been stretched too far to heal without surgery. That's not even touching on the subject of the potentially torn supraspinatus tendon. The MRI was unclear, but it's hard to ignore the way it feels. *Has felt.*

I don't think I can brush away the problem any longer.

I rub my shoulder, grateful to know Chad will never judge me for this moment of weakness. He always thought I pushed myself too hard anyway. "I don't know what to do," I admit.

"Can you play?"

I shake my head. "Maybe a few innings, but I don't think I can last a whole game anymore."

"They never should have played you so hard. You're a starter, not the end-all be-all."

"That was always by choice." At least, it was in the beginning. I wanted to prove that I was strong enough to carry my team to victory. To be worthy of the role of captain.

Chad hums, resting his elbows on his knees as Darcy emerges from the bucket of water victorious, an apple clamped in her mouth as the others cheer. "Have you talked to Darcy about all of this? What did she think?"

"She doesn't know. She barely knows anything about baseball to begin with, and I don't want to dump something like this on her when we haven't even been on a date yet."

"Haven't you?"

I'm not sure I can call lunch at Big Henry's with fifteen screaming boys a date, especially compared to what I've done with Tamlin recently. Between trivia night, dancing at the gala, and today's lunch, I've been awfully good at creating imbalance when it comes to my relationships.

It's no wonder I've been torn between the two. I want to get to know Darcy, but I've been spending all my time with Tamlin.

"I'll tell her about my shoulder," I say, if only to get that judging look out of Chad's eyes. "Eventually. And I don't think you should be giving dating advice when you just spent two weeks in the woods with a girl and came back empty handed."

Chad grimaces. "Micah doesn't know everything," he says, referring to our group chat and Micah's insistence that he's been falling in love since the day he got to Laketown. He scrubs a hand along his jaw, looking older than usual. He's been good about hiding his tension for the most part, but I spent most of my childhood idolizing my big brother. I know when something's bothering him.

We never talk about our dating lives—except when Chad gives me lectures on how to treat women—but maybe we've grown up enough to have an adult conversation. "Want to talk about it?" There has to be a good reason he's back in Sun City. I got the impression he was going to stay in the small town for a while.

His grimace shifts into a scowl. As if sensing his master's frustration, Duke hops up from his bed in the corner and plants his head on Chad's knee.

"There's nothing to talk about," Chad says, growling the words. "She's just a woman who was in the house next to mine, and she clearly doesn't know what she wants. No one can be perfect, but she expects a relationship to be rainbows and sunshine and no bad days. Good things take work, and patience, and sacrifice. Running away from her problems isn't going to get her anywhere."

"Yep," I say with a grin. "You don't want to talk at all."

He rolls his eyes, leaning his back against the stairs and stretching his legs out. He lets out another groan as he covers his eyes with the back of his wrist. "I messed up. A lot. I thought I would have this kind of thing figured out by now, you know? I'm not getting any younger."

"Yeah, you're right. You're ancient."

He kicks my foot. "Shut up. I just mean it should get easier."

"I don't know. I've had more relationships than I can count, and I've never been more terrified of messing things up."

Chad doesn't look at me. "How long have you been in love with her?"

So maybe I'm not imagining things. If Chad sees something there, it must be real. "I don't know. It's only been a couple of weeks, but I feel like I've known her my whole life." Talking to her on the porch after trivia night was one of the best nights I've had in a long time, and she's even easier to talk to than Jordan. It's so easy to imagine us staying up late and talking like that every night.

Just as easy as it is to imagine waking up every morning next to her.

"Why do you think she doesn't know anything about baseball?" Chad asks.

That's a strange question, but it's pretty in line with the way Chad operates. Except, usually when he asks things like that, he's digging for a secret. But there's no secret here. I don't *want* there to be a secret. I want to get over my issues and trust Darcy because she hasn't given me a reason to do otherwise. Even the Jesse thing panned out.

"Because we've talked about it," I say, frowning. "She uses all the wrong terms, and she came to a Little League game last week and looked totally lost."

Darcy stands in the kitchen, munching on her apple as she watches Jordan attempt to get two apples at once. There's something in the way she's holding the fruit that pricks at something in my mind, but I can't quite place it. Pretty sure Chad is just making me paranoid.

Chad sits up again, following my gaze. "She can definitely hold her own against our chaos," he says. "And she's different from the women you usually bring around."

"That's why I like her."

"What about that reporter?"

I tense. "How do you know about—"

Chad laughs. "Do you really think I wouldn't get a play-by-play of trivia night from Micah? She may have been reading things wrong—"

"Wouldn't be the first time," I grumble.

"—but she said there was some serious tension between you two."

I appreciate the fact that he didn't throw the word *sexual* in there even though odds are high that Micah did when she was describing the night's events. She wouldn't be wrong, but I think there's a very fine line between attraction and hatred. This week, I crossed that line.

"I'll admit Tamlin is beautiful," I say before Chad can call me out on it. "And she's a genius. Plus, she played baseball in high school, which is hotter than I'd care to admit."

"But?" Chad prompts.

"But we're meant to be friends. She's almost too perfect." I won't even get into that switch she makes when she's on camera. I haven't seen that side of her lately, but I can't forget how easily and quickly she can become something else. "It's almost like she's not real."

"Hmm." Chad's fingers tap his pocket, where his phone has miraculously remained all night. His gaze is in the kitchen as he gets a thoughtful look on his face.

I know that look a little too well.

I wince. "Don't," I beg. "Don't go digging into my life. I'm having a hard enough time trusting Darcy to begin with, and I don't need you putting thoughts into my head."

"I thought we were talking about Tamlin."

Great. He's already got me saying things I didn't want to say. Jordan can know that I've had some doubts—doubts that Darcy unknowingly soothed when she mentioned Jesse—but Chad? Chad is a fixer. He can't leave something alone if it isn't working, which likely explains why he's back here instead of in Laketown with the mysterious girl who got him all ruffled.

Not everything needs fixing. The flaws are what give something character.

"Can you not be a detective for a minute and let me be happy?"

"Are you happy?"

"Yes." Okay, well, even I didn't believe that one, but I'm blaming my lack of confidence on my shoulder. And the fact that my dad is going to be loose again soon, which is dredging up old hurts and fears that I may end up like him. And I'm worried that things might be moving too fast with Darcy but I can't stop this train now that I'm on it.

"Go outside, Duke," Chad says after some kids shout something outside in front of the house. The dog trots off immediately, slipping through his door and disappearing into the darkness of the backyard.

"That is the most well-behaved dog I have ever seen," I mutter.

Chad chuckles. "If only people responded as easily. I know you don't want me to do any digging, but people are complicated, Hou. Sometimes it helps to understand where they're coming from." The doorbell rings, and he grunts and gets up, grabbing the candy bowl on his way to the door. "Think about it."

Instead of a chorus of little voices shouting, "Trick or treat!" after the door opens, only silence fills the living room until Chad says, "Oh."

Not only does that catch my attention, but it pulls the others over too, and we all crowd together to get a glimpse of whoever's at the door. I can barely see her behind Chad's bulk, but she looks around Micah's age, her features soft and delicate. She and Chad definitely know each other, though; they can't take their eyes off one another.

"Hi," the girl says quietly.

Chad folds his arms. "Where are the kids?"

Kids? There are kids involved in whatever this is? I glance at Brook, who shrugs before turning her attention back to the door.

"They're with my aunt," the girl says. "You left Laketown."

"I didn't see a reason to stay."

"So you just left? Without saying anything?"

"You left first."

"For two days! I came back."

This? *This* is the girl Chad is pining over? But she has to be at least a decade younger than him. And if she has kids, that makes this a lot more complicated than Chad probably likes. He's a simple man, and I always thought he would need a simple relationship and work his way up to the family part.

The girl's eyes leave Chad's face for the first time, and she turns bright red when she sees all of us watching.

Chad doesn't even give us a glance. Stepping out onto the porch, he shuts the door behind him and cuts us off from the rest of the conversation.

"I'm going to the window," Micah says, but Fischer and I both hold her back.

"I think Chad needs to do this on his own," I say, surprised by my own self-control. I'm dying of curiosity, just like everyone else.

"Uh, who's ready to carve pumpkins?" Jordan asks, though I'm pretty sure he is tempted to sneak upstairs and open the window in the hall bathroom so he can listen in on all the drama happening on the porch. He can rarely resist a bit of intrigue.

We all shuffle to the table and start picking out pumpkins from the box in the corner of the dining room. We're all being exceptionally quiet as if we might hear some of Chad's conversation. Even Darcy has picked up on the fact that Chad in a new relationship is a big deal, so she's silent along with the rest of us. I give her a look that says I'll explain later, and she replies with a smile and a shrug.

Fischer clears his throat, clearly reluctant to break the silence even though he's probably the least interested in what is happening outside. "Should I grab a—"

"Shh!" Micah hisses and claps her hand over his mouth.

He pulls away. "It's not like we can hear anything. And we need somewhere to put all the seeds."

"You're hopeless," Micah says with a huff, and they shift into a glaring contest that Fischer is definitively winning. Micah keeps turning redder the longer they stare at each other.

I'm the first one to crack, my laugh escaping in a snort that breaks Brook's resolve, and then all of us are busting up because this whole thing is ridiculous. Fischer's right, and we can't hear a thing outside because Chad would never let us overhear a conversation like this one.

"I'll grab a bowl," Brook says to Fischer, and then we dive into carving.

"There's going to be a contest," I tell Darcy as I spin my pumpkin, deciding which side has the optimal carving space.

I love the way she instantly gives her own pumpkin more attention. "What sort of contest? Most intricate? Most realistic?"

"Yeah, we need details," Jordan adds. "You've never let me join in on this before."

"It's a people's choice award," Micah says. "We all put in our vote for whichever we think is our favorite."

Fischer frowns, already elbow deep in pumpkin guts. He seemed eager to carve until I mentioned the contest. "Won't we all just vote for ourselves?"

"You would think so," Brook replies, "but someone always comes out the winner."

"It's because Chad never votes for himself," Micah says as if it should be obvious.

But that can't be right because, "I never vote for myself either," I say, pausing with my hand inside my pumpkin. "But I've still won a couple of times." Even when my pumpkins come out horrible every year. I turn my gaze to Brooklyn, who flushes bright red and focuses a little too hard on picking pumpkin string off her pinky. "Brook. You always do the final tally."

Micah gasps. "Brooklyn! Have you been *cheating the system all this time?*"

Jordan busts up again, planting a kiss on Brook's cheek as she mumbles, "I didn't want anyone to feel left out."

"My entire life is a lie," I say dramatically and throw a handful of slimy pumpkin seeds at her.

She screams but retaliates quickly, only her aim is way off and she pelts Darcy right in the face, leaving sticky orange strings stretched across Darcy's face. "Oh my goodness, Darcy! I'm so—"

A handful of guts flies out of Darcy's hand and lands in Brook's hair.

"Nice shot!" I say, offering Darcy a pumpkiny high five right before Jordan defends his girlfriend by grabbing a leftover chicken wing and thwacking me in the side of the head with it. "Oh, you're going down," I growl, and in two seconds flat we're all throwing food and pumpkin guts like there's no tomorrow.

"Stay behind me!" I tell Darcy, choosing to be the dashing hero.

Instead, she hops up onto a chair like Micah and flings her seeds with impressive coverage. Then she leaps onto my back and ducks, letting me take the brunt of the return fire. "I need more ammo!" she orders, and I comply, hurrying into the kitchen and ducking behind the counter to give her access to the food while attempting to protect myself.

Duke comes barreling in from the yard amidst our shouts and screams, barking like crazy but looking like he's having the time of his life as he starts chowing down on our fallen offerings.

"Stand!" Darcy shouts, and I do, receiving a face full of spinach dip from Micah at the same time Darcy squirts whipped cream directly into Jordan's hair while he scoops from his pumpkin.

He's just about to unleash his gloppy handful directly down my leotard when a whistle pierces the air. Duke isn't the only one who freezes, though no one else flops to the floor like he does.

Chad stands just inside the dining room, murder in his eyes as he takes in the scene of carnage. The woman at his side—who clings to his hand, I should add—looks a lot more entertained than he does.

"I don't want to ask," Chad grumbles and then turns and walks right back out the front door with his lady in tow, slamming the door behind him.

"Oops," Jordan says, which sends us all into fits of laughter again.

It feels good to laugh like this, and it's been a long time since all of my siblings were this happy. Though this cleanup is going to be a beast, I can't stop thinking about how Darcy fits right in with our chaos as she hangs on my back with her cream canister still at the ready.

Hopefully she wants to stay.

GREY
BIRD
TAVERN

Chapter Twenty-Five

Darcy

I ALWAYS WANTED TO be in a food fight. Movies make them look so fun, but my parents would have killed Carissa and me if we'd ever tried something like that. Now that I'm sitting on Houston's shoulders, scraping semi-dried pumpkin strings from the top of the cabinet, I can see why it is such a forbidden game. We've spent the last hour trying to make Chad's kitchen shine, but I'm pretty sure he's going to be finding stray pumpkin seeds until next Halloween.

"How?" Fischer asks in exasperation when he finds yet another seed inside the closed Tupperware drawer. He'd only opened it to grab some containers to pack up any food that didn't get decimated, but that turned into a deep clean because somehow there is pumpkin *everywhere*.

No one in the movies ever talks about how food fights are ten seconds of fun followed by a hundred times that in cleanup time.

Houston laughs and adjusts his hold on my legs, sending a shock through me just like he has every time he reminds me he's there. Not that I could have forgotten. I am impossibly tall up here, and he's been holding me long enough that I know he has to be getting tired. That hasn't stopped me from running my hands through his thick hair multiple times under the pretext of removing pumpkin strings and other food items.

This may not be how I pictured Halloween going, but I'm not complaining.

"How's it looking up there?" Houston asks me. "And how long do you think we should let Jordan and Brook make out in the pantry before we tell them we know they're not looking for more towels?"

"The cabinets are squeaky-clean," I say, my cheeks hurting from smiling as much as I have tonight. "I can't say the same for the pantry."

Someone bumps the pantry door from inside, and Houston rolls his eyes before slapping his palm against the door twice. "That's enough, you two," he says loudly before moving to the counter and setting me on my feet. As soon as he ducks out from underneath me, he holds out his arms to help me down.

I eagerly slide into his hold, letting him slip his hands beneath my legs and hold me bridal style, just like he did in the backyard back home. "Thanks," I say just as Brooklyn and Jordan come out of the pantry.

They try to look innocent, but the way Brooklyn's lips look slightly swollen beneath her mussed up hair is pretty strong evidence that Houston was right.

"Couldn't find any towels," Jordan says, and he gives Houston a wink.

Houston groans. "Do you really have to be like that when I'm around?"

For an answer, Jordan grabs Brooklyn again and plants a kiss on her mouth. Thankfully, for Houston's sake, he keeps it pretty tame. "Love isn't worth hiding," he says.

Houston looks at me at the same time I look at him, which has us both blushing. He puts me on my feet and gives me a nervous smile that I kind of love. At least I'm not the only one who's nervous.

"I think it's sweet," Micah says from her place on the floor. She's been picking seeds out of Duke's fur for the last five minutes, though now it looks like she's just giving the food-drunk dog a belly rub. "No one should be afraid of how they feel."

"I am not afraid," Fischer replies immediately. "I just don't think the whole world needs to know the depth of my love for you. That's solely for you."

Fischer might be generally quiet, but he is clearly madly in love with Micah. I'm pretty sure he didn't throw any food during the fight, but he ended up just as covered as the rest of us even though he could have left the room and spared himself.

Micah *awws* and hops over to give Fischer a kiss.

"I'm not following the pattern," Houston mutters to me, taking my hand. "Our first kiss doesn't need witnesses."

As heat floods my face, I try not to sound as overwhelmed as I feel. "I appreciate that," I say. "We're a little crowded here."

Fire flashes in his eyes. "I couldn't agree more." Tucking my arm through his, he clears his throat and grabs the attention of his siblings. "We're taking off."

"But what about the pumpkin contest?" Micah asks.

"Brook will just cheat again."

"I will not!" Brooklyn complains. "Not now that you know the truth."

"Then I'm going to lose anyway," Houston says as he tugs me toward the door. "Jordan, you're going to need a ride to my house to get your truck back."

Jordan salutes.

When we make it outside, Chad is sitting on the porch swing with the young woman tucked under his arm, and he seems far calmer than he did when he caught us flinging food around his house.

Houston grins at the sight of them, but it's more of a warm smile than a teasing one, and one that Chad matches. I wonder what they talked about while they were sitting on the stairs and if it had anything to do with relationships. Did they talk about me?

"Is my house still a disaster?" Chad asks calmly.

Houston chuckles. "You taught us too well. I'm pretty sure it's cleaner than when we started."

"Good."

Houston shoots a pointed look toward the woman beside Chad. "Are you going to introduce us?"

Chad smirks. "Nope."

I expect the woman to protest, but she just smiles and rests her head on Chad's shoulder like she is perfectly okay with remaining anonymous. If I had to guess, she's probably only in her early twenties, but she looks like she fits so well next to Chad. And Chad is more relaxed than he was when the party started, like everything is better now that she's here.

Houston seems a little weirded out by his brother's refusal, but he gets over it pretty quickly. "Well, we're headed out. Are you going back to Laketown?"

Chad glances at the woman, and she grins at him like there's some joke I missed. "We'll see." When he turns to me, there's something off about his smile. "It was nice to meet you, Darcy Paxton." Maybe he always calls people by their full names, but I don't like being under his gaze. I'll have to ask Houston what Chad does for work. When we're far away from here, obviously, and I'm not being stared down by a lumberjack.

Once we're on our way, I relax in my seat. It's not that Houston's family isn't great, but feeling like I have to hide such a large part of my-self—especially because most of them have met Tamlin—is completely exhausting. I don't know why it's never felt that way with Houston on his own.

He's always easy.

As he drives, he keeps glancing at me, like he's making sure I'm still there. "So, did my family scare you off, or...?"

Not yet, but Chad might. "Nah. Your family is great."

"They clearly like you."

I swear his expression says he likes me too, which has me blushing and floundering to change the subject. Looking around Jordan's truck for something to say, I ask the question I've wanted to ask him since the moment I first saw *his* truck.

"Why do you keep your old truck instead of buying a new one like this?"

"Technically I did buy this one." He winks. Then shrugs. "I like my old truck. I bought it in high school, after my stepdad started paying me to do yard work because I wouldn't accept money as a gift."

"Why not? Most kids would gladly take money. I had a great aunt who sent me twenty bucks on my birthday every year, and it was the best gift ever."

He chuckles, reaching over for my hand and relaxing as soon as he has a hold of me. "We had next to nothing when I was a kid, and my dad was awful with money. The contrast between living with him and living with my stepdad, Lloyd, was almost painful. And, nice as that life was, I wanted to prove to myself that I could be better than my dad. That I was stronger. I wanted to be the one taking care of the people I loved, not the other way around."

How is he such a good guy? He's always looking out for other people, and I wonder if it's because he felt so alone as a kid. There is so much to this man that I never would have guessed if Connor hadn't sent me here to befriend him.

Connor didn't intend for me to develop *feelings* for Houston, though. That's a problem all on its own.

"We didn't have a lot of money growing up either," I admit, filling the silence between us. "My dad runs a tiny hardware store, and it's always been hard to compete with the chains, especially in recent years. He's well past retiring age, but he keeps working so he can take care of my mom."

"Sounds like you have a good dad." Houston rubs my thumb, a thoughtful look on his face. Thoughtful, but with a healthy dose of worry mixed in there too. "Do you ever wonder how much we pick up from our parents genetically?"

Okay, this feels big. And deep. And probably beyond my level of expertise. I may have a psychology degree, but that doesn't make me a therapist. "Well, I don't think you're bad with money," I say lightly.

Houston snorts and glances over at me. "Are you trying to get me to tell you how much money I have?"

I bet people ask him that all the time. I know his yearly salary—a lot of people do—but there are plenty of athletes with multimillion-dollar paychecks that bleed themselves dry.

"Let's see," I say with mock thoughtfulness. "You drive a terrible truck—"

"Hey!"

"—and live in a duplex. But you also own a bunch of businesses and pay for lunch for an entire team and their families."

His head snaps over to me, jerking the truck a bit with it. "Who told you that?"

"Little Henry and I became buds while you were out playing catch."

Houston grumbles something that sounds a lot like, "Traitor."

"I think it's really sweet, Houston." I squeeze his hand, loving that he squeezes right back. "And it makes you a ridiculously good man. I'm not sure how I can keep up."

He's shaking his head before I even finish my sentence. "You just said the word *buds* in a sentence with Little Henry. He doesn't have friends. And my brother likes you, which means you're doing something right. He doesn't like anyone."

I didn't get the feeling that Chad likes me, at least not at the end there, but I keep that to myself. Chad's approval seems important to Houston. "Your family really is great, Houston. Thank you for letting me meet them."

He smiles as he pulls up in our driveway; I have no idea how we got here so fast. "I don't know about you," he says slowly, "but I'm not ready for tonight to end. But I could also use a shower."

I can feel my hair plastered together in several places, not to mention I'm pretty sure there's a pumpkin seed stuck in my bra. "A shower sounds great." And then heat floods through my face when I realize how that sounds. "Separately!" I add quickly. "My own shower." He probably wasn't even implying a shower *together* but now I've put it into his head and he's going to think that I'm thinking about it and—

"Darcy." Houston rubs his thumb along mine, his eyes warm and soft in the light from the porch. "I am fully planning on kissing you tonight, but that's it. Is that okay?"

Who would have thought a line like that would be so dizzyingly perfect? "Yeah," I breathe, which doesn't exactly sound confident.

He crosses the space between us, and for a second I think he's going to kiss me right now, in Jordan's truck. But he presses his lips to my forehead—good thing I took the hat off soon after the food fight—taking his time with the moment. "Meet you out back in half an hour?" he whispers.

The only thing I can get out is another airy, "Yeah."

It only takes me twenty minutes to get myself pumpkin-free and my hair secured in a braid so it doesn't frizz out of control. I don't bother reapplying makeup when I'm only going to wash it off again before I go to bed, and I'm slightly curious to see how Houston reacts to the base version of me with nothing but sweats and a t-shirt to recommend myself.

I can't wait another ten minutes stuck in the house, so I head out to the back patio to wait under the stars. Only, Houston beat me out there, and he somehow had time to set up candles along the side of the pool and a cozy little blanket pile on the tiny stretch of lawn off to the side. He's currently making sure the blankets and pillows are just right—wearing his awful slippers beneath a pair of sweats that hug his thighs and a t-shirt that looks a size too small—and I've never seen a more romantic sight. It's such a sweet gesture that it almost hurts.

When he notices me standing on the patio, he snaps to attention and speaks an octave too high. "Hey! Hi. You look..." He clears his throat. "Beautiful, as always. I hope this isn't too much. The neighbors left these candles when they moved out of your place, and since you like the stars I thought—"

I bound toward him and throw my arms around his neck, pulling myself in tight. I don't know why this is hitting so hard, but it is. I'm nearly in tears. "No one has ever done something like this for me."

He tightens the embrace. "Never?"

"I was one of the guys," I whisper, choking on the words. "I guess they assumed I wouldn't like the romantic stuff."

"You seem to like it," Houston says into my neck.

"I really do. Thank you."

Without letting go, he lifts me off my feet and crosses the last few feet to the blankets. "Wouldn't want you to step on a scorpion," he says, though he seems reluctant to put me down. "And don't worry. I'll keep you safe tonight."

To prove it, he stretches himself out on the side of the blanket pile that is closest to the edge of the yard and the desert beyond, leaving me the side with nothing but cement and the pool.

I'm not actually all that worried about getting stung tonight, but it sounds like a great excuse to get close to him. Not that I need one. As he gets himself comfortable and puts one arm behind his head, he puts his whole body on display, all of his lean lines and curved muscles pulling me in. He's got an easy smile on his face, no ounce of pressure in his expression. I could probably stand here all night and he wouldn't question it.

Well, he would probably question it, but he would find a way to make sure I'm comfortable on my feet. I can't imagine Houston ever making me feel dumb or prudish because I'm good at choosing my boundaries.

Tonight, my boundaries are right beside him.

After taking in the delicious sight of him for three more seconds, I settle down next to him, shoulder to shoulder and hip to hip. He grins when I take his hand, like that's all he's ever wanted, and then he shifts so our heads are touching because apparently everything else isn't close enough for him.

"I used to do this all the time as a kid," he says and then takes a deep breath of the cool night air. "Usually in the middle of the night, when I couldn't sleep. I would sneak out into my dad's backyard and lie there for hours, imagining what it would be like to be up in the stars."

I love that he's telling me this. "Did you want to be an astronaut as a kid?"

"Who didn't?"

"I didn't. I wanted to be a veterinarian."

"Really? Even when you didn't have any pets?"

I laugh, amazed that he remembered that detail from last week at Big Henry's. "My stuffed animals got a lot of doctoring back in the day."

"What changed your mind?"

I've never really thought about it, and I take a second to examine my life and the path it has taken. "I guess it was a gradual thing," I say. A breeze blows over us, and I shiver.

Houston immediately grabs another blanket and throws it over me, taking the time to make sure it covers all of me. For half a second, he's up on one elbow with his face only an inch or two away from mine. He pauses, eyes locked on my lips, before he slides his arm behind my head and settles back down beside me.

"What's your dream now?" he asks.

I can't tell him that I'm living it, traveling the country as a sports journalist. So I smile and roll closer, resting my head more on his shoulder than his arm. "My dream is to stay up all night and learn everything there is to know about Houston Briggs."

He laughs and presses a kiss to the top of my head. "I don't think it will take that long. I'm a pitcher who can't cook and drives a crappy truck."

I snicker. "I already know those things."

"You don't know that I'm deathly afraid of bees and have never been stung so I don't know if I'm allergic. And I really am afraid of spiders. Not so much of socks. You already know everything else worth knowing."

Though his fingers begin a distracting dance across my back and threaten to put me to sleep, I do my best to stay focused. "That's not true. There are a lot of things I don't know. Like, what's your favorite movie?"

"*Field of Dreams.*"

"Seriously?"

"Don't judge."

"When did you give up the astronaut dream?"

"When I realized I was bad at math but good at baseball. Next question."

Just like on the porch last week, we talk for hours. About everything. Movies, music, food, embarrassing childhood memories and our best friends growing up. Houston tells me all about his mom and how she was the strongest person he's ever known, even though he didn't get to know her for long before she died. I tell him about my sister and how excited she is to be a physical therapist and always has been, and I tell him about the way my mom is always looking out for other people.

It doesn't matter if the topics are inconsequential or significant—talking to Houston is so easy, like we inherently trust each other with everything, no matter how much it means to us.

I don't think there's ever a moment that Houston isn't actively touching me, whether it's rubbing his thumb along mine or massaging my neck with his strong fingers. Sometimes he runs his palm up and down my arm, and at one point he pulls the scrunchie out of my hair and runs his fingers through it, probably making it an utter mess but I don't even care. He's so good at making himself present that I enjoy every second of being in this backyard, to the point that I don't want to leave and go back to real life.

But when Houston pauses in telling a story of him and Brooklyn going trick-or-treating without telling Chad and says, "You should probably go to bed, Darce," I know he's right. I'm falling asleep in his arms, and if I let myself do that, I'm going to want to do it again and again.

Still, I groan and hide my face in his shoulder. "How are you not tired?"

"The curse of constantly being on the road. I never fall asleep easily."

"Just give me, like, five more minutes."

He laughs, and the sound echoes through his chest. "I don't think you realize how tempted I am to let you fall asleep and keep you here all night," he says, brushing my hair away from my face with his whole hand. "But if I don't walk you to your door, how am I going to kiss you goodnight?"

That wakes me right up. "Oh. Yeah. Cool." And I've already made things awkward. *Great.*

As I sit up, immediately missing his body warmth, I haphazardly wrap a blanket around myself and try to ignore the fact that it's twisted at my back. I can do this. Not be awkward. It's not my first kiss, and it's not like I don't know if he wants it. I'm not even usually this flustered by the idea of kissing someone, and yet as I struggle to my feet while clinging to this stupid blanket, I am terrified.

What is Houston going to think? Am I going to be good at it? He's had so much experience, and the last time I kissed a guy was before I became Tamlin. Ugh, has it really been more than two years? That means I'm out of practice, and I'm going to be terrible at it, and I'm walking to the door without realizing it until Houston laughs and catches up to me, pulling me to a stop and wrapping me up in a hug from behind.

"You don't have to kiss me if you don't want to," he says, his voice low and rough. "But I hope you do." I expect him to kiss my neck or cheek—he has perfect access with the way he leans his head over my shoulder—but instead he loosens his hold, giving me a chance to escape if I want to.

Why in the world would I want that? I love that he's giving me this control, and it's enough to kick my insecurities to the curb as I spin in his arms and press my lips to his. But he accepts my offering with less enthusiasm than I would have expected after all the build-up to it tonight. It's like he's afraid to truly kiss me.

It's short and sweet and *absolutely not enough*. A little moan escapes me, a cry for more, and Houston responds, capturing my mouth again, this time with more eagerness. His hands find my face, thumbs brushing my cheeks as he pulls me closer. He's so gentle, but I can feel his restraint slipping the longer he explores my lips. His hands slide down, painstakingly slow as he touches my shoulders, my arms, my wrists and fingers, leaving a trail of fire in their wake. Then they find my hips, tugging me against his body as he tilts his head and deepens the kiss in a delicious show of command that I don't want to fight because I'm always the one who has to make things happen. I surrender, letting him take charge of this moment as I get lost in his kiss.

I've wanted to be a sports journalist since my first high school baseball game, when I heard the announcer make several comments about me when I was at bat the first time. Not because of my skill but because I was a girl among boys. An outsider. A gimmick to bring attention to our team. I shut him up when I hit a home run, but I decided that night that the world of sports needed more women. More people who will praise an athlete's talents and perseverance no matter their gender or background. I love my job, and I love that I might have a chance to bring light and happiness to a judgmental sphere of media. I am on the cusp of running my own division and having the power to focus only on the good things, and it's like all of my dreams are within reach.

But here, kissing Houston Briggs, I'm thinking about giving that all up. When the man said he wanted to live deliberately, he clearly meant it, and there is nothing impulsive about the way he kisses me. Every touch, every taste, means something, and I would give anything to learn everything he wants to say. Who needs a dream job when they can have a man like this?

He breaks away first, taking a full step back as his gaze burns through me. "Sleep," he rasps, stuffing his hand into his hair. I'm pretty sure I've already mussed it up plenty on my own, and his hair is a wild mess. As he watches me admire my handiwork with what I'm sure is a slightly crazed and dazed smile, Houston groans and comes back in, this time kissing me frantically, like he can't get enough. I'm not angry about it in the slightest, and I badly want to see Houston when he drops all inhibitions. I match his eagerness with my own, grabbing onto anything I can to keep him close.

But then he pulls away again, looking pained.

With one hand still hooked onto the collar of his t-shirt, I press the other hand to my mouth, as if that might stop me from kissing him again. Mostly I can't get over how absolutely perfect it feels to kiss him. It's like we were destined to be together, designed to fill in the gaps of the other person.

He laughs, showing off his dimples as he covers my hand with his own. "Thanks for that. And goodnight, Darcy." This time he kisses my forehead, so tenderly that I might cry. How am I supposed to leave him behind?

I only make it one shaky step inside the dark dining room of my side of the house when he says, "What are you doing tomorrow?" He leans on my door frame, looking way too attractive.

I grin. "You mean you're not sick of me yet?"

He answers with a quick kiss that leaves me breathless. The man absolutely knows what he's doing.

That makes it far more difficult to say what I say next. "I have to go to Albuquerque for work tomorrow."

He frowns. "Albuquerque? Really? What kind of work?"

I probably should have given him a job that actually existed rather than telling him some vague nonsense that technically applies to journalism if you think really hard. I control a lot of data every time I do an interview. But I do my best to offer up some sort of explanation that isn't the truth—that I'm going to be interviewing the putter designer. "We have some people in Albuquerque, and I have some training I need to do." Technically it's true. Connor wants me to test out a new camerawoman who has applied to work at Enhance and happens to be from Albuquerque.

Houston's eyebrows dip as he considers what I said. "But that's, like, three hours away. You're going by yourself?"

"I do things by myself all the time."

His expression saddens, and he grabs my hand like he worries about letting me go. "But you don't have to."

"Houston." I brush my hand along his jaw. How is he real? "It's just a business trip. I'll only be gone tomorrow and Saturday."

That doesn't help the puppy-dog look he's giving me. "You're going to miss the Scorpions' game? I was hoping you could come again this week."

That was never going to happen. Not when he's planning on Tamlin running her story on him coaching the team. No face masks could get me to be in the same place twice. Still, I really hate disappointing him like this when he isn't shy about telling me how much he wants me there. But what can I do? Nothing except tell him the truth, and I haven't found my story yet. Nor do I *actually* want to lose my job, no matter how much I like him. If not for my contract...

He drops his head when he realizes my unavailability probably isn't going to change no matter how much he begs. "So I have to wait until Sunday to see you again?"

How is a man who is paid millions to throw a ball at insane speeds this cute? "Let's not go crazy," I say, leaning up on my toes and putting myself within prime kissing distance again. "I'll be back Saturday night. You can last two days, right?"

He moans and then claims my mouth yet again, leaving me feeling like the most valuable person in the world. Every place he touches lights on fire, yet his hands are impossibly gentle as he works hard to make me forget that we both need to go to bed. Who needs sleep? I need to explore this man's mouth and never leave his side.

Houston is the one to find the will to walk away again, though I can see in his eyes that he really doesn't want to. He walks the few steps to his own back door, never taking his eyes off me. "Goodnight, Darcy. Don't forget me when you're in Albuquerque."

I grin. "You're such a dork. Goodnight, Hou."

As I head upstairs to get ready for bed, I can't help but imagine a future where I don't have to say goodnight to Houston Briggs because I'm not leaving his side. I don't know if I could ever find a better man than him, so why would I ever look farther than next door?

This has been one of the best nights of my life, and nothing could dampen my mood.

Right as I climb into bed, I get a text from a number I don't recognize.

> Unknown Number:
>
> So, are you going to tell him, or am I?

Well, spam has certainly gotten creepier recently. But right before I'm about to set my phone on the nightstand and go to sleep, hopefully to dream about Houston, another text makes my stomach drop.

> Unknown Number:
>
> Houston deserves better than someone who can so easily lie to him about who she is.

I swallow, all of the happiness from what happened on the porch dissipating with these words. I don't know who figured out my secret, but whoever they are, they might ruin things before I'm ready. What if they tell Houston before I can find a way to explain why I've been lying to him without actually telling him the truth and breaking my contract?

I don't know if it even matters. Houston and I were never meant to be endgame. But that doesn't make the ache in my chest go away, nor does it do anything to dim the tingling sensation in my lips that lingers even now.

But the anonymous texter is right. Houston deserves better, and I have to let him go before I hurt us both. I'm just not sure I can.

Chapter Twenty-Six

Houston

November 1

"Briggs!"

I snap to attention, lifting my mitt just in time to avoid a ball hitting me in the ribs. It's the third time in the last hour that I've zoned out, and the guys are starting to notice. Hopkins looks ready to hit me in the side of the head with a bat, and Badir is practically glaring at me from behind home plate.

I shake my head, but it only moderately clears thoughts of Darcy from my mind. I knew it was going to be hard to concentrate on practice today, but I didn't think I would be this lost.

With the number of women I've kissed over the years, last night shouldn't have been a big deal. But it was. I've never talked with someone like that in my life, and it felt like I was laying myself bare and asking Darcy to hold my heart for me because I have nothing left to protect it. No shields or walls that she hasn't broken through. And the way she kissed me...

I'm not sure I'll ever recover.

"Yo, Briggs, are you going to throw the ball, or what?"

This isn't working. How am I supposed to concentrate on baseball when I'm already thinking she's a pretty good reason to give it up for good?

Thankfully, one of the coaches waves me off the field and tells me the manager wants me in his office. He must have noticed me staring off into space for most of the morning, but I barely care that I'm about to get a lecture.

But when I get to Fujimura's office, the team's physical therapist, Solano, is there as well, and my heart sinks. This doesn't bode well.

"Sit," Fujimura says, pointing to the chair next to Solano.

Solano winces when he gets a good look at my face as I sit next to him. "I had to tell him," he says. "You and I both know it's not getting better."

I try to convey with a look that I don't blame him for doing his job; my tongue feels like cotton in my mouth, so speaking isn't going to come easily.

Fujimura sighs, pulling my attention to him again. "How long, Briggs?"

If I don't answer honestly, Solano will probably do it for me. "The pain started about fourteen months ago."

Fujimura's eyes nearly bug out of his head, and he swears loudly. "You've been losing your arm for over a year and didn't say anything? You played the whole season!"

"I didn't want to disappoint anyone." Maybe that makes me sound pathetic or like a pushover, but it's the truth. My whole life, I've just wanted to be needed. Valuable. Someone who wouldn't get left behind again. "It's fine."

"It's not fine, Briggs. You may have done irreparable damage by ignoring this problem."

I glance at Solano, wondering just how much he told the manager because there is no "may have" in this situation. My arm is shot—pretty much has been since August—and even if I get the surgery to repair the torn ligaments, I'll probably be dealing with scar tissue and limited mobility the rest of my life. I'm pretty sure that's part of the reason I've been ignoring the problem for so long. The minute I admit the problem exists is the minute I'm officially done.

"So, what now?" Fujimura asks, rubbing his temples. "You still have a year on your contract. Can you play?"

"Yes," I say at the same time Solano emphatically says, "No." He glares at me. "You tore a tendon, Briggs. That's not a minor thing."

I cringe. "Barely tore it. Maybe." But he and I both know that continuing to pitch with the tear has only made it worse. What he doesn't know is that I played several weeks before he even found out about the injury. The only reason he knows about it is because that last Series game nearly did me in. He forced me to go to the clinic for the MRI the next day, though I almost didn't go. "I'm fine."

Fujimura glances between us. "Normally, I'd trust Solano's opinion, but you just won us a Series with a bum arm, Briggs. You clearly know your own limits. If you say you can play, then you'll play, but I'm finding us a new starting pitcher no matter what you do. We have a small rotation as it is."

He's practically asking me if I plan to retire, but for some reason I can't say one way or the other. This shouldn't be a difficult decision. I might be able to throw a few good pitches, but what use can I really be? I could barely hold Darcy in my arms last night without the pain creeping in. And yet I keep my mouth shut.

Whatever I'm trying to prove, it's going to be my end.

"So?" Fujimura says, looking between me and Solano again as he waits for a definitive answer on whether I'll be one of the starting pitchers next season.

If only I had one to give. "I'll let you know," I mutter, rising to my feet before anyone can guilt me into making a decision I'm clearly not ready to make.

"Briggs." Fujimura pierces me with his dark eyes. He took a chance on a twenty-year-old kid back when the Red-tails drafted me, and I like to think I was worth the risk. But I can see in his eyes that he's not ready to let me go, which makes this all so much harder. "Sooner than later, if you please."

Nodding, I slip out of his office and take a moment in the empty hallway to breathe. To think. Solano is right, and I will barely be able to play next season. But how can I abandon the guys? They made me a team captain for a reason, and I'm more than just a pitcher to some of them. A few of us have played together from the beginning, brothers brought together by a game we all love. And I'm supposed to just walk away without warning?

Heart sinking, I trudge to my locker to see if Darcy made it to Albuquerque safely because I need something at least moderately happy, even if that something is a couple hundred miles away. Sure enough, I've got a few texts from Darcy, and a bit of the tightness eases in my chest at the sight of her name.

She sent a picture of a chipmunk chowing down on a cracker.

I can't help but smile at the way she so easily changes my mood just by being her. I should really get back out to the field—should I, though?—but there's no way I'm going to be able to wait until later to let her know I can't get her out of my head.

Me:

> You only seem to be unlucky if I'm not around. Good thing there's an easy solution to making sure you have all the luck you need. We officially need to spend as much time together as possible, for your own safety. ;)

Me:

> I'm glad you made it to Burque in one piece, but remind me to teach you how to change a tire when you get back. Only 31 hours to go...

I haven't flirted over text since high school, but this is remarkably fun. And it's nice that I can be a total dork without worrying that Darcy might start a smear campaign against me on Twitter as soon as I don't live up to the hype.

I wait a couple of minutes to see if she'll respond, but she must be busy doing whatever training she's got. Right as I'm about to return my phone to my locker and head back outside, I get a text from Chad, which is as rare as it is concerning. Literally the last time he texted me outside of our sibling group chat was over three months ago.

Chad:

> Free to do lunch today?

"Well, this is new," I mutter, trying to come up with a reason Chad would want to get together like this. He's always been a workaholic—one could say the same about me—so we pretty much only see each other during family events. It's not that I don't want to hang with my big brother. I just don't know what his goal is.

Guess I'll have to find out. It could easily be that his girlfriend is as good for him as mine has been for me.

I send a reply, telling him what time I should be done with practice and asking for a ride since John still has my truck until I can get it back from him on Saturday.

He's waiting for me when I leave the stadium, leaning against his truck and looking perfectly calm and casual. I know better than to think his outward appearance has anything to do with what he's actually feeling, but at least he doesn't look angry. Chad may be a bit grumpy, but he rarely gets angry. When he does, it's terrifying.

"Missed me that much?" I say as I toss my gear into the truck bed. "What about your lady friend?"

"Don't call her that." He waits until we're both seated and on our way to wherever he's taking us to say anything else. When he does speak, he's hesitant. "Her name is Hope."

"And who, pray tell, is Hope?"

The slightest shade of red rises up his neck. I didn't know Chad could even *get* embarrassed. "She's…"

"Your lady friend," I repeat and brace for his punch. The hit is only half-hearted, which I appreciate. "It seems like she makes you happy. I'm happy for you, man."

"She has two kids."

"And?" If any of us were meant to be a parent, Chad was. He practically raised Brook and me, and Micah looks up to him just as much as she does her dad.

Chad lets out a deep and weary sigh, like he's finally realizing that holding up the world is exhausting. "What if I can't be enough for her? I've already messed things up once, and we're going to give things another try. But I'm not sure if…"

I don't think Chad has ever confided in me like this before, and I really don't want to waste this opportunity to help him the way he's helped me so many times in the past, whether he knew it or not.

"I'm going to be serious for a second, okay?"

He glances at me. "Is that possible?"

"Only on rare occasions."

"Blow me away, Texas."

He's the only one who still regularly calls me that, and I grin at the nickname. "I know for a fact I haven't ever thanked you, but you were the best big brother anyone could have asked for."

He pulls into the tiny parking lot of our favorite Mexican restaurant, but he doesn't look away from the windshield even after he turns off the truck. I doubt he expected me to say anything like that.

So I keep going. "You got the short end of the straw, being so much older than us, and when Mom died, you never got a chance to really mourn." As if he isn't fully aware of all of this. "The State made us go back with Dad, which meant you suddenly became a parent at fifteen, but I never once heard you complain. You may think we didn't realize how crazy it was that a teenager would have to get a job to make sure there was food on the table, but we did."

There's definitely something stuck in my throat, which is ridiculous because I haven't eaten anything all morning. There's no way it's emotion choking me up. Not a chance.

"It might make me sound ungrateful," I say, quieter now, "but I was mad when Lloyd worked the courts so he could take us in. I felt like he was shoving it in your face that he was so much better than you, even if that's stupid."

"It's not stupid," Chad mumbles. "I hated him for the first few years because he did what I couldn't. I didn't have the stability to get guardianship after I turned eighteen."

"But you tried?" I hadn't even considered the notion that Chad might have tried to get custody of Brook and me once he became an adult, even if that's exactly what I wanted as a kid.

He nods, staring at the steering wheel now instead of out the window. I can't imagine how hard he must have taken that. Years of taking care of us, and the government told him he wasn't good enough?

I clear my throat. "My point is you've always looked out for us, and you are always going to do what's best for the people you love. Even if that means letting our rich stepdad try to buy me a Charger when I graduated."

Chad chokes, looking over at me in alarm. "He did that?"

"*Tried* is the key word. I refused it, obviously."

"You and I have different notions of obvious."

"Can we get back on track? You're clearly in love with Hope, and I don't think there's anyone in the world who will try harder to give her the life she wants. As long as she looks out for you too, then I'm happy for you."

"She's twenty-four."

It's my turn to choke, only I manage to get a mouthful of saliva into my lungs and nearly suffocate trying to clear it so I can breathe again. "Oh," is all I manage to get out.

Chad smiles, shaking his head. "I know twelve years is a lot. I never planned on my relationship with her being anything more than platonic.

Or reluctantly civil. But she crawled under my skin and made herself comfortable."

"That is the grossest metaphor."

He punches my arm. "Shut up. Hungry?"

"Starving. Are you going to tell me why you're treating me to lunch?"

"You're definitely picking up the bill, Texas. Unless you're still going to try to convince me your wallet isn't as big as your ego."

Laughing, I follow him inside and buy enough tacos to make us both sick.

"But seriously," I say as we settle in a corner booth—Chad likes to face the door and watch the whole room. "As much as I enjoyed that unexpected heart-to-heart, I know you had other motives. You and I aren't exactly buddy-buddy."

"But we could be, right?" For the first time, Chad looks a little nervous. "I mean, you trust me, yeah?"

I grimace. There could only be one reason he is now looking at me with pity, and I'm pretty sure I don't want to hear what he came to say. "What did you do?"

"How much do you really know about Darcy Paxton?"

Now I regret buying him tacos. "I told you not to look into her! We're not talking about this, Chad." Even if a morbid curiosity is creeping up now that I know there's something. It could be completely inconsequential, even though I can't deny the fact that Chad is usually pretty good about ignoring the details that don't matter and focusing on the important stuff.

Or whatever he found could explain the reason for my hesitation up until last night. I had to have the gut feeling of distrust for a reason beyond my issues, right?

Chad watches me as if waiting for me to give him the green light to ruin the best relationship I've ever had. Sure, it just started, but up until thirty seconds ago I was pretty dang happy.

I groan, dropping my head onto the table. "Do I have reason to be worried?"

"I'm not sure."

"Then why bring this up?"

"Because I don't like not being sure. I'm just looking out for you, Hou."

"Is she dangerous or something?" That's pretty hard to imagine. Darcy is the kind of girl who stops and feeds a chipmunk because it's cute. Who makes friends with tired, working parents who do whatever they can to make sure their boys get to have some fun in a game they love. Who nearly convinces me that leaving baseball won't be the end of the world every time she gives me a smile.

Chad sighs. "Again, I'm not sure. It depends on how you define dangerous."

"Just tell me."

"I don't think you really want to know. If I tell you, it's not something you can unknow."

I slowly lift my head, wishing I had been a worse brother and ignored his text. I could have still been living in my happy bubble. "Then don't tell me. If it's important, I'll figure it out on my own."

"Even if it might be too late?"

It might already be too late. I've fallen for her, and I doubt there is much that will get in the way of that outside of something truly shocking. I don't think Darcy is capable of lying, though she may be good at stretching the truth or skirting around issues. Is that any better? I don't know. But I don't want my brother putting a rift between us that doesn't need to be there.

Chad's phone pings, and he pulls up some sort of video.

I recognize Tamlin's voice immediately and roll my eyes. "You set up an alert for Tamlin Park? Why?"

"Because you took an interest in her. And she's clearly interested in you." He goes quiet as he turns up the volume on a live video on Tamlin's social media page, turning his phone so I can see.

"Harrison claims he has designed the perfect putter," she says brightly as she stands in the middle of a sunny golf course, "and so far it has lived up to the hype. Why don't you tell us about this putter, Mr. Harrison."

The guy—a middle aged man with a subdued demeanor—quietly explains some of the details about the putter and all of the tests he put it through before he settled on what he thinks is the perfect design.

"And how about you demonstrate it a few times and show us how it makes the shot every time?"

The guy does so, moving around to several balls that have already been placed at different distances around the hole. He hits each one in with precision, and Tamlin gets more excited every time. I don't know if I've ever seen her smile this much while on camera. Especially not this real smile. There isn't a single trace of fake in that smile, and she's practically glowing out there in the sunshine.

"Isn't that amazing?" Tamlin says to whomever is holding the camera. "Now, let's see if I can make it work. I happen to be a pretty good golfer, but I'm hoping this putter will help me qualify for The Masters."

She lines up her shot—from the looks of things, she really does have some skills with the sport—but her swing is just a little too hard and the ball overshoots the hole. Her next shot rolls along the hole's edge but doesn't make it in. Her final putt looks like it's going to be perfect, but then it stops just shy of falling in.

Though Harrison looks horrified, Tamlin is more excited than ever.

"Well, you're not trying very hard," Harrison mumbles. I don't think he remembered he's got a mic attached to his collar.

Tamlin's smile doesn't falter. "Tell you what," she says. "If I don't make this shot, I owe you a hundred bucks. I don't like to lose."

I know that much about her, and I chuckle a little thinking about how competitive she was at trivia night. If I had swallowed my ego and let her answer more questions, we probably would have won.

I really should send her a picture of my tutu. She'd get a kick out of that.

Harrison agrees to the bet, and Tamlin drops another golf ball about three yards from the hole. She lines up, sticking her tongue between her lips, and hits the ball. Yet again, it rolls right to the edge of the hole but doesn't make it in.

Harrison looks devastated, like he's about ready to tear the mic off and head straight back to his workshop.

Tamlin, on the other hand, puts her hand on his arm and sends him a warm smile that looks so familiar, even if I've barely been around her enough to get a natural smile like that. That smile feels like it's a part of me somehow. "How about this?" she says and tosses a few more balls onto the green. "If you can sink all of these, I'll give you a thousand bucks."

Harrison's eyes nearly bug out of his head. "What? Why? It's clearly not a perfect putter."

"Humor me. We may still prove there's a perfect putter here."

I get what she's going for. Harrison has probably spent so much time testing his putters that he'll be able to hit every single ball in without problem, no matter which club he uses. Did Tamlin expect that the whole time? She must have, with the way she's ready to prove her point.

Sure enough, Harrison hits one, two, three balls in perfectly. He lines up to the fourth, sweat beading on his forehead, and takes his time with this one. He shouldn't have worried. The ball rolls right into the hole along with the others, and Tamlin grins so wide she looks like she might start laughing.

"Well, there you have it," she tells the camera. "No tool can be perfect, but if you take the time to practice like Larry Harrison, *you* could be. I'm Tamlin Park from Enhance Media, enjoying the sun here in Albuquerque. Hey Harrison, how about a round of golf? Just know, I'm nowhere near as talented as you, so I'll probably need some pointers. Until next time!" She salutes the camera, and the video ends.

That's the kind of stories she should be telling. The ones that celebrate the average athlete or the people who have worked hard to get to where they are. I can't imagine she enjoys tearing people down the way she has been over the last couple of years. And the way she smiled? I could get used to a smile like that.

Chad clears his throat. *Right*. Lunch.

I sit up—I'd been leaning closer to the screen apparently—just in time for our tacos to arrive. "What?"

He raises an eyebrow. "If only you could see the stupid smile on your face. You sure you don't have any interest in the reporter?"

Is he serious? "I'm dating Darcy."

"You are apparently dating Tamlin too. How was La Bella, anyway? I've always wanted to go there."

My jaw drops. "Did you look into me too? What the hell, Chad?"

"Language."

"Shut up."

"Hou, I'm just trying to—"

"You're not my dad." As soon as those words leave my mouth, I regret them. And not just because it makes me sound thirteen instead of twenty-eight. I've hurt him, even if he tries to play it off as nothing.

I swallow, my appetite gone. "I didn't mean that. You're a hundred times the man he is, and I know you're trying to help me. But this is the first time I really feel like I've been in charge of my own life. I just need to figure this out on my own, okay?"

My dating life isn't the only decision I need to make in my life right now, and Fujimura's words echo in my head, giving me a headache. Why did all of this have to happen at once? Why couldn't I have figured out my future and *then* met Darcy? Or Tamlin? Whichever one isn't going to end up breaking my heart. As it stands right now, I might be the one to break my own heart if I keep being so confused about everything.

I'm not supposed to be interested in Tamlin, but every time I see her, it's like I'm pulled closer in her orbit because I learn something new. I see more of the real woman beneath the perfect mask.

"You okay, Texas?"

"Probably not," I admit. "It shouldn't be possible to fall for two women at the same time, right?"

He almost smiles, which isn't what I expected. "It's unlikely," he agrees.

"I like Darcy. A lot. I feel like I can be myself around her without any expectations, and she's always been so genuine." And then there's the fact that I really like kissing her and can't wait to do it again when I see her tomorrow night.

"But?"

I never thought I'd see the day when I went to *Chad* for dating advice. He dated the same awful woman for six years up until about seven months ago, and before that I rarely saw him go out. And yet here I sit, desperate for him to tell me what I should do.

I shove my hands into my hair. "But you might be right about the way I feel about Tamlin. I'm more excited to see her tomorrow than I realized. I thought we'd both decided that we would work better as friends, but I'm clearly not thinking of us as just friends."

As he grabs a taco, Chad mutters something that sounds like, "You're not the only one."

And I go on high alert. "What is that supposed to mean?" I ask right as he stuffs the entire taco in his mouth.

He takes his time chewing, something I know he does on purpose because Chad is generally a vacuum cleaner, especially when it comes to good Mexican food. "I thought you wanted to figure things out on your own," he finally says after swallowing.

Is he trying to drive me crazy? Because it's working. "You are infuriating," I grumble.

"I'm your brother. I'm supposed to be infuriating. Are you going to make me eat all of these on my own?"

"Definitely not. You're fat enough as it is."

We spend the next twenty minutes eating in silence and watching highlights from last night's Lobos game, and a text comes in from Darcy right as we're heading back to Chad's truck.

Darcy:

Twenty-eight more hours.

Warmth spreads through me knowing she's counting down the hours like I am. But there's a bit of unease churning in my stomach as well. (I'm hoping that's just too much hot sauce and not actual foreboding.) A lot can happen in a day, and I'm going to be spending a good chunk of tomorrow with Tamlin.

Let's hope I'm not as much of an idiot as I think I am, or I'm going to ruin everything by being indecisive.

GREY
BIRD
TAVERN

Chapter Twenty-Seven

Darcy

November 2

I SPEND MY SATURDAY morning on the baseball field making a game plan with the cameraman I borrowed from a local news network, all the while eagerly anticipating the moment Houston arrives. I shouldn't be this excited, considering I'm dressed as Tamlin right now and can't kiss him like I've been wanting to do for the last day and a half. But I am. Every moment I get to spend with him is a good moment, and I don't know how many more I'm going to get.

I haven't heard anything else from my mysterious texter, but it's only a matter of time.

I feel like everything is coming to a head, like the storm that's been brewing in the distance is just a few miles away. Technically, my contract prohibits me from telling anyone outside of Enhance that Darcy and Tamlin are the same person—something Connor reminded me *again* after he complimented me on yesterday's putter story—but how am I supposed to keep lying to Houston when I'm pretty sure I'm in love with him?

I would think falling that fast would be impossible if my parents hadn't known on their first date that they were meant to be. Dad may have been a good deal older than Mom, but they talked about their future lives together over the ice cream they shared that first date. If that can lead into a strong thirty-year marriage, surely it's not so crazy that after a couple of weeks of spending most of my time either with or thinking about someone, I'm head over heels. Right?

It probably doesn't matter. The moment I tell Houston I've been lying to him this whole time is the moment I lose him, and that's exactly what I deserve.

"You good, Miss Park?" Ricardo, the cameraman, raises an eyebrow at me, which means I've probably been standing here lost in thought for way too long.

I give my body a shake, hoping to shake my growing dread. "Sorry, it's been a long couple of weeks. Do you have any questions? Think you can keep the kids out of focus?"

He nods with a smile, and I admire his confidence. Most local cameramen tend to be intimidated by me, like the one in Albuquerque who either stared at me or refused to make eye contact. "Like I said, if we keep you and Briggs here in this spot, I'll have enough space to frame everything how you want. Easy peasy."

"Perfect. Thanks for being willing to come out on a Saturday. I'll make sure you get that autograph from Briggs." Hopefully Houston is okay with that...

Five minutes later, the first coach arrives with a couple of the boys, and we shift over to the side to stay out of the way until Houston gets here and can talk through everything before we start. I hope to get everything done while the kids are warming up so we don't disrupt their game.

I know the minute Houston arrives, even before I see him. The air shifts, like it crackles with electricity that makes the hair on the back of my neck stand up. Shivering with anticipation, I force myself to remain seated on my bench, even after he comes around the bleachers and catches sight of me.

I meet his smile, the full-dimpled one that I've missed the last day and a half. "You ready for this, Coach?" I ask when he comes up to me.

He eyes Ricardo, who nearly vibrates with excitement. "You're going to let me control what info goes out?" he asks, though I don't think it's because he doesn't trust me. I think he's just generally worried about compromising these boys because there's a lot of pressure on his shoulders with this story.

I stand and step closer to him, lowering my voice so only he can hear me. "This is all you. I wish I didn't have to tell the story, but..."

"But the secret is out regardless," he finishes for me. Okay, but why is he looking at me so intently? Did I forget my contacts or something?

No, because Jesse is ridiculously good at his job and doesn't allow a hair out of place before I go on camera. He refused to let me go to Albuquerque without him yesterday, even though I insisted I'd be fine as long as he made me up before I left. He spent an extra ten minutes on me before Harrison and I started talking, just to make sure I looked absolutely perfect.

So, there has to be some other reason that Houston is looking at me like I've got a cooler full of ice-cold drinks on a hot day.

"Uh, Ricardo was hoping you could sign his hat," I say, feeling too warm beneath Houston's gaze.

Glancing at my cameraman again, Houston flashes a quick smile and holds out his hand. "Sure. You a fan?"

Ricardo nearly drops his camera—I grab it for him, and dang this thing is heavy—as he scrambles to pull a Sharpie out of his pocket while simultaneously dropping his hat three times. "Yes! Yes, sir! Been to nearly every Red-tails game here in Sun City!" Then he launches into a recap of the final World Series game while Houston gives me an amused look.

I didn't realize he was that big of a fan, I silently tell him.

Whether he understands me or not, Houston's return expression seems to say, *How come you never fawned over me like this?* I'm probably projecting, but when I think about it, I don't really have an answer. I had plenty of respect and admiration for Houston Briggs before meeting him at the last Series game, but the moment he stepped into the press tent, any awe or inadequacy I might have been feeling just vanished. Not in a bad way, but in a way that made me realize he was human.

I think that's what has made it so easy to fall for him. He's just a guy—insanely attractive and athletic, yes—and I'm just a girl. What more does anyone need?

"I'm going to get everyone going on warmups," Houston says as he hands Ricardo's hat back to him, now sporting a swirling signature on the brim. "Then I'll be good to go."

"I'll be here," I reply and nearly swoon at the smile he gives me. That man's lips should not be allowed to do so many knee-weakening maneuvers.

Before I know it, Houston and I are side by side as boys throw balls to each other behind us. Ricardo gives me a thumbs up, and I lift up my microphone like I've done a hundred times before. But this feels so much different. Usually, it's me and them. I have a plan going into it, and the athletes I talk to are sweating bullets. But Houston is pretty relaxed beside me, all things considered, and I am far too aware of the fact that his arm keeps brushing against mine every time one of us moves. He doesn't have to stand that close, but he does it anyway.

We're in this *together*.

"Good morning from gorgeous Sun City, New Mexico! I'm Tamlin Park from Enhance Media, and I'm here with none other than Houston Briggs, top starting pitcher for the Sun City Red-tails. He's hot off his win at the World Series, but an unstoppable arm is not the only secret weapon in Houston's arsenal. We're here on one of many baseball fields scattered across the state, where kids of all ages learn not only the skills to play an exciting game of baseball, but also how to be part of a team. Houston, what can you say about the Little League circuit here in Sun City?"

For a second, I think maybe he's gotten nervous and isn't sure what to say, but when I glance at him, he's staring at me with a little half-grin that has my face heating. He clears his throat and looks back at the camera. "Here in Sun City, we have so many Little League teams that some of these kids only play against each other once or twice in their entire League careers. I guess you could say we have a lot of Red-tails fans."

"Or Houston Briggs fans," I counter with a wink.

He chuckles. "I'm only part of the team. It takes all of us to win games, just like it does with these kids."

"And what do you have to do with all of this?" I ask. I really should be focusing on the camera, but that would be a lot easier to manage if Houston wasn't so focused on *me*.

"Well, I really don't get much of a chance to come out to games and practices during the season, but when I do have free time, I like to come out and help coach. A lot of these kids need a good role model, so I'm here to show them what *not* to do."

I snort a little laugh, then cover my mouth with my hand in horror. I have never *snorted* on TV before.

Houston laughs. "No, I really just want to do whatever I can to help these kids succeed, whether it's in baseball or school or anything else. They need all the support they can get, and I'm sure every team would love some more fans."

I force myself to turn back to the camera. "They've already converted one new fan. I'll be right there in the stands, rooting for all of these kids no matter which side they're on."

"You mean you're not going to cheer for *my* team?" Houston asks, eyes dancing as he pulls my attention to him again as he folds his arms. "I thought I'd managed to turn you to the dark side."

Oh goodness, he should not be looking at me like that. A shiver runs through me, which is ridiculous because I'm pretty sure the temperature just rose to a hundred degrees over the last ten seconds.

Ricardo clears his throat.

I jump, turning back to the camera and plastering on a smile. "Well, maybe I'm hoping a certain team wins, but no matter who scores the most runs, all of these kids are winners in my book. I'm Tamlin Park for Enhance. Until next time!"

As soon as Ricardo lowers the camera, I consider running away from TV and never looking back because that was completely awful. *Connor* is going to see that. He's going to watch that clip and immediately order me to get on a plane back to Missouri. He'll tell me that I've lost all sense of professionalism and that the director spot is going to go to Stan in marketing who gets nervous when he has to ask someone to move when they're standing in front of the vending machine and I'll be stuck training interns for the rest of my life and watching them move on to bigger and better things like I never will and—

"I think that was great!" Houston says, clapping his hands. "Ricardo, what do you think?"

Ricardo flushes red but nods. "Looked like a winner to me. Maybe people will start coming out to games. I didn't know there were that many teams in SC."

"What's your take, Tam?"

I jump when Houston touches my arm. "What?"

He grins. "Think we spun the story the right way?"

"Oh, absolutely. Definitely. Undoubt..." I stop myself before I get too far.

And now I have a choice to make. I could run back home and turn myself back into Darcy in time to catch the end of the game and pretend I managed to come back early. Or I could stay put and not waste a minute of getting to watch Houston in his element as the part of me that actually understands the sport. Tamlin won't have to play dumb, but Darcy is more likely to get a kiss.

What do I really want here? A friend or a boyfriend?

I wish I could have both.

"Mind if I stick around for the game?" I ask. "Ricardo, you can send that footage to Enhance, right?"

"Yes, ma'am. Thanks for hiring me, and thank you for the autograph, Mr. Briggs."

Houston grimaces. "You can call me Houston."

Ricardo nearly squeals, which is not the sound I would have expected from a burly man of forty. "Thank you! It's an honor! I'll get that footage sent right away, Miss Park."

He scurries off, looking like he's just had the best ten minutes of his life.

"You're going to stay and watch the game?" Houston asks.

He sounds so surprised that when I turn to look at him, I spin so fast that I nearly twist right into him. He catches my arm, and I'm pretty sure his touch leaves a brand on my bare skin. No way I'm looking to check.

"If that's okay," I say, rethinking my decision not to tap out and let Darcy take the reins for the rest of today.

Houston is still holding my arm, though I'm not entirely sure he realizes that. "I was hoping you would."

Does he want Darcy or Tamlin at this game? Because he's said pretty much the same to both, and now he's not the only one who is confused. Houston Briggs isn't a player, as far as I know, and neither does he know my secret. He's definitely not good at hiding something big like that. Then again, he probably thinks the same thing about me.

"Houston!" One of the other coaches waves him over.

Houston hesitates for only a moment, and then he presses a kiss to my cheek that knocks me down to the bench behind me as he runs off to gather the boys for a pregame speech or something. I. Am. In. Trouble.

But not as much trouble as I'm about to be in. Halfway through the game, two texts come in. One from the same unknown number as Halloween, and the other from my boss. The first one gives me some measure of relief but with a healthy dose of new nerves as I read it.

Unknown Number:

My brother may be in love with both sides of you, but you know this is going to hurt him when he finds out the truth. I'd rather it didn't come from me, and I don't think you want him to figure it out on his own. Tell him who you are before this destroys him. Please.

The latter absolutely ties my stomach into knots.

Connor:

That story was great! Very impressed people over here, though it's going to need a bit of editing before we post it. It's clear you're no longer impartial when it comes to Briggs. I'm giving you until Wednesday to figure out why Briggs isn't throwing pitches at practice, or I'm pulling you out. For your own safety.

GREY
BIRD
TAVERN

Chapter Twenty-Eight

Darcy

THE NUMBER OF TIMES I nearly got up and disappeared without giving Houston any warning was only exceeded by the number of parents who came up to me to tell me how much they like watching me on TV because I tell it how it is. And I thought about running *a lot.* Chad—I'm assuming that's who texted me—has me spooked. Not because he's a private investigator—thank you, Google—and apparently knows that Tamlin and Darcy are the same person. (I'll admit it's a little freaky how quickly he figured that out.) No, Chad's text scared me because I'm pretty sure he means Houston is likely going to figure out my secret pretty soon.

I mean, how can he not? Houston's not an idiot. Even if he hasn't fully pieced it together yet, I'm pretty sure it's lurking in the back of his mind. The more interest he shows in me, the more he's going to notice that beneath the faux surface I'm the same person I've always been.

The same lying, selfish woman who just spent the last hour watching Houston interact with each boy individually in a way that makes it impossible to deny how I feel about him.

As the Scorpions scrape out a win against the Mountain Lions, I consider texting Chad back and asking him for advice on how to admit the truth to Houston. There are so many layers of pathetic to that idea, though. I don't think Chad would take kindly to learning I'm winging this as I go, and he would probably ask why I've been lying in the first place. He seems like the kind of guy who values relationships over a career, so I don't imagine him being sympathetic to my reasoning unless I were to explain the ins and outs of the whole situation.

That's too much to put into a text to a guy I've only been around for a couple of hours.

I keep to the bleachers while the boys clear the field and parents follow them. Houston hasn't left the diamond. It's like he's waiting for something, but I don't know what... He turns, meeting my gaze, and gestures for me to join him.

My feet are on their way before I can stop them, bringing me right up to Houston's side.

"Congratulations on win—"

"Want to play?" He holds up a bat and smirks at me, almost like he's taunting me.

Not *like*. He *is* taunting me, raising an eyebrow at me like he knows I'm going to refuse because I'm in slacks and wedge heels.

Competitiveness creeps up, red hot and heady, and I snatch the bat out of his hand. "Don't go easy on me, Briggs."

"Never in the plan," he replies, and he picks up a few balls before heading to the pitcher's mound. I have no idea what his intention is, but I'm abnormally excited to see what it's like to be on the receiving end of one of his pitches.

But now Connor is in my head, asking questions I didn't know needed to be asked. Is Houston really not throwing any pitches at practice? How does Connor even know that? Why haven't I been trying harder to figure out what this story is so I have a better idea of what might happen going down the road?

Does Houston look worried about pitching to me? I'm probably projecting again. He's not even going to be throwing that hard, and I doubt he—

Houston suddenly winds up and throws a pitch that zooms past me at a terrifying speed. It's been a while since I went to the batting cages, and I never put the speed on the machine up to pro levels. He may be slower than most pitchers—the curse of being a lefty as well as on the high end of average player age—but that doesn't mean he's slow.

I glare at him. "Trying to intimidate me, Briggs?"

His grin lights up in a way that I know he's never done in a game. He might be enjoying teasing me, but I'm pretty sure he also just loves playing baseball without all the pressure. "Just getting warmed up, Park."

He picks up another ball, and this time I'm ready for him. But my bat hits nothing but air.

"I thought you said you played," he says with a wink.

"Yeah, well, it's been a few years." I fix my stance, adjusting my grip on the bat and wishing Jesse had put my hair up today. I'm always too afraid to mess up the wig to do anything with it myself. But I can make this work. "Bring it, superstar."

I clip the edge of the ball this time, sending it up and over the small fence between the bleachers and the diamond. Improvement! But not good enough.

Houston smirks at me, knuckling the next ball as he waits for me to get ready. "You sure you're up for this?" he asks, as if he wasn't the one who challenged me in the first place.

"Throw the dang ball!"

He does, and I catch the signs of a curve ball just in time to adjust my swing. The ball collides with the bat with a crack and sails over Houston's head. Even though I am absolutely not dressed for this, I take off running around the bases. We'll pretend the diamond is regulation size instead of adapted smaller for the kids. Just to make me feel better.

I'm rounding third and on my way to home when Houston returns with the ball, trying to beat me back. I consider sliding despite what I'm wearing, but I'd rather not have to pay for the damage that would bring to these clothes. Besides, Houston is faster than me.

Instead of simply tagging me out, he slips into my path and wraps his arm around my waist, swinging me around as my momentum keeps me going. We spin twice before settling just before home plate, Houston pinning me to his side as he heaves for breath.

"Dang, Park," he gasps, and he doesn't seem to be trying to hide how winded he is. It's like he wants me to know how hard he had to try to catch me.

I don't care about that. I care that he's holding me so close, his face only inches from mine. We breathe together, chests rising and falling in unison, and his fingers tighten around my waist as he finds a way to pull me even closer. I feel every part of him that touches me, like my body has become attuned to his. His bicep flexes beneath my fingers, warm and solid through his sleeve, his breath brushes my hair, and his eyes never once stray from mine, leaving me dizzy.

If I wasn't dressed as Tamlin, I would know exactly how to respond to this moment, but I feel completely lost when it comes to this man. What am I supposed to do?

When his brow dips, his gaze growing confused, I pull from his hold and pick up the bat, holding it out to him like nothing intimate just happened even though the Darcy side of me is screaming. Why am I the confused one when Houston has every right to be completely bewildered?

"Thanks for pitching a slow one for me," I say, giving him a neutral smile.

That just confuses him more, though he seems to shake his confusion away as he settles on the nearest bench. "That wasn't slow."

I roll my eyes, sitting beside him. "Of course it wasn't."

"No, really. All of those were my regular pitches."

I'm about to argue when he lifts his eyebrows. "Wait, are you serious? I hit one of your actual pitches?"

"I'm as surprised as you are."

I punch him in the arm. "Are you insinuating I wasn't a good batter in high school?"

"I'm insinuating you haven't been on a team in almost a decade," Houston says with a chuckle. "So forgive me for being surprised that you managed to hit the curve that struck out twelve different players last season."

"Not that you were keeping track or anything."

"It is kind of my job, so of course I was keeping track."

"What would you do if you weren't playing baseball?" The question slips off my tongue before I can hold it back.

I expect Houston to be caught off guard, which he clearly is when his eyes go wide. But what I don't expect is the way his right hand goes to his left shoulder and grips the muscle for half a second before he brings his hand back to his lap.

"I haven't really thought about it," he says.

Liar.

"I mean, I'll have to think about it eventually. Can't play forever." The way he winces when he says that feels like a hand closing around my heart and giving it a painful squeeze. His entire adult life—and most of his childhood—has been baseball, and I can't imagine it will be an easy transition into something else. But is that transition going to be sooner or later?

"You only have a year left on your contract, right?" I ask.

He shrugs, poorly hiding another wince as if that movement was too much for his shoulder. He *did* just throw some intense pitches without warming up, but if Connor was right about him not pitching at practice, something tells me this is more than a little discomfort.

Pitchers' arms go out all the time, but no one has mentioned anything about Houston losing mobility. Unless Houston himself mentioned something? When he answered that phone call the other day, he threw out that scientific word I didn't understand. I have no idea how to spell what he said, but maybe Carissa could tell me what it is if I remember it right. Super-something?

If Enhance got wind of Houston Briggs being injured before any other news outlets figured it out, our site would explode.

"Yeah, just a year," Houston says, speaking with his voice carefully controlled. He's hiding something in that.

"Think you'll continue playing if the Red-tails want to keep you when it's over?"

He tries to smile but doesn't do a great job with it. "When did this turn into an interview? Speaking of interviews, that story you did yesterday with the golfer was awesome."

I freeze, my heart sinking. And not just because he's changing the subject, which probably means I'm on the right track. No, my heart sinks because I'm quickly realizing I made a mistake in telling him Darcy was going to Albuquerque. Did I mention in the video that I was in Albuquerque? I'm pretty sure I did. But maybe he didn't make the connection. "You watched it?"

Houston fights a more natural smile as he watches me try not to panic. "Yeah. Why is that so terrifying?"

Maybe I'm safe? "I guess it feels weird to connect to a viewer. They're usually faceless masses in my head."

"So, I'm just a viewer?"

Oh, he's definitely more than that.

Houston nudges my arm when I don't reply. "Well, it really was great. You should do more inspirational stories like that. You really seemed to enjoy that one."

He's not wrong. Harrison was so sweet after he realized what I was saying, and he tried to refuse the money that I offered him. Or, he did until he realized it was part of a sponsorship by a company hoping to help patent his putter. "The putter may not have been perfect, but it was really well made," I tell Houston. "Regardless, I knew going into it that Harrison was probably the reason the ball went in every time, but he was convinced it couldn't be skill over craftsmanship. I felt like someone needed to acknowledge his talent."

Houston lets his smile loose, hitting me with its full force and almost making me glad for the change in subject. "Are you going to tell more stories like that?"

I decide to be brave and take one step toward admitting the truth. Chad is right, and my time is running out. I'd rather Houston hear the truth straight from me, but that's impossible. "I'm actually trying to get a director spot over a new segment that will focus on people who defy the odds and do great things."

"That's amazing! You're a shoo-in, I'm sure."

"Well, that depends."

"On what?"

"On the story I find here."

Frowning, he glances around the empty diamond as if he might find the story lurking about. "Little League?"

If only… "No, there's something else here. Something big. I'm not sure what it is yet, but the board is looking to see what I do with it when I find it."

As he considers that, Houston's eyes go distant. Wherever he's gone, it's taken his smile away, and I really don't like that. But how do I get it back?

"What are you thinking about?" I ask instead of assuming I can read him at all right now. It is way too dangerous for me to start thinking his shoulder is going out when I don't have any hard evidence to support that theory.

He surprises me with his ready answer. "I'm thinking about how you're going to go back to St. Louis as soon as your job is done here."

He's…what? "That was always the plan," I say, too confused to think of anything else. Why would that matter? For Darcy, sure, but Tamlin? We've only been friends, if that, though my mind wanders back to the way he held me at the gala. And the look he just gave me on the diamond. Both are moments I'll relive for the rest of my life. "I need to get back to my office eventually."

"What if you didn't?" He turns, blue eyes boring into mine.

And even if the question could easily be an innocent one, my heart doesn't listen. It beats *mine mine mine* in my chest until I can't help but cross the distance and press my lips to his.

At first, he's frozen, understandably shocked by my forwardness. But then he slides a hand behind my neck and dives into the kiss. For about five seconds. Then he jerks away and touches his thumb to his lips as he stares at me like I'm the culprit here.

I am. He's right. That was so completely stupid!

"I'm sorry," I gasp, and I mean it. I shouldn't have done that. It wasn't good for my sanity, and worst of all it only complicates things for Houston. He's probably beating himself up inside because two women are throwing themselves at him and he can't figure out why he's attracted to both of us. Maybe that's entirely wrong and I am in over my head with this whole thing.

That last part is definitely true.

"I'm sorry," I say again because the first time didn't feel like enough. "I know we said we're only friends. And that's good. It *should* be that way. I didn't mean to—"

His mouth is on mine before I can finish that sentence, hungrily searching for an answer to a question he didn't ask. Though a voice in the back of my head tells me to quit before this blows up in my face, Houston's lips speak louder. He's drowning out all of my thoughts, pulling me deeper and deeper until the only thing I'm aware of is how familiar this is. It doesn't matter that our first kiss was only two days ago or that Houston thinks *this* is our first; Houston Briggs feels like home, and a future, and every dream coming true with each brush of his lips on mine.

When he breaks away, a little moan escapes out of me, missing the contact I just shared with him. I'm being greedy, and I barely care.

Houston cares. His gaze is hard and full of concentration as he examines my face. Touches my lips with his fingertips. Leans in close again.

And then suddenly he's gone, stalking toward the parking lot without looking back.

I could be wrong, but if that kiss felt familiar to me, odds are high it felt familiar to him too. Houston isn't stupid, and makeup only goes so far. If anyone is stupid, it's me for thinking it wouldn't be dangerous to fall in love with a man who deserves so much more than a liar.

Chapter Twenty-Nine

Houston

I POUND ON THE front door of a house I've never been to and don't stop, not even when my fist starts to ache from its impact with the wood. I don't even know if he's home, but I couldn't think of where else to go and I'm desperate for him to tell me what to do.

When Kit opens the door, I nearly break down with relief. "Houston?" he says, eyes going wide. "What are you doing here?"

"I couldn't..." Nope. There aren't any words to capture all the things that have gone through my head during the last two hours it took to drive here. (Maybe it was an hour and a half. Don't judge my speeding; I'm in crisis.)

Kit steps back, allowing me into his house. "Just breathe," he says gently.

You'd think I would have gotten over the initial shock by now, but no. Being stuck in my truck with no company except my thoughts got me overthinking to the point that I nearly had to pull over in the middle of nowhere and scream into the desert void.

"What's going on?" It isn't Kit who asks that. It's one of his friends, the ones he calls Wonder Friends or something like that. I've met them only once, when they came to a game last year, but I can't remember any of their names. I liked this one. He played baseball in high school and looks like a personal trainer. Actually, now that I think about it, he might *be* a personal trainer.

"Cam," Kit says as his friend joins his side while I stand here on the verge of hyperventilating. "You remember Houston Briggs, right?"

Cam coughs out a laugh. "Is that a trick question? You okay, man?"

I shake my head. I am so not okay. Not when everything I thought I knew might be a lie.

"Sit." Cam says that in such a commanding tone that I instantly obey, falling onto the couch in Kit's front room. "Take a breath."

I do my best, though it feels pretty pathetic. I swear I can do better than that.

As he crouches down in front of me, eyebrows low, Cam holds out a set of keys. "Hang on to these for me for a second, okay?"

I don't understand, but I'm too tired to argue. The keys are warm from being in his pocket, and I rub my thumb along the edge of one, feeling each ridge as I go.

Cam nods as if I need him to praise my key-holding skills, and then he turns to Kit. "Does it smell like the brownies are done?"

I don't smell any brownies. Have I lost my sense of smell? Am I dying?

"I don't smell them yet," Kit says with a shrug.

"At least you got your thermostat fixed so it's no longer freezing in here," Cam says.

It's definitely too warm in here. Or, it was when I got here. Compared to outside, at least. It's amazing how just a couple of hours of driving can completely change the temperature. Diamond Springs is at a much higher elevation than Sun City, and the air outside has a crisp quality that I didn't think about until now. I love fall, but it's only just starting to cool down in Sun City. I think I'm starting to cool down too.

"We should make brownies for real," Kit says. "That sounds delicious."

Wait, what? "There aren't any brownies?" I ask, oddly disappointed by this news.

Laughing, Cam pats my knee before standing back to his full height. "Welcome back. You can keep my keys if you need to."

I glance down to where I'm still rubbing my thumb along the key's rough edge. I can breathe again in a way I haven't been able to for the last two hours.

Since I kissed Tamlin and realized she might be...

I gulp. So much for breathing.

"So, are we going to talk about why Houston Briggs is having a panic attack in your living room?" someone new asks.

I cringe as two more guys come into the room after poking their heads around the corner. I came here to get Kit's advice, not to be stared at by his friends. Wonder *Boys.* That's what they call themselves; I have no idea why. It sounds ridiculous. The one who spoke throws his arms over Kit's and Cam's shoulders, even though he's several inches shorter than them, and gives me a searching look as if he expects me to answer that question.

I didn't even realize I was having a panic attack. I'm not sure I can explain why it was happening any more than I can come up with a reason Darcy would completely lie to me about who she is. Or Tamlin. Honestly, I'm not convinced I know which one is the real person.

The one thing I'm almost certain of is they are the *same* person. And I was an idiot for not figuring that out sooner.

"Something tells me we need brownies," the new guy says with a frown. "Ben, you know how to make brownies, right?"

The fourth guy rolls his eyes at the same time Cam says, "Are you seriously assuming I don't know how to make brownies, Oliver?"

"I'm sure you do, but you'd probably throw spinach or protein powder in them or something. That's the last thing this guy needs."

Before I can say anything to the contrary—anyone who can put those things in brownies and make them taste good deserves a medal—Kit frees himself from Oliver's arm and approaches me, holding out his hand. "We can go for a walk or move into the kitchen. Either way, we're talking. What'll it be?"

As intimidating as it feels to insert myself into this group of friends who I'm pretty sure have known each other for years, this situation feels big enough that having multiple perspectives might be nice.

"Kitchen," I say, though it comes out more like a question.

"You only get to pick once," Kit warns.

I examine the three guys for a moment, realizing if they have Kit Morgan for a friend, they have to be decent guys. They look nice enough, and Cam did just talk me down from a panic attack without me even realizing what he was doing.

"I could use all the help I can get," I mutter and grasp Kit's wrist, letting him pull me up onto shaky legs.

It isn't until I'm settled on a barstool between Oliver and Ben that I notice it's just the guys here. "Where's Skyler?" I ask Kit as he and Cam go about gathering ingredients and mixing bowls.

"Girls' night," all four guys say at once.

A glance around the room tells me all of them are married, and something in my chest throbs. "Do they do that often?"

"Every other Saturday," Oliver says, twisting back and forth on his stool. "You unfortunately picked my wife's turn to have the kid."

"Why is that unfortunate?" I'm not sure I would be able to handle a kid right now.

Kit chuckles. "Because my nephew is ridiculously adorable and would have melted away all your problems by smiling at you and calling you Dada."

"It's so stupid," Oliver moans, dropping his head onto the counter. "Orion knows, like, a hundred words. Why does he call everyone Dada but me?"

I frown. "What does he call you?"

Everyone except Oliver snickers.

"He calls him Poopy," Ben says lightly.

"I'm pretty sure he's going for Papa but missed the mark," Oliver groans. "I swear he's smart."

"On that note," Kit says, "how about you give us the CliffsNotes version of why you're here, Houston."

I don't even know where to start. "I'm in love."

"Yes, a great reason to panic," Cam says as he measures out flour. He sounds serious, but he must have a really deadpan sarcasm or something because he's wearing a wedding ring like the rest of them.

I push forward despite the confusing response. "With my next-door neighbor. Well, my tenant, actually."

Ben winces beside me. "That sounds complicated."

"That's not the worst part. You know that reporter, Tamlin Park?"

"The hot one?" Cam cringes as soon as the words leave his mouth. "Ignore me."

"She's beautiful," Kit agrees. "But I thought you didn't like her."

"I..." This is all too confusing, and though it's not what I mean to say, what comes out of my mouth is, "I'm in love with her too."

Cam stops measuring cocoa to glower at me, which is not the kind of look anyone should be on the receiving end of. If he was intimidating before, now he's terrifying.

"You can't be in love with two people at the same time," Oliver says warily, like he's worried how I might react to that. Or maybe he's worried he might witness a murder with the way Cam is glaring at me. "You can *love* two people, but you can't be *in love* with them."

I meet Kit's gaze. He seems on the verge of following Cam's example and punching me for being a tool, but I think he recognizes that there's more to this than what I've said. "Talk," he orders, pointing a whisk at me.

This is going to sound completely crazy. "I think...I think they're the same person."

The silence that follows my claim is perfectly understandable, and a part of me wishes I hadn't said it out loud.

"Tamlin Park lives in Sun City?" Cam asks eventually. Thank goodness he's willing to keep listening rather than trying to murder me with his eyes. "I thought Enhance Media was back east somewhere."

"Missouri. She's been in New Mexico for the last couple of weeks." I take a slow breath. This would probably be easier if any of them knew Darcy, but I can try to explain. "Darcy moved into my duplex around the same time Tamlin showed up."

"So, naturally they're the same person," Oliver says, raising his eyebrow. "Do they look the same?"

I don't like the way he asks that question like I'm stupid. "No, they don't. But at the same time, they do. I don't...I've never seen Tamlin without a lot of makeup."

"Makeup," Ben repeats. He's the quietest of the bunch, but his skepticism somehow hurts more.

"I think she wears colored contacts," I say, my voice rising in pitch in my desperation. "And a wig? I've never seen them in the same place, even when they were both in the house at the same time. Tamlin wouldn't give me her phone number, even when I took her on a date, and she's really good at flipping a switch and being something different. Darcy always has vague answers to questions about her job, and they were both in Albuquerque yesterday. When I kissed Tamlin today, it felt just like when I kissed Darcy on Halloween."

"I'm going to stop you there," Cam says. Apparently he's forgotten about the brownies, now leaning his hands on the counter in a total power move as he stares me down. "You kissed Darcy on Halloween, two days ago, and say you're in love with her. Why in the world would you kiss someone else today? I thought you were one of the good ones, Briggs."

"I am! I mean, I try to be. And I didn't kiss her. She kissed me."

Well, that isn't entirely true. Tamlin kissed me first, but something snapped in me and made me forget where I was and who I was with. It was like deep down I already knew that it was Darcy underneath the perfect surface, and I was desperate to kiss her again. And it all felt so right, like I had known her my entire life and had found my center in her. Just like I felt with Darcy. Either I am desperate for connection and a complete jerk for playing with the emotions of two great women, or she kissed me because it has been two days since our kiss under the stars and she couldn't wait any longer.

I moan, stuffing my hands into my hair. "This is such a mess. If they're not the same, I don't want to hurt either of them, but it's like half of me wants the familiarity and friendship I feel with Tamlin while the other half wants the stability and comfort I feel with Darcy. Tamlin shares my passions, but Darcy understands me. Am I just trying to convince myself they're the same person so I don't have to choose?"

Could I really be that terrible of a person? It's what my dad did. He said he loved my mom until someone new came along, and he didn't bother waiting until the divorce before he rushed off to find his pleasures elsewhere. More than ten years of marriage thrown away for a month-long fling. I wouldn't have even known about the affair if Chad hadn't gotten drunk after his own cheating girlfriend of six years dumped him. I picked him up from the bar and took him home, and he spent the whole drive cursing himself for falling into the same trap our mom did. I never knew why she left dad—not until Chad spilled the beans—and I still haven't decided if knowing is a blessing or a curse.

I already hated my dad, but finding out what he did to hurt my mom made me hate him more. And fear him. What if I turn out just like him? Learning about the affair is the reason I started thinking I should change my ways and find real connection, but what if that's not enough?

"This Tamlin Park person works for Enhance Media?" Oliver asks, pulling his phone out of his pocket. "Give me a minute."

"Are you going to hack into their records or something?" Cam asks, and he seems both curious and appalled.

"I have never *hacked* anything in my life," Oliver replies, turning slightly red. "I'll leave that to Isla's boyfriend."

I meet Kit's gaze, and I'm pretty sure we're both wondering if Oliver lied just now. (Whoever Isla is, I hope her boyfriend doesn't actually hack anything.) I can't imagine Kit would be friends with someone who did anything illegal, but what do I know? I also didn't think Brook would ever go for someone shameless and loud like Jordan, and they're probably going to end up being a long-term thing with the way Jordan looks at my sister. Nor did I think Chad could fall so head-over-heels for someone so quickly.

Whatever those two found—whatever Kit and his friends have with their wives—I want that. Am I going to find it with Darcy? Or is this budding relationship about to fall apart and leave me alone at the worst possible time?

I'm already losing my career, and my siblings have all found significant others and don't need me as a seventh wheel. If not baseball and my family, what do I even have? Several businesses that don't need me because they're already run by the people who started them. A bank account full of more money than I could ever spend in a lifetime. A heart that feels like it's on the verge of breaking.

The kitchen is mostly silent as Oliver taps away at his phone. Cam continues working on the brownie mix, while Kit and Ben seem to have a silent conversation between the two of them.

Ben clears his throat. "How's baseball going?" he asks me.

I groan and drop my head on my arms. That movement pulls at my tight shoulder, and I groan again, this time from the pain. I shouldn't have thrown like I did at the park today. At least not without warming up. The tendons in my shoulder are still just as strained as they were a week ago, and without warming up my arm, I exacerbated the problem. Wanting to see what Tamlin could do not only made me wildly more attracted to her but also hurt like crazy.

"I'm done," I say into my arms, not sure why it's so easy to admit that to these men who are basically strangers. "I don't even know if I have another game in my shoulder, but I hate that I'll be abandoning my team if I retire a year early. We don't have another good pitcher to take my place in the starting rotation, so what are they going to do if I tap out? What am *I* going to do?"

When no one says anything, I slowly lift my head and take in their expressions. Ben looks mildly sympathetic, but I'm pretty sure he's not really a sports guy. Cam should understand since he played ball in school, though he was a shortstop if I remember right and probably didn't have any issues. Besides, with how fit he is, he looks like the kind of guy who will still be spry at eighty.

Oliver is still swiping around on his phone and likely didn't listen to a word I said. But Kit? Kit is *smiling*.

He leans on the counter, commanding my attention with his warm expression. "Do you remember when we met last year?"

"You came to my family reunion pretending to be engaged to my stepsister," I reply, as if he might have forgotten that part.

"The week before that, I got laid off. I'd been teaching third grade for the last seven years, and I had been planning on doing that for the rest of my life." He shudders. "I also got a new nephew that week, and Cam and Ben were both getting married soon. When Sky found me, my whole life had fallen apart."

I'm not sure how this could possibly count as a pep talk. "That sucks, Morgan."

He chuckles. "I know. But you know what? I had to get rid of all of those things that were holding me back in order for me to find the life I really wanted."

"You just said Ben and I were holding you back," Cam points out as he grabs a glass cake pan.

"You know that's not what I meant," Kit replies, rolling his eyes. Then he turns his attention to me again. "What I'm trying to say, Houston, is there is always another door. If one closes, you just have to find the next one."

"I kind of hate metaphors," I mumble back, but he's right. Micah would probably slap me if she knew how pessimistically I was looking at my life. Suddenly I wonder what the queen of optimism would say if I had come to her with all my problems instead of driving to another state for advice from a bunch of dudes I don't know.

"How much are you really wanting an answer to your problem?" Oliver asks suddenly, placing his phone screen-down on the counter.

My entire focus fixates on that phone, and I have never wanted to know something more than I do right now. "You're saying I'm right? They're the same person?"

Oliver shrugs. "No, I'm not saying that. But I am saying I found a forum where someone is claiming none of the reporters at Enhance actually exist. Legally, I mean. There aren't any payrolls or social security records or birth certificates for any of them. The comment got deleted and buried, probably by Enhance, but nothing can completely vanish once it's on the internet. I think it was a former employee who made the claim, so take that as you will."

If Tamlin doesn't legally exist, that would mean she's an alias. Which means the chances of me being right are so much higher than I thought. My heart pounds in my chest, but I can't decide if it's good or bad. What do I actually want the outcome to be here? Either I have to choose between these two women, or Darcy has been lying to me this whole time.

"Have you asked Chad about this?" Kit asks. "As a private investigator, he probably—"

"I think he already knows," I say. "But he decided he didn't want to tell me. I think..." Man, my brother is a good guy. "He thought it would be better if I figured it out myself. Or maybe he wanted Darcy to tell me. If he'd told me they were the same person, I probably wouldn't have believed him, and that would have made this whole thing so much messier."

"Messier than a woman catfishing you with her own alter-ego?" Cam says, raising an eyebrow.

Okay, yeah, that sounds pretty convoluted. I run a hand down my face, exhausted. "What am I supposed to do? What if she's been lying to me since the day we met?"

"Maybe it depends on *why* she's been lying," Ben says.

"I don't think anyone should lie about who they are," Cam says.

"She could be working under a contract and legally can't say any-thing," Kit replies, making me wonder if I should ask Skyler if that's a thing. She used to be a lawyer; she probably knows how binding some-thing like that could be.

"I totally get why a company like Enhance would create fake identities for their crews," Oliver throws in. "Seeing some of the comments people have made about Tamlin Park, I'm surprised she's willing to get on TV at all. There are literal death threats all over the internet because of some of the stories she's broadcasted."

I snatch Oliver's phone, blood boiling. "There's *what*?"

He laughs. "Easy, Fastball. People on the internet are a lot braver than they are in real life."

I still want to punch anyone who would ever try to hurt a woman like Tamlin. Or Darcy. Whoever she is. Doesn't even have to be her. Anyone who threatens violence deserves to be beaten to a pulp.

Including me, apparently.

I force a deep breath, trying to stay rational. "So, you think she dresses up as Tamlin to protect herself?"

"It would make sense," Oliver replies. "It's probably similar to the reason Kit never uses his real name in his woodworking videos or talks about where he lives, except for him it's to avoid public humiliation."

Kit whacks Oliver on the side of the head. "We can theorize all we want, but if you want to know the truth, you're going to have to ask her, Houston. You know that, right?"

It would be so much easier to make assumptions and avoid any confrontation by cutting ties and saving myself from potential hurt, but he's right. If I want to be living my life deliberately, I can't take the easy way out. I want to see if things could work between Darcy and me, even if it comes with the risk of discovering everything about her has been a ploy to get information for her big story.

It's the only reason I can figure she would move in next door. If she really is Tamlin, that can't have been a coincidence. She said she's here for a story, and with all the time she has spent with me, that story has to be centered around me. Does she know about my shoulder? I don't think so, or she would have told that story already. Maybe she's just waiting for some evidence to validate her claim that I'm just a washed-up has-been who is too old and broken to play anymore.

Is she going to be my doom?

Honestly, I'm not sure it matters. Whether or not she tells the story, I'm out. Finished. Done.

"Houston?" Kit pierces me with one of his all-knowing stares.

"I think I need a distraction," I say, feeling another panic attack coming on.

"Video games?" Kit suggests. "I warn you—you will lose."

"I don't care. That could be distracting enough to make it worth it."

For the next several hours, Kit and his friends do everything they can to keep me occupied, whether it's with video games, eating enough brownies to make me want to puke, or a terrible game of two-on-two basketball in the backyard that nearly results in several broken bones because Kit and Cam get so competitive that Ben has to act as referee and keep them from playing dirty.

I don't think anything could actually make me forget about my complicated situation with Darcy and Tamlin, but the Wonder Boys keep it pushed to the back of my mind until Ben gets a text from his wife telling him that their girls' night is over.

Immediately, all three of Kit's friends say they need to return home.

I would hate it if it wasn't clear they were all eager to see their wives.

Kit sees them out, and when it's just the two of us left, I know my time is up. Skyler will be home soon, and they were bad enough with displays of affection when they were dating. I don't need to experience their newly married life at home.

"I should head back before it gets too late," I mutter, moving toward the door.

Kit steps in my way. "Uh, if you think I'm letting you drive home in this state, you don't know me at all. Give me your keys."

"They're…" I have to think about it. "I think they're still in the ignition."

Kit rolls his eyes before heading outside to retrieve them, and I'm too tired to stop him. He's probably right; driving home would be dangerous. When he comes back in, he holds my phone out to me and says, "Don't ask her about things tonight. This should be a face-to-face conversation."

He's right, but when I see half a dozen texts from Darcy, the urge to demand she explain things is almost overwhelming.

I stuff the phone back into Kit's hand. "What did she say?"

Though he gives me a look that says, *Are you serious?*, he still opens up the messages and skims through them. "She said she got back from Albuquerque earlier than she thought she would and wants to know when you're free. Then she said something about a chipmunk being at the same rest stop and waiting for her." He snickers a little at something he doesn't read out loud, and then he winces. "She texted about ten minutes ago, asking when you'll be home because she wants to talk."

I've told her before that those are some of the most terrifying words in existence. Or maybe that was Tamlin. At this point, I'm all sorts of mixed up. "What am I supposed to say to her? I'm terrified to talk to her. What if I'm wrong?"

"Maybe she wants to tell you the truth."

"Maybe she is moving out of state sooner than expected."

"Back to Missouri?"

"What if I'm wrong?" I repeat. "Tamlin is great, she really is. But Darcy makes me feel seen. I don't want her to leave, but I can't help feeling like no matter what the truth is, I'm going to lose her."

Kit puts his hand on my shoulder, and the gesture seems to steady me where I stand. "You don't know enough to panic about this yet. And you haven't lost her yet either. There's a lot of power in those three letters—*yet*—but don't let them control you. Use them to your advantage and keep believing everything will be okay."

I swallow the emotion that seems ready to choke me. "How did you get so wise, Morgan?"

Kit smiles. "I have three incredible friends who married three incredible women, just like I did. I pay attention, so I've learned a lot by knowing them. Maybe take a page out of Micah's book and hope for the best." He types out a text on my phone and hits send. "I'll give this back in the morning, but for now you should probably try to get some sleep. I'll tell Sky to be quiet when she gets home so she doesn't disturb you. It'll probably be pretty late because she's obsessed with our nephew and never wants to put him down. Hang out here for a sec, and I'll grab you a blanket and a change of clothes."

"Kit?" I stop him before he can head upstairs. "Thanks. You didn't have to drop everything to help me, but I appreciate that you did."

He smiles. "It's what family does, Houston."

"Your friends are really great."

"They are," he agrees, his smile growing. "Get some sleep. I think you'll feel better about things in the morning."

I really hope he's right.

Chapter Thirty

Darcy

November 3

ONCE UPON A TIME, I used to sleep on the couch pretty much every night because I spent so much of my free time studying that I would pass out in the middle of reading a textbook chapter about organizational behavior or something. I could wake up in time for class in the morning no problem and even throw in a workout before doing it all over again.

At some point between now and then, I got old. And I regret everything. My back is killing me.

I meant to go up to bed last night, but I kept waiting for Houston to text me again. Or for him to come home. The only text I got from him yesterday was as cryptic as it was adorable, and I'm pretty sure I barely slept because of my thoughts swirling around while my back decided to tell me I shouldn't play baseball in heels or sleep on couches anymore.

Houston:

I've been thinking about you all day. I'm not in a place to talk right now, but I'll see you tomorrow?

What does he mean by that? Not in a place to talk? Is that mentally, emotionally, physically? I mean, I watched him drive away in his truck, so I know he didn't come home by the time I fell asleep. But with the way he kissed me yesterday, it could be an emotional distance. What if he has changed his mind and would rather date Tamlin than me? I know it doesn't matter, but at the same time it does. If he prefers the falsely beautiful woman to the real and plain girl, what does that say about him? What does it say about me that I'm jealous of myself?

Love shouldn't be this complicated.

Stretching, I force myself to slide off the couch and head up to the bathroom to try to freshen up and give myself some motivation to face today. I should have said more to Houston than just, "Yes," in my text reply, but I had too many questions about why he would disappear when on Friday he was so anxious to see Darcy again.

By the time I've brushed my teeth and washed my face, Jesse is awake and in the hallway, looking bleary-eyed and bitter about being up this early. He was up almost as late as I was, inking people, and his expression is pretty easy to read.

When can I go home?

I know he signed up for this—or at the very least is being paid well to be here on this extended job—but I can't blame him for wanting the comfort of his own apartment.

"Soon," I say right as someone knocks on the front door.

As my heart leaps into my throat, Jesse puts his hand on my shoulder, reminding me of what he said when he told me I could be happy here with Houston.

Let's hope he's right. No matter what, I have to tell Houston who I really am, and then I can move on with my life. Whether he's still in it is up to him.

"Good luck," Jesse says, as if he knows exactly who is at the door.

When I open the front door, Houston stands there with a plate of steaming waffles topped with strawberries and whipped cream. His expression is fairly neutral, which makes it so hard to guess what he might be thinking.

"Trying to impress me with your purchasing skills again?" I ask, hoping the tease will put us on familiar ground.

His face doesn't change as he glances down at the plate in his hands. "I made these. I forced Jordan to wake up unnaturally early and teach me his secret recipe in person."

"Oh. That's...that's actually really sweet."

Finally, a smile peeks out on his lips. "What do you mean *actually*? I'm always sweet. Can I come in?"

"Yes! Yeah, of course."

Handing me the waffles, he slips past me and sends a waft of his clean and fresh scent washing over me. He is newly showered, his hair still damp, and I wish I changed from my pajamas so I don't look so disheveled comparatively. He sits on the couch and looks so enticing that it takes a lot of willpower for me to hang on to the waffles as I sit beside him instead of launching myself at him. I know I'm being awkward, but I can't help it. After the way he left things yesterday, I'm on edge.

"So," he says when I fail to work up the courage to start up the conversation. His eyes slip to the waffles on my lap.

Feeling obligated to at least taste them, even though I feel like I might throw up from nerves, I pull off a piece and pop it into my mouth. "Oh!" I say when it hits my tongue. It's somehow soft but crispy, sweet but not, and the texture is so fluffy and perfect that it brings literal tears to my eyes. (I'm already feeling emotional, and breakfast food is my favorite, okay?) "This is so good, Houston!"

His smile widens as he watches me pull off another bite. "I guarantee I'll never be able to make them again. Jordan doesn't believe in recipes. He says cooking should be done with the heart, not the head."

"I can taste your heart in these." I grimace. "Well, that sounded entirely creepy."

"Are you Tamlin Park?"

The waffles slide off my lap and onto the floor with a splat, along with any ounce of calm I might have been feeling before that question left his tongue. "What?"

I'm pretty sure my breathless response answers his question for me; he purses his lips and drops his gaze to his knees. "You are." Not a question this time.

This is what I wanted, but I can feel my heart breaking with every passing second that he won't look at me. "Yes. Houston, let me—"

He's on his feet in a flash, slipping out the front door without a word. He doesn't slam the door, but neither does he look back.

And that's that. My short-lived romance with the baseball superstar with a heart of gold has come to an end, and I don't think he'll give me a chance to say goodbye or explain why I had to do what I did. Why would he? I've been lying to him for the last two weeks.

I slump into the back of the couch, my heart aching. Not being able to explain even a little is the part I hate the most. Maybe he wouldn't have listened to me, but if I could have just...

I jump to my feet. "What am I doing?" I ask out loud, as if someone might be around to answer me. I can't just sit here and let Houston make all the decisions when this is *my* story as much as it is his. I march to the door, making my plan as I go. If he doesn't let me in, I'll just come grab the key he gave me and force him to hear me out. Whether or not he accepts my reasons for doing what I did won't change my need to come clean. He can't deny me a chance to be honest.

When I grab the doorknob and pull it open, I do it with the full force of my righteous anger. That's great and all, except the door opens without my added force, and I fly backwards at the same time Houston comes tumbling inside. We crash together, both of us trying to keep us on our feet until we slam into the wall. Houston's arms lock me in, but it's the intensity of his gaze that holds me captivated. I have no idea what thoughts are going through his head, but they are many.

And all I can think about is how he came back.

"I'm sorry I couldn't tell you," I whisper, knowing there's so much more I need to say. I have to start somewhere. "I wanted to—"

But then Houston locks his lips onto mine, fingers sliding into my hair as he pulls me into a kiss so desperate that I can't breathe. Who needs oxygen? He shifts, hands wrapping around my hips and lifting me up until my legs lock around his waist to keep me in the perfect spot to dive into this kiss. His arms slide around my back, pulling me closer, and I grip the long hair at the back of his neck. He groans and deepens the kiss, pressing me into the wall as he gives me the best kiss of my life. We're molded together, lips moving in a choreographed dance that we've known our whole lives but never had the right partner until now.

Eventually he breaks away, and we both fight to breathe. "I'm so relieved," he gasps, resting his forehead against mine.

My heart soars. Did I just hear what I think I heard? "I thought you were going to hate me," I whisper.

He shakes his head, letting his nose brush against mine before he pulls me in for another kiss, no less glorious than the last one even though he's more controlled now. "Honestly? Knowing the truth solves all my problems. I was so afraid I was falling in love with two people." My breath hitches, and he nods. "Yeah, I'm in love with you, Darcy. Tamlin. Whoever you are."

"I'm both," I say, needing him to understand. "I never pretended to be something I wasn't."

Grinning, he tucks some hair behind my ear. "I'm pretty sure you were pretending to be a brunette, Darce. And..." He glances down at our chests pressed together and turns a healthy shade of red.

I bite my lip. "Okay, those might be fake too."

"That's not..." Houston snorts a laugh as he drops his head onto my shoulder. "I don't care. However you look, you're beautiful. But it's *you* I'm in love with, Darcy. Not the way you look."

Okay, well, a girl could get used to a guy saying stuff like that, but it all feels too good to be true. "You really don't hate me? I thought that was why you walked out."

He slowly lowers me back to my feet, wrapping his arms around my waist to keep me close. "No. I just needed a second to process it all. Though, it would be nice if you told me there was a contract or something that prevented you from telling me before I figured it out."

"There was! Is, technically." But I need to be honest with him, especially with how cool he's being about all of this. "But I was also scared."

"Why?"

Reaching up, I run my fingers along the light scruff he didn't shave this morning, remembering the feel of it scratching my cheeks as he kissed me. "You had these ideas of who I was in your head, and when you started to like both sides, I was worried you wouldn't like it all together. Like my flaws as Darcy and my flaws as Tamlin would somehow add up to be too many for you to want them."

Goodness, he looks gutted as he stares at me with those baby blues of his. "You thought I couldn't love all of the pieces of you that make you perfect? Darcy..."

He steps back, taking his warmth with him, and runs a hand through his hair as he starts to pace. "You are one of the sweetest people I've ever met, but you're not afraid to stand up for yourself and make sure stupid men like me know you can be both crazy smart and insanely beautiful. You feed chipmunks and befriend literally anyone you come in contact with, and you can hit a curveball thrown by a professional pitcher. You know sports better than I do and see potential in people when they can't see it themselves, and if you think there is anything about you that I do not love with everything I have in me, you're just wrong."

I'm not generally a crier on my own, but Houston has me breaking down with all these incredible words. Tears spill from my eyes as I stand there wishing I knew what I could say that would ever compare to all of that.

The only thing I can get out is, "Well, I'm incredibly unlucky, so…"

He shakes his head before wrapping his big arms around me and pulling me to his chest in a hug that shuts out the world. "I have literally never seen that to be true. I meant it when I said you might as well just stick with me forever so your luck can change."

I think he's right. Whenever I'm with him, everything seems to go well. I could use that in my life, given how much of it is wrong right now.

"Can I tell you something?" I ask, listening to his heart pound in my ear.

"Always."

"I've been paying my sister's student loans. And my dad needs in-home care or maybe even to move into a facility because he's losing mobility, and my parents can't afford that. That's one of the reasons I've been trying so hard to get this promotion. So I can help them pay for it all."

Saying that out loud feels like handing over a backpack full of bricks, something I've been carrying for so long without even knowing how heavy it has become. Connor knows how much I help my family and probably fought to get me in the running for the promotion, but there's only so much he can do when it comes to the emotional side of carrying that burden. Yes, I love laughing with Houston and talking sports, and I absolutely enjoy kissing him. But this? Unloading a weight from my shoulders is something I've never experienced before.

"I don't know why I told you that," I whisper, pulling myself tighter into his hold.

Houston matches my movement, wrapping me up more securely. "Because that's what boyfriends are for, I think."

My heart does a sort of fish-flopping motion in my chest. "Are you my boyfriend?"

"I hope so. I did just tell you I love you, and that was kind of my end goal. At least for now, until I'm ready to ask for more."

Holy promises, Batman. What is he saying?

This has been the longest hug of my life, and I don't want it to end. So I burrow in deeper, and Houston chuckles.

"I'm freaking you out, aren't I?" he says. "Don't worry. I'm freaking myself out too. This is so far beyond what I'm used to. I didn't really sleep last night, so it could be exhaustion talking, but it gave me a lot of time to think. I'm never going to find anyone more perfect for me than you, and I don't want to let you go."

This can't be real. This is all just some weird fever dream from sleeping on the couch as a twenty-six-year-old.

"And there was also all that thinking time while I was driving back this morning. Apparently the radio is broken in my truck, and two hours is a long time to—"

"Two hours?" I pull away, staring at him. "Where did you go?"

He blinks, turning slightly red. "Uh. Diamond Springs."

"Colorado? Why?"

"I needed advice."

"You ran away?"

"I was panicking!"

I can't help but laugh, shaking my head. "Kissing me made you panic?"

"When I thought you were two different people, yeah. But the more I thought about Tamlin's kiss..."

It's my turn to blush, and I bury myself back in his arms even though it makes him laugh. "I'm a little mortified when I think about how bad I was at separating my feelings for you from who I was supposed to be at the time. Have I said sorry yet for lying to you?"

"Just promise me you won't lie to me in the future, and we'll be good."

That's more than fair, though now I'm thinking about the future. And thinking about the future reminds me about my story, which reminds me about him not throwing at practice, which reminds me I have very little time left to find the story that will get me promoted, which has me thinking about what happens if I *do* get promoted because Houston is here in Sun City and my job is in Missouri, and—

"Okay, what's happening right now?" Houston asks, pushing me to arm's length and studying me with so much intention that I can practically feel his eyes on my face. "I feel like you're overthinking something."

I bite the insides of my lips. I'm overthinking, but what if telling him what I'm thinking about spooks him? He may say he's in this for the long haul, but those are just words. I haven't given him many reasons to stick around.

Swallowing, I take one of his hands from my shoulder and lace my fingers with his, hoping the contact helps him know that I'm not out to get him. "You know that mystery story I told you about?"

He nods. "The one that will get you promoted. Did you figure it out?"

I don't like this any more than he's going to. "You tell me," I say and press my palm against his left shoulder.

I can see each emotion as it crosses his face in rapid succession. Fear first in his wide eyes, followed by anger in the clenching of his jaw. His lips purse at the same time his eyebrows dip down, both speaking volumes to the uncertainty he must be feeling.

Right as he opens his mouth, I touch my fingers to his lips. "Don't say anything you don't want me to put in a story. I got sent here because of you, and the last thing I want to do is ruin what game time you have left. I can find another way to help my family, and this won't be my only chance to tell the stories I want to tell, so don't you dare think about me when you decide what to tell me, if anything at all. Understand?"

His eyes have grown heavy while I speak, and though he nods against my fingers, he keeps his mouth shut. I might be disappointed by that, but if he thinks it's better not to tell me anything, I'll trust him. With the way he responded to learning my secret, I'll trust him with just about anything.

"I should clean up those waffles," I say, wanting to give myself a moment to think about what I'm going to do next. "Or maybe eat them off the floor because they're so good. I think—"

Houston doesn't release my hand when I walk away. Instead, he tugs me back to his side and gives me a slow and gentle kiss. "I can't pitch anymore," he says against my lips, like a whispered secret he's afraid to share. "I've torn a tendon—a few places, probably—and it'll take surgery to repair the damage. I'll be out most of the season, and by that point..."

I squeeze his hand, my heart aching for him. "At that point you really will be too old to play," I finish for him. I hate that players—especially pitchers—rarely make it to thirty in the major leagues, but I hate more that Houston has been sitting on this for so long. "What are you going to do?"

"That's the question everyone wants an answer to," he says on a sigh.

"Do the Red-tails even have a backup pitcher to take your spot?" I only pay attention to the players who actually take the field, and for the last several years, Houston has been the best Red-tails pitcher on the mound. The other starting pitchers are fine, but I know the team counts on their small rotation so Houston can play (and therefore win) more games.

"We do," Houston says, "but he's notorious for pitching home runs."

"So, not great."

"None of the relief pitchers have what it takes to do what I do. There's a reason I've been playing whole games, and it's not because I'm awesome."

I raise an eyebrow.

"Not *entirely* because I'm awesome." The smile that stretches across his mouth is so tempting that I can't help but swoop in and claim it for myself. He doesn't stop smiling, even while I kiss him, which makes the whole thing exceptionally difficult. Difficult, but no less enjoyable.

Eventually, Houston pulls me to the couch and lays down, pulling me down with him until we're stretched out together with me held securely in his arms. He lets out a heavy sigh, his whole body relaxing behind me.

"Thank you," he says softly. "For listening. For being someone I can trust with this."

"You must be exhausted from keeping it to yourself."

"You have no idea." He sounds like he's falling asleep.

I snuggle in closer. "And you really didn't sleep last night?"

He buries his nose into my neck. "I was too busy thinking about you," he murmurs, his voice soft and velvety.

"Me too."

"You were thinking about you?"

I snort a laugh, but when he doesn't say anything else, I realize he's already fallen asleep, his breaths coming in a slow, steady rhythm. He must have been completely exhausted! It makes sense, after how late we were up on Thursday, and if he didn't sleep at all last night, he should probably spend all of this Sunday off sleeping.

Which means I'm stuck here. Not a bad place to be, but now that I know how bad his shoulder really is, my brain is running at full speed. If I had my phone with me, I could start planning out how I'm going to spin this, though I'll need Houston's input at some point.

"Jesse!" I whisper-call. When Jesse doesn't answer and Houston doesn't stir, I call a little louder.

After the third call, Jesse appears on the stairs with obvious reluctance, but he relaxes as soon as he sees Houston sound asleep. *Good news?* his eyes seem to say.

I grin. "I need my phone. I finally found out what the story is, and I'm..." I look at Houston's large arms that have me trapped. "Can you get it for me? The sooner I get this planned out, the sooner you can go home."

He turns, preferably on his way to grab my phone, but then he pauses and looks back at me. "You," he says, and it takes me a second to figure out what he means. I said the sooner *you* can go home. Not *we*.

"I don't know if I'm going home yet," I say, and I mean that. I'm not sure I can abandon my job, but I *know* I can't abandon Houston. I'll need Jesse one more time for when I report the story, but hopefully I won't need Tamlin after that. Hopefully I can just be me.

Chapter Thirty-One

Houston

November 4

I DON'T THINK I've ever had to do anything worse than walking into the clubhouse on Monday morning. Okay, so maybe attending my mother's funeral was worse, but I barely remember that day because I was only seven. After spending all of Sunday with Darcy—if we weren't sleeping on the couch we were either making out or talking like we did on Halloween—going back to the real world feels like stepping into a dream.

It's like none of this is my life anymore, and I'm just going through the motions and comprehending none of it. When Darcy dropped me off (her idea to spend as much time with me as possible), I almost couldn't leave her because she feels so much more important than anything.

Everything in my life has changed.

"Yo, Briggs."

I stop when Badir calls my name, his gaze hard as he leans one shoulder against his locker. He and I used to spend a lot of time together off the field, before I started cleaning up my life a bit, but I've pulled away over this last year or so. He's a good guy and an excellent catcher, and he always calls the right pitches. But I don't like the way he's looking at me right now. Like I've betrayed him.

"What's going on with you? It's like the season ended and you disappeared."

I could tell him about my shoulder. It's going to come out tonight anyway when Darcy does an exclusive interview with me. But I'd like one more day with my team that feels semi-normal, so I don't.

Instead, I grin. "I met a girl."

Badir laughs. "You meet girls all the time."

"Not like this."

"Briggs!" Fujimura barks my name from his office, and Badir winces, probably thinking I'm about to get chewed out for being distracted the last few days.

Maybe he's right, but it doesn't matter. Darcy and I made a plan, and she's already talked to her boss about doing a press release tonight. I wasn't thinking of changing my mind, but at this point I basically can't. Not without hurting her chances, which is more than enough reason to keep going down this path.

"Duty calls," I say to Badir, tossing my stuff into my locker before heading over to the manager's office. "Sir?"

He waits until he's closed the door behind me and we're both seated on either side of his desk. He looks nervous, probably because he knew this moment was coming as soon as Solano told him about my shoulder. "Have you made a decision, Briggs?"

I didn't think I would feel this calm. My heart beats with peaceful steadiness, telling me this is the right decision. "Yes, sir. I can't play, and I don't feel right about getting paid to sit on the sidelines. I'm done."

He sighs, pinching the bridge of his nose. "I was afraid of that. I hoped I'd get at least another year out of you."

"I know. That's what made this decision so difficult. I owe everything I am to you. You took a chance on me, and—"

"And you were worth every penny and more, Houston." He sighs again. "How am I supposed to find another player like you? You were perfect."

That gets a laugh out of me, which thankfully brings a smile to Fujimura's face too. "I really wasn't, but thanks. I'm sure there's another rookie out there just waiting to be discovered. Roundy already has some prospects to replace me on his roster."

"That's cold."

"We all knew I already hit my prime," I say, rolling my eyes. "You can't blame him for wanting to keep his paychecks coming."

Sitting back in his chair, he studies me for a long time. Whatever he's looking for, I try to let him find it. "What's next for you?" he asks, and I have a feeling he doesn't usually do this with his players. He's not a sentimental guy, and I don't think I've ever had a conversation with him that didn't revolve around baseball.

I shrug. "Not sure yet. But I'll figure it out. I'll be announcing my retirement tonight, but I was hoping you could keep this quiet. Especially with the guys. I want one more day before I walk away."

"You can still change your mind."

"No. I can't. Thanks for everything, sir."

He shakes my outstretched hand, and that feels like it seals the end of my baseball career.

Oddly, I feel fine.

By the time practice ends, I do *not* feel fine. I thought spending one last practice with the guys would be bittersweet, but it only stabs me in the gut every time I throw a ball or make eye contact with one of them. I'm pretty sure I come close to crying more than once, which is ridiculous, and when Hopkins says something about tomorrow's practice, emotion chokes my throat and leaves me completely speechless.

I'm sure some of my teammates notice—they would be blind not to—but no one says a word until Badir spreads the news about my new lady friend. Then multiple guys joke about how she's turned me soft and got me whipped, and I just go along with their ribbing because it's easier than trying to hide my growing misery.

By the time I grab my stuff and head out to meet Darcy, I'm feeling raw and uncertain, and I rush from the clubhouse because I know she'll be able to make me feel better about all of this.

But when I slip through a side door and head for the parking lot, a familiar voice pulls me to a dead stop.

"How was practice, son?"

I don't bother turning around to look at him. I haven't seen him in over a decade, since the last time I was forced to visit him, but he sounds the same, still with that weakness in his voice that came from losing control of his life.

"What are you doing here, Dad?" I ask and grip the strap of my bag, forcing myself to keep breathing. Of all the times for him to show up, it had to be now? I'm more likely to blow up on him than have a civil conversation, and I'm exhausted from keeping things in during practice. I won't be able to hold back now, and already a familiar resentment is bubbling up inside me.

I don't think this can end well for either of us.

He clears his throat. "I was hoping to see you practice, but I couldn't get in."

"That's for a reason," I growl.

"Houston."

Gritting my teeth, I finally turn and grace him with a glance. He looks better than the last time I saw him, though anything is better than drug-addicted and violent. He's gained some healthy weight, gotten a haircut, put on some clothes that actually fit.

"How long have you been out?" I ask reluctantly. If I had my truck, I could walk away from this conversation instead of having it, but maybe this is good for me. I can get all the forced pleasantries out of the way and never speak to him again. Everything will be up from here on out.

Dad ducks his head, clearly embarrassed by the fact that he just got out of prison. Or maybe he's just feeling the strain of this as much as I am. "'Bout a week ago," he grunts.

"Do the others know?"

He nods. "I went and saw Brooklyn yesterday." He must see the way my hands clench into fists at the idea of him being anywhere near my sister without me there because he lifts a hand. "Jordan was with her. And I called first."

I make a mental note to hug Jordan, though I'm a little hurt that Brook didn't tell me that our dad was here. She must have had a reason. Maybe she just knows me too well. "Chad?" I ask.

He shakes his head, and I'm surprised by the sadness in his navy eyes. We all got our blond hair and blue eyes from him, but he has always looked dim and dull compared to my siblings. That hasn't changed much, even with his forced rehabilitation, but this expression reminds me so much of Chad that it hits me harder than I'd like. He's still my dad, no matter what he's done.

"Chad won't talk to me," he says.

I doubt that will ever change. Chad already made his peace with our father years ago, but that doesn't mean he wants to reconcile. I know he's forgiven him, but I don't think I've ever heard Chad talk about him willingly. He saw too much of the damage Dad caused and had to pick up all of the pieces, and that burden is something that can never go away.

"So," I say, shifting my weight and praying Darcy shows up soon. "You're out."

He nods. He's fidgety as he stands there, though whether he's nervous or uncomfortable, I'm not sure. "Yeah. On probation, obviously. I was hoping..." He swallows. "I was hoping we could catch up, like I did with Brooklyn."

"Nope." That word comes out easily. "If Brook lets you in, that's her choice, but I don't need you in my life."

I have never been more relieved to see my truck appear at the other end of the parking lot, though I wish I had a way to get rid of my dad before he can see Darcy.

I grip my duffel tighter. "You missed my whole life up until now, so I don't see why you deserve to be a part of the rest of it."

"Houston."

I have nowhere to go, so I reluctantly meet his gaze again.

"Congrats on winning the Series. That's really amazing."

I resist the urge to roll my eyes. If he thinks that's enough to get me to reconsider, he's going to have to do better than Google my name. "Thanks," I mutter, wishing Darcy would just gun it across the parking lot. Then again, I don't think my truck can actually go that fast.

Dad keeps talking, as if he knows that as soon as that truck pulls up, he's out of chances. "And that game two seasons ago where you caught the ball that came right at you instead of ducking away from it? Incredible."

Darcy finally arrives, pulling up to the curb.

I make it two steps before Dad speaks again. "Remember that perfect game you threw in college? And three strike-outs in a row. As soon as I saw that, I knew you were meant for great things. But it was the game before that that told me you had become a good man. When you apologized for hitting that batter with the ball even though him walking cost you the game."

I'm frozen in place. I remember that game vividly, though most people forgot about it because it was a loss. I don't think there were any stories written about my apology, but I remember the moment being on local TV. The newscasters mentioned my good conduct and then moved on. But if Dad knows about that, it means...

I turn back, staring at him. "You watched my games?" I croak. That was after he went to jail, when he was at his lowest.

Nodding, he stuffs his hands into his pockets as if he knows he needs to keep his distance still. But I can see the eagerness in his eyes. "All of them. Whenever I could. I'm so proud of you, Houston."

Ask me ten minutes ago if I would have wanted to hear those words, I would have emphatically said no. But as I stand here staring at the tears in my dad's eyes, a tiny crack forms in the armor I've kept around my heart specifically to defend against him. He'll never make up for failing as a father my entire childhood, but maybe I can find it in myself to forgive him and move on. Like my siblings did.

"Thanks," I say weakly. It's about all I can muster after the day I've had so far.

"Houston?" Darcy says my name warily. She can probably see my tension clear as day as she stands on the driver's side of the truck.

I turn to give her a smile but flinch instead. She's dressed as Tamlin, which I should have expected, but a part of me wonders if yesterday was a dream and she's still a different person.

As if reading my thoughts, she gives me an easy smile and says, "I told Jordan that he has to make us waffles for lunch today because I ruined the last batch." Her false blue eyes flick to my dad, who's looking back at her with curiosity.

And while I know they're both expecting an introduction, my dad is one part of my life that I'd like to keep separated from the rest as long as I can. Turning to face him, I give him a single nod. "Maybe I'll be in touch," I say, which is as much as I'll give him until I've had time to process the fact that he hasn't been as completely absent as I always thought. Watching my games isn't much, but it's something.

"As for *you*," I tell Darcy and round the truck to get to her side. Dropping my duffel, I pull her out of view and then bend down to kiss her like I've been wanting to do all morning. She responds eagerly, running her hands through my hair the same way she did yesterday and solidifying the fact that she's the same woman I'm in love with, no matter how she looks.

When I pull away, she laughs and uses her thumb to wipe her lipstick from my mouth. "I should have told Jesse to go with a long wear lip stain," she says with a wink. "He insisted I needed this shade to match my dress."

I know my dad's still standing on the other side of the truck, but I like pretending we're completely on our own right now. I don't have anything else to say to him anyway. I take a step back, giving myself the opportunity to examine Darcy without reservation. It's still hard to wrap my brain around the idea that Darcy is underneath all of this, especially when her body shape is so different.

Something clicks in my brain suddenly. "Wait, *Jesse* does your makeup?"

She laughs. "There is no way I could do all this myself. He had his last shift at the tattoo place tonight, so I had to enlist him earlier than I would have liked. I hope you don't mind."

I shake my head. "You're still Darcy, right?"

"Always."

"Then I don't mind. Want to get out of here? You get me for three hours before Roundy starts tracking me down."

Her smirk pulls me back in, though she speaks before I can kiss her. "I can think of a lot of things we can do in three hours. But you're not allowed to touch my face. Lipstick, I can do, but the rest?" She crosses the space between us, giving me a kiss that puts all of her in danger, not just her face.

I groan and lift my hands behind my head before they get ahead of themselves. "Got any ideas that aren't this?"

"I was thinking mini golf so I can prove to someone that I really do know how to putt. I hate that I didn't make any shots in Albuquerque."

That sounds like a fantastic way to spend the afternoon. "Something tells me the full version of you is a little scary." I make sure she sees my smile so she knows I'm only halfway serious. "I thought you were perfect before—both of you—and now that I know you're the full package, I'm going to feel insignificant by comparison."

Scoffing, she hooks a finger in the collar of my t-shirt and pulls me flush against her. "Don't even pretend you're not Mr. Perfect yourself. I fell in love with you for a reason."

My breath catches. That's a word she didn't use yesterday, something I hadn't really noted until I heard it today. I wasn't expecting her to say it, as much as I wanted it, but hearing it now sends my heart into a frenzy. "Say that again," I whisper.

She turns a bright pink. Maybe she didn't realize what she just said, but she's aware of it now. What if she didn't mean it?

She smiles after taking in my probably panicked expression. "Yes, I'm in love with you, Houston Briggs."

"Why?" I clap a palm to my face. Of all the stupid things I could have said... "You don't have to—"

Placing her hand over my mouth, Darcy gives me one of her honest and genuine smiles. I can't believe I didn't recognize that smile before; it's so Darcy, and it doesn't matter how much makeup she wears or how many fancy dresses she squishes herself into. She's still the same person.

"I love you because you make me feel beautiful on the inside," she says gently. "Because you care so much about everyone around you. Because one of the biggest reasons you had such a hard time giving up baseball didn't have anything to do with yourself. You are the most selfless, respectful, generous man I have ever met. And you brought me nachos."

Then she pulls me into a kiss that is a thousand times better than Grey Bird nachos. And that's saying something.

Chapter Thirty-Two

Houston

At some point, Darcy—Tamlin, to everyone else—arranged a whole setup for my announcement. There's a stage erected at the stadium with a Red-tails banner behind it. She's got lighting set up and a fancy camera ready to go, and she even went through my closet this morning and picked out her favorite shirt and jacket for me to wear. The team's owner has shown up along with all of the coaches, and half the team is here too, which makes me wonder how they found out about this.

Still, it's kind of nice to see familiar faces as I stand off to the side with Roundy. It would have been harder to talk to just a camera, even with Darcy right there next to me.

"Last chance to change your mind," Roundy says quietly, and there's a bit of pleading in his voice that I didn't expect. He's been with me from the beginning; almost nine years is nothing to laugh at, and I know I'm the reason he's become such a big name in the world of sports agencies. I was his first big client, and we owe each other a lot.

I clap a hand on his shoulder. "Thanks for getting me here, Alan. I couldn't have done it without you."

He grunts, and his eyes find Darcy across the room, where she's talking to Fujimura. "It's because of her, isn't it? She forced you into this."

When I told Roundy that I would only talk to Tamlin Park, he immediately asked if she was blackmailing me. I didn't tell him much, so I can see why he still thinks she's the reason I finally made my decision. He's not wrong.

"Yes and no," I admit. "This choice is the one I need to make, for myself and for the team. But she helped me be at peace with it. She gave me a reason to look forward to the future."

Darcy turns right then and meets my gaze, and her whole face lights up with a smile that I can't help but match.

Roundy clears his throat. "Does that reason happen to live in St. Louis?"

There's really no point in denying that one, even if I'm not positive what this future with Darcy is going to look like. It all depends on whether she gets that promotion, which depends on how this story plays out tonight. My retirement is a big deal, but anyone could tell my story. I'm curious to see how Darcy puts her own spin on it to prove that she's the right person for the inspirational side of Enhance.

"Maybe," I say.

Then Roundy surprises me. "I'm happy for you," he says and then takes a seat, his phone in his hand.

Darcy appears just a moment later. "You ready?"

Probably not, but I nod anyway. Delaying this will only make me more nervous, and I want the country to know that I'm making the best decision for myself. That means I need to have confidence.

We get wired up with mics, and Darcy takes a second to test sound levels with the Enhance cameraman they flew in from St. Louis. Everyone takes their seats, and suddenly it's time for me to admit that I'm broken and jobless.

Darcy reaches over and gives my hand a squeeze. "You've got this," she says gently. "Just be yourself, and I'll be right here the whole time."

I know it's stupid, but I still ask. "Promise?"

She grins, but then she turns to the camera and flips that switch that I've seen so many times. Suddenly she's Tamlin Park, the most intimidating sports journalist I've ever spoken to. "Hello, and welcome to the Salverditos Stadium in Sun City, New Mexico. I'm Tamlin Park with Enhance Media, and I'm sitting here with Houston Briggs, top starting pitcher for the Sun City Red-tails. I've got some big news for the world of baseball, so you're going to want to stick around. How are you feeling tonight, Houston?"

"Like I might puke," I say without meaning to.

The guys in the audience chuckle, and Darcy gives me a smirk that weirdly settles my nerves a bit. A few weeks ago, that saucy smile would have sent me running. Now that I know her, and what motivates her, there's nothing she could do that would scare me.

"Well," she says, "that could make this interview interesting. That's one way to go viral! How about we start with this last season? How do you feel about how the Red-tails played on their journey to the World Series?"

Darcy is seriously good at her job. We talk about the highs and lows of the season, revisiting some of my best moments as well as my worst, and she manages to praise most of the rest of the team in subtle ways as we talk, calling many out by name without taking the focus away from my own career.

Then she pulls up a video on a tablet, holding it up so both the camera and I can see what's on it. "Let's talk about this moment in your first game against the Angels last August."

My heart skips a beat when she hits play. I know exactly which game this is, and while it wasn't the first time I wondered if I might have an injury, it was the first time I thought I'd done some serious damage. It was near the end of the game, and I watch as I throw a pitch that flies off course.

The video pauses right before the camera cuts to the batter, and my pain is clear as day in my face. At the time, it felt like my arm tried to detach from the rest of me, and it was one of the few times I thought about letting a relief pitcher take over the rest of the game.

"What happened here?" Darcy asks gently.

My hand shifts to my shoulder, which aches from the memory of that pitch. "I tore my supraspinatus tendon," I mutter.

The team breaks into a buzz of murmured conversations behind the cameras.

With a sympathetic grimace, Darcy hits play again, and the video goes through a quick montage of the rest of my pitches throughout that game. "You kept playing."

"I couldn't let my team down," I say. But I'm also stubborn and stupid, two things I keep to myself.

"But the rest of the season?" Darcy frowns. "You played every inning of your games this year without fail, but with an injury like that, I can't imagine your arm got much of a chance to heal."

"No," I admit, and I can't decide if this makes me sound like a hero or an idiot. "Like I said, the guys were counting on me, and I'm not one to back down from a promise."

"There have been rumors that you've been placed on temporary rest and haven't been pitching during practices since the season ended," Dar-

cy says, and I know she's gearing up for me to make my big announcement. "Do you think you'll have enough recovery time to be ready for
spring training?"

"Actually." I swallow and glance at the camera. Look at Roundy.
Make eye contact with Fujimura. "I've decided that it is in my best
interest to retire before the season starts."

The Red-tails burst into shouts of surprise and anger, but I only
focus on Darcy and the gentle smile she gives me. She doesn't care if
I'm a famous pitcher or a washed up former pro athlete, so why would
it matter what anyone else thinks of my choice? She's the only person
whose opinion I care about.

When the audience finally quiets down, Darcy continues with her
questions. "I can't imagine this was an easy decision for you. You've been
playing baseball your entire life. What brought you to this conclusion?"

"It was a lot of things. For one, I don't think I'd be able to play more
than a few innings at a time. For another, some people think I'm too old
to keep playing anyway." I wink at her, chuckling when she scowls at my
callback to our first interview. "Mostly, I was starting to feel unsteady in
life, like I was lost at sea without an anchor."

"Are you going to miss playing?"

I laugh. "That's like asking me if I would miss my arm. Yeah, hitting
the end of my career sucks. It was going to happen eventually, but it
seems the universe was ready for that end before I was."

"Are you disappointed that you didn't play enough years to qualify
for the Hall of Fame?"

That question catches me off guard. "Oh. I haven't thought about it."

Darcy cringes and mouths, "Sorry."

But I smile. "As cool as that would be, it was never really my end goal.
Baseball was something I did for me, as a way to push myself to be better
than I was the year before. That's just going to look different now."

"So, what's next?"

"I thought it might be time to settle down and start building a life with
someone."

She grins, though I can tell she's fighting it. One of the things we
talked about yesterday was which side of her I would be dating. Darcy
still needs Tamlin to tell her stories until things hopefully change with
her career, but she doesn't want to have to dress up every time we go out.

I'll probably be in the spotlight for a while, until someone else becomes more interesting, so people will be paying attention to who I'm with.

Basically, I'm dating Darcy. So I should really stop smiling at Tamlin and giving the country a front and center view of how I feel about this woman.

"Anyone you have in mind?" Darcy asks, smirking a little.

I'm going to get her back for this. I don't know how, but I will. "Yeah, I have someone who makes me want to be a better man. She sees me for who I am and is the best part of my life."

Darcy's eyes fill with tears, which she somehow manages to cover up by taking a drink of water. "She sounds great, and she's certainly lucky to have someone like you."

"Not as lucky as I am."

Darcy clears her throat. "Well, I have one more question for you, Houston. If there's one thing you've learned playing with the Red-tails, what is it?"

I like this question, but even though I knew she was going to ask it, I didn't have an answer until now. Seeing my team beyond the cameras, the way they all have supportive smiles on their faces now that the news has sunk in, I realize I shouldn't have gone through all of this alone. How much easier might this have been if I had told my family about what I was going through?

I look at Darcy and give her a small smile. "I learned that the best way to go through life is to trust your team. Whether that's in sports, or your friends, co-workers, family... We're all in this together, and no one should have to go through life on their own. I've been lucky to have such an incredible team behind me, both on the field and at home, and that's not something I would trade for the world." My voice breaks, but I let myself feel the bittersweet ache of leaving this life behind.

Darcy looks ready to throw caution to the wind and throw her arms around me. "Well," she says with emotion to match my own, "I'm sure I speak for your fellow Red-tails as well as all your fans when I say I'm going to miss seeing you on the mound."

I grin. "It's someone else's turn to help take the team to victory."

"I'll be here when they do."

"I hope you are. I have a feeling you have a knack for finding the players worth knowing and giving them their time to shine."

Now Darcy looks ready to kiss me. Or maybe punch me for getting her emotional and *then* kiss me. As long as there's a kiss involved, I don't really care. "On that note," she says, turning to the camera, "I'm Tamlin Park with Enhance Media, and we've just hit the end of an era. He may be done pitching, but I have a feeling this isn't the last we'll see of Houston Briggs. Until next time!"

The instant the cameraman signals the end of the recording, the area bursts into activity. Players swarm Roundy, probably hoping to take my spot on his roster, and they go for the coaches too, likely for answers to who's going to pitch next season. For a moment, Darcy and I are completely alone, and I'm not going to waste this chance to escape before I'm surrounded.

I scramble to get rid of the microphone, glad to see Darcy doing the same. The moment we're both wire-free, I grab her hand and pull her around to the other side of the backdrop.

Darcy frowns, looking around. "I thought we'd get farther than this," she admits, which pulls a laugh out of me.

"Roundy won't let me get far. He's got other press coming in an hour, but I wanted Enhance to be the first to air the news."

Darcy starts to cry again, this time letting it out despite the damage it could do to her makeup. "How are you so great?" she whispers before wrapping her arms around my neck in a tight embrace that I happily return.

"Because you make me want to be great."

"How long do you think you'll have to stick around doing interviews?"

Too long. "I told Roundy I'm only giving his people an hour."

"Good. Then what?"

I hadn't really thought about it, but I have a feeling Chad is going to find the Enhance video pretty quickly if he hasn't already. He'll tell everyone else, and I'm going to have all of my siblings descending on my house to demand an explanation. I'm fine with that, as long as they don't stay all night.

But until they show up?

"How about a nap?" I suggest with a chuckle. "I just made the biggest announcement of my life, and I want to hide from it all for a little bit.

And hold you in my arms." I nuzzle into her neck, glad she's in such monstrous heels so she isn't so far below me.

Laughing, she plays with the hair at the nape of my neck and sends a shiver through me. "You don't think we spent enough time on my couch yesterday already? It's really not that comfortable."

Oh, she does not want me to go there. But I go there anyway. "Well, my bed is pretty comfortable," I say in a low voice that makes her shiver. "But there are a couple things that should probably happen before we get to that point."

She doesn't even flinch, merely pulling herself closer. "Such as?"

"Such as the fact that I've never had a woman in my bed because the only woman I want there is my wife."

This time she does react, pulling back enough to look up at me with wide eyes. "Really? Never?"

I nod. "Surprising, right?"

"You're telling me you never...not even with Bonnie Aiken?"

I tuck some hair behind her ear, loving how easy this conversation is. Some of my past girlfriends thought I was crazy for waiting, especially back when I was convinced I didn't want to settle down. They made some compelling arguments, but I'm glad I never changed my mind. "I promised my mom I would never treat a woman poorly," I say quietly. "And I've always thought something like that should be shared with someone I am deeply in love with. Someone I'm fully committed to. I never felt like that about anyone, so I never wanted to go too far into a relationship that I didn't think would last. Not until you. You're a forever kind of deal, Darcy Paxton."

Her breath hitches. "Are you asking me to marry you, Houston Briggs?"

Chuckling, I kiss the tip of her nose. "Not tonight. But someday I will." And then I press my lips to hers, feeling like everything in my life is falling into place and settling into something truly wonderful.

GREY
BIRD
TAVERN

Epilogue
Darcy

July 2

"YOU SHOULD HAVE WARNED me how hot it gets in Sun City in July. I'm sweating like a pig." I wave my hands over my armpits as if that might help.

Houston, on the other hand, looks cool as a cucumber with his arms stretched out along the backs of the seats and his hat tugged low on his head to hide his face. I tried to convince him to contact the manager before we showed up and do an interview or something, but he said he was just here to enjoy some baseball.

This calm of his is fake. This is the first time he's been around the Red-tails since he retired last fall, and he hasn't hidden his nerves well. He's been nervous for days.

"You say that like Missouri isn't at ninety-eight percent humidity right now," he says. "Dry heat is so much easier to handle."

"Maybe, but I already miss the way your hair curls in St. Louis." I brush my fingers through what hair I can see poking out beneath his hat. He's due for a haircut, but he keeps telling me he's waiting for the right moment because he hates getting his hair trimmed. Apparently, Chad tried to cut his hair once when he was eight, and it was a complete disaster. He's never recovered, and haircuts only happen by necessity. I'm not sure what constitutes a necessity, but I'll leave it be. Until Jesse starts looking at him with disgust, it probably isn't that bad.

Houston grins at me before returning his attention to the game, but he doesn't say anything about my hair comment. He's been unusually quiet today, which makes me wonder if something is bothering him.

"Are you glad to be back home?" I ask him, grateful for the noise of the crowd around us because it makes my question feel less frightening.

Houston glances at me. "Of course. It's always nice to visit."

Okay, but it's not technically visiting. He still lives here in New Mexico, even if he spends most of his time with me in Missouri or on the road when I've got a story. I don't travel a lot lately, saving my limited free time for the really juicy stories. The ones that make people cry because they're so full of heart. The rest of the time, I'm busy coordinating my team and finding the next promising athletic talent. Technically, I only managed to get away from the office for this trip because the Red-tails' new starting pitcher has been taking the league by storm. I'll never tell Houston, but this kid is possibly the best pitcher the team has had in a decade.

Though he's clearly distracted by the game, Houston leans in and kisses my cheek. "I'm happy to be wherever you are," he assures me.

It would be a lot easier to make that happen if he wasn't renting an apartment thirty minutes across town from me in St. Louis. He swears the distance is an important and crucial part of his goal to live deliberately, but every night that I have to say goodbye to him gets that much harder, and I can see his reluctance each time he drives away.

He has invested in a couple of businesses in St. Louis that keep him fairly busy while I'm at work, and he keeps looking for more people who could use his help. But there's still a part of me that wonders how long he's going to stay. Nothing about his situation is permanent, and I haven't been brave enough to ask what his plan is. For now, I'm happy that he spends so much time with me when he could be with his family here in Sun City.

As the crowd breaks into groans and boos, Houston grabs his hat and tosses it to the ground at his feet. "He was safe!" he shouts at the umpire despite being too far to be heard. "That should have been a run!"

Unfortunately, the Red-tails take to the outfield while the Astros get ready to bat. The rookie is on the mound, and I'm eager to see him throw even though I feel like Houston is still acting strangely.

A song by Sixpence None the Richer blasts over the speakers at the same time the announcer shouts that it's time for the Kiss Cam, and Houston leans back in his seat, now hatless. He has definite hat hair, and he runs his fingers through the waves as if he knows it.

I lean into him as the first couple comes on screen. "Is it weird that I love these?" I ask, watching the shy pair give each other a peck.

Houston smirks, shifting in his seat and digging into his pocket. "I thought maybe you would."

The next couple look like they're about eighty, and their kiss is surprisingly juicy. The announcer calls them fans for life, and I want to be that cool in fifty years.

"Speaking of fans," the announcer continues as Houston shifts again, like he can't get comfortable, "we have a local hero in our midst. Everyone give a warm welcome to the one and only Houston Briggs!"

The crowd goes crazy at the same time the jumbotron shows me and Houston. Why is Houston barely in the frame? I look over at him, and my heart stops.

He's down on one knee, a little velvet box in his shaking hands. He pries it open to reveal the most gorgeous ring I've ever seen. It's a solitaire cut set in a twisted rose gold band that is both understated and elegant, the perfect mix of simple and dazzling.

"Houston," I gasp.

He grins, flashing those dimples I love. "I told you this question was coming."

"I didn't think you were serious!" Maybe in a year or two, but not after we've only been dating for eight months.

"Let's give her some encouragement, folks," the announcer says.

I don't know which camera is trained on me, so I glare at all of them in turn, generating laughter from the cheering crowd.

Houston hasn't moved, and despite his nerves, he's so calm. Like he's known what my answer will be since the day he warned me about the question. "I am so deeply, madly in love with you, Darcy Paxton," he says. "You challenge me and lift me up, and I will follow you to the ends of the earth and back again if you let me be your husband."

"Let you be..." I don't know why, but him asking to be my husband rather than asking if I'll be his wife makes me burst into tears because it's so perfect. "Hou."

He purses his lips. "You don't have to say yes right now. Or at all. I know I'm putting a lot of pressure on this question by doing this here, but I—"

"Yes." The word squeaks out of me like I'm some chipmunk on the side of the road. "Yes, of course you can be my husband!" I throw my arms around his neck and pull myself in.

The cheer starts directly around us, spreading throughout the stadium as everyone figures out that I said yes. Despite the jumbotron documenting all of this, I give Houston the kiss of his life and wonder, like I've done so many times, how I got so lucky to fall in love with him.

Eventually, the announcer returns to the game and the crowd settles, and I figure I should give Houston a chance to breathe. Besides, I want to watch the rookie pitch. As we return to our seats with our hands clasped together, Houston pulls his hat back on his head as if that might help people forget that he's sitting there. I'm torn between watching the game and admiring the absolutely perfect ring he picked out, and then there's the people around us, who start crowding us and patting Houston on the back in congratulations.

After about two minutes of constant interaction, Houston looks at me. "Sorry," he whispers. "I know you prefer watching games from the bleachers, but I did get a box if..."

He's right, and games are so much better out in the open and in the thick of things. The crowd is as much a part of the game as the players. But maybe not this crowd; they're all fans of Houston Briggs. Nodding, I let him lead me up the stairs and through the disappointed spectators until we're on the mezzanine behind the seats. Anyone who's back there to get a hot dog or nachos recognizes Houston right away and starts swarming, so we break into a run until we burst through the door of the private box he rented, both of us laughing too hard to breathe.

A cheer in front of us makes me jump. Looking up, I recognize both our families, and my heart swells. "Mom! Dad!" I embrace them first because they're closest, and Mom's tears unleash my own.

"I'm so happy for you!" she says as she gives me a bone-crushing hug. When I first brought Houston to Philly, she was entirely wary—apparently she Googled him before we made it to the house—but Houston charmed her quickly. Especially when I told her that he helped me get my dream job. Now that she can actually see me on TV sometimes, she understands better why I love what I do. Plus, Houston sweet-talked her into letting him pay for some home renovations and treatments to help my dad and give my mom a break when it comes to his care.

Dad's hug is stronger than I expected, which only makes me cry harder. "You found the best of men," he tells me. "He makes you shine."

I grin. "I know."

Then Carissa tackles me. My little sister has gotten strong from her days in her physical therapy office and nearly knocks me off my feet, but I manage to keep us upright as she squeals into my ear. "You're getting married!"

As if I hadn't realized that part, my heart rate goes haywire. "I'm getting married," I gasp. "Sweet cherry pie, I'm going to marry Houston Briggs!"

Carissa squeals again, and the two of us jump up and down as we hold on to each other. Another pair of arms wraps around me as Houston's sister, Micah, joins our excitement.

"You're going to be my sister!" she shrieks.

The room fills with laughter. I figure I should greet Houston's family as well as my own—they're going to be my family too—so I wrap Micah up in a hug and laugh when she koala hugs me back. It's a good thing she's tiny or I would fall over trying to hold her.

Brooklyn is a lot calmer as she hugs me, tears in her eyes. I've spent a lot of time with Houston's twin anytime I'm here in Sun City, and she's basically my best friend at this point. I know how worried she's been over the years that Houston would never put down roots. "I'm so glad you found each other," she tells me.

"Thank you. Me too." Then I move on to have a hug battle with Chad's wife, Hope.

We like to see who can squeeze the other the hardest, and I always win. But today, Hope keeps her embrace light, so I follow suit, and based on the way Chad lingers nearby with watchful eyes, I have a pretty good idea why. My eyes go wide, and I glance down at her stomach. "Are you...?"

Hope grins, turning pink. "Yeah. I'm due in January."

I scream, and then Micah screams, and then all of us girls are screaming together as we collide in one big embrace, Hope's daughter, Zelda, included.

"What just happened?" Houston asks with wide eyes.

Chad chuckles. Though he's leaning against the wall and pretending to be calm, he can't stop smiling. "Hope is pregnant."

"Dude!" Houston leaps onto Chad, and I can't decide if he's trying to hug him or tackle him to the ground. Maybe both.

Laughing, Chad fights him off. "What about your arm?"

Houston rolls his eyes, though Chad is right. He's only a few months off of his surgery and should probably be taking it easy. "My arm is fine. You're going to be a dad! Again!"

"I'm going to be a big brother," a little voice says, and Link appears from behind Chad. Has he been there the whole time? I really haven't interacted with Chad's kids much, but since Link started playing Little League, he has really opened up. The one game I went to, he was more interested in a raccoon on the edge of the field than the game itself, but at least he's having fun and making friends.

Finally, after hugging Jordan and giving Fischer a high five, I make it back into Houston's arms, and he holds me like he's afraid to let me go.

"We're getting married," I say into his chest. Then I turn my head to give me a slightly better view of the field.

Houston laughs. "You want to watch the game, don't you?"

"Unless you have any other surprises?"

"Nope." Kissing me first—it's almost enough to thoroughly distract me from the game—Houston leads me to the seats at the front of the box. The Red-tails have already left the field, which means I probably missed some impressive plays, but it's hard to care about baseball when I have so much to love here in the box with me.

I lean into Houston, resting my head on his shoulder. It's the shoulder that brought us together, and it's one of my favorite parts of him. "I love you. Like, a lot."

Resting his cheek on my head, Houston runs his thumb along mine. "A lot? That doesn't sound like very much."

"You're such a dork."

"I'm just saying, I love beating Kit in trivia a lot. And I love watching you when you're telling an inspiring story a lot."

Sitting up, I pull him in and kiss him like we don't have a whole audience behind us. "I love you more than Jordan's waffles," I whisper against his lips. "I love you more than baseball. I love you more than Grey Bird nachos."

"Now we're talking." Houston kisses me again.

Let's be real. With Houston beside me, I don't see much of the game at all.

And I don't care in the slightest.

The End

Also by Dana LeCheminant

Love in Sun City
Kiss Me if You Can (a novella)
She Likes It, Hey Micah
The Chad Next Door
Crossing the Brooklyn Briggs
Houston, We Have a Problem

The Wonder Boys
Love on Camera
Love in Writing
Love on Display
Love in Disguise

Simple Love Stories (Sweet Love Stories)
Simplicity
Growing Young
Bittersweet Brews
In Front of Me
As Long as You Love Me
Dear Dalia
Let Go

Terms of Inheritance (Sweet Romance)
Forever You and Me
Holding On to Everything
A World without You
Love, Strictly Speaking

Historical Romances
The Thief and the Noble
A Twist of Christmas (part of The Holly and the Ivy anthology)
What Dreams May Come
This Above All

About the Author

Dana LeCheminant has been telling stories since she was old enough to know what stories were. After spending most of her childhood reading everything she could get her hands on, she eventually realized she could write her own books too, and since then she always has plots brewing and characters clamoring to be next to have their stories told. A lover of all things outdoors, she finds inspiration while hiking the remote Utah backcountry and cruising down rivers. Until her endless imagination runs dry, she will always have another story to tell.